MEMNOCH
THE DEVIL

MEMNOCH
THE DEVIL

The Vampire Chronicles

ANNE RICE

ALFRED A. KNOPF CANADA

PUBLISHED BY ALFRED A. KNOPF CANADA

Copyright © 1995 by Anne O'Brien Rice

Canadian Cataloguing in Publication Data

Rice, Anne.
Memnoch the devil
ISBN 0-394-28126-8
I. Title.
PS3568.I265M45   1995   813'.54   C95-931580-2

First Canadian Edition

Manufactured in the United States of America

For
Stan Rice, Christopher Rice
and
Michele Rice

For
John Preston

For
Howard and Katherine Allen O'Brien

For
Katherine's brother John Allen,
Uncle Mickey
and for
Uncle Mickey's son, Jack Allen,
and all the descendants
of Jack

And for
Uncle Marian Leslie,
who was in Corona's Bar on that night

With love for you
and for
all our kith and kin
this book
is
dedicated

WHAT GOD DID NOT PLAN ON

Sleep well,
Weep well,
Go to the deep well
As often as possible.
Bring back the water,
Jostling and gleaming.
God did not plan on consciousness
Developing so
Well. Well,
Tell Him our
Pail is full
And He can
Go to Hell.

Stan Rice

24 June 93

THE OFFERING

To the somethingness
Which prevents the nothingness
Like Homer's wild boar
From thrashing this way and that
Its white tusks
Through human beings
Like crackling stalks
And to nothing less
I offer this suffering of my father

Stan Rice

16 Oct 93

DUET ON IBERVILLE STREET

The man in black leather
Buying a rat to feed his python
Does not dwell on particulars.
Any rat will do.
While walking back from the pet store
I see a man in a hotel garage
Carving a swan in a block of ice
With a chain saw.

Stan Rice
30 Jan 94

MEMNOCH
THE DEVIL

Prologue

LESTAT here. You know who I am? Then skip the next few paragraphs. For those whom I have not met before, I want this to be love at first sight.

Behold: your hero for the duration, a perfect imitation of a blond, blue-eyed, six-foot Anglo-Saxon male. A vampire, and one of the strongest you'll ever encounter. My fangs are too small to be noticed unless I want them to be; but they're very sharp, and I cannot go for more than a few hours without wanting human blood.

Of course, I don't need it that often. And just how often I do need it, I don't know, because I've never put it to the test.

I'm monstrously strong. I can take to the air. I can hear people talking on the other side of the city or even the globe. I can read minds; I can bind with spells.

I'm immortal. I've been virtually ageless since 1789.

Am I unique? By no means. There are some twenty other vampires in the world of whom I know. Half of these I know intimately; one half of those I love.

Add to this twenty a good two hundred vagabonds and strangers of whom I know nothing but now and then hear something; and for good measure another thousand secretive immortals, roaming about in human guise.

Men, women, children—any human being can become a vampire. All it takes is a vampire willing to bring you into it, to suck out most of your blood, and then let you take it back, mixed with his or her own. It's not all that simple; but if you survive, you'll live forever. While you're young, you'll thirst unbearably, probably have to kill each night. By the time you're a thousand years old, you'll look and sound wise, even if you were a kid when you started, and you will drink and kill because you cannot resist it, whether you need it anymore or not.

If you live longer than that, and some do, who knows? You'll get tougher, whiter, ever more monstrous. You'll know so much about suffering that you will go through rapid cycles of cruelty and kindness, insight and maniacal blindness. You'll probably go mad. Then you'll be sane again. Then you may forget who you are.

I myself combine the best of vampiric youth and old age. Only two hundred years old, I have been for various reasons granted the strength of the ancients. I have a modern sensibility but a dead aristocrat's impeccable taste. I know exactly who I am. I am rich. I am beautiful. I can see my reflection in mirrors. And in shopwindows. I love to sing and to dance.

What do I do? Anything that I please.

Think about it. Is it enough to make you want to read my story? Have you perhaps read my stories of the vampires before?

Here's the catch: it doesn't matter here that I'm a vampire. It is not central to the tale. It's just a given, like my innocent smile and soft, purring French-accented voice and graceful way of sauntering down the street. It comes with the package. But what *happened* here could have happened to a human being; indeed, it surely has happened to humans, and it will happen to them again.

We have souls, you and I. We want to know things; we share the same earth, rich and verdant and fraught with perils. We don't—either of us—know what it means to die, no matter what we might say to the contrary. It's a cinch that if we did, I wouldn't be writing and you wouldn't be reading this book.

What does matter very much, as we go into this story together, is that I have set for myself the task of being a hero in this world. I maintain myself as morally complex, spiritually tough, and aesthetically relevant—a being of blazing insight and impact, a guy with things to say to you.

So if you read this, read it for that reason—that Lestat is talking again, that he is frightened, that he is searching desperately for the lesson and for the song and for the raison d'être, that he wants to understand his own story and he wants you to understand it, and that it is the very best story he has right now to tell.

If that's not enough, read something else.

If it is, then read on. In chains, to my friend and my scribe, I dictated these words. Come with me. Just listen to me. Don't leave me alone.

1

I SAW him when he came through the front doors. Tall, solidly built, dark brown hair and eyes, skin still fairly dark because it had been dark when I'd made him a vampire. Walking a little too fast, but basically passing for a human being. My beloved David.

I was on the stairway. The grand stairway, one might say. It was one of those very opulent old hotels, divinely overdone, full of crimson and gold, and rather pleasant. My Victim had picked it. I hadn't. My victim was dining with his daughter. And I'd picked up from my victim's mind that this was where he always met his daughter in New York, for the simple reason that St. Patrick's Cathedral was across the street.

David saw me at once—a slouching, blond, long-haired youth, bronze face and hands, the usual deep violet sunglasses over my eyes, hair presentably combed for once, body tricked out in a dark-blue, doubled-breasted Brooks Brothers suit.

I saw him smile before he could stop himself. He knew my vanity, and he probably knew that in the early nineties of the twentieth century, Italian fashion had flooded the market with so much shapeless, hangy, bulky, formless attire that one of the most erotic and flattering garments a man could choose was the well-tailored navy-blue Brooks Brothers suit.

Besides, a mop of flowing hair and expert tailoring are always a potent combination. Who knows that better than I?

I didn't mean to harp on the clothes! To hell with the clothes. It's just I was so proud of myself for being spiffed up and full of gorgeous contradictions—a picture of long locks, the impeccable tailoring, and a regal manner of slumping against the railing and sort of blocking the stairs.

He came up to me at once. He smelled like the deep winter outside, where people were slipping in the frozen streets, and snow had turned to filth in the gutters. His face had the subtle preternatural gleam which only I could detect, and love, and properly appreciate, and eventually kiss.

We walked together onto the carpeted mezzanine.

Momentarily, I hated it that he was two inches taller than me. But I was so glad to see him, so glad to be near him. And it was warm in here, and shadowy and vast, one of the places where people do not stare at others.

"You've come," I said. "I didn't think you would."

"Of course," he scolded, the gracious British accent breaking softly from the young dark face, giving me the usual shock. This was an old man in a young man's body, recently made a vampire, and by me, one of the most powerful of our remaining kind.

"What did you expect?" he said, tête-à-tête. "Armand told me you were calling me. Maharet told me."

"Ah, that answers my first question." I wanted to kiss him, and suddenly I did put out my arms, rather tentatively and politely so that he could get away if he wanted, and when he let me hug him, when he returned the warmth, I felt a happiness I hadn't experienced in months.

Perhaps I hadn't experienced it since I had left him, with Louis. We had been in some nameless jungle place, the three of us, when we agreed to part, and that had been a year ago.

"Your first question?" he asked, peering at me very closely, sizing me up perhaps, doing everything a vampire can do to measure the mood and mind of his maker, because a vampire cannot read his maker's mind, any more than the maker can read the mind of the fledgling.

And there we stood divided, laden with preternatural gifts, both fit and rather full of emotion, and unable to communicate except in the simplest and best way, perhaps—with words.

"My first question," I began to explain, to answer, "was simply going to be: Where have you been, and have you found the others, and did they try to hurt you? All that rot, you know—how I broke the rules when I made you, et cetera."

"All that rot," he mocked me, the French accent I still possessed, now coupled with something definitely American. "What rot."

"Come on," I said. "Let's go into the bar there and talk. Obviously no one has done anything to you. I didn't think they could or they would, or that they'd dare. I wouldn't have let you slip off into the world if I'd thought you were in danger."

He smiled, his brown eyes full of gold light for just an instant.

"Didn't you tell me this twenty-five times, more or less, before we parted company?"

We found a small table, cleaving to the wall. The place was half crowded, the perfect proportion exactly. What did we look like? A couple of young men on the make for mortal men or women? I don't care.

"No one has harmed me," he said, "and no one has shown the slightest interest in it."

Someone was playing a piano, very tenderly for a hotel bar, I thought. And it was something by Erik Satie. What luck.

"The tie," he said, leaning forward, white teeth flashing, fangs completely hidden, of course. "This, this big mass of silk around your neck! This is not Brooks Brothers!" He gave a soft teasing laugh. "Look at you, and the wing-tip shoes! My, my. What's going on in your mind? And what is this all about?"

The bartender threw a hefty shadow over the small table, and murmured predictable phrases that were lost to me in my excitement and in the noise.

"Something hot," David said. It didn't surprise me. "You know, rum punch or some such, whatever you can heat up."

I nodded and made a little gesture to the indifferent fellow that I would take the same thing.

Vampires always order hot drinks. They aren't going to drink them; but they can feel the warmth and smell them if they're hot, and that is so good.

David looked at me again. Or rather this familiar body with David inside looked at me. Because for me, David would always be the elderly human I'd known and treasured, as well as this magnificent burnished shell of stolen flesh that was slowly being shaped by his expressions and manner and mood.

Dear Reader, he switched human bodies before I made him a vampire, worry no more. It has nothing to do with this story.

"Something's following you again?" he asked. "This is what Armand told me. So did Jesse."

"Where did you see them?"

"Armand?" he asked. "A complete accident. In Paris. He was just walking on the street. He was the first one I saw."

"He didn't make any move to hurt you?"

"Why would he? Why were you calling to me? Who's stalking you? What is all this?"

"And you've been with Maharet."

He sat back. He shook his head. "Lestat, I have pored over manuscripts such as no living human has seen in centuries; I have laid my hands on clay tablets that . . ."

"David, the scholar," I said. "Educated by the Talamasca to be the perfect vampire, though they never had an inkling that that is what you'd become."

"Oh, but you must understand. Maharet took me to these places where she keeps her treasures. You have to know what it means to hold in your hands a tablet covered in symbols that predate cuneiform. And Maharet herself, I might have lived how many centuries without ever glimpsing her."

Maharet was really the only one he had ever had to fear. I suppose we both knew it. My memories of Maharet held no menace, only the mystery of a survivor of Millennia, a living being so ancient that each gesture seemed marble made liquid, and her soft voice had become the distillation of all human eloquence.

"If she gave you her blessing, nothing else much matters," I said with a little sigh. I wondered if I myself would ever lay eyes upon her again. I had not hoped for it nor wanted it.

"I've also seen my beloved Jesse," said David.

"Ah, I should have thought of that, of course."

"I went searching for my beloved Jesse. I went crying out from place to place, just the way you sent out the wordless cry for me."

Jesse. Pale, bird-boned, red-haired. Twentieth-century born. Highly educated and psychic as a human. Jesse he had known as a human; Jesse he knew now as an immortal. Jesse had been his human pupil in the order called the Talamasca. Now he was the equal of Jesse in beauty and vampiric power, or very near to it. I really did not know.

Jesse had been brought over by Maharet of the First Brood, born as a human before humans had begun to write their history at all or barely knew that they had one. The Elder now, if there was one, the Queen of the Damned was Maharet and her mute sister, Mekare, of whom no one spoke anymore much at all.

I had never seen a fledgling brought over by one as old as Maharet. Jesse had seemed a transparent vessel of immense strength when last I saw her. Jesse must have had her own tales to tell now, her own chronicles and adventures.

I had passed onto David my own vintage blood mixed with a strain even older than Maharet's. Yes, blood from Akasha, and blood from the ancient Marius, and of course my own strength was in my blood, and my own strength, as we all knew, was quite beyond measure.

So he and Jesse must have been grand companions, and what had it meant to her to see her aged mentor clothed in the fleshly raiment of a young human male?

I was immediately envious and suddenly full of despair. I'd drawn David away from those willowy white creatures who had drawn him into their sanctuary somewhere far across the sea, deep in a land where their treasures might be hidden from crisis and war for generations. Exotic names came to mind, but I could not for the moment think where they had gone, the two red-haired ones, the one ancient, the one young. And to their hearth, they had admitted David.

A little sound startled me and I looked over my shoulder. I settled back, embarrassed to have appeared so anxious, and I focused silently for a moment on my victim.

My Victim was still in the restaurant very near us in this hotel, sitting with his beautiful daughter. I wouldn't lose him tonight. I was sure enough of that.

I sighed. Enough of him. I'd been following him for months. He was interesting, but he had nothing to do with all this. Or did he? I might kill him tonight, but I doubted it. Having spied the daughter, and knowing full well how much the Victim loved her, I had decided to wait until she returned home. I mean, why be so mean to a young girl like that? And how he loved her. Right now, he was pleading with her to accept a gift, something newly discovered by him and very splendid in his eyes. However, I couldn't quite see the image of the gift in her mind or his.

He was a good victim to follow—flashy, greedy, at times good, and always amusing.

Back to David. And how this strapping immortal opposite me must have loved the vampire Jesse, and become the pupil of Maharet. Why didn't I have any respect for the old ones anymore? What did I want, for the love of heaven? No, that was not the question. The question was . . . did something want me right now? Was I running from it?

He was politely waiting for me to look at him again. I did. But I didn't speak. I didn't begin. And so he did what polite people often do, he talked slowly on as if I were not staring at him through the violet glasses like one with an ominous secret.

"No one has tried to hurt me," he said again in the lovely calm British manner, "no one has questioned that you made me, all have treated me with respect and kindness, though everyone of course wanted to know all the details firsthand of how you survived the Body Thief. And I don't think you know quite how you alarmed them, and how much they love you."

This was a kindly reference to the last adventure which had brought us together, and driven me to make him one of us. At the time, he had not sung my praises to Heaven for any part of it.

"They love me, do they?" I said of the others, the remnants of our revenant species around the world. "I know they didn't try to help me." I thought of the defeated Body Thief.

Without David's help, I might never have won that battle. I could not think of something that terrible. But I certainly didn't want to think of all my brilliant and gifted vampiric cohorts and how they'd watched from afar and done nothing.

The Body Thief himself was in Hell. And the body in question was opposite me with David inside it.

"All right, I'm glad to hear I had them a little worried," I said. "But the point is, I'm being followed again, and this time it's no scheming mortal who knows the trick of astral projection and how to take possession of someone else's body. I'm being *stalked.*"

He studied me, not so much incredulous as striving perhaps to grasp the implications.

"Being stalked," he repeated thoughtfully.

"Absolutely." I nodded. "David, I'm frightened. I'm actually frightened. If I told you what I think this thing is, this thing that's stalking me, you'd laugh."

"Would I?"

The waiter had set down the hot drinks, and the steam did feel glorious. The piano played Satie ever so softly. Life was almost worth living, even for a son of a bitch of a monster like myself. Something crossed my mind.

In this very bar, I'd heard my victim say to his daughter two nights ago, "You know I sold my soul for places just like this."

I'd been yards away, quite beyond mortal hearing, yet hearing every word that fell from my Victim's lips, and I was enthralled with the daughter. Dora, that was her name. Dora. She was the one thing this strange and succulently alluring Victim truly loved, his only child, his daughter.

I realized David was watching me.

"Just thinking about the victim who brought me here," I said. "And his daughter. They're not going out tonight. The snow's too deep and the wind too cruel. He'll take her back up to their suite, and she'll look down on the towers of St. Patrick's. I want to keep my victim in my sights, you know."

"Good heavens, have you fallen in love with a couple of mortals?"

"No. Not at all. Just a new way of hunting. The man's unique, a blaze of individual traits. I adore him. I was going to feed on him the first time I saw him, but he continues to surprise me. I've been following him around for half a year."

I flashed back on them. Yes, they were going upstairs, just as I thought. They had just left their table in the restaurant. The night was too wretched even for Dora, though she wanted to go to the church and to pray for her father, and beg him to stay there and pray too. Some memory played between them, in their thoughts and fragmentary words. Dora had been a little girl when my Victim had first brought her to that cathedral.

He didn't believe in anything. She was some sort of religious leader. Theodora. She preached to television audiences on the seriousness of values and nourishment of the soul. And her father? Ah, well, I'd kill him before I learnt too much more, or end up losing this big trophy buck just for Dora's sake.

I looked back at David, who was watching me eagerly, shoulder resting against the dark satin-covered wall. In this light, no one could have known he wasn't human. Even one of us might have missed it. As for me, I probably looked like a mad rock star who wanted all the world's attention to crush him slowly to death.

"The victim's got nothing to do with it," I said. "I'll tell you all that another time. It's just we're in this hotel because I followed him here. You know my games, my hunts. I don't need blood any more than Maharet does, but I can't stand the thought of not having it!"

"And so what is this new sort of game?" he said politely in British.

"I don't look so much for simple, evil people, murderers, you know, so much as a more sophisticated kind of criminal, someone with the mentality of an Iago. This one's a drug dealer. Highly eccentric. Brilliant. An art collector. He loves to have people shot, loves to make billions in a week off cocaine through one gateway and heroin through another. And then he loves his daughter. And she, she has a televangelist church."

"You're really enthralled with these mortals."

"Look right now, past me, over my shoulder. See the two people in the lobby moving towards the elevators?" I asked.

"Yes." He stared at them fixedly. Perhaps they'd paused in just the right spot. I could feel, hear, and smell both of them, but I couldn't know precisely where they were unless I turned around. But they were there, the dark smiling man with his pale-faced eager and innocent little girl, who was a woman-child of twenty-five if I had reckoned correctly.

"I know that man's face," said David. "He's big time. International. They keep trying to bring him up on some charges. He pulled off an extraordinary assassination, where was it?"

"The Bahamas."

"My God, how did you happen on him? Did you really see him in person somewhere, you know, like a shell you found on the beach, or did you see him in the papers and the magazines?"

"Do you recognize the girl? Nobody knows they're connected."

"No, I don't recognize her, but should I? She's so pretty, and so sweet. You're not going to feed on her, are you?"

I laughed at his gentlemanly outrage at such a suggestion. I wondered if David asked permission before sucking the blood of his victims, or at least insisted that both parties be properly introduced. I had no idea what his killing habits were, or how often he fed. I'd made him plenty strong. That meant it didn't have to be every night. He was blessed in that.

"The girl sings for Jesus on a television station," I said. "Her church will someday have its headquarters in an old, old convent building in New Orleans. Right now she lives there alone, and tapes her programs out of a studio in the French Quarter. I think her show goes through some ecumenical cable channel out of Alabama."

"You're in love with her."

"Not at all, just very eager to kill her father. Her television appeal is peculiar. She talks theology with gripping common sense, you know, the kind of televangelist that just might make it all work. Don't we all fear that someone like that will come along? She dances like a nymph or a temple virgin, I suppose I should say, sings like a seraph, invites the entire studio audience to join with her. Theology and ecstasy, perfectly blended. And all the requisite good works are recommended."

"I see," he said. "And this makes it more exciting for you, to feast on the father? By the way, the father is hardly an unobtrusive man. Neither seem disguised. Are you sure no one knows they're connected?"

The elevator door had opened. My Victim and his daughter were rising floor after floor into the sky.

"He slips in and out of here when he wants. He's got bodyguards galore. She meets him on her own. I think they set it up by cellular phone. He's a computer cocaine giant, and she's one of his best-protected secret operations. His men are all over the lobby. If there'd been anyone nosing around, she would have left the restaurant alone first. But he's a wizard at things like that. There'll be warrants out for him in five states and he'll show up ringside for a heavyweight match in Atlantic City, right in front of the cameras. They'll never catch him. I'll catch him, the vampire who's just waiting to kill him. And isn't he beautiful?"

"Now, let me get this clear," David said. "You're being stalked by something, and it's got nothing to do with this victim, this, er, drug dealer, or whatever, or this televangelist girl. But something is following you, something frightening you, but not enough to make you stop tracking this dark-skinned man who just got into the elevator?"

I nodded, but then I caught myself in a little doubt. No, there couldn't be any connection.

Besides, this thing that had me rattled to the bone had started before I saw the Victim. It had "happened" first in Rio, the stalker, not long after I'd left Louis and David and gone back to Rio to hunt.

I hadn't picked up this Victim until he'd walked across my path in my own city of New Orleans. He'd come down there on a whim to see Dora for twenty minutes; they'd met in a little French Quarter bar, and I had been walking past and seen him, sparkling like a fire, and her white face and large compassionate eyes, and wham! It was fatal hunger.

"No, it's got nothing to do with him," I said. "What's stalking me started months before. He doesn't know I'm following him. I didn't catch on right away myself that I was being followed by this thing, this. . . ."

"This what?"

"Watching him and his daughter, it's like my miniseries, you know. He's so intricately evil."

"So you said, and what *is* stalking you? Is this a thing or a person or . . . ?"

"I'll get to that. This Victim, he has killed so many people. Drugs. Such people wallow in numbers. Kilos, kills, coded accounts. And the girl, the girl of course turned out not to be some dim-witted little miracle worker telling diabetics she can cure them with the laying on of hands."

"Lestat, your mind's wandering. What's the matter with you? Why are you afraid? And why don't you kill this victim and get that part over?"

"You want to go back to Jesse and Maharet, don't you?" I asked suddenly, a feeling of hopelessness descending on me. "You want to study for the next hundred years, among all those tablets and scrolls, and look into Maharet's aching blue eyes, and hear her voice, I know you do. Does she still always choose blue eyes?"

Maharet had been blind—eyes torn out—when she was made a vampire queen. She took eyes from her victims and wore them until they could see no more, no matter how the vampiric blood tried to preserve them. That was her shocking feature—the marble queen with the bleeding eyes. Why had she never wrung the neck of some vampire fledgling and stolen his or her eyes? It had never occurred to me before. Loyalty to our own kind? Maybe it wouldn't work. But she had her scruples, and they were as hard as she was. A woman that old remembers when there was no Moses and no Hammurabi's Code. When only the Pharaoh got to walk through the Valley of Death. . . .

"Lestat," David said. "Pay attention. You must tell me what you are talking about. I've never heard you admit so readily that you were afraid. You did say afraid. Forget about me for the moment. Forget that victim and the girl. What's up, my friend? Who's after you?"

"I want to ask you some more questions first."

"No. Just tell me what's happened. You're in danger, aren't you? Or you think you are. You sent out the call for me to come to you here. It was an unabashed plea."

"Are those the words Armand used, 'unabashed plea'? I hate Armand."

David only smiled and made a quick impatient gesture with both hands. "You don't hate Armand and you know you don't."

"Wanna bet?"

He looked at me sternly and reprimandingly. English schoolboy stuff probably.

"All right," I said. "I'll tell you. Now, first, I have to remind you of something. A conversation we had. It was when you were alive still, when we last talked together in your place in the Cotswolds, you know, when you were just a charming old gentleman, dying in despair—"

"I remember," he said patiently. "Before you went into the desert."

"No, right after, when we knew I couldn't die as easily I thought I could, when I'd come back burnt. You cared for me. Then you started talking about yourself, your life. You said something about an experience you'd had before the war, you said, in a Paris café. You remember? You know what I'm talking about?"

"Yes. I do. I told you that when I was a young man I thought I'd seen a vision."

"Yes, something about the fabric of life ripping for a moment so you glimpsed things you shouldn't have seen."

He smiled. "You're the one who suggested that, that the fabric had ripped somehow and I'd seen through the rip accidentally. I thought then and I still think now that it was a vision I was meant to see. But fifty years have passed since then. And my memory, my memory is surprisingly dim of the whole affair."

"Well, that's to be expected. As a vampire, you will remember everything that happens to you from now on vividly, but the details of mortal life will slip rather fast, especially anything that had to do with the senses, you'll find yourself chasing after it—what did wine taste like?"

He motioned for me to be quiet. I was making him unhappy. I hadn't meant to do this.

I picked up my drink, savored the fragrance. It was some sort of hot Christmas punch. I think they called it wassail in England. I set down the glass. My hands and face were still dark from that excursion into the desert, that little attempt to fly into the face of the sun. That helped me pass for human. What an irony. And it made my hand a little more sensitive to the warmth.

A ripple of pleasure ran through me. Warmth! Sometimes I think I get my money out of everything! There's no way to cheat a sensualist like me, somebody who can die laughing for hours over the pattern of the carpet in a hotel lobby.

I became aware again of his watching me.

He seemed to have collected himself somewhat or forgiven me for the one thousandth time for having put his soul into a vampire's body without his permission, indeed against his will. He looked at me, almost lovingly suddenly, as if I needed that reassurance.

I took it. I did.

"In this Paris café, you heard two beings talking to each other," I said, going back to his vision of years before. "You were a young man. It all happened gradually. But you realized they weren't 'really' there, the two, in a material sense, and the language they were speaking was understandable to you even though you didn't know what it was."

He nodded. "That's correct. And it sounded precisely like God and the Devil talking to each other."

I nodded. "And when I left you in the jungles last year, you said I wasn't to worry, that you weren't going off on any religious quest to find God and the Devil in a Paris café. You said you'd spent your mortal life looking for such things in the Talamasca. And now you would take a different turn."

"Yes, that's what I said," he admitted agreeably. "The vision's dimmer now than it was when I told you. But I remember it. I still remember it, and I still believe I saw and heard something, and I'm as resigned as ever that I'll never know what it was."

"You're leaving God and the Devil to the Talamasca, then, as you promised."

"I'm leaving the Devil to the Talamasca," he said. "I don't think the Talamasca as a psychic order was ever that interested in God."

All this was familiar verbal territory. I acknowledged it. We both kept our eye on the Talamasca, so to speak. But only one member of that devout order of scholars had ever known the true fate of David Talbot, the former Superior General, and now that human being was dead. His name had been Aaron Lightner. This had been a great sadness to David, the loss of the one human who knew what he was now, the human who had been his knowing mortal friend, as David had been mine.

He wanted to pick up the thread.

"You've seen a vision?" he asked. "That's what's frightening you?"

I shook my head. "Nothing as clear as that. But the Thing is stalking me, and now and then it lets me see something in the blink of an eye. I hear it mostly. I hear it sometimes talking in a normal conversational voice to another, or I hear its steps behind me on the street, and I spin around. It's true. I'm terrified of it. And then when it shows itself, well, I usually end up so disoriented, I'm sprawled in the gutter like a common drunk. A week will pass. Nothing. Then I'll catch that fragment of conversation again. . . ."

"And what are the words?"

"Can't give the fragments to you in order. I'd been hearing them before I realized what they were. On some level, I knew I was hearing a voice from some other locale, so to speak, you knew it wasn't a mere mortal in the next room. But for all I knew, it could have had a natural explanation, an electronic explanation."

"I understand."

"But the fragments are things like two people talking, and one says—*the one,* that is—says, 'Oh, no, he's perfect, it has nothing to do with vengeance, how could you think I wanted mere vengeance?' " I broke off, shrugged. "It's, you know, the middle of a conversation."

"Yes," he said, "and you feel this Thing is letting you hear a little of it . . . just the way I thought the vision in the café was meant for me."

"You've got it exactly right. It's tormenting me. Another time, this was only two days ago, I was in New Orleans; I was sort of spying on the Victim's daughter, Dora. She lives there in the convent building I mentioned. It's an old 1880s convent, unoccupied for years, and gutted, so that it's like a brick castle, and this little sparrow of a girl, this lovely little woman, lives there fearlessly, completely alone. She walks about the house as if she were invincible.

"Well, anyway, I was down there, and I had come into the courtyard of this building—it's, you know, a shape as old as architecture, main building, two long wings, inner courtyard."

"The rather typical late-nineteenth-century brick institution."

"Exactly, and I was watching through the windows, the progress of that little girl walking by herself through the pitch-black corridor. She was carrying a flashlight. And she was singing to herself, one of her hymns. They're all sort of medieval and modern at the same time."

"I believe the phrase is 'New Age,' " David suggested.

"Yes, it's somewhat like that, but this girl is on an ecumenical religious network. I told you. Her program is very conventional. Believe in Jesus, be saved. She's going to sing and dance people into Heaven, especially the women, apparently, or at least they'll lead the way."

"Go on with the story, you were watching her. . . ."

"Yes, and thinking how brave she was. She finally reached her own quarters; she lives in one of the four towers of the building; and I listened as she threw all the locks. And I thought, not many mortals would like to go prowling about this dark building, and the place wasn't entirely spiritually clean."

"What do you mean?"

"Little spirits, elementals, whatever, what did you call them in the Talamasca?"

"Elementals," he said.

"Well, there are some gathered about this building, but they're no threat to this girl. She's simply too brave and strong.

"But not the Vampire Lestat, who was spying her. He was out in the courtyard, and he heard the voice right next to his ear, as if Two Men were talking at his right shoulder and the other one, the one who is not following me, says quite plainly, 'No, I don't see him in the same light.' I turned round and round trying to find this Thing, close in on it mentally and spiritually, confront it, bait it, and then I realized I was shaking all over, and you know, the elementals, David, the little pesky spirits . . . the ones I could feel hanging about the convent . . . I don't think they even realized this person, or whoever he was, had been talking in my ear."

"Lestat, you do sound as if you've lost your immortal mind," he said. "No, no, don't get angry. I believe you. But let's backtrack. Why were you following the girl?"

"I just wanted to see her. My Victim, he's worried—about who he is, what's he done, what the officials know about him. He's afraid he'll blemish her when the final indictment comes and all the newpaper stories. But the point is, he'll never be indicted. I'm going to kill him first."

"You are. And then it actually might save her church, is that not right? Your killing him speedily, so to speak. Or am I mistaken?"

"I wouldn't hurt her for anything on this earth. Nothing could persuade me to do that." I sat silent for a moment.

"Are you sure you are not in love? You seem spellbound by her."

I was remembering. I had fallen in love only a short time ago with a mortal woman, a nun. Gretchen had been her name. And I had driven her mad. David knew the whole story. I'd written it; written all about David, too, and he and Gretchen had passed into the world in fictional form. He knew that.

"I would never reveal myself to Dora as I did with Gretchen," I said. "No. I won't hurt Dora. I learnt my lesson. My only concern is to kill her father in such a way that she experiences the least suffering and the maximum benefit. She knows what her father is, but I'm not sure she's prepared for all the bad things that could happen on account of him."

"My, but you are playing games."

"Well, I have to do something to keep my mind off this Thing that's following me or I'll go mad!"

"Shhhh . . . what's the matter with you? My God, but you're rattled."

"Of course I am," I whispered.

"Explain more about the Thing. Give me more fragments."

"They're not worth repeating. It's an argument. It's about me, I tell you. David, it's like God and the Devil are arguing about *me.*"

I caught my breath. My heart was hurting me, it was beating so fast, no mean feat for a vampiric heart. I rested back against the wall, let my eyes range over the bar—middle-aged mortals mostly, ladies in old-style fur coats, balding men just drunk enough to be loud and careless and almost young.

The pianist had moved on into something popular, from the Broadway stage, I think. It was sad and sweet, and one of the old women in the bar was rocking slowly to the music, and mouthing the words with her rouged lips as she puffed on a cigarette. She was from that generation that had smoked so much that stopping now was out of the question. She had skin like a lizard. But she was a harmless and beautiful being. All of them were harmless and beautiful beings.

My victim? I could hear him upstairs. He was still talking with his daughter. Would she not take just one more of his gifts? It was a picture, a painting perhaps.

He would move mountains for his daughter, this victim, but she didn't want his gift, and she wasn't going to save his soul.

I found myself wondering how late St. Patrick's stayed open. She wanted so badly to go there. She was, as always, refusing his money. It's "unclean," she said to him now. "Roge, I want your soul. I can't take the money for the church! It comes from crime. It's filthy."

The snow fell outside. The piano music grew more rapid and urgent. Andrew Lloyd Webber at his best, I thought. Something from *Phantom of the Opera.*

There was that noise again out in the lobby, and I turned abruptly in my chair and looked over my shoulder, and then back at David. I listened. I thought I heard it again, like a footstep, an echoing footstep, a deliberately terrifying footstep. I did hear it. I knew I was trembling. But then it was gone, over. There came no voice in my ear.

I looked at David.

"Lestat, you're petrified, aren't you?" he asked, very sympathetically.

"David, I think the Devil's come for me. I think I'm going to Hell."

He was speechless. After all, what could he say? What does a vampire say to another vampire on such subjects? What would I have said if Armand, three hundred years older than me, and far more wicked, had said the Devil was coming for him? I would have laughed at him. I would have made some cruel joke about his fully deserving it and how he'd meet so many of our kind down there, subject to a special sort of vampiric torment, far worse than mere damned mortals ever experienced. I shuddered.

"Good God," I said under my breath.

"You said you've seen it?"

"Not quite. I was . . . somewhere, it's not important. I think New York again, yes, back here with him—"

"The victim."

"Yes, following him. He had some transaction at an art gallery. Midtown. He's quite a smuggler. It's all part of his peculiar personality, that he loves beautiful and ancient objects, the sort of things you love, David. I mean, when I finally do make a meal of him, I might bring you one of his treasures."

David said nothing, but I could see this was distasteful to him, the idea of purloining something precious from someone whom I had not yet killed but was surely to kill.

"Medieval books, crosses, jewelry, relics, that's the sort of thing he deals in. It's what got him into the dope, ransoming church art that had been lost during the Second World War in Europe, you know, priceless statues of angels and saints that had been pillaged. He's got his most valued treasures stashed in a flat on the Upper East Side. His big secret. I think the dope money started as a means to an end. Somebody had something he wanted. I don't know. I read his mind and then I tire of it. And he's evil, and all those relics have no magic, and I'm going to Hell."

"Not so fast," he said. "The Stalker. You said you saw something. What did you see?"

I fell silent. I had dreaded this moment. I had not tried to describe these experiences even to myself. But I had to continue. I had called David here for help. I had to explain.

"We were outside, out there on Fifth Avenue; he—the Victim— was traveling in a car, uptown, and I knew the general direction, the secret flat where he keeps his treasures.

"I was merely walking, human style. I stopped at a hotel. I went inside to see the flowers. You know, in these hotels you can always find flowers. When you think you're losing your mind on account of winter, you can go into these hotels and find lavish bouquets of the most overwhelming lilies."

"Yes," he said with a little soft, halfhearted sigh. "I know."

"I was in the lobby. I was looking at this huge bouquet. I wanted to . . . to, ah . . . leave some sort of offering, as if it were a church . . . to those who'd made this bouquet, something like that, and I was thinking to myself, Maybe I should kill the Victim, and then . . . I swear this is the way it was, David—

"—the ground was gone. The hotel was gone. I wasn't anywhere or anchored to anything, and yet I was surrounded by people, people howling and chattering and screaming and crying, and laughing, yes, actually laughing, and all this was happening simultaneously, and the light, David, the light was blinding. This wasn't darkness, this wasn't the clichéd flames of the inferno, and I reached out. I didn't do this with my arms. I couldn't find my arms. I reached out with everything, every limb, every fiber, just trying to touch something, to regain equilibrium, and then I realized I was standing on terra firma, and this Being was in front of me, its shadow was falling over me. Look, I don't have any words for this. It was horrific. It was very certainly the worst thing I've ever seen! The light was shining behind it, and it stood between me and this light and it had a face, and the face was dark, extremely dark, and as I looked at it I lost all control. I must have roared. Yet I have no idea if in the real world I made a sound.

"When I came to my senses, I was still there, in the lobby. Everything looked ordinary, and it was as if I'd been in that other place for years and years, and all sorts of fragments of memory were slipping away from me, flying away from me, so fast that I couldn't catch any one thought or finished proposition or suggestion.

"All I could remember with any certainty is what I just told you. I stood there. I looked at the flowers. Nobody in the lobby noticed me. I pretended everything was normal. But I kept trying to remember, kept chasing these fragments, beset by bits and pieces of talk, or threat or description, and I kept seeing very clearly this truly ugly dark Being before me, exactly the sort of demon you'd create if you wanted to drive someone right out of his reason. I kept seeing this face and. . . ."

"Yes?"

". . . I've seen him twice again."

I realized I was mopping my forehead with the little napkin the waiter had given me. He'd come again. David placed an order. Then he leant close to me.

"You think you've seen the Devil."

"There's not much else that could frighten me, David," I said. "We both know that. There isn't a vampire in existence who could really frighten me. Not the very oldest, not the wisest, not the cruelist. Not even Maharet. And what do I know of the supernatural other than us? The elementals, the poltergeists, the little addlebrained spirits, we all know and see . . . the things you called up with Candomble witchcraft."

"Yes," he said.

"This was *The Man Himself*, David."

He smiled, but it was by no means unkind or unsympathetic. "For you, Lestat," he teased softly, seductively, "for you, it would have to be the Devil Himself."

We both laughed. Though I think it was what writers call a mirthless laugh. I went on.

"The second time it was in New Orleans. I was near home, our flat in the Rue Royale. Just walking. And I started to hear those steps behind me, like something deliberately following me and letting me know it. Damn it, I've done this to mortals myself and it's so vicious. God! Why was I ever created! And then the third time, the Thing was even closer. Same scenario. Huge, towering over me. Wings, David. Either it has wings or I in my fear am endowing it with wings. It is a Winged Being, and it is hideous, and this last time, I kept hold of the image long enough to run from it, to flee, David, like a coward. And then I woke up, as I always do, in some familiar place, where I started actually, and everything's just the way it was. Nobody has a hair out of place."

"And it doesn't talk to you when it appears like this?"

"No, not at all. It's trying to drive me crazy. It's trying to . . . to make me do something, perhaps. Remember what you said, David, that you didn't know why God and the Devil had let you see them."

"Hasn't it occurred to you that it *is* connected with this victim you're tracking? That perhaps something or someone does not want you to kill this man?"

"That's absurd, David. Think of the suffering in the world tonight. Think of those dying in Eastern Europe, think of the wars in the Holy Land, think of what's happening in this very city. You think God or the Devil gives a damn about one man? And our kind, our kind preying for centuries on the weak and the attractive and the unlucky. When has the Devil ever interfered with Louis, or Armand, or Marius, or any of us? Oh, would that it were so easy to summon his august presence and know once and for all!"

"Do you want to know?" he asked earnestly.

I waited, thought about it. Shook my head. "Could be something explainable. I detest being afraid of it! Maybe this is madness. Maybe that's what Hell is. You go mad. And all your demons come and get you just as fast as you can think them up."

"Lestat, it is evil, you are saying that?"

I started to answer and then stopped. Evil.

"You said it was hideous; you described intolerable noise, and a light. Was it evil? Did you feel evil?"

"Well, actually, no. I didn't. I felt the same thing I feel when I hear those bits of conversation, some sort of sincerity, I suppose is the word for it, sincerity and purpose, and I'll tell you something,

David, about this Being, this Being who's stalking me—he has a sleepless mind in his heart and an insatiable personality."

"What?"

"A sleepless mind in his heart," I insisted, "and an insatiable personality," I had blurted out. But I knew it was a quote. I was quoting it from something, but what I had no idea, some bit of poetry?

"What do you mean?" he asked patiently.

"I don't know. I don't even know why I said it. I don't even know why those words came into my mind. But it's true. He does have a sleepless mind in His heart, and He has an insatiable personality. He's not mortal. He's not human!"

" 'A sleepless mind in his heart,' " David quoted the words. " 'Insatiable personality.' "

"Yes. That's The Man, all right, the Being, the male Thing. No, wait, stop, I don't know if it's male; I mean . . . why, I don't know what gender it is . . . it's not distinctly female, let's put it that way, and not being distinctly female, it seems therefore . . . to be male."

"I understand."

"You think I've gone mad, don't you? You hope so, don't you?"

"Of course I don't."

"You ought to," I said. "Because if this being doesn't exist inside my head, if he exists outside, then he can get you too."

This made him very obviously thoughtful and distant and then he said strange words to me I didn't expect.

"But he doesn't want me, does he? And he doesn't want the others, either. He wants you."

I was crestfallen. I am proud, I am an egomaniac of a being; I do love attention; I want glory; I want to be wanted by God and the Devil. I want, I want, I want, I want.

"I'm not upbraiding you," he said. "I'm merely suggesting that this thing has not threatened the others. That in all of these hundreds of years, none of the others . . . none that we know has ever spoken of such a thing. Indeed, in your writing, in your books, you've been most explicit that no vampire had ever seen the Devil, have you not?"

I admitted it with a shrug. Louis, my beloved pupil and fledgling, had once crossed the world to find the "eldest" of the vampires, and Armand had stepped forward with open arms to tell him that there was no God or Devil. And I, half a century before that, had made my own journey for the "eldest" and it had been Marius, made in the days of Rome, who had said the very same thing to me. No God. No Devil.

I sat still, conscious of stupid discomforts, that the place was stuffy, that the perfume was not really perfume, that there were no lilies in these rooms, that it was going to be very cold outside, and I couldn't think of rest until dawn forced me to it, and the night was long, and I was not making sense to David, and I might lose him . . . and that Thing might come, that Thing might come again.

"Will you stay near me?" I hated my own words.

"I'll stand at your side, and I'll try to hold on to you if it tries to take you."

"You will?"

"Yes," he said.

"Why?"

"Don't be foolish," he said. "Look, I don't know what I saw in the café. Never again in my life did I ever see anything like that or hear it. You know, I told you my story once. I went to Brazil, I learned the Candomble secrets. The night you . . . you came after me, I tried to summon the spirits."

"They came. They were too weak to help."

"Right. But . . . what is my point? My point is simply that I love you, that we're linked in some way that none of the others is linked. Louis worships you. You're some sort of dark god to him, though he pretends to hate you for having made him. Armand envies you and spies on you far more than you might think."

"I hear Armand and I see him and I ignore him," I said.

"Marius, he hasn't forgiven you for not becoming his pupil, I think you know that, for not becoming his acolyte, for not believing in history as some sort of redemptive coherence."

"Well put. That is what he believes. Oh, but he's angry with me for much greater things than that, you weren't one of us when I woke the Mother and the Father. You weren't there. But that's another tale."

"I know all of it. You forget your books. I read your work as soon as you write it, as soon as you let it loose into the mortal world."

I laughed bitterly. "Maybe the Devil's read my books too," I said. Again, I loathed being afraid. It made me furious.

"But the point is," he said, "I'll stand with you." He looked down at the table, drifting, the way he so often had when he was mortal, when I could read his mind yet he could defeat me, consciously locking me out. Now it was simply a barrier. I would never again know what his thoughts felt like.

"I'm hungry," I whispered.

"Hunt."

I shook my head. "When I'm ready, I'll take the Victim. As soon as Dora leaves New York. Soon as she goes back to her old convent. She knows the bastard's doomed. That's what she will think after I've done it, that one of his many enemies got him, that his evil came back on him, very Biblical, when all the time it was just a species of killer roaming the Savage Garden of the Earth, a vampire, looking for a juicy mortal, and her father had caught my eye, and it's going to be over, just like that."

"Are you planning to torture this man?"

"David. You shock me. What an impolite question."

"Will you?" he asked more timidly, more imploringly.

"I don't think so. I just want to. . . ." I smiled. He knew now well enough. Nobody had to tell him anymore about drinking the blood, the soul, the memory, the spirit, the heart. I wouldn't know that wretched mortal creature until I took him, held him against my chest, opened up the only honest vein in his body, so to speak. Ah, too many thoughts, too many memories, too much anger.

"I'm going to stay with you," he said. "Do you have rooms here?"

"Nothing proper. Find something for us. Find it close to . . . close to the cathedral."

"Why?"

"Well, David, you should know why. If the Devil starts chasing me down Fifth Avenue, I'll just run into St. Patrick's and run to the High Altar and fall on my knees before the Blessed Sacrament and beg God to forgive me, not to sink me into the river of fire up to my eyes."

"You are on the verge of being truly mad."

"No, not at all. Look at me. I can tie my shoelaces. See? And my tie. Takes some care, you know, to get it all around your neck and into your shirt and so forth, and not look like a lunatic with a big scarf around your neck. I'm together, as mortals so bluntly state it. Can you find us some rooms?"

He nodded.

"There's a glass tower, right over there somewhere, beside the cathedral. Monstrous building."

"The Olympic Tower."

"Yes, could you get us some rooms there? Actually I have mortal agents who can do this sort of thing, I don't know why in the world I'm whining like a fool in this place, asking you to take care of humiliating particulars. . . ."

"I'll take care of it. It's probably too late tonight, but I can swing it tomorrow evening. It will be under the name David Talbot."

"My clothes. There's a stash of them here under the name Isaac Rummel. Just a suitcase or two, and some coats. It's really winter, isn't it?" I gave him the key to the room. This was humiliating. Rather like making a servant of him. Perhaps he'd change his mind and put our new lodgings under the name of Renfield.

"I'll take care of it all. We'll have a palatial base of operations by tomorrow. I'll see that keys are left for you at the desk. But what are you going to be doing?"

I waited, I was listening for the Victim. Still talking to Dora. Dora was leaving in the morning.

I pointed upwards. "Killing that bastard. I think I'll do it tomorrow right after sunset if I can zone in on him quickly enough. Dora will be gone. Oh, I am so hungry. I wish she'd take a midnight plane out of here. Dora, Dora."

"You really like this little girl, don't you?"

"Yes. Find her on television sometime, you'll see. Her talent's rather spectacular, and her teaching has that dangerous emotional grip to it."

"Is she really gifted?"

"With everything. Very white skin, short black hair, bobbed, long thin yet shapely legs, and she dances with such abandon, arms flung out, rather makes one think of a whirling dervish or the Sufis in their perfection, and when she speaks it's not humble precisely, it's full of wonder and all very, very benign."

"I should think so."

"Well, religion isn't always, you know. I mean she doesn't rant about the coming Apocalypse or the Devil coming to get you if you don't send her a check."

He reflected for a moment, then said meaningfully, "I see how it is."

"No, you don't. I love her, yes, but I'll soon forget her completely. It's just that . . . well, there's a convincing version of something there, and delicacy, and she really believes in it; she thinks Jesus walked on this earth. She thinks it happened."

"And this thing that's following you, it's not connected in any way with this choice of victim, her father?"

"Well, there is a way to find out," I said.

"How?"

"Kill the son of a bitch tonight. Maybe I'll do it after he leaves her. My Victim won't stay here with her. He's too scared of bringing danger to her. He never stays in the same hotel with her. He has three different apartments here. I'm surprised he's stayed this long."

"I'm staying with you."

"No, go on, I have to finish this one. I need you, I really need you. I needed to tell you, and to have you with me, the age-old venerable human needs, but I don't need you at my side. I know you're thirsting. I don't have to read your mind to feel that much. You starved as you came here, so that you wouldn't disappoint me. Go prowl the city." I smiled. "You've never hunted New York, have you?"

He shook his head in the negative gesture. His eyes were changing. It was the hunger. It was giving him that dull look, like a dog who had caught the scent of the bitch in heat. We all get that look, the bestial look, but we are nothing as good as bestial, are we? Any of us.

I stood up. "The rooms in the Olympic Tower," I said. "You'll get them so that they look down on St. Patrick's, won't you? Not too high up, low if you can do it, so that the steeples are close."

"You are out of your brilliant preternatural mind."

"No. But I'm going out into the snow now. I hear him up there. He's planning to leave her, he's kissing her, chaste and loving kisses. His car is prowling around out front. He'll go way uptown to that secret place of his where the relics are kept. He thinks his enemies in crime and government know nothing of it, or believe it's just the junk shop of a friend. But I know of it. And what all those treasures mean to him. If he goes up there, I'll follow. . . . No more time, David."

"I've never been so completely confused," he said. "I wanted to say God go with you."

I laughed. I leant to give him a quick kiss on the forehead, so swift others would not make anything of it if they saw it, and then swallowing the fear, the instantaneous fear, I left him.

In the rooms high above, Dora cried. She sat by the window watching the snow and crying. She regretted refusing his new present for her. If only. . . . She pushed her forehead against the cold glass and prayed for her father.

I crossed the street. The snow felt rather good, but then I'm a monster.

I stood at the back of St. Patrick's, watching as my handsome Victim came out, hurriedly through the snow, shoulders hunched, and plunged into the backseat of his expensive black car. I heard him give the address very near to that junk-shop flat where he kept his treasures. All right, he'd be alone up there for a while. Why not do it, Lestat?

Why not let the Devil take you? Go ahead! Refuse to enter Hell in fear. Just go for it.

2

I REACHED his house on the Upper East Side before he did. I'd tracked him here numerous times. I knew the routine. Hirelings lived on the lower and upper floors, though I don't think they knew who he was. It wasn't unlike a vampire's usual arrangement. And between those two flats was his long chain of rooms, the second story of the town house, barred like a prison, and accessible by him through a rear entrance.

He never had a car let him out in front of the place. He'd get out on Madison and cut deep into the block to his back door. Or sometimes he got out on Fifth. He had two routes, and some of the surrounding property was his. But nobody—none of his pursuers—knew of this place.

I wasn't even sure that his daughter, Dora, knew the exact location. He'd never brought her there in all the months I'd been watching him, savoring and licking my lips over his life. And I'd never caught from Dora's mind any distinct image of it.

But Dora knew of his collection. In the past, she had accepted his relics. She had some of them scattered about the empty convent castle in New Orleans. I'd sensed a glimmer or two of these fine things the night when I'd pursued her there. And now my Victim was still lamenting that she'd refused the latest gift. Something truly sacred, or so he thought.

I got into the flat simply enough.

One could hardly call it a flat, though it did include a small lavatory, dirty in the way barren, unused places become dirty, and then room after room was crammed with trunks, statues, bronze figures, heaps of seeming trash that no doubt concealed priceless discoveries.

It felt very strange to be inside, concealed in the small rear room, because I had never done more than look through the windows. The place was cold. When he came, he would create heat and light simply enough.

I sensed he was only halfway up Madison in a crush of traffic, and I began to explore.

At once, a great marble statue of an angel startled me. I came round out of the door and almost ran smack into it. It was one of those angels that used to stand inside church doors, offering holy water in half shells. I had seen them in Europe and in New Orleans.

It was gigantic, and its cruel profile stared blindly into the shadows. Far down the hall, the light came up from the busy little street that ran into Fifth. The usual New York songs of traffic were coming through the walls.

This angel was poised as if he had just landed from the skies to offer his sacred basin. I slapped his bent knee gently and went around him. I didn't like him. I could smell parchment, papyrus, various kinds of metal. The room opposite appeared to be filled with Russian icons. The walls were veritably covered with them and the light was playing on the halos of the sad-eyed Virgins or glaring Christs.

I went on to the next room. Crucifixes. I recognized the Spanish style, and what appeared to be Italian Baroque, and very early work which surely must have been very rare—the Christ grotesque and poorly proportioned yet suffering with appropriate horror on the worm-eaten cross.

Only now did I realize the obvious. It was *all* religious art. There was nothing that wasn't religious. But then it's rather easy to say that about all art from the end of the last century backwards, if you think about it. I mean, the great majority of art is religious.

The place was utterly devoid of life.

Indeed, it stank of insecticide. Of course, he had saturated it to save his old wooden statues, he would have had to do that. I could not hear or smell rats, or detect any living thing at all. The lower flat was empty of its occupants, though a small radio chattered the news in a bathroom.

Easy to blot out that little sound. On the floors above, there were mortals, but they were old, and I caught a vision of a sedentary man, with earphones on his head, swaying to the rhythm of some esoteric German music, Wagner, doomed lovers deploring the "hated dawn" or some heavy, repetitive, and distinctly pagan foolishness. Leitmotiv be damned. There was another person up there, but she was too feeble to be of any concern, and I could catch only one image of her and she appeared to be sewing or knitting.

I didn't care enough about any of this to bring it into loving focus. I was safe in the flat, and He'd be coming soon, filling all these rooms with the perfume of his blood, and I'd do my damnedest not to break his neck before I'd had every drop. Yes, this was the night.

Dora wouldn't find out until she got home tomorrow anyway. Who would know that I'd left his corpse here?

I went on into the living room. This was tolerably clean; the room where he relaxed and read and studied and fondled his objects. There were his comfortable bulky couches, fitted with heaps of pillows, and halogen lamps of black iron so delicate and light and modern and easy to maneuver that they looked like insects poised on tables and on the floor itself, and sometimes on top of cardboard boxes.

The crystal ashtray was full of butts, which confirmed he preferred safety to cleanliness, and I saw scattered glasses in which the liquor had long ago dried to a glaze that was now flaked like lacquer.

Thin, rather frowsy drapes hung over the windows, making the light soiled and tantalizing.

Even this room was jammed with statues of saints—a very lurid and emotional St. Anthony holding a chubby Child Jesus in the crook of his arm; a very large and remote Virgin, obviously of Latin American origin. And some monstrous angelic being of black granite, which even with my eyes I could not fully examine in the gloom, something resembling more a Mesopotamian demon than an angel.

For one split second this granite monster sent the shivers through me. It resembled . . . no, I should say its wings made me think of the creature I'd glimpsed, this Thing that I thought was following me.

But I didn't hear any footsteps here. There was no rip in the fabric of the world. It was a statue of granite, that's all, a hideous ornament perhaps from some gruesome church full of images of Hell and Heaven.

Lots of books lay on the tables. Ah, he did love books. I mean, there were the fine ones, made of vellum and very old and all that, but current books, too, titles in philosophy and religion, current affairs, memoirs of currently popular war correspondents, even a few volumes of poetry.

Mircea Eliade, history of religions in various volumes, might have been Dora's gift, and there, a brand-new *History of God*, by a woman named Karen Armstrong. Something else on the meaning of life—*Understanding the Present*, by Bryan Appleyard. Hefty books. But fun, my kind, anyway. And the books had been handled. Yes, it was his scent on these books, heavily his scent, not Dora's.

He had spent more time here than I ever realized.

I scanned the shadows, the objects, I let the air fill my nostrils. Yes, he'd come here often and with someone else, and that person . . . that person had died here! I hadn't realized any of this before, of course, and it was just more preparation for the meal. So the murderer drug dealer had loved a young man in these digs once, and it hadn't been all clutter. I was getting flashes of it in the worst way, more emotion than image, and I found myself fairly fragile under the onslaught. This death hadn't occurred all that long ago.

Had I passed this Victim in those times, when his friend was dying, I would never have settled on him, just let him go on. But then he was so flashy!

He was coming up the back steps now, the inner secret stairway, cautiously taking each step, his hand on the handle of his gun inside his coat, very Hollywood style, though there wasn't much else about him that was predictable. Except, of course, that many who deal in cocaine are eccentric.

He reached the back door, saw that I'd opened it. Rage. I slipped over into the corner opposite that overbearing granite statue, and I stood back between two dusty saints. There wasn't enough light for him to see me right off. He'd have to turn on one of the little halogens, and they were spots.

Right now, he listened, he sensed. He hated it that someone had broken open his door; he was murderous and had no intention of not investigating, alone; a little court case was held in his mind. No, no one could possibly know about this place, the judge decided. Had to be a petty thief, goddamn it, and those words were heaped in rage upon the accidental.

He slipped the gun out, and he started going through his rooms, through rooms I'd skipped. I heard the light switch, saw the flash in the hall. He went on to another and another.

How on earth could he tell this place was empty? I mean, anyone could be hiding in this place. I knew it was empty. But what made him so sure? But maybe that's how he'd stayed alive all this time, he had just the right mixture of creativity and carelessness.

At last came the absolutely delicious moment. He was satisfied he was alone.

He stepped into the living-room door, his back to the long hall, and slowly scanned the room, failing to see me, of course, and then he put his large nine-millimeter gun back in his shoulder holster, and he slipped off his gloves very slowly.

There was enough light for me to note everything I adored about him.

Soft black hair, the Asian face that you couldn't clearly identify as Indian or Japanese, or Gypsy; could even have been Italian or Greek; the cunning black eyes, and the remarkably perfect symmetry of the bones—one of the very few traits he'd passed on to his daughter, Dora. She was fair skinned, Dora. Her mother must have been milk white. He was my favorite shade, caramel.

Suddenly something made him very uneasy. He turned his back to me, eyes quite obviously locked to some object that had alarmed him. Nothing to do with me. I had touched nothing. But his alarm had thrown up a wall between my mind and his. He was on full alert, which meant he wasn't thinking sequentially.

He was tall, his back very straight, the coat long, his shoes those Savile Row handmade kind that takes the English shops forever. He took a step away from me, and I realized immediately from a jumble of images that it was the black granite statue that had startled him.

It was perfectly obvious. He didn't know what it was or how it had gotten here. He approached, very cautious, as though someone might be hiding in the vicinity of the thing, then pivoted, scanned the room, and slowly drew out his gun again.

Possibilities were passing through his mind in rather orderly fashion. He knew one art dealer who was stupid enough to have delivered the thing and left the door unlocked, but that dealer would have called him before ever coming.

And this thing? Mesopotamian? Assyrian? Suddenly, impulsively, he forgot all practical matters and put his hand out and touched the granite. God, he loved it. He loved it and he was acting stupid.

I mean, there could have been one of his enemies here. But then why would a gangster or a federal investigator come bearing a gift such as that?

Whatever the case, he was enthralled by the piece. I still couldn't see it clearly. I would have slipped off the violet glasses, which would have helped enormously, but I didn't dare move. I wanted to see this, this adoration of his for the object that was new. I could feel his uncompromising desire for this statue, to own it, to have it here . . . the very sort of desire which had first attracted him to me.

He was thinking only about it, the fine carving, that it was recent, not ancient, for obvious stylistic reasons, seventeenth century perhaps, a fleshed-out rendering of a fallen angel.

Fallen angel. He did everything but step on tiptoe and kiss the thing. He put his left hand up and ran it all over the granite face and the granite hair. Damn, I couldn't see it! How could he put up with this darkness? But then he was smack up against it, and I was twenty feet away and stuffed between two saints, without a good perspective.

Finally, he turned and switched on one of the halogen lamps. Thing looked like a preying mantis. He moved the thin black iron limb so the beam shone up on the statue's face. Now I could see both profiles beautifully!

He made little noises of lust. This was unique! The dealer was of no importance, the back door forgiven, the supposed danger fled. He slipped the gun in the holster again, almost as if he wasn't even thinking about it, and he did go up on tiptoe, trying to get eye level with this appalling graven image. Feathered wings. I could see that now. Not reptilian, feathered. But the face, classical, robust, the long nose, the chin . . . yet there was a ferocity in the profile. And why was the statue black? Maybe it was only St. Michael pushing devils into hell, angry, righteous. No, the hair was too rank and tangled for that. Armour, breastplate, and then of course I saw the most telling details. That it had the legs and feet of a goat. Devil.

Again there came a shiver. *Like the thing I'd seen.* But that was stupid! And I had no sense of the Stalker being near me now. No disorientation. I wasn't even really afraid. It was just a frisson, nothing more.

I held very still. Now take your time, I thought. Figure this out. You've got your Victim and this statue is just a coincidental detail that further enriches the entire scenario. He turned another halogen beam on the thing. It was almost erotic the way he studied it. I smiled. Erotic the way I was studying him—this forty-seven-year-old man with a youth's health and a criminal's poise. Fearlessly he stood back, having forgotten any threat of any kind, and looked at this new acquisition. Where had it come from? Whom? He didn't give a damn about the price. If only Dora. No, Dora wouldn't like this thing. Dora. Dora, who had cut him to the heart tonight refusing his gift.

His entire posture changed; he didn't want to think about Dora again, and all the things Dora had said—that he had to renounce what he did, that she'd never take another cent for the church, that she couldn't help but love him and suffer if he did go to court, that she didn't want the veil.

What veil? Just a fake, he'd said, but one of the best he'd found so far. Veil? I suddenly connected his hot little memory with something hanging on the far wall, a framed bit of fabric, a painted Christface. Veil. Veronica's veil.

And just an hour ago he'd said to Dora, "Thirteenth century, and so beautiful, Dora, for the love of heaven. Take it. If I can't leave these things to you, Dora. . . ."

So this Christface had been his precious gift?

"I won't take them anymore, Daddy, I told you. I won't."

He had pressed her with the vague scheme that this new gift could be exhibited for the public. So could all his relics. They could raise money for the church.

She had started to cry, and all this had been going on back at the hotel, whilst David and I had been in the bar only yards from them.

"And say these bastards do manage to pick me up, some warrant, something I haven't covered, you're telling me you won't take these things? You'll let strangers take them?"

"Stolen, Daddy," she had cried. "They are not clean. They are tainted."

He really could not understand his daughter. It seemed he'd been a thief ever since he was a child. New Orleans. The boardinghouse, the curious mixture of poverty and elegance and his mother drunk most of the time. The old captain who ran the antique shop. All this was going through his mind. Old Captain had had the front rooms of the house, and he, my Victim, had brought the breakfast tray each morning to Old Captain, before going on to school. Boardinghouse, service, elegant oldsters, St. Charles Avenue. The time when the men sat on the galleries in the evening and the old ladies did, too, with their hats. Daylight times I'd never know again.

Such reverie. No, Dora wouldn't like this. And he wasn't so sure he did either, suddenly. He had standards which were often difficult to explain to people. He began some defense as though talking to the dealer who'd brought this. "It's beautiful, yes, but it's too Baroque! It lacks that element of distortion that I treasure."

I smiled. I loved this guy's mind. And the smell of the blood, well. I took a deliberate breath of it, and let it turn me into a total predator. Go slowly, Lestat. You've waited for months. Don't rush it. And he's such a monster himself. He'd shot people in the head, killed them with knives. Once in a small grocery he had shot both his enemy and the proprietor's wife with utter indifference. Woman in the way. And he had coolly walked out. Those were early New York days, before Miami, before South America. But he remembered that murder, and that's why I knew about it.

He thought a lot about those various deaths. That's why I thought about them.

He was studying the hoofed feet of this thing, this angel, devil, demon. I realized its wings reached the ceiling. I could feel that shiver again if I let myself. But again, I was on firm ground, and there was nothing from any other realm in this place.

He slipped off his coat now, and stood in shirtsleeves. That was too much. I could see the flesh of his neck, of course, as he opened his collar. I could see that particularly beautiful place right below his ear, that special measure between the back of the neck of a human and the lobe of his ear, which has so much to do with male beauty.

Hell, I had not invented the significance of necks. Everyone knew what those proportions meant. He was all over pleasing to me, but it was the mind, really. To hell with his Asian beauty and all that, even his vanity which made him glow for fifty feet in all directions. It was the mind, the mind that was locked onto the statue, and had for one merciful moment let thoughts of Dora go.

He reached for another one of the little halogen spots and

clamped his hand over the hot metal and directed it full on the demon's wing, the wing I could best see, and I too saw the perfection he was thinking about, the Baroque love of detail; no. He did not collect this sort of thing. His taste was for the grotesque, and this thing was only grotesque by accident. God, it was hideous. It had a ferocious mane of hair, and a scowl on its face that could have been designed by William Blake, and huge rounded eyes that fixed on him in seeming hatred.

"Blake, yes!" he said suddenly. He turned around. "Blake. The damned thing looks like one of those drawings by Blake."

I realized he was staring at me. I had projected the thought, carelessly, yes, obviously with purpose. I felt a shock of connection. He saw me. He saw the glasses perhaps, and the light, or maybe my hair.

Very slowly I stepped out, with my arms at my sides. I wanted nothing so vulgar as his reaching for his gun. But he hadn't reached for it. He merely looked at me, blinded perhaps by the bright little lights so near to him. The halogen beam threw the shadow of the angel's wing on the ceiling. I came closer.

He said absolutely nothing. He was afraid. Or rather, let me say, he was alarmed. He was more than alarmed. He felt this might very well be his last confrontation. Someone had gotten by him totally! And it was too late to be reaching for guns, or doing anything so literal, and yet he wasn't actually in fear of me.

Damned if he didn't know I wasn't human.

I came swiftly towards him, and took his face in both my hands. He went into a sweat and tremble, naturally, yet he reached up and pulled the glasses off my eyes and they fell on the floor.

"Oh, it's gorgeous, finally," I whispered, "to be so very close to you!"

He couldn't form words. No mortal in my grip like this could have been expected to utter anything but prayers, and he had no prayers! He stared right into my eyes, and then very slowly took my measure, not daring to move, his face still fixed in both my cold, cold hands, and he knew. Not human.

It was the strangest reaction! Of course I'd confronted recognition before, in lands the world over; but prayer, madness, some desperate atavistic response, something always accompanied it. Even in old Europe where they believed in the nosferatu, they'd scream out a prayer before I sank my teeth.

But this, what was this, his staring at me, this comical criminal courage!

"Going to die like you lived?" I whispered.

One thought galvanized him. *Dora.* He went into a violent struggle, grabbing at my hands, realizing they felt like stone, and then convulsing, as he tried to pull himself loose, held mercilessly by the face. He hissed at me.

Some inexplicable mercy came over me. Don't torture him like this. He knows too much. Understands too much. God, you've had months of watching him, you don't have to stretch this out. On the other hand, when will you find another kill like this one!

Well, hunger overcame judgment. I pressed my forehead against his neck first, shifting my hand to the back of his head, let him feel my hair, heard him draw in his breath, and then I drank.

I had him. I had the gush, and him and Old Captain in the front room, the streetcar crashing past outside, and him saying to Old Captain, "You ever show it to me again or ask me to touch it and I won't ever come near you." And Old Captain swearing he never would. Old Captain taking him to the movies, and to dinner at the Monteleone, and on the plane to Atlanta, having vowed never to do it again, "Just let me be around you, son, just let me be near you, I'll never, I swear." His mother drunk in the doorway, brushing her hair. "I know your game, you and that old man, I know just what you're doing. He bought you those clothes? You think I don't know." And then Terry with the bullet hole in the middle of her face, a blond-haired girl turning to the side and crumpling to the floor, the fifth murder and it has to be you, Terry, you. He and Dora were in the truck. And Dora knew. Dora was only six and she knew. Knew he'd shot her mother, Terry. *And they'd never, never spoken a word about it.* Terry's body in a plastic sack. Ah, God, plastic. And him saying, "Mommy's gone." Dora hadn't even asked. Six years old, she knew. Terry screaming, "You think you can take my daughter from me, you son of a bitch, you think you can take my child, I'm leaving tonight with Jake and she's going with me." Bang, you're dead, honey. I couldn't stand you anyway. In a heap on the floor, the very flashy cute kind of common girl with very oval pale pink nails, and lipstick that always looks extraordinarily fresh, and hair from a bottle. Pink shorts, little thighs.

He and Dora driving in the night, and they never had spoken a word.

*What are you doing to me! You are killing me! You are taking my blood,
not my soul, you thief, you . . . what in the name of God?*

"You talking to me?" I drew back, blood dripping from my lips,
Good God, he *was* talking to me! I bit down again, and this time I did
break his neck, but he wouldn't stop.

*Yes, you, what are you? Why, why this, the blood? Tell me, damn you
into hell! Damn you!*

I had crushed the bones of his arms, twisted his shoulder out of
the socket, the last blood I could get was there on my tongue. I stuck
my tongue into the wound, give me, give me, give me. . . .

But what, what is your name, under God, who are you?

He was dead. I dropped him and stepped back. Talking to me!
Talking to me during the kill? Asking *me* who *I* was? Piercing the
swoon?

"Oh, you are so full of surprises," I whispered. I tried to clear my
head. I was warmly full of blood. I let it stay in my mouth. I wanted to
pick him up, tear open his wrist, drink anything that was left, but that
was so ugly, and the truth was, I had no intention of touching him
again! I swallowed and ran my tongue along my teeth, getting the last
taste, he and Dora in the truck, she six years old, Mommy dead, shot
in the head, with Daddy now forever.

"That was the fifth killing!" he'd said aloud to me, I'd heard him.
"Who are you?"

"Talking to me, you bastard!" I looked down at him, ooh, the
blood was just flooding my fingertips finally and moving down my
legs; I closed my eyes, and I thought, Live for this, just for this, for
this taste, this feeling, and his words came back to me, words to Dora
in a fancy bar, "I sold my soul for places like this."

"Oh, for Godsakes, die, damn it!" I said. I wanted the blood to
keep burning, but enough of him, hell, six months was plenty for a
love affair between vampire and human! I looked up.

The black thing wasn't a statue at all. It was alive. And it was
studying me. It was living and breathing and watching me under its
furious shining black scowl, looking down at me.

"No, not true," I said aloud. I tried to fall into the deep calm that
danger often produces in me. *Not true.*

I nudged his dead body on the floor deliberately just to be sure I
was still there, and not going mad, and in terror of the disorientation,
but it didn't come, and then I screamed.

I screamed like any kid.

And I ran out of there.

I tore out of there, down the hall, out of the back and into the wide night.

I went up over the rooftops, and then in sheer exhaustion slipped down in a narrow alley, and lay against the bricks. No, that couldn't have been true. That was some last image he projected, my Victim; he threw that image out in death, a sweet vengeance. Making that statue look alive, that big dark winged thing, that goat-legged. . . .

"Yeah," I said. I wiped my lips. I was lying in dirty snow. There were other mortals in this alley. Don't bother us. I won't. I wiped my lips again. "Yeah, vengeance; all his love," I whispered aloud, "for all the things in that place, and he threw that at me. He knew. He knew what I was. He knew how. . . ."

And besides, the Thing that stalked me had never been so calm, so still, so reflective. It had always been swelling and rising like so much thick, stinking smoke and those voices . . . That had been a mere statue standing there.

I got up, furious with myself, absolutely furious for having fled, for having passed up the last little trick involved in the whole kill. I was furious enough to go back there, and kick his dead body and kick that statue, which no doubt returned to granite the instant that conscious life went completely out of the dying brain of its owner.

Broken arms, shoulders. As if from the bloody heap I'd made of him, he'd called up that thing.

And Dora will hear about this. Broken arms, shoulders. Neck broken.

I went out onto Fifth Avenue. I walked into the wind.

I stuffed my hands in the pockets of my wool blazer, which was far too light to look appropriate in this quiet blizzard, and I walked and walked. "All right, damn it, you knew what I was, and for a moment, you made that thing look alive."

I stopped dead still, staring over the traffic at the dark snow-covered woods of Central Park.

"If it *is* all connected, come for me." I was talking not to him now, or the statue, but to the Stalker. I simply refused to be afraid. I was just completely out of my head.

And where was David? Hunting somewhere? Hunting . . . as he had so loved to do as a mortal man in the Indian jungles, hunting, and I'd made him the hunter of his brothers forever.

I made a decision.

I was going back at once to the flat. I'd look at the damned statue, and see for myself that it was utterly inanimate, and then I'd do what I ought to do for Dora—that is, get rid of her father's corpse.

It took me only moments to get back, to be going up the narrow pitch-dark back stairs again, and into the flat. I was past all patience with my fear, simply furious, humiliated and shaken, and at the same time curiously excited—as I always am by the unknown.

Stench of his freshly dead body. Stench of wasted blood.

I could hear or sense nothing else. I went into a small room which had once been an active kitchen and still contained the remnants of housekeeping from the time of that dead mortal whom the Victim had loved. Yes, just what I wanted under the sink pipes where mortals always shove it, a box of green plastic garbage sacks, just perfect for his remains.

It suddenly hit me that he had chucked his murdered wife, Terry, into such a bag, I'd seen it, smelled it, when I was feasting on him. Oh, hell with it. So he'd given me the idea.

There were a few pieces of cutlery around, though nothing that would allow a surgical or artistic job. I took the largest of the knives, carbon-steel blade, and went into the living room, deliberately without hesitation, and turned and looked at the mammoth statue.

The halogens were still shining; bright, deliberate beams in the shadowy clutter.

Statue; goat-legged angel.

You idiot, Lestat.

I went up to it and stood before it, looking coldly at the details. Probably *not* seventeenth-century. Probably contemporary, executed by hand, yes, but it had the utter perfection of something contemporary, and the face did have the William Blake sublime expression—an evil, scowling, goat-legged being with the eyes of Blake's saints and sinners, full of innocence as well as wrath.

I wanted it suddenly, would liked to have kept it, gotten it down some way to my rooms in New Orleans as a keepsake for practically falling down dead in fear at its feet. Cold and solemn it stood before me. And then I realized that all these relics might be lost if I didn't do something with them. As soon as his death was known, all this would be confiscated, that was his whole point with Dora, that this, his true wealth, would pass into indifferent hands.

And Dora had turned her narrow little back to him and wept, a waif consumed with grief and horror and the worst frustration, the inability to comfort the one she most loved.

I looked down. I was standing over his mangled body. He still looked fresh, wrecked, murdered by a slob. Black hair very soft and mussed, eyes half open. His white shirtsleeves were stained an evil pinkish color from the little blood that oozed out of the wounds I'd accidentally inflicted, crushing him. His torso was at a hideous angle in relation to his legs. I'd snapped his neck, and snapped his spine.

Well, I'd get him out of here. I'd get rid of him, and then for a long time no one would know. No one would know he was dead; and the investigators couldn't pester Dora, or make her miserable. Then I'd think about the relics, perhaps spiriting them away for her.

From his pockets I took his identification. All bogus, nothing with his real name.

His real name had been Roger.

I knew that from the beginning, but only Dora had called him Roger. In all his dealings with others, he'd had exotic aliases, with odd medieval sounds. This passport said Frederick Wynken. Now that amused me. Frederick Wynken.

I gathered all identifying materials and put them in my pockets to be totally destroyed later.

I went to work with the knife. I cut off both his hands, rather amazed at their delicacy and how well-manicured were his nails. He had loved himself so much, and with reason. And his head, I hacked that off, more through brute strength forcing the knife through tendon and bone than any sort of real skill. I didn't bother to close his eyes. The stare of the dead holds so little fascination, really. It mimics nothing living. His mouth was soft without emotion, and cheeks smooth in death. The usual thing. These—the head, and the hands—I put into two separate green sacks, and then I folded up the body, more or less, and crammed it into the third sack.

There was blood all over the carpet, which I realized was only one of many, many carpets layering this floor, junk-shop style, and that was too bad. But the point was, the body was on its way out. Its decay wouldn't bring mortals from above or below. And without the body, no one might ever know what had become of him . . . best for Dora, surely, than to have seen great glossy photographs of a scene such as I had made here.

I took one last look at the scowling countenance of the angel, devil, or whatever he was with his ferocious mane and beautiful lips and huge polished eyes. Then, hefting the three sacks like Santa Claus, I went out to get rid of Roger piece by piece.

This was not much of a problem.

It gave me merely an hour to think as I dragged myself along through the snowy, empty black streets, uptown, searching for bleak chaotic construction sights, and heaps of garbage, and places where rot and filth had accumulated and were not likely to be examined anytime soon, let alone cleared away.

Beneath a freeway overpass, I left his hands buried in a huge pile of trash. The few mortals hovering there, with blankets and a little fire going in a tin can, took no notice of what I did at all. I shoved the plastic-wrapped hands so deep in the rubble no one could conceivably try to retrieve them. Then I went up to the mortals, who didn't so much as look up at me, and I dropped a few bills down by the fire. The wind almost caught the money. Then a hand, a living hand, of course, the hand of one of these bums, flashed out in the firelight and caught the bills and drew them back into the breathing darkness.

"Thanks, brother."

I said, "Amen."

The head I deposited in a similar manner much farther away. Back door dumpster. Wet garbage of a restaurant. Stench. I took no last look at the head. It embarrassed me. It was no trophy. I would never save a man's head as a trophy. The idea seemed deplorable. I didn't like the hard feel of it through the plastic. If the hungry found it, they'd never report it. Besides, the hungry had been here for their share of the tomatoes and lettuce and spaghetti and crusts of French bread. The restaurant had closed hours ago. The garbage was frozen; it rattled and clattered when I shoved his head deep into the mess.

I went back downtown, still walking, still with this last sack over my shoulder, his miserable chest and arms and legs. I walked down Fifth, past the hotel of the sleeping Dora, past St. Patrick's, on and on, past the fancy stores. Mortals rushed through doorways beneath awnings; cabbies blew their horns in fury at hulking, slow limousines.

On and on I walked. I kicked at the sludge and I hated myself. I could smell him and hated this too. But in a way, the feast had been so divine that it was just to require this aftermath, this cleaning up.

The others—Armand, Marius, all my immortal cohorts, lovers,

friends, enemies—always cursed me for not "disposing of the remains." All right, this time Lestat was being a good vampire. He was cleaning up after himself.

I was almost to the Village when I found another perfect place, a huge warehouse, seemingly abandoned, its upper floors filled with the pretty sparkle of broken windows. And inside it, refuse of every description, in a massive heap. I could smell decayed flesh. Someone had died in there weeks ago. Only the cold kept the smell from reaching human nostrils. Or maybe no one cared.

I went farther into the cavernous room—smell of gasoline, metal, red brick. One mountain of trash stood as big as a mortuary pyramid in the middle of the room. A truck was there, parked perilously close to it, the engine still warm. But no living beings were here.

And there was decayed flesh aplenty in the largest pile. I reckoned by scent at least three dead bodies, scattered through the rubble. Perhaps there were more. The smell was utterly loathsome to me, so I didn't spend a great deal of time anatomizing the situation.

"Okay, my friend, I give you over to a graveyard," I said. I shoved the sack deep, deep among the broken bottles, smashed cans, bits of stinking fruit, heaps and stacks of cardboard and wood and trash. I almost caused an avalanche. Indeed there was a small trash quake or two and then the clumsy pyramid re-formed itself quietly. The only sounds were the sounds of rats. A single beer bottle rolled on the floor, a few feet free of the monument, gleaming, silent, alone.

For a long moment, I studied the truck; battered, anonymous, warm engine, smell of recent human occupants. What did I care what they did here? The fact is they came and went through the big metal doors, ignoring or occasionally feeding this charnel heap. Most likely ignoring it. Who would park next to one's own murder victims?

But in all these big dense modern cities, I mean the big-time cities, the world-class dens of evil—New York, Tokyo, Hong Kong—you can find the strangest configurations of mortal activity. Criminality had begun to fascinate me in its many facets. That's what had brought me to him.

Roger. Good-bye, Roger.

I went out again. The snow had stopped falling. It was desolate here, and sad. A bare mattress lay on the corner of the block, the snow covering it. The streetlamps were broken. I wasn't certain precisely where I was.

I walked in the direction of the water, to the very end of the island, and then I saw one of those very ancient churches, churches that went back to the Dutch days of Manhattan, with a little fenced grave-yard attached to it with stones that would read awesome statistics such as 1704, or even 1692.

It was a Gothic treasure of a building, a tiny bit of the glory of St. Patrick's, and possibly even more intricate and mysterious, a welcome sight for all its detail and organization and conviction amid the big-city blandness and wastes.

I sat on the church steps, rather liking the carved surfaces of the broken arches, rather liking to sink back in the darkness against sanctified stone.

I realized very carefully that the Stalker was nowhere about, that tonight's deeds had brought me no visits from another realm, or horrifying footsteps, that the great granite statue had been inanimate, and that I still had Roger's identification in my pocket, and this would give Dora weeks, perhaps even months, before her peace of mind was disturbed by her father's disappearance, and she would now never know the details.

So much for that. The end of the adventure. I felt better, far better than when I'd spoken with David. Going back, looking at that monstrous granite thing, it had been the perfect thing to do.

Only problem was that Roger's stench clung to me. Roger. He'd been "the Victim" until when? Now I was calling him Roger. Was that emblematic of love? Dora called him Roger and Daddy and Roge and Dad. "Darling, this is Roge," he'd say to her from Istanbul. "Can you meet me in Florida, just for a few days. I have to talk to you. . . ."

I pulled out the phony identification. The wind was harsh and cold, but no more snow, and the snow that was on the ground was hardening. No mortal would have sat here like this, in this shallow high broken arch of a church door, but I liked it.

I looked at this fake passport. Actually it was a complete set of false papers, some of which I didn't understand. There was a visa for Egypt. Smuggling from there, no doubt! And the name Wynken made me smile again because it is one of those names that makes even children laugh when they hear it. Wynken, Blinken, and Nod. Wasn't that the poem?

It was a simple matter to tear all this into tiny fragments, and let it blow away into the night, over the tiny upright stones of the small graveyard. What a gust. It went like ashes, as if his identity had been cremated and the final tribute was being paid.

I felt weary, full of blood, satisfied, and foolish now for having been so afraid when I talked to David. David no doubt thought I was a fool. But what had I really ascertained? Only that the Thing stalking me wasn't particularly protective of Roger, the Victim, or had nothing to do with Roger. Hadn't I already known this? It didn't mean the Stalker was gone.

It just meant the Stalker chose his own moments and maybe they had nothing to do with what I did.

I admired the little church. How priceless and ornate and incongruous among the other buildings of lower Manhattan, except that nothing in this strange city is exactly incongruous anymore because the mix of Gothic and ancient and modern is so very thick. The nearby street sign said Wall Street.

Was I at the very foot of Wall Street? I rested back against the stones, closed my eyes. David and I would confer tomorrow night. And what of Dora? Did Dora sleep like an angel in her bed in the hotel opposite the cathedral? Would I forgive myself if I took one last secret, safe, forlorn peek at Dora in her bed before letting go of the whole adventure? Over.

Best to get the idea of the little girl out of my mind; forget the figure moving through the huge dark corridors of that empty New Orleans convent with the electric torch in hand, brave Dora. Not at all like the last mortal woman I'd loved. No, forget about it. Forget about it, Lestat, you hear me?

The world was full of potential victims, when you began to think in terms of an entire life pattern, an ambience to an existence, a complete personality, so to speak. Maybe I'd go back down to Miami if I could get David to go with me. Tomorrow night David and I could talk.

Of course he might be thoroughly annoyed that I'd sent him to seek refuge in the Olympic Tower and was now ready to move south. But then maybe we wouldn't move south.

I became acutely aware that if I heard those footsteps now, if I sensed the Stalker, I'd be trembling tomorrow night in David's arms. The Stalker didn't care where I went. And the Stalker was real.

Black wings, the sense of something dark accumulating, thick smoke, and the light. Don't dwell on it. You have done enough grue-some thinking for one night, haven't you?

When would I spot another mortal like Roger? When would I see another light shining that bright? And the son of a bitch talking to me through it all, talking through the swoon! Talking to *me*! And managing to make that statue look alive somehow with some feeble telepathic impulse, damn him. I shook my head. Had I brought that on? Had I done something different?

By tracking Roger for months had I come to love him so much that I was talking to him as I killed him, in some soundless sonnet of devotion? No. I was just drinking and loving him, and taking him into myself. Roger in me.

A car came slowly through the darkness, stopping beside me. Mortals who wanted to know if I needed shelter. I gave a wave of my head, turned, crossed the little graveyard, stepping on grave after grave as I made my way through the headstones, and was off towards the Village, moving so fast probably they could not have even seen me go.

Imagine it. They see this blond young man in a double-breasted navy-blue blazer, with a flaming scarf around his neck, sitting in the cold on the steps of the quaint little church. And then the figure vanishes. I laughed out loud, loving the sound of it as it went up the brick walls. Now I was near music, people walking arm in arm, human voices, the smell of cooking. There were young people about, healthy enough to think that bitter winter could be fun.

The cold had begun to annoy me. To be almost humanly painful. I wanted to go inside.

3

I WALKED on only a few steps, saw revolving doors, pushed into the lobby of someplace or other, a restaurant I think, and found myself sitting at the bar. Just what I wanted, half empty, very dark, too warm, bottles glittering in the center of the circular counter. Some comforting noise from the diners beyond the open doors.

I put my elbows on the bar, my heels hooked on the brass rail. I sat there on the stool shivering, listening to mortals talk, listening to nothing, listening to the inevitable sloth and stupidity of a bar, head down, sunglasses gone—damn, I had lost my violet glasses!—yes, nice and dark here, very, very dark, a kind of late-night languor lying over everything, a club of some sort? I didn't know, didn't care.

"Drink, sir?" Lazy, arrogant face.

I named a mineral water. And as soon as he set down the glass, I dipped my fingers into it and washed them. He was gone already. Wouldn't have cared if I had started baptizing babies with the water. Other customers were scattered at tables in the darkness . . . a woman crying in some far-off corner and a man telling her harshly that she was attracting attention. She wasn't. Nobody gave a damn.

I washed my mouth off with the napkin and water.

"More water," I said. I pushed the polluted glass away from me. Sluggishly, he acknowledged my request, young blood, bland personality, ambitionless life, then drifted off.

I heard a little laugh nearby . . . the man to my right, two stools away, perhaps, who'd been there when I came in, youngish, scentless. Utterly scentless, which was most strange.

In annoyance I turned and looked at him.

"Going to run again?" he whispered. It was the Victim.

It was Roger, sitting there on the stool.

He wasn't broken or battered or dead. He was complete with his head and his hands. He wasn't there. He only appeared to be there, very solid and very quiet, and he smiled at me, thrilled by my terror.

"What's the matter, Lestat?" he asked in that voice I so loved after six months of listening to it. "No one in all these centuries has ever come back to haunt you?"

I said nothing. Not there. No, not there. Material, but not the same material as anything else. David's word. Different fabric. I stiffened. That's a pathetic understatement. I was rigid with incredulity and rage.

He got up and moved over onto the stool close to me. He was getting more distinct and detailed by the second. Now I could catch something like a sound coming from him, a sound of something alive, or organized, but certainly no breathing human being.

"And in a few minutes more I'll be strong enough perhaps to ask for a cigarette or a glass of wine," he said.

He reached into his coat, a favorite coat, not the one in which I'd killed him, another coat made for him in Paris, that he liked, and he drew out his flashy little gold lighter and made the flame shoot up, very blue and dangerous, butane.

He looked at me. I could see that his black curly hair was combed, his eyes very clear. Handsome Roger. His voice sounded exactly the way it had when he was alive: international, originless, New Orleans–born and world-traveled. No British fastidiousness, and no Southern patience. His precise, quick voice.

"I'm quite serious," he said. "You mean in all these years, not one single victim has ever come back to haunt you?"

"No," I said.

"You're amazing. You really won't tolerate being afraid for a moment, will you?"

"No."

Now he appeared completely solid. I had no idea whether anyone else could see him. No idea, but I suspected they could. He looked like anyone might look. I could see the buttons on his white cuffs, and the soft white flash of his collar at the back of the neck, where the fine hair came down over it. I could see his eyelashes, which had always been extraordinarily long.

The bartender returned and set down the water glass for me, without looking at him. I still wasn't sure. The kid was too rude for that to be proof of anything except that I was in New York.

"How are you doing this?" I asked.

"The same way any other ghost does it," he said. "I'm dead. I've been dead for over an hour and a half now, and I have to talk to you! I don't know how long I can stay here, I don't know when I'll start to . . . God knows what, but you have to listen to me."

"Why?" I demanded.

"Don't be so nasty," he whispered, appearing truly hurt. "You murdered me."

"And you? The people you've killed, Dora's mother? She ever come back to demand an audience with you?"

"Ooh, I knew it. I knew it!" he said. He was visibly shaken. "You know about Dora! God in Heaven, take my soul to Hell, but don't let him hurt Dora."

"Stop being absurd. I wouldn't hurt Dora. It was you I was after. I've followed you around the world. If it hadn't been for a passing respect for Dora, I would have killed you long before now."

The bartender had reappeared. This brought the most ecstatic smile to my companion's lips. He looked right at the kid.

"Yes, my dear boy, let me see, the very last drink unless I'm very badly mistaken, make it bourbon. I grew up in the South. What do you have? No, I'll tell you what, son, just make it Southern Comfort." His laugh was private and convivial and soft.

The bartender moved on, and Roger turned his furious eyes on me. "You have to listen to me, whatever the Hell you are, vampire, demon, devil, I don't care, you cannot hurt my daughter."

"I don't intend to hurt her. I would never hurt her. Go on to hell, you'll feel better. Good night."

"You smug son of a bitch. How many years do you think I had?" Droplets of sweat were breaking out on his face. His hair was moving a little in the natural draft through the room.

"I couldn't give less of a damn!" I said. "You were a meal worth waiting for."

"You've got quite a swagger, don't you?" he said acidly. "But you're nothing as shallow as you pretend to be."

"Oh, you don't think so? Try me. You may find me 'as sounding brass or a tinkling cymbal.' "

That gave him pause.

It gave me pause too. Where did those words come from? Why did they roll off my tongue like that? I was not likely to use that sort of imagery!

He was absorbing all this, my preoccupation, my obvious self-doubt. How did it manifest itself, I wonder? Did I sag or fade slightly as some mortals do, or did I merely look confused?

The bartender gave him the drink. Very tentatively now, he was trying to put his fingers around it and lift it. He managed and got it to his lips and took a taste. He was amazed, and thankful, and suddenly so full of fear that he almost disintegrated. The illusion was almost completely dispersed.

But he held firm. This was so obviously the person I had just killed, hacked to pieces and buried all over Manhattan, that I felt physically sick staring at him. I realized only one thing was saving me from panic. He was talking to me. What had David said once, when he was alive, about talking to me? That he wouldn't kill a vampire because the vampire could talk to him? And this damned ghost was talking to me.

"I have to talk to you about Dora," he said.

"I told you I will never hurt her, or anyone like her," I said. "Look, what are you doing here with me! When you appeared, you didn't even know that I knew about Dora! You wanted to tell me about Dora?"

"Depth, I've been murdered by a being with depth, how fortunate, someone who actually keenly appreciated my death, no?" He drank more of the sweet-smelling Southern Comfort. "This was Janis Joplin's drink, you know," he said, referring to the dead singer whom I, too, had loved. "Look, listen to me out of curiosity, I don't give a damn. But listen. Let me talk to you about Dora and about me. I want you to know. I want you to really know who I was, not what you might think. I want you to look out for Dora. And then there's something back at the flat, something I want you. . . ."

"Veronica's veil in the frame?"

"No! That's trash. I mean, it's four centuries old, of course, but it's a common version of Veronica's veil, if you have enough money. You did look around my place, didn't you?"

"Why did you want to give that veil to Dora?" I asked.

This sobered him appropriately. "You heard us talking?"

"Countless times."

He was conjecturing, weighing things. He looked entirely reasonable, his dark Asian face evincing nothing but sincerity and great care.

"Did you say 'look out for Dora'?" I asked. "Is that what you asked me to do? Look out for her? Now that's another proposition and why the hell do you want to tell me the story of your life! You're running through your personal afterdeath judgment with the wrong guy! I don't care how you got the way you were. The things at the flat, why would a ghost care about such things?"

This was not wholly honest on my part. I was being far too flippant and we both knew it. Of course he cared about his treasures. But it was Dora that had made him rise from the dead.

His hair was a deeper black now, and the coat had taken on more texture. I could see the weave of the silk and the cashmere in it. I could see his fingernails, professionally manicured, very neat and buffed. Same hands I threw in the garbage! I don't think all these details had been visible moments ago.

"Jesus Christ," I whispered.

He laughed. "You're more afraid than I am."

"Where are you?"

"What are you talking about?" he asked. "I'm sitting next to you. We're in a Village bar. What do you mean, where am I? As for my body, you know where you dumped the pieces of it as well as I."

"That's why you're haunting me."

"Absolutely not. Couldn't give less of a damn about that body. Felt that way the moment I left it. You know all this!"

"No, no, I mean, what realm are you in now, what is it, where are you, what did you see when you went . . . what. . . ."

He shook his head with the saddest smile.

"You know the answer to all that. I don't know where I am. Something's waiting for me, however. I'm fairly certain of that. Something's waiting. Perhaps it's merely dissolution. Darkness. But it seems personal. It's not going to wait forever. But I don't know how I know.

"And I don't know why I'm being allowed to get through to you, whether it's sheer will, my will, I mean, of which I have a great deal by the way, or whether it's some sort of grant of moments, I don't know! But I went after you. I followed you from the flat and back to it and then out with the body and I came here and I have to talk to you. I'm not going to go without a struggle, until I've spoken with you."

"Something's waiting for you," I whispered. This was awe. Plain and simple. "And then, after we've had our chat, if you don't dissolve, where exactly are you going to go?"

He shook his head and glared at the bottle on the center rack, flood of light, color, labels.

"Tiresome," he said crossly. "Shut up."

It had a sting to it. Shut up. Telling me to shut up.

"I can't go looking out for your daughter," I said.

"What do you mean?" He threw an angry glance at me, and took another sip of his drink, then gestured to the bartender for another.

"Are you going to get drunk?" I asked.

"I don't think I can. You *have* to look out for her. It's all going to go public, don't you see? I have enemies who'll kill her, for no other reason than that she was my child. You don't know how careful I've been, and you don't know how rash she is, how much she believes in Divine Providence. And then there's the government, the hounds of government, and my things, my relics, my books!"

I was fascinated. For about three seconds, I'd utterly forgotten that he was a ghost. Now my eyes gave me no evidence of it. None. But he was scentless, and the faint sound of life that emanated from him still had little to do with real lungs or a real heart.

"All right, let me be blunt," he said. "I'm afraid for her. She has to get through the notoriety; enough time has to pass that my enemies forget about her. Most of them don't know about her. But somebody might. Somebody's bound to know, if you knew."

"Not necessarily. I'm not a human being."

"You have to guard her."

"I can't do such a thing. I won't."

"Lestat, will you listen to me?"

"I don't want to listen. I want you to go."

"I know you do."

"Look, I never meant to kill you, I'm sorry, it was all a mistake, I should have picked someone. . . ." My hands were shaking. Oh, how fascinating all this would sound later, and right now I begged God, of all people, please make this stop, all of it, stop.

"You know where I was born, don't you?" he asked. "You know that block of St. Charles near Jackson?"

I nodded. "The boardinghouse," I said. "Don't tell me the story of your life. There's no reason. Besides, it's over. You had your chance to write it down when you were alive, just like anyone else. What do you expect me to do with it?"

"I want to tell you the things that count. Look at me! Look at me, please, try to understand me and to love me and to love Dora for me! I'm begging you."

I didn't have to see his expression to understand this keen agony, this protective cry. Is there anything under God that can be done to us that will make us suffer as badly as seeing our child suffer? Our loved ones? Those closest to us? Dora, tiny Dora walking in the empty convent. Dora on a television screen, arms flung out, singing.

I must have gasped. I don't know. Shivered. Something. I couldn't clear my head for a moment, but it was nothing supernatural, only misery, and the realization that he was there, palpable, visible, expecting something from me, that he had come across, that he had survived long enough in this ephemeral form to demand a promise of me.

"You do love me," he whispered. He looked serene and intrigued. Way beyond flattery. Way beyond me.

"Passion," I whispered. "It was your passion."

"Yes, I know. I'm flattered. I wasn't run down by a truck in the street, or shot by a hit man. You killed me! You, and you must be one of the best of them."

"Best of what?"

"Whatever you call yourself. You're not human. Yet you are. You sucked my blood out of my body, took it into your own. You're thriving on it now. Surely you're not the only one." He looked away. "Vampires," he said. "I saw ghosts when I was a boy in our house in New Orleans."

"Everybody in New Orleans sees ghosts."

He laughed in spite of himself, a very short, quiet laugh. "I know," he said, "but really I did and I have, and I've seen them in other places. But I never believed in God or the Devil or Angels or Vampires or Werewolves, or things like that, things that could affect fate, or change the course of some chaotic-seeming rhythm that governed the universe."

"You believe in God now?"

"No. I have the sneaking suspicion that I'll hold firm as long as I can in this form—like all the ghosts I've ever glimpsed—then I'll start to fade. I'll die out. Rather like a light. That's what's waiting for me. Oblivion. And it isn't personal. It just feels that way because my mind, what's left of it, what's clinging to the earth here, can't comprehend anything else. What do you think?"

"It terrifies me either way or any way." I was *not* going to tell him about the Stalker. I was *not* going to ask him about the statue. I knew now he had had nothing to do with the statue seeming animate. He had been dead, going up.

"Terrifies you?" he asked respectfully. "Well, it's not happening to you. You make it happen to others. Let me explain about Dora."

"She's beautiful. I'll . . . I'll try to look out for her."

"No, she needs something more from you. She needs a miracle."

"A miracle?"

"Look, you're alive, whatever you are, but you're not human. You can make a miracle, can't you? You could do this for Dora, it would be no problem for a creature of your abilities at all!"

"You mean some sort of fake religious miracle?"

"What else? She's never going to save the world without a miracle and she knows it. You could do it!"

"You're remaining earthbound and haunting me in this place to make a sleazy proposition like this!" I said. "You're unsalvageable. You are dead. But you're still a racketeer and a criminal. Listen to yourself. You want me to fake some spectacle for Dora? You think Dora would want that?"

He was flabbergasted, clearly. Much too much so to be insulted.

He put the glass down and sat there, composed and calm, appearing to scan the bar. Looking dignified and about ten years younger than he had been when I killed him. I don't guess anyone wants to come back as a ghost except in beautiful form. It was only natural. And I felt a deepening of my inevitable and fatal fascination, this, my Victim. *Monsieur, your blood is inside me!*

He turned.

"You're right," he said in the most torn whisper. "You're absolutely right. I can't make some deal with you to fake miracles for her. It's monstrous. She'd hate it."

"Now you're talking like the Grateful Dead," I said.

He gave another little contemptuous laugh. Then with a low sombre emotion, he said, "Lestat, you have to take care of her . . . for a while."

When I didn't answer, he persisted gently:

"Just for a little while, until the reporters have stopped, and the horror of it is over; until her faith is restored, and she's whole and Dora after all, and back to her life. She has her life, yet. She can't be hurt because of me, Lestat, not because of me, it's not fair."

"Fair?"

"Call me by my name," he said. "Look at me."

I looked at him. It was exquisitely painful. He was miserable. I didn't know whether human beings could express this same intensity of misery. I actually didn't know.

"My name's Roger," he said. He seemed even younger now, as though he were traveling backwards in time, in his mind, or merely becoming innocent, as if the dead, if they are going to stick around, have a right to remember their innocence.

"I know your name," I said. "I know everything about you, Roger. Roger, the Ghost. And you never let Old Captain touch you; you just let him adore you, and educate you, and take you places, and buy you beautiful things, and you never even had the decency to go to bed with him."

I said those things, about the images I'd drunk with his blood, but without malice. I was just talking in wonder of how bad we all are, the lies we tell.

He said nothing for the moment.

I was overwhelmed. It was grief veritably blinding me, and bitterness and a deep ugly horror for what I had done to him, and to others, and that I had ever harmed any living creature. Horror.

What was Dora's message? How were we to be saved? Was it the same old canticle of adoration?

He watched me. He was young, committed, a magnificent semblance of life. Roger.

"All right," he said, the voice soft and patient, "I didn't sleep with Old Captain, you're right, but he never really wanted that of me, you see, it wasn't like that, he was far too old. You don't know what it was really like. You might know the guilt I feel. But you don't know later how much I regretted not having done it. Not having known that with Old Captain. And that's not what made me go wrong. It wasn't that. It wasn't the big deception or heist that you imagine it to be. I loved the things he showed me. He loved me. He lived two, three more years, probably because of me. Wynken de Wilde, we loved Wynken de Wilde together. It should have turned out different. I was with Old Captain when he died, you know. I never left the room. I'm faithful that way when I am needed by those I loved."

"Yeah, you were with your wife, Terry, too, weren't you?" It was cruel of me to say this, but I'd spoken without thinking, seeing her face again as he shot her. "Scratch that, if you will," I said. "I'm sorry. Who in the name of God is Wynken de Wilde?"

I felt so utterly miserable. "Dear God, you're haunting me," I said. "And I'm a coward in my soul! A coward. Why did you say that strange name? I don't want to know. No, don't tell me—This is enough for me. I'm leaving. You can haunt this bar till doomsday if you want. Get some righteous individual to talk to you."

"Listen to me," he said. "You love me. You picked me. All I want to do is fill in the details."

"I'll take care of Dora, somehow or other, I'll figure some way to help her, I'll do something. And I'll take care of all the relics, I'll get them out of there and into a safe place and hold on to them for Dora, until she feels she can accept them."

"Yes!"

"Okay, let me go."

"I'm not holding you," he said.

Yes, I did love him. I did want to look at him. I did want him to tell me everything, every last little detail! I reached out and touched his hand. Not alive. Not human flesh. Something with vitality, however. Something burning and exciting.

He merely smiled.

He reached across with his right hand and clamped his fingers around my right wrist and drew near. I could feel his hair touching my forehead, teasing my skin, just a loose wisp of hair. Big dark eyes looking at me.

"Listen to me," he said again. Scentless breath.

"Yes. . . ."

He started talking to me in a low, rushed voice. He began to tell me the tale.

4

THE POINT is, Old Captain was a smuggler, a collector. I spent years with him. My mother had sent me to Andover, then brought me home, couldn't live without me; I went to Jesuit, I didn't belong with anyone or anywhere, and maybe Old Captain was the perfect person. But Wynken de Wilde, that started with Old Captain and the antiques he sold through the Quarter, usually small, portable things.

"And I'll tell you right now, Wynken de Wilde amounts to nothing, absolutely nothing, except a dream I had once, a very perverse plan. I mean my lifelong passion—aside from Dora—has been Wynken de Wilde, but if you don't care about him after this conversation, no one will. Dora does not."

"What was this Wynken de Wilde all about?"

"Art, of course. Beauty. But I got it mixed up in my head when I was seventeen that I was going to start a new religion, a cult—free love, give to the poor, raise one's hand against no one, you know, a sort of fornicating Amish community. This was of course 1964, the time of the flower children, marijuana, Bob Dylan seeming to be singing all the time about ethics and charity, and I wanted a new Brethren of the Common Life, one in tune with modern sexual values. Do you know who the Brethren were?"

"Yes, popular mysticism, late Middle Ages, that anyone could know God."

"Yes! Ah, that you know such a thing."

"You didn't have to be a priest or monk."

"Exactly. And so the monks were jealous, but my concept of this as a boy was all wound up with Wynken, whom I knew to have been influenced by German mysticism and all those popular movements, Meister Eckehart, et cetera, though he worked in a scriptorium and still did old-fashioned parchment prayer books of devotion by hand. Wynken's books were completely different from those of others. I thought if I could find all Wynken's books I'd have it made."

"Why Wynken, what made him different?"

"Let me tell it my way. See, this is how it happened, the boarding-house was shabby-elegant, you know the kind, my mother didn't get her own hands dirty, she had three maids and an old colored man who did everything; the old people, the boarders—they were on hefty private incomes, limousines garaged around the Garden District, three meals a day, red carpets. You know the house. Henry Howard designed it. Late Victorian. My mother had inherited it from her mother."

"I know it, I've seen it, I've seen you stop in front of it. Who owns it now?"

"I don't know. I let it slip away. I ruined so many things. But picture this: drowsy summer afternoon there, I'm fifteen and lonely, and Old Captain invites me in, and there on the table in the second parlour—he rents the two front parlours—he lives in a sort of wonderland of collectibles and brass and such—"

"I see it."

"—and there are these books on the table, medieval books! Tiny medieval prayer books. Of course, I know a prayer book when I see it; but a medieval codex, no; I was an altar boy when I was very little, went to Mass every day for years with my mother, knew liturgical Latin as was required. The point is, I recognize these books as devotional and rare, and something that Old Captain is inevitably going to sell.

" 'You can touch them, Roger, if you're careful,' he tells me. For two years, he had let me come and listen to his classical records, and we'd taken walks together. But I was just becoming sexually interesting to him, though I didn't know it, and it's got nothing to do with what I have to say until later on.

"He was on the phone talking to somebody about a ship in the harbour.

"Within a few minutes we were off to the ship. We used to go on these ships all the time. I never knew what we were doing. It had to be smuggling. All I remember is Old Captain sitting at a big round table with all the crew, they were Dutch, I think, and some nice officer with a heavy accent giving me a tour of the engine room, the map room, and the radio room. I never tired of it. I loved the ships. The New Orleans wharves were active then, full of rats and hemp."

"I know."

"Do you remember those long ropes that ran from the ships to the dock, how they had the round steel rat shields on them—disks of steel that the rats couldn't climb over?"

"I remember."

"We get home that night and instead of going to bed as I would have done, I beg him to let me come in and see those books. I have to see them before he sells them. My mother wasn't in the hallway, so I supposed she'd gone to bed.

"Let me give you an image of my mother and this boardinghouse. I told you it was elegant, didn't I? You can imagine the furnishings, heavy Renaissance revival, machine-made pieces, the kind that junked up mansions from the 1880s on."

"Yes."

"The house has a glorious staircase, winding, set against a stained-glass window, and at the foot of the stairs, in the crook of it, this masterpiece of a stairs of which Henry Howard must have been profoundly proud—in the stairwell—stood my mother's enormous dressing table, imagine, and she'd sit there in the main hall, at the dressing table, brushing her hair! All I have to do is think of that and my head aches. Or it used to when I was alive. It was such a tragic image, and I knew it, even though I grew up seeing it every day; that a dressing table of marble and mirrors and sconces and filigree, and an old woman with dark hair, does not belong in a formal hallway. . . ."

"And the boarders just took it in?" I asked.

"Yes, because the house was gobbled up for this one and that one, Old Mister Bridey, living in what had once been a servants' porch, and Blind Miss Stanton in the little fainting room upstairs! And four apartments carved out of the servants' quarters in back. I am keenly sensitive to disorder; you find around me either perfect order or the neglected clutter of the place in which you killed me."

"I realize that."

"But if I were to inhabit that place again. . . . Ah, this is not important. The point I'm trying to make is that I believe in order and when I was young I used to dream about it. I wanted to be a saint, well, a sort of secular saint. Let me return to the books."

"Go on."

"I hit the sacred books on the table. One of them I took from its own little sack. I was charmed by the tiny illustrations. I examined each and every book that night, planning to thereafter take my time. Of course the Latin was unreadable to me in that form."

"Too dense. Too many pen strokes."

"My, you do know things, don't you?"

"Maybe we're surprising each other. Go on."

"I spent the week thoroughly examining all of them. I cut school all the time. It was so boring. I was way ahead of everybody, and wanted to do something exciting, you know, like commit a major crime."

"A saint or a criminal."

"Yes, I suppose that does seem a contradiction. Yet it's a perfect description."

"I thought it was."

"Old Captain explained things about the books. The book in the sack was a girdle book. Men carried such books with them. And this particular one was a prayer book, and another of the illuminated books, the biggest and thickest, was a Book of the Hours, and then there was a Bible in Latin, of course. He was casual about all of it.

"I was incredibly drawn to these books, can't tell you why. I have always been covetous of things that are shining and bright and seemingly valuable, and here was the most condensed and seemingly unique version of such I'd ever beheld."

I smiled. "Yes, I know exactly."

"Pages full of gold, and red, and tiny beautiful little figures. I took out a magnifying glass and started to study the pictures in earnest. I went to the old library at Lee Circle—remember it?—and I studied up on the entire question. Medieval books. How the Benedictines had done them. Do you know Dora owns a convent? It isn't based on the plan of St. Gall, but it's just about the nineteenth-century equivalent."

"Yes, I saw it, I saw her there. She's brave and doesn't care about the darkness or the aloneness."

"She believes in Divine Providence to the point of idiocy and she can make something of herself only if she isn't destroyed. I want another drink. I know I'm talking fast. I have to."

I gestured for the drink. "Continue, what happened, who's Wynken de Wilde?"

"Wynken de Wilde was the author of two of these precious books that Old Captain had in his possession. I didn't figure that out for months. I was going over the little illustrations, and gradually I determined two of the books were done by the same artist, and then in spite of Old Captain insisting that there would be no signature, I found his name, in several places in both books. Now you know Captain sold these types of things. I told you. He dealt in them through a shop on Royal Street."

I nodded.

"Well, I lived in terror of the day he was going to have to sell these two books! These books weren't like the other books. First off, the illustrations were exceedingly detailed. One page might contain the motif of a flowering vine, with blossoms from which birds drank, and in these blossoms there were human figures intertwined, as if in a bower. Also, these were books of psalms. When you first examined them you thought they were psalms of the Vulgate, you know, the Bible we accept as canonical."

"Yes. . . ."

"But they weren't. They were psalms that never appeared in any Bible. I figured that much out, simply by comparing them to other Latin reprints of the same period that I got out of the library. This was some sort of original work. Then the illustrations, the illustrations contained not only tiny animals and trees and fruit but naked people, and the naked people were doing all sorts of things!"

"Bosch."

"Exactly, like Bosch's *Garden of Earthly Delights*, that kind of luscious sensuous paradise! Of course, I hadn't seen Bosch's painting yet in the Prado. But it was here in miniature in these books. Little figures frolicking beneath the abundant trees. Old Captain said, 'Garden of Eden imagery,' that it was very common. But two books full of it? No. This was different. I had to crack these books, get an absolutely clear translation of every word.

"And then Old Captain did the kindest thing for me he'd ever done, the thing that might have made a great religious leader out of me, and may still make one in Dora, though hers is wholly another creed."

"He gave you the books."

"Yes! He gave me the books. And let me tell you more. That summer, he took me all over the country to look at medieval manuscripts! We went to the Huntington Library in Pasadena, and the Newbury Library in Chicago. We went to New York. He would have taken me to England, but my mother said no.

"I saw all types of medieval books! And I came to know that Wynken's were unlike any others. Wynken's were blasphemous and profane. And nobody, nobody at any of these libraries had a book by Wynken de Wilde, but the name was known!

"Captain still let me keep the books! And I set to work on translating them right away. Old Captain died in the front room, the first week of my senior year. I didn't even start school till after he was buried. I refused to leave him. I sat there with him. He slipped into a coma. By the third day of the coma, you could not have told who he was, his face had so changed. He didn't close his eyes anymore, and didn't know they were open, and his mouth was just a slack sort of oval, and his breath came in even gasps. I sat there. I told you."

"I believe you."

"Yes, well, I was seventeen, my mother was very sick, there wasn't any money for college, which every other senior boy at Jesuit was talking about, and I was dreaming of flower children in the Haight Ashbury of California, listening to the songs of Joan Baez, and thinking that I would go to San Francisco with the message of Wynken de Wilde, and found a cult.

"This was what I knew then through translation. And in that regard I had had the help of an old priest at Jesuit for quite some time, one of those genuinely brilliant Latin scholars who has to spend half the day making boys behave. He had done the translation for me gladly, and of course there was a little of the usual promise in it of my proximity and intimacy, he and I being alone and close for hours."

"So you were selling yourself again, even before Old Captain died?"

"No. Not really. Not the way you think. Well, sort of. Only this priest was a genuine celibate, Irish, almost impossible to understand now, this sort of priest. They never did anything to anyone. I doubt they even masturbated. It was all being near boys and occasionally breathing heavily or something. Nowadays religious life doesn't attract that particular kind of robust and completely repressed individual. A man like that could no more molest a child than he could get up on the altar at Mass and start to shout."

"He didn't know he felt an attraction for you, that he was giving you special favors."

"Precisely, and so he spent hours with me translating Wynken. He kept me from going crazy. He always stopped in to visit with Old Captain. If Old Captain had been Catholic, Father Kevin would have given him the Last Rites. Try to understand this, will you? You can't judge people like Old Captain and Father Kevin."

"No, and not boys like you."

"Also, my mother had a disastrous new boyfriend that last year, a sugar-coated mock gentleman, actually, one of those people who speaks surprisingly well, has overly bright eyes, and is obviously rotten inside, and from a totally unconvincing background. He had too many wrinkles in his youngish face; they looked like cracks. He smoked du Maurier cigarettes. I think he thought he was going to marry my mother for the house. You follow me?"

"Yes, I do. So after Old Captain died, you had only the priest."

"Right. Now you get it. Father Kevin and I worked a lot at the boardinghouse, he liked that. He'd drive up, park his car on Philip Street and come around and we'd go up to my room. Second floor, front bedroom. I had a great view of the parades on Mardi Gras. I grew up thinking that was normal, for an entire city to go mad two weeks out of every year. Anyway, we were up there during one of the night parades, ignoring it as natives can do, you know, once you've seen enough papier-mâché floats and trinkets and flambeaux—"

"Horrible, lurid flambeaux."

"Yes, you said it." He stopped. The drink had come and he was gazing at it.

"What is it?" I asked him. I was alarmed because he was alarmed. "Look at me, Roger. Don't start fading, keep talking. What did the translation of the books reveal? Were they profane? Roger, talk to me!"

He broke his frigid meditative stillness. He picked up the drink, tossed down half of it. "Disgusting and I adore it. Southern Comfort was the first thing I ever drank when I was a boy."

He looked at me, directly.

"I'm not fading," he assured me. "It's just I saw and smelled the house again. You know? The smell of old people's rooms, the rooms in which people die. But it was so lovely. What was I saying? All right, it was during Proteus, one of the night parades, that Father Kevin made the incredible breakthrough that both these books had been dedicated by Wynken de Wilde to Blanche De Wilde, his patron, and that she was obviously the wife to his good brother, Damien; it was all embedded in the designs of the first few pages. And that threw an entirely different light on the psalms. The psalms were filled with lascivious invitations and suggestions and possibly even some sort of secret codes for clandestine meetings. Over and over again there appeared paintings of the same little garden—understand we're talking miniatures here—"

"I've seen many examples."

"And in these little tiny pictures of the garden there would always be one naked man and five women dancing around a fountain within the walls of a medieval castle, or so it seemed. Magnify it five times and it was just perfect. And Father Kevin began to laugh and laugh.

" 'No wonder there isn't a single saint or biblical scene in any of this,' Father Kevin said, laughing. 'Your Wynken de Wilde was a raving heretic! He was a witch or a diabolist. And he was in love with this woman, Blanche.' He wasn't shocked so much as amused.

" 'You know, Roger,' he said, 'if you did get in touch with one of the auction houses, very likely these books could put you through Loyola, or Tulane. Don't think of selling them down here. Think about New York; Butterfield and Butterfield, or Sotheby's.'

"He had in the last two years copied out by hand about thirty-five different poems for me in English, the best sort of translation—straight prose from the Latin—and now we went over them, tracing repetitions and imagery, and a story began to emerge.

"First thing we realized was that there had been many books originally, and what we possessed were the first and third. By the third, the psalms reflected not mere adoration for Blanche, who was again and again compared to the Virgin Mary in her purity and brightness, but also answers to some sort of correspondence about what the lady was suffering at the hands of her spouse.

"It was clever. You have to read it. You have to go back to the flat where you killed me and get those books."

"Which means you didn't sell them to go to Loyola or Tulane?"

"Of course not. Wynken, having orgies with Blanche and her four friends! I was fascinated. Wynken was my saint by virtue of his talent, and sexuality was my religion because it had been Wynken's and in every philosophical word he wrote he encoded a love of the flesh! You have to realize I didn't believe any orthodox creed really, I never had. I thought the Catholic Church was dying. And that Protestantism was a joke. It was years before I understood that the Protestant approach is fundamentally mystic, that it is aiming for the very oneness with God that Meister Eckehart would have praised or that Wynken wrote about."

"You are being generous to the Protestant approach. And Wynken *did* write about oneness with God?"

"Yes, through union with the women! It was cautious but clear; 'In thine arms I have known the Trinity more truly than men can teach,' like that. Oh, this was the new way, I was sure. But then I knew Protestantism only as materialism, sterility and Baptist tourists who got drunk on Bourbon Street because they could not dare do it in their hometowns."

"When did you change your opinion?" I asked.

"I'm speaking in broad generalities. I mean, I saw no hope for religions in existence in the West at our time. Dora feels very much the same, but we'll come to Dora."

"Did you finish the entire translation?"

"Yes, just before Father Kevin was transferred. I never saw him again. He did write to me later, but by that time I had run away from home.

"I was in San Francisco. I'd left without my mother's blessing, and taken the Trailways Bus because it was a few cents cheaper than the Greyhound. I didn't have seventy-five dollars in my pocket. I'd squandered everything Captain ever gave me. And when he died, did those relatives of his from Jackson, Mississippi, ever clean out those rooms!

"They took everything. I always thought Captain had left something for me, you know. But I didn't care. The books were his greatest gift and all those luncheons at the Monteleone Hotel when we had had gumbo together, and he let me break up all my saltine crackers in the gumbo till it was porridge. I just loved it.

"What was I saying? I bought the ticket to California and saved a small balance for pie and coffee at each stop. A funny thing happened. We came to a point of no return. That is, when we passed through some town in Texas I realized I didn't have enough money to go back home, even if I wanted to. It was the middle of the night. I think it was El Paso! Anyway, then I knew there was no going back.

"But I was headed for San Francisco and the Haight Asbury, and I was going to found a cult based on the teachings of Wynken in praise of love and union and claiming that sexual union was godlike union and I would show his books to my followers. It was my dream, though to tell you the truth, I had no personal feeling about God at all.

"Within three months, I had discovered that my credo was by no means unique. The entire city was full of hippies who believed in free love, and panhandling, and though I gave regular lectures to large loose circles of friends on Wynken, holding up the books and reciting the psalms—these are very tame, of course—"

"I can imagine."

"—my principle job was that of business manager and boss of three rock musicians who wanted to become famous and were too stoned to remember their bookings, or collect the proceeds at the door. One of them, Blue, we called him, could really sing well. He had a high tenor, and quite a range. The band had a sound. Or at least we thought it did.

"Father Kevin's letter found me when I was living up in the attic of the Spreckles Mansion on Buena Vista Park, do you know that house?"

"I do know it. It's a hotel."

"Exactly, and it was a private home in those days, and the top floor had a ballroom with bath and kitchenette. This was well before any restoration. Nobody had invented 'bed and breakfast,' and I just rented the ballroom and the musicians played there and we all used the filthy bath and kitchen, and in the day, when they were asleep all over the floor, I'd dream about Wynken and think about Wynken and wonder how I would ever find out more about this man and what these love poems were. I had all sorts of fantasies about him.

"That attic, I wonder about it now. It had windows at three points of the compass, and deep window seats with tattered old velvet cushions. You could see San Francisco in every direction but east as I remember, but I don't have a good sense of direction. We loved to sit in those window alcoves and talk and talk. My friends loved to hear about Wynken. We were going to write some songs based on Wynken's poems. Well, that never happened."

"Obsessed."

"Completely. Lestat, you must go back for those books, no matter what you believe of me when we're finished here. All of them are in the flat. Every single one that Wynken ever did. It was my life's work to get those books. I got into dope for those books. Even back in the Haight.

"I was telling you about Father Kevin. He wrote me a letter, said that he had looked up Wynken de Wilde in some manuscripts and found that Wynken had been the executed leader of a heretical cult. Wynken de Wilde had a religion of strictly female followers, and his works were officially condemned by the church. Father Kevin said all that was 'history,' and I ought to sell the books. He'd write more later. He never did. And two months later I committed multi-murder completely on the spur of the moment, and it changed the course of things."

"The dope you were dealing?"

"Sort of, only I wasn't the one who made the slipup. Blue dealt more than me. Blue carried around grass in suitcases. I was into little sacks of it, you know, it made just about as much as the band made for me. But Blue bought by the kilo and lost two kilos. Nobody knew what happened to them. He actually lost them in a taxi, we figured, but we never knew.

"There were a lot of stupid kids walking around then. They would get into 'dealing' never realizing that the supply was originating with some vicious individual who thought nothing of shooting people in the head. Blue thought he could talk his way out of it, he'd make some explanation, he'd been ripped off by friends, that sort of thing. His connections trusted him, he said, they'd even given him a gun.

"The gun was in the kitchen drawer, and they'd told him they might need him to use it sometime, but of course he would never do that. I guess when you are that stoned, you think everybody else is stoned. These men, he said, they were just heads like us, nothing to worry about, that had been just talk. We would all be as famous as Big Brother and the Holding Company and Janis Joplin very soon.

"They came for him during the day. I was the only one home, except for him.

"He was in the big room, the ballroom, at the front door, giving these two men the runaround. I was out of sight in the kitchen, hardly listening. I might have been studying Wynken, I'm not sure. Anyway, very gradually I realized what they were talking about out there in the ballroom.

"These two men were going to kill Blue. They kept telling him in very flat voices that everything was okay, and please come with them, and come on, they had to go, and no, he had to come now, and no, he had to come along quickly. And then one of them said in a very low, vicious voice, 'Come on, man!' And for the first time Blue stopped jabbering in hippie platitudes, like it will all come around, man, and I have done no evil, man, and there was this silence, and I knew they were going to take Blue and shoot him and dump him. This had already happened to kids! It had been in the papers. I felt the hair stand up on the back of my neck. I knew Blue didn't have a chance.

"I didn't think about what I was doing. I completely forgot about the gun in the kitchen drawer. This surge of energy overtook me. I walked into the big room. Both these men were older, hard-looking guys, not hippies, nothing hippified about them. They weren't even Hell's Angels. They were just killers. And both sort of visibly sagged when they discovered there was an impediment to dragging my friend out of the room.

"Now, you know me, that I am as vain as you are probably, and then I was truly convinced of my special nature and destiny, and I came glistening and flashing towards these two men, you know, throwing off sparks, making a dance out of the walk. If I had any idea in my head, it was this: If Blue could die, that would mean I could die. And I couldn't let something like that be proven to me then, you know?"

"I can see it."

"I started talking to these characters very fast, chattering in a kind of intense, pretentious manner, as if I were a psychedelic philosopher, throwing out four-syllable words and walking right towards them all the time, lecturing them on violence, and implying that they had disturbed me and 'all the others' in the kitchen. We were having a class out there, me and the others.

"And suddenly one of them reached into his coat and pulled out his gun. I think he thought it would be a slam dunk. I can remember this so distinctly. He simply pulled out the gun and pointed it at me. And by the time he had it aimed, I had both hands on it, and I yanked it away from him, kicked him as hard as I could, and shot and killed both men."

Roger paused.

I didn't say anything. I was tempted to smile. I liked it. I only nodded. Of course it had begun that way with him, why hadn't I realized it? He hadn't instinctively been a killer; he would never have been so interesting if that had been the case.

"That quick, I was a killer," he said. "That quick. And a smashing success at it, no less, imagine."

He took another drink and looked off, deep into the memory of it. He seemed securely anchored in the ghost body now, revved up like an engine.

"What did you do then?" I asked.

"Well, that's when the course of my life changed. First I was going to go to the police, going to call the priest, going to go to hell, phone my mother, my life was over, call Father Kevin, flush all the grass down the toilet, life finished, scream for the neighbors, all of that.

"Then I just closed the door and Blue and I sat down and for about an hour I talked. Blue said nothing. I talked. I prayed, meanwhile, that nobody had been in a car outside waiting for those two, but if there came a knock I was ready because I had their gun now, and it had lots of bullets, and I was sitting directly opposite the door.

"And as I talked and waited and watched and let the two bodies lie there, and Blue simply stared into space as if it had been a bad LSD trip, I talked myself into getting the hell out of there. Why should I go to jail for the rest of my life for those two? Took about an hour of expressed logic."

"Right."

"We cleaned out that pad immediately, took everything that had belonged to us, called the other two musicians, got them to pick up their stuff at the bus station. Said it was a drug bust coming down. They never knew what happened. The place was so full of fingerprints from all our parties and orgies and late-night jam sessions, nobody would ever find us. None of us had ever been printed. And besides, I kept the gun.

"And I did something else, too, I took the money off the men. Blue didn't want any of it, but I needed bucks to get out of there.

"We split up. I never saw Blue again. I never saw Ollie or Ted, the other two. I think they went to L.A. to make it big. I think Blue probably became a drug crazy. I'm not sure. I went on. I was totally different from the instant it happened. I was never the same again."

"What made you different?" I asked. "What was the source of the change in you, I mean, what in particular? That you'd enjoyed it?"

"No, not at all. It was no fun. It was a success. But it wasn't fun. I've never found it fun. It's work, killing people, it's messy. It's hard work. It's fun for *you* to kill people, but then you're not human. No, it wasn't that. It was the fact that it had been possible to do it, to just walk up to that son of a bitch and make the most unexpected gesture, to just take that gun from him like that, because it was the last thing he ever expected could happen, and then to kill them both without hesitation. They must have died with surprise."

"They thought you were kids."

"They thought we were dreamers! And I was a dreamer, and all the way to New York I kept thinking, I do have a great destiny, I am going to be great, and this power, this power to simply shoot down two people had been the epiphany of my strength!"

"From God, this epiphany."

"No, from fate, from destiny. I told you I never really had any feeling for God. You know they say in the Catholic Church that if you don't feel a devotion to the Blessed Virgin Mary, well, they fear for your soul. I never had any devotion to her. I never had any devotion to any real personal deity or saint. I never felt it. That's why Dora's development surprised me in that particular, that Dora is so absolutely sincere. But we'll get to that. By the time I got to New York, I knew my cult was to be of this world, you know, lots of followers and power and lavish comforts and the licentiousness of this world."

"Yes, I see."

"That had been Wynken's vision. Wynken had communicated this to his women followers, that there was no point in waiting until the next world. You had to do everything now, every kind of sin . . . this was a common conception of heretics, wasn't it?"

"Yes, of some. Or so their enemies said."

"The next killing I did purely for money. It was a contract. I was the most ambitious boy in town. I was managing some other band again, a bunch of no-accounts, we weren't making it, though other rock stars were making it overnight. I was into dope again, and was being a hell of a lot smarter about it, and developing a personal distaste for it. This was the real early days, when people flew the grass across the border in little planes, and it was almost like cowboy adventures.

"And the word came down that this particular man was on the shit list of a local power broker who'd pay anyone thirty thousand dollars for the killing. The guy himself was particularly vicious. Everybody was scared of him. He knew they wanted to kill him. He was walking around in broad daylight and everyone was scared to make a move.

"I guess everybody else figured that somebody else would do it. How connected these people were to what and to whom I had no idea. I just knew the guy was game, you know? I made sure.

"I figured a way to do it. I was nineteen by then. I dressed up like a college boy in a crew-neck sweater, a blazer, flannel slacks, had my hair cut Princeton style, and carried a few books with me. I found out where the man lived on Long Island, and walked right up to him in his back driveway as he got out of his car one evening, and shot him dead five feet from where his wife and kids were eating dinner inside."

He paused again, and then said with perfect gravity, "It takes a special kind of animal to do something so vicious. And not to feel any remorse."

"You didn't torture him the way I tortured you," I said softly. "You know everything you've done, don't you? You really understand! I didn't get the whole picture when I was following you. I imagined you were more intimately perverse, wrapped up in your own romance. An arch self-deceiver."

"Was that torture, what you did to me?" he asked. "I don't remember pain being involved in it, only fury that I was going to die. Whatever the case, I killed this man in Long Island for money. It meant nothing to me. I didn't even feel relief afterwards, only a kind of strength, you know, of accomplishment, and I wanted to test it again soon and I did."

"And you were on your way."

"Absolutely. And in my style too. The word was out. If the task seems impossible, get Roger. I could get into a hospital dressed like a young doctor, with a name tag on my coat and a clipboard in my hand, and shoot some marked guy dead in his bed before anyone was the wiser. I did that, in fact.

"But understand, I didn't make myself rich as a hit man. It was heroin first, and then cocaine, and with the cocaine it was going back to some of the very same cowboys I'd known in the beginning, who flew the cocaine over the border same fashion, same routes, same planes! You know the history of it. Everyone does today. The early dope dealers were crude in their methods. It was 'cops and robbers' with the government guys. The planes would outrun the government planes, and when the planes landed, sometimes they were so stuffed with cocaine the driver couldn't wriggle out of the cockpit, and we'd run out and get the stuff, and load it up and get the hell out of there."

"So I've heard."

"Now there are geniuses in the business, people who know how to use cellular phones and computers and laundering techniques for money which no one can trace. But then? I was the genius of the dopers! Sometimes the whole thing was as cumbersome as moving furniture, I tell you. And I went in there, organizing, picking my confidants and my mules, you know, for crossing the borders, and even before cocaine ever hit the streets, so to speak, I was doing beautifully in New York and L.A. with the rich, you know, the kind of customers to whom you deliver personally. They never have to even leave their palatial homes. You get the call. You show up. Your stuff is pure. They like you. But I had to move out from there. I wasn't going to be dependent upon that.

"I was too clever. I made some real-estate deals that were pure brilliance on my part, and having the cash on hand, and you know those were the days of hellish inflation. I really cleaned up."

"But how did Terry get involved in it, and Dora?"

"Pure fluke. Or destiny. Who knows? Went home to New Orleans to see my mother, brushed up against Terry and got her pregnant. Damned fool.

"I was twenty-two, my mother was really dying this time. My mother said, 'Roger, please come home.' That stupid boyfriend with the cracked face had died. She was all alone. I'd been sending her plenty of money all along.

"The boardinghouse was now her private home, she had two maids and a driver to take her around town in a Cadillac whenever she felt the desire. She'd enjoyed it immensely, never asking any

questions about the money, and of course I'd been col.
Wynken. I had two more books of Wynken by that time and my
sure storehouse in New York already, but we can get to that later c
Just keep Wynken in the back of your mind.

"My mother had never really asked me for anything. She had the
big bedroom upstairs now to herself. She said she talked to all the
others who had gone on ahead, her poor old sweet dead brother
Mickey, and her dead sister, Alice, and her mother, the Irish maid—
the founder of our family, you might say—to whom the house had
been willed by the crazy lady who lived there. My mother was also
talking a lot to Little Richard. That was a brother that died when he
was four. Lockjaw. Little Richard. She said Little Richard was walking around with her, telling her it was time to come.

"But she wanted me to come home. She wanted me there in that
room. I knew all this. I understood. She had sat with boarders that
were dying. I had sat with others than Old Captain. So I went home.

"Nobody knew where I was headed, or what my real name was, or
where I came from. So it was easy to slip out of New York. I went to
the house on St. Charles Avenue and sat in the sickroom with her,
holding the little vomit cup to her chin, wiping her spittle, and trying
to get her on the bedpan when the agency didn't have a nurse to send.
We had help, yes, but she didn't want the help, you know. She didn't
want the colored girl, as she called her. Or that horrible nurse. And I
made the amazing discovery that these things didn't disgust me
much. I washed so many sheets. Of course there was a machine to put
them in, but I changed them over and over for her. I didn't mind.
Maybe I was never normal. In any event, I simply did what had to be
done. I rinsed out that bedpan a thousand times, wiped it off, sprinkled powder on it, and set it by the bed. There is no foul smell which
lasts forever after all."

"Not on this earth at least," I murmured. But he didn't hear me,
thank God.

"This went on for two weeks. She didn't want to go to Mercy
Hospital. I hired nurses round the clock just for backup, you know, so
they could take her vital signs when I got frightened. I played music
for her. All the predictable things, said the rosary out loud with her.
Usual deathbed scene. From two to four in the afternoon she tolerated visitors. Old cousins came. 'Where is Roger?' I stayed out of
sight."

"You weren't torn to pieces by her suffering."

"I wasn't crazy about it, I can tell you that. She had cancer all through her and no amount of money could save her. I wanted her to hurry, and I couldn't bear watching it, no, but there has always been a deep ruthless side to me that says, Do what you have to do. And I stayed in that room without sleep day in and day out and all night till she died.

"She talked a lot to the ghosts, but I didn't see them or hear them. I just kept saying, 'Little Richard, come get her. Uncle Mickey, if she can't come back, come get her.'

"But before the end came Terry, a practical nurse, as they called them then, who had to fill in when we could not get the registered nurse because they were in such demand. Terry, five foot seven, blonde, the cheapest and most alluring piece of goods I had ever laid eyes on. Understand. This is a question of everything fitting together precisely. The girl was a shining perfect piece of trash."

I smiled. "Pink fingernails, and wet pink lipstick." I had seen her sparkle in his mind.

"Every detail was on target with this kid. The chewing gum, the gold anklet, the painted toenails, the way she slipped off her shoes right there in the sickroom to let me see the toenails, the way the cleavage showed, you know, under her white nylon uniform. And her stupid, heavy-lidded eyes beautifully painted with Maybelline eye pencil and mascara. She'd file her nails in there in front of me! But I tell you, never have I seen something that was so completely realized, finished, ah, ah, what can I say! She was a masterpiece."

I laughed, and so did he, but he went on talking.

"I found her irresistible. She was a hairless little animal. I started doing it with her every chance I had. While Mother slept, we did it in the bathroom standing up. Once or twice we went down the hall to one of the empty bedrooms; we never took more than twenty minutes! I timed us! She'd do it with her pink panties around her ankles! She smelled like Blue Waltz perfume."

I gave a soft laugh.

"Do I ever know what you're saying," I mused. "And to think you knew it, you fell for her and you knew it."

"Well, I was two thousand miles away from my New York women and my boys and all, and all that trashy power that goes along with dealing, you know, the foolishness of bodyguards scurrying to open doors for you, and girls telling you they love you in the backseat of the limousine just because they heard you shot somebody the night before. And so much sex that sometimes right in the middle of it, the best oral job you've ever had, you can't keep your mind on it anymore."

"We are more alike than I ever dreamed. I've lived a lie with the gifts given me."

"What do you mean?" he asked.

"There isn't time. You don't need to know about me. What about Terry? How did Dora happen?"

"I got Terry pregnant. She was supposed to be on the Pill. She thought I was rich! It didn't matter whether I loved her or she loved me. I mean this was one of the dumbest and most simpleminded humans I have ever known, Terry. I wonder if you bother to feed upon people that ignorant and that dull."

"Dora was the baby."

"Yeah. Terry wanted to get rid of it if I didn't marry her. I made a bargain. One hundred grand when we marry (I used an alias, it was never legal except on paper and that was a blessing because Dora and I are in no way legally connected) and one hundred grand when the baby was born. After that I'd give her her divorce and all I wanted was my daughter."

" 'Our daughter,' she said.

" 'Sure, our daughter,' I said. What a fool I was. What I didn't figure on, the very obvious and simple thing, what I didn't figure on was that this woman, this little nail filing, gum chewing, mascara-wearing nurse in her rubber-soled shoes and diamond wedding ring, would naturally feel for her own child. She was stupid, but she was a mammal, and she had no intention of letting anybody take her baby. Like hell. I wound up with visitation rights.

"Six years I flew in and out of New Orleans every chance I had just to hold Dora in my arms, talk to her, go walking with her in the evenings. And understand, this child was mine! I mean she was flesh of my flesh from the start. She started running towards me when she saw me at the end of the block. She flew into my arms.

"We'd take a taxi to the Quarter and go through the Cabildo; she adored it; the cathedral, of course. Then we'd go for muffaletas at the Central Grocery. You know, or maybe you don't, the big sandwiches full of olives—"

"I know."

"—She'd tell me everything that had happened in the week since I'd been there. I'd dance with her in the street. Sing to her. Oh, what a beautiful voice she had from the beginning. I don't have a good voice. My mother had a good voice, and so did Terry. And this child got the voice. And the mind she had. We'd ride the ferry together over the river and back, and sing, as we stood by the rail. I took her shopping at D. H. Holmes and bought her beautiful clothes. Her mother never minded that, the beautiful clothes, and of course I was smart enough to pick up something for Terry, you know, a brassiere dripping with lace or a kit of cosmetics from Paris or some perfume selling for one hundred dollars an ounce. Anything but Blue Waltz! But Dora and I had so much fun. Sometimes I thought, I can stand anything if I can just see Dora within a few days."

"She was verbal and imaginative, the way you were."

"Absolutely, full of dreams and visions. Dora is no naif, now, you have to understand. Dora's a theologian. That's the amazing part. The desire for something spectacular? That I engendered in her, but the faith in God, the faith in theology? I don't know where that came from."

Theology. The word gave me pause.

"Meantime, Terry and I began to hate each other. When school-time came, so did the fights. The fights were hell. I wanted Sacred Heart Academy for Dora, dancing lessons, music lessons, two weeks away with me in Europe. Terry hated me. I wasn't going to make her little girl into a snot. Terry had already moved out of the St. Charles Avenue house, calling it old and creepy, and settled for a shack of a ranch-style tract home on some naked street in the soggy suburbs! So my kid was already snatched from the Garden District and all those colors, and settled in a place where the nearest architectural curiosity was the local 7-Eleven.

"I was getting desperate and Dora was getting older, old enough perhaps to be stolen effectively from her mother, whom she did love in a very protective and kind way. There was something silent between those two, you know, talking had nothing to do with it. And Terry was proud of Dora."

"And then this boyfriend came into the picture."

"Right. If I had come to town a day later, my daughter and my wife would have been gone. She was skipping out on me! To hell with my lavish checks. She was going with this bankrupt electrician boyfriend of hers to Florida!

"Dora knew from nothing and was outside playing down the block. They were all packed! I shot Terry and the boyfriend, right in that stupid little tract house in Metairie where Terry had chosen to bring up my daughter rather than on St. Charles Avenue. Shot them both. Got blood all over her polyester wall-to-wall carpet, and her Formica-top kitchen breakfast bar."

"I can imagine it."

"I dumped both of them in the swamps. It had been a long time since I'd handled something like this directly, but no matter, it was easy enough. The electrician's truck was in the garage anyway, and I bagged them up, and I took them out that way, into the back of the truck. I took them way out somewhere, out Jefferson Highway, I don't even know where I dumped them. No, maybe it was out Chef Menteur. Yeah, it was Chef Menteur. Somewhere around one of the old forts on the Rigules River. They just disappeared in the muck."

"I can see it. I've been dumped in the swamps myself."

He was too excited to hear my mumblings. He continued.

"Then I went back for Dora, who was by then sitting on the steps with her elbows on her knees wondering why nobody was home, and the door was locked so she couldn't get in, and she started screaming, "Daddy! I knew you'd come. I knew you would!" the minute she saw me. I didn't risk going inside to get her clothes. I didn't want her to see the blood. I put her with me in the boyfriend's pickup truck and out of New Orleans we drove, and we left the truck in Seattle, Washington. That was my cross-country odyssey with Dora.

"All those miles, insanity, just the two of us together talking and talking. I think I was trying to tell Dora everything that I had learned. Nothing evil and self-destructive, nothing that would ever bring the darkness near her, only the good things, what I had learned about virtue and honesty and what corrupts people, and what was worthwhile.

" 'You can't just simply do nothing in this life, Dora,' I kept saying, 'you can't just leave this world the way you found it.' I even told her how when I was young I was going to be a religious leader, and what I did now was collect beautiful things, church art from all over Europe and the Orient. I dealt in it, to keep the few pieces I wanted. I led her to believe, of course, that is what had made me rich, and by then, oddly enough, it was partly true."

"And she knew you'd killed Terry."

"No. You got the wrong idea on that one. All those images were tumbling in my mind. I felt it when you were taking my blood. That wasn't it. She knew I'd gotten rid of Terry, or I'd freed her from Terry, and now she could be with Daddy forever, and fly away with Daddy when Daddy flew away. That's a different thing from knowing Daddy murdered Terry. That she does not know. Once when she was twelve, she called, sobbing, and said, 'Daddy, will you please tell me where Mother is, where did she and that guy go when they went to Florida.' I played it off, that I hadn't wanted to tell her that Terry was dead. Thank God for the phone. I do very well on the phone. I like it. It's like being on the radio.

"But back to Dora of six years old. Daddy took Dora to New York and got a suite at the Plaza. After that, Dora had everything Daddy could buy."

"She cry for Terry even then?"

"Yes. And she was probably the only one who ever did. Before the wedding, Terry's mother had told me Terry was a slut. They hated each other. Terry's father had been a policeman. He was an okay guy. But he didn't like his daughter either. Terry wasn't a nice person. Terry was mean by nature; Terry wasn't even a good person to bump into in the street, let alone to know or to need or to hold.

"Her family back there thought she'd run off to Florida and abandoned Dora to me. That's all they ever knew till the day the old man and woman died, Terry's parents. There's some cousins. They still believe that. But they don't know who I am, really, it's all rather difficult to explain. Of course by now maybe they've seen the articles in the papers and magazines. I don't know, that's not important. Dora cried for her mother, yes. But after that big lie I told her when she was twelve, she never asked about anything again.

"But Terry's devotion to Dora had been as perfect as that of any mammalian mother! Instinctive; nurselike; antiseptic. She'd feed Dora from the four food groups. She'd dress Dora up in beautiful clothes, take her to dancing school, and sit there and gossip with the other mothers. She was proud of Dora. But she rarely ever spoke to Dora. I think they could go for days without their eyes meeting. It was mammalian. And for Terry, probably everything was like that."

"This is rather funny, that you should get mixed up with a person like this, you know."

"No, not funny. Fate. We made Dora. She gave the voice to Dora, and the beauty. And there is something in Dora from Terry which is like hardness, but that's too unkind a word. Dora is a mixture of us, really, an optimum mixture."

"Well, you gave her your own beauty too."

"Yes, but something far more interesting and marketable happened when the genes collided. You've seen my daughter. My daughter is photogenic, and beneath the flash and dash I gave her, there is the steadiness of Terry. She converts people over the airwaves. 'And what is the true message of Christ!' she declares, staring right into the camera. 'That Christ is in every stranger you meet, the poor, the hungry, the sick, the people next door!' And the audience believes it."

"I've watched. I've seen her. She could just rise to the top."

He sighed.

"I sent Dora to school. By this time I was making big, big money. I had to put lots of miles between me and my daughter. I switched Dora among three schools overall before graduation, which was hard for her, but she didn't question me about these maneuvers, or the secrecy surrounding our meetings. I led her to believe I was always on the verge of having to rush to Florence to save a fresco from being destroyed by idiots, or to Rome to explore a catacomb that had just been found.

"When Dora began to take a serious interest in religion, I thought it was spiritually elegant, you know. I thought my growing collection of statues and books had inspired her. And when she told me at eighteen that she had been accepted to Harvard and that she meant to study comparative religion, I was amused. I made the usual sexist assumption: study what you want and marry a rich man. And let me show you my latest icon or statue.

"But Dora's fervor and theological bent were developing far beyond anything I had ever experienced. Dora went to the Holy Land when she was nineteen. She went back twice before she graduated. She spent the next two years studying religions all over the world. Then she proposed the entire idea of her television program: she wanted to talk to people. Cable had made possible all these religion channels. You could tune in to this minister or that Catholic priest.

" 'You serious about this?' I asked. I hadn't known she believed it all. But she was out to be true to ideals that I had never fully understood myself yet somehow passed on to her.

" 'Dad, you get me one hour on television three times a week, and the money to use it the way I want,' she said, 'and you'll see what happens.' She began to talk about all kinds of ethical questions, how we could save our souls in today's world. She envisioned short lectures or sermons, punctuated by ecstatic singing and dancing. The abortion issue—she makes impassioned logical speeches that both sides are right! She explains how each life is sacrosanct yet a woman must have dominion over her own body."

"I've seen the program."

"You realize seventy-five different cable networks have picked up this program! You realize what news of my death may do to my daughter's church?"

He paused, thinking, then resumed as rapid-fire as before.

"You know, I don't think I ever had a religious aspiration, a spiritual goal, so to speak, that wasn't drenched in something materialistic and glamorous, do you know what I mean?"

"Of course."

"But with Dora, it's different. Dora really doesn't care about material things. The relics, the icons, what do they mean to Dora? Dora believes against impossible psychological and intellectual odds that God exists." He stopped again, shaking his head with regret.

You were right in what you said to me earlier. I am a racketeer. Even for my beloved Wynken I had an angle, what they call now an agenda. Dora is no racketeer."

I remembered his remark in the barroom, "I think I sold my soul for places like this." I had known what he was talking about when he said it. I knew it now.

"Let me get back to the story. Early on, as I told you, I gave up that idea of a secular religion. By the time Dora started in earnest, I hadn't thought about those ambitions in years. I had Dora. And I had Wynken as my obsession. I chased down more of Wynken's books, and managed through my various connections to purchase five different letters of the period which made clear mention of Wynken de Wilde and Blanche De Wilde and her husband, Damien, as well. I had searchers digging for me in Europe and America. Rhineland mysticism, dig into it.

"My researchers found a capsule version of Wynken's story in a couple of German texts. Something about women practicing the rites of Diana, witchcraft. Wynken dragged out of the monastery and publicly accused. The record of the trial, however, was lost.

"It had not survived the Second World War. But in other places there were other documents, caches of letters. Once you had the code word Wynken—once you knew what to look for—you were on the way.

"When I had a free hour I sat down and looked at Wynken's little naked people, and I memorized his poems of love. I knew his poems so that I could sing them. When I saw Dora for weekends—and we met somewhere whenever possible—I would recite them to Dora and maybe even show her my latest find.

"She tolerated my 'Burnt-out hippie version of free love and mysticism,' as she called it. 'I love you, Roge,' she'd say. 'But you're so romantic to think this bad priest was some sort of saint. All he did was sleep with these women, didn't he? And the books were ways of communicating among the others . . . when to meet.'

" 'Ah, but Dora,' I would say, 'there was not a vicious or ugly word in the work of Wynken de Wilde. You see for yourself.' Six books I had by then. It was all about love. My present translator, a professor at Columbia, had marveled at the mysticism of the poetry, how it was a blending of love of God and the flesh. Dora didn't buy it. But Dora was already obsessed with her own religious questions. Dora was reading Paul Tillich and William James and Erasmus and lots of books on the state of the world today. That's Dora's obsession, the State of the World Today."

"And Dora won't care about those books of Wynken's if I get them to her."

"No, she won't touch *any* of my collection, not now!" he said.

"Yet you want *me* to protect all these things," I said.

"Two years ago," he sighed. "A couple of news articles! No connection to her, you understand, but with her, my cover was blown forever. She'd been suspecting. It was inevitable, she said, that she'd figure out my money wasn't clean."

He shook his head. "Not clean," he said again. He went on. "The last thing she let me do was buy the convent for her. One million for the building. And one million to gut it of all the modern desecrations and leave it the way it had been for the nuns in the 1880s, with chapel and refectory and dormitory rooms and wide corridors. . . .

"But even that, she took with reluctance. As for the artwork, forget it. She may never take from me the money she needs to educate her followers there, her order or whatever the hell a televangelist calls it. The cable TV connection is nothing compared to what I could have made it, fixing up that convent as the base. And the collection—the statues, icons—imagine it. 'I could make you as big as Billy Graham or Jerry Falwell, darling,' I said to her. 'You can't turn away from my money, not for Jesus' sake.' "

He shook his head despairingly. "She meets with me now out of compassion, and of that my beautiful daughter has an endless supply. Sometimes she'll take a little gift. Tonight, she would not. Once when the program almost went under, she accepted just enough to get it over the hump. But my saints and angels, she won't touch them. My books, my treasures, she won't look at them.

"Of course, we both knew the threat to her reputation. You've helped by eliminating me. But there'll be news of my disappearance soon, has to be. 'Televangist financed by cocaine king.' How long can her secrecy last? It has to survive my death and she has to survive my death. At all costs! Lestat, you hear what I'm saying."

"I am listening to you, Roger, to every word you say. They aren't on to her yet, I can assure you."

"My enemies are a ruthless lot. And the government . . . who knows who the hell the government is or what the hell the government does."

"She's afraid of this scandal?"

"No. Brokenhearted, yes, afraid of scandal, never. She'd take what would come. What she wanted was for me to give it all up! That became her attack. She didn't care that the world might find out we were father and daughter. She wanted me to renounce everything. She was afraid for me, like a gangster's daughter would be, like a gangster's wife.

" 'Just let me build the church,' I kept pleading. 'Take the money.' The television show has proved her mettle. But no more . . . things are in ruins around her. She's a little one-hour program three times a week. The ladder to heaven is hers alone to climb. I'm out of it. She's relying on her audience to bring the millions needed to her.

"And the female mystics she quotes, you've heard her read from them, Hildegard of Bingen, and Julian of Norwich. Teresa of Avila. You've read any of those women?"

"All of them," I said.

"Smart females who want to hear smart females listen to her. But she's beginning to attract everyone. You cannot make it in this world if you speak to only one gender. That isn't possible. Even I know that, the marketeer in me knows that, the Wall Street genius, and I am that, too, have no doubt. She attracts everyone. Oh, if I only had those last two years to do over, if only I could have launched the church before she discovered—"

"You're looking at this all wrong. Stop regretting. If you'd made the church big, you would have precipitated your exposure and the scandal."

"No, once the church was big enough, the scandal wouldn't have mattered. That's just the catch. She stayed small, and when you're small, a scandal can do you in!" He shook his head again, angrily. He was becoming too agitated, but the image of him only grew stronger. "I cannot be allowed to destroy Dora. . . ." His voice drifted off again. He shuddered. He looked at me:

"What does it come to, Lestat?" he asked.

"Dora herself must survive," I said. "She has to hang on to her faith after your death is discovered!"

"Yes. I'm her biggest enemy, dead or alive. And her church, you know, she walks a thin line; she's no puritan, my daughter. She thinks Wynken's a heretic, but she doesn't know how much her own modern compassion for the flesh is just what Wynken was talking about."

"I get it. But what about Wynken, am I supposed to save Wynken too? What do I do with Wynken?"

"She is a genius in her own way, actually," he went on, ignoring me. "That's what I meant when I called her a theologian. She's done the near impossible thing of mastering Greek and Latin and Hebrew, even though she was not bilingual as a small child. You know how hard it is."

"Yes, it's not that way for us, but. . . ." I stopped. A horrible thought had occurred to me with full force.

The thought interrupted everything.

It was too late to make Roger immortal. He was dead!

I hadn't even realized that I was assuming all this time, all this time, as we talked and his story poured out, that I could, if I wanted to, actually bring him to me, and keep him here, and stop him from going on. But suddenly I remembered with a ferocious shock that Roger was a ghost! I was talking to a man who was already dead.

The situation was so hideously painful and frustrating and utterly abnormal that I was thunderstruck and might have begun to groan, if I hadn't had to cover it up so that he would go on.

"What's the matter with you?" he asked.

"Nothing. Talk more about Dora to me. Tell me the sort of things Dora says."

"She talks about the sterility of now, and how people need the ineffable. She points to rampant crime and goalless youth. She's going to make a religion where nobody hurts anybody else. It's the American dream. She knows Scripture inside and out, she's covered all the Pseudepigrapha, Apocrypha, the works of Augustine, Marcion, Moses Maimonides; she's convinced that the prohibition against sex destroyed Christianity, which is hardly original with her, of course, and certainly appeals to the women who listen to her, you know. . . ."

"Yes, I understand all that, but she must have felt some sympathy for Wynken."

"Wynken's books weren't a series of visions to her as they are to me."

"I see."

"And by the way, Wynken's books are not merely perfect, they are unique in a number of ways. Wynken did his work in the last twenty-five years before the Gutenberg printing press. Yet Wynken did everything. He was scribe, rubicator, that is, the maker of the fancy letters, and also the miniaturist who added all the naked people frolicking in Eden and the ivy and vine crawling over every page. He had to do every step himself at a time when scriptoria divided up these functions.

"Let me finish Wynken. You have Dora now in your mind. Let me go to Wynken. Yeah, you have to get those books."

"Great," I said dismally.

"Let me bring you right up to date. You're going to love those books, even if Dora never does. I have all twelve of his books, as I think I told you. He was Rhineland Catholic, forced into the Benedictines as a young man, and was in love with Blanche de Wilde, his brother's wife. She ordered the books done in the scriptorium and that's how it all started, her secret link with her monk lover. I have letters between Blanche and her friend Eleanor. I have some incidents decoded from the poems themselves.

"Most sad of all, I have the letters Blanche wrote to Eleanor after Wynken was put to death. She had the letters smuggled out to Eleanor, and then Eleanor sent them on to Diane, and there was another woman in it, but there are very few extant fragments of anything in her hand.

"This is what went down. They used to meet in the garden of the De Wilde castle to perform their rites. It wasn't the monastery garden at all, as I'd once supposed. How Wynken got there I don't know, but there are a few mentions in some of the letters that indicate he simply slipped out of the monastery and followed a secret way into his brother's house.

"And this made sense, of course. They'd wait till Damien de Wilde was off doing whatever such counts or dukes did, and then they'd meet, do their dance around the fountain, and make love. Wynken bedded each of the women in turn; or sometimes they celebrated various patterns. All this is recorded more or less in the books. Well, they got caught.

"Damien castrated and stabbed Wynken in front of the women and put them to rout. He kept the remains! Then, after days of interrogation, the frightened women were bullied into confessing to their love for Wynken and how he had communicated through the books; and the brother took all those books, all twelve of the books of Wynken de Wilde, everything this artist had ever created, you understand—"

"His immortality," I whispered.

"Exactly, his progeny! His books! And Damien had them buried with Wynken's body in the castle garden by the fountain that appears in all the little pictures in the books! Blanche could look out on it every day from her window, the place in the ground where Wynken had been laid to rest. No trial, no heresy, no execution, nothing like that. He just murdered his brother, it was as simple as that. He probably paid the monastery huge amounts of money. Who knows if it was even necessary? Did the monastery love Wynken? The monastery is a ruin now where tourists come to snap pictures. As for the castle, it was obliterated in the bombing of the First World War."

"Ah. But what happened after that, how did the books get out of the coffin? Do you have copies? Are you speaking of. . . ."

"No, I have the originals of every one. I have come across copies, crude copies, made at the behest of Eleanor, Blanche's cousin and confidante, but as far as I know they stopped this practice of copies. There were only twelve books. And I don't know how they surfaced. I can only guess."

"And what is your guess?"

"I think Blanche went out in the night with the other women, dug up the body, and took the books out of the coffin, or whatever poor

Wynken's remains had been placed in, and put everything back right the way it was."

"You think they'd do that?"

"Yes, I think they did it. I can see them doing it, by candlelight in the garden, see them digging, the five women together. Can't you?"

"Yes."

"I think they did it because they felt the way I do! They loved the beauty and the perfection of those books. Lestat, they knew they were treasures, and such is the power of obsession and such is the power of love. And who knows, maybe they wanted the bones of Wynken. It's conceivable. Maybe one woman took a thigh bone and another the bones of his fingers and, ah, I don't know."

It seemed a ghastly picture suddenly, and it put me in mind, without a second's hesitation, of Roger's hands, which I had chopped off sloppily with a kitchen knife and dumped, wrapped in a plastic sack. I stared at the image of these hands before me, busy, fretting with the edge of the glass, tapping the bar in anxiety.

"How far back can you trace the journey of the books?" I asked.

"Not very far at all. But that's often the case in my profession, I mean antiquities. The books have turned up one, maybe two at a time. Some from private collections, two from museums bombed during the wars. Once or twice I've paid almost nothing for them. I knew what they were the minute I laid eyes on them, but other people didn't. And understand, everywhere I went I put out the search for this sort of medieval codex. I am an expert in this field. I know the language of the medieval artist! You have to save my treasures, Lestat. You can't let Wynken get lost again. I'm leaving you with my legacy."

"So it seems. But what can I do with these, and all the other relics, if Dora will have no part of it?"

"Dora's young. Dora will change. See, I still have this vision—that maybe somewhere in my collection—forget about Wynken—that maybe somewhere among all the statues and relics is a central artifact that can help Dora with her new church. Can you gauge the value of what you saw in that flat? You have to make Dora touch those things again, examine them, catch the scent of them! You have to make her realize the potency of the statues and paintings, that they are expressions of the human quest for truth, the very quest that obsesses her. She just doesn't know yet."

"But you said Dora never cared for the paint and the plaster."

"Make her care."

"Me? How! I can conserve all this, yes, but how am I to make Dora love a work of art? Why would you even suggest such a thing, I mean—my having contact with your precious daughter?"

"You'll love my daughter," he said in a low murmur.

"Come again?"

"Find something miraculous in my collection for her."

"The Shroud of Turin?"

"Oh, I like you. I really do. Yes, find her something that's significant, something that will transform her, something that I, her father, bought and cherished, that will help her."

"You're as insane dead as you were alive, you know it? Are you still racketeering, trying to buy your way into salvation with a hunk of marble or a pile of parchment? Or do you really believe in the sanctity of all you've collected?"

"Of course I believe in the sanctity of it. It's *all* I believe in! That's my point, don't you see? It's all you believe in too . . . what glitters and what is gold."

"Ah, but you do take my breath away."

"That's why you murdered me there, among the treasures. Look, we have to hurry. We don't know how much time we have. Back to the mechanics. Now, with my daughter, your trump card is her ambition.

"She wanted the convent for her own female missionaries, her own Order, which was to teach love, of course, with the same unique fire as other missionaries have taught it; she would send her women into the poor neighborhoods and into the ghettoes and into the working districts, and they would hold forth on the importance of starting a movement of love from the core of the people that would reach eventually to all governments in power, so that injustice would end."

"What would distinguish these women from other such orders or missionaries, from Franciscans or any sort of preachers . . . ?"

"Well, one that they would be women, and preaching women! Nuns have been nurses, teachers for little children, servants, or locked in the cloister to bray at God like so many boring sheep. Her women would be doctors of the church, you see! Preachers. They would work up the crowds with personal fervor; they would turn to the women, the impoverished and the depotentiated women, and help them to reform the world."

"A feminist vision, but coupled with religion."

"It had a chance. It had as much of a chance as any such movement. Who knows why one monk in the 1300s became a crazy? And another one a saint? Dora has ways to show people how to think. I don't know! You have to figure this all out, you have to!"

"And meanwhile save the church decorations," I said.

"Yes, until she will accept them or until she can turn them to some good. That's how you get her. Talk about good."

"That's how you get anybody," I said sadly. "That's how you're getting me."

"Well, you'll do it, won't you? Dora thinks I was misguided. She said, 'Don't think you can save your soul after all you've done by passing on these church objects to me.' "

"She loves you," I affirmed. "I saw that every time I saw her with you."

"I know. I need no such assurances. There's no time now to go into all the arguments. But Dora's vision is immense, remember that. She's small-time now, but wants to change the entire world. I mean, she isn't satisfied to have a cult the way I wanted it, you know, to be a guru with a retreat full of pliant followers. She really wants to change the world. She thinks somebody has to change the world."

"Doesn't every religious person believe that?"

"No. They don't dream of being Mohammed or Zoroaster."

"And Dora does."

"Dora knows that that is what's required."

He shook his head, took another little bit of the drink, and looked off over the half-empty room. Then he made a little frown as if pondering it still.

"She said, 'Dad, religion doesn't come from relics and texts. They are the expression of it.' She went on and on. After all her studying of Scripture, she said it was the inner miracle that counted. She put me to sleep. Don't make any cruel jokes!"

"Not for the world."

"What's going to happen to my daughter!" he whispered desperately. He wasn't looking at me. "Look at her heritage. See it in her father. I'm fervent and extremist and gothic and mad. I can't tell you how many churches I've taken Dora to, how many priceless crucifixes

I've shown to her, before turning them around for a profit. The hours Dora and I have spent looking at the ceilings of Baroque churches in Germany alone! I have given Dora magnificent relics of the true cross embedded in silver and rubies. I have bought many veils of Veronica, magnificent works that would take your breath away. My God."

"Was there ever—with Dora, I mean—a concept of atonement in all of this, a guilt?"

"You mean, for letting Terry disappear without explanation, for never asking, until years later? I thought of that. If it was there in the beginning, Dora's passed it a long time ago. Dora thinks the world needs a new revelation. A new prophet. But you just don't become a prophet! She says her transformation must come with seeing and feeling; but it's no Revival Tent experience."

"Mystics never think it's a Revival Tent experience."

"Of course not."

"Is Dora a mystic? Would you say that?"

"Don't you know? You followed her, you watched her. No, Dora hasn't seen the face of God or heard His voice and would never lie about it, if that's what you mean. But Dora's looking for it. She's looking for the moment, for the miracle, for the revelation!"

"For the angel to come."

"Yes, exactly."

We were both quiet suddenly. He was probably thinking of his initial proposition; so was I, that I fake a miracle, I, the evil angel that had once driven a Catholic nun to madness, to bleeding from her hands and feet in the Stigmata.

Suddenly he made the decision to continue, and I was relieved.

"I made my life rich enough," he said, "that I stopped caring about changing the world if ever I really thought of it; I made a life, you see, you know, a world unto itself. But she really has opened her soul in a sophisticated way to . . . to something. My soul's dead."

"Apparently not," I said. The thought that he would vanish, had to, sooner or later, was becoming intolerable to me, and far more frightening than his initial presence had ever been.

"Let's get back to the basics. I'm getting anxious. . . ." he said.

"Why?"

"Don't freak on me, just listen. There is money put aside for Dora that has no connection to me. The government can't touch it, besides, they never got an indictment against me let alone a conviction, you saw to that. The information's in the flat. Black leather folders. File cabinet. Mixed right in with sales slips for all sorts of paintings and statues. And you have to save all that somewhere for Dora. My life's work, my inheritance. It's in your hands for her. You can do it, can't you? Look, there's no hurry, you've done away with me in a rather clever way."

"I know. And you're asking me now to function as a guardian angel, to see that Dora receives this inheritance untainted. . . ."

"Yes, my friend, that's precisely what I'm begging you to do. And you can do it! And don't forget about my Wynken! If she won't take those books, you keep those books!"

He touched my chest with his hand. I felt it, the little knock upon the door of the heart.

He continued. "When my name drops out of the papers, assuming it ever makes it from the FBI files to the wire service, you get the money to Dora. Money can still create Dora's church. Dora is magnetic. Dora can do it all by herself, if she has the money! You follow me? She can do it the way Francis did it or Paul or Jesus. If it wasn't for her theology, she would have become the charismatic celebrity long ago. She has all the assets. She thinks too much. Her theology is what sets her apart."

He took a breath. He was talking very rapidly, and I was beginning to shiver. I could hear his fear like a low emanation from him. *Fear of what?*

"Here," he said. "Let me quote something to you. She told me this last night. We've been reading a book by Bryan Appleyard, a columnist for the papers in England, you've heard of him? He wrote some tome called *Understanding the Present.* I have the copy she gave me. And in it he said things that Dora believed . . . such as that we are 'spiritually impoverished.' "

"Agreed."

"But it was something else, something about our dilemma, that you can invent theologies, but for them to work they have to come from some deeper place inside a person . . . I know what she called it . . . Appleyard's words . . . 'a totality of human experience.' " He stopped. He was distracted.

I was desperate to reassure him that I understood this. "Yes, she's looking for this, courting it, she's opening herself for it."

I suddenly realized that I was holding on to him as tightly as he was holding on to me.

He was staring off.

I was filled with a sadness so awful that I couldn't speak. I'd killed this man! Why had I done it? I mean, I knew he'd been interesting and evil, but Christ, how could I have . . . but then what if he stayed with me the way he was! What if he could become my friend exactly the way he was.

Oh, this was too childish and selfish and avaricious! We were talking about Dora, about theology. Of course I understood Appleyard's point. *Understanding the Present.* I pictured the book. I'd go back for it. I filed it in my preternatural memory. Read at once.

He hadn't moved or spoken.

"Look, what are you scared of?" I asked. "Don't fade on me!" I clung to him, very raw, and small, and almost crying, thinking that I had killed him, taken his life, and now all I wanted to do was hold on to his spirit.

He gave no response. He looked afraid.

I wasn't the ossified monster I thought I was. I wasn't in danger of being inured to human suffering. I was a damned jibbering empath!

"Roger? Look at me. Go on talking."

He only murmured something about maybe Dora would find what he had never found.

"What?" I demanded.

"Theophany," he whispered.

Oh, that lovely word. David's word. I'd only heard it myself a few hours ago. And now it slipped from his lips.

"Look, I think they're coming for me," he said suddenly. His eyes grew wide. He didn't look afraid now so much as puzzled. He was listening to something. I could hear it too. "Remember my death," he said suddenly, as if he'd just thought of it most distinctly. "Tell her how I died. Convince her my death has cleansed the money! You understand. That's the angle! I paid with my death. The money is no longer unclean. The books of Wynken, all of it, it's no longer unclean. Pretty it up. I ransomed it all with my blood. You know, Lestat, use your clever tongue. Tell her!"

Those footsteps.

The distinct rhythm of Something walking, slowly walking. . . .

and the low murmur of the voices, the singing, the talking, I was getting dizzy. I was going to fall. I held on to him and on to the bar.

"Roger!" I shouted aloud. Surely everybody in the bar heard it. He was looking at me in the most pacific manner, I don't even know if his face was animate anymore. He seemed puzzled, even amazed. . . .

I saw the wings rise up over me, over him. I saw the immense obliterating darkness shoot up as if from a volcanic rip in the very earth and the light rise behind it. Blinding, beautiful light.

I know I cried out. "Roger!"

The noise was deafening, the voices, the singing, the figure growing larger and larger.

"Don't take him. It's my fault." I rose up against It in fury; I would tear It to pieces if I had to, to make It let him go! But I couldn't see him clearly. I didn't know where *I* was. And It came rolling, like smoke again, thick and powerful and absolutely unstoppable, and in the midst of all this, looming above him as he faded, and towards me, the face, the face of the granite statue for one second, the only thing visible, his eyes—

"Let him go!"

There was no bar, no Village, no city, no world. Only all of them!

And perhaps the singing was no more than the sound of a breaking glass.

Then blackness. Stillness.

Silence.

Or so it seemed, that I had been unconscious in a quiet place for some time.

I woke up outside on the street.

The bartender was standing there, shivering, asking me in the most annoyed and nasal tone of voice, "Are you all right, man?" There was snow on his shoulders, on the black shoulders of his vest, and on his white sleeves.

I nodded, and stood up, just so he'd go away. My tie was still in place. My coat was buttoned. My hands were clean. There was snow on my coat.

The snow was falling very lightly all around me. The most beautiful snow.

I went back through the revolving door into the tiled hallway and stood in the door of the bar. I could see the place where we had talked, see his glass still there. Otherwise the atmosphere was unchanged. The bartender was talking in a bored way to someone. He hadn't seen anything, except me bolt, probably, and stumble out into the street.

Every fiber in me said, Run. But where will you run? Take to the air? Not a chance, it will get you in an instant. Keep your feet on the cold earth.

You took Roger! Is that what you followed me for? Who are you!

The bartender looked up over the empty, dusty distance. I must have said something, done something. No, I was just blubbering. A man crying in a doorway, stupidly. And when it is this man, so to speak, that means blood tears. Make your exit quick.

I turned and walked out into the snow again. It was going to be morning soon, wasn't it? I didn't have to walk in the miserable punishing cold until the sky brightened, did I? Why not find a grave now, and go to sleep?

"Roger!" I was crying, wiping my tears on my sleeve. "What are you, damn it!" I stood and shouted, voice rolling off the buildings. "Damn it!" It came back to me suddenly in a flash. I heard all those mingled voices, and I fought it. The face. It has a face! *A sleepless mind in its heart and an insatiable personality.* Don't get dizzy, don't try to remember. Somebody in one of the buildings opened a window and shouted at me to move on. "Stop screaming out there." Don't try to reconstruct. You'll lose consciousness if you do.

I suddenly envisioned Dora and thought I might collapse where I was, shuddering and helpless and jabbering nonsense to anyone who came to help me.

This was bad, this was the worst, this was simply cosmically awful!

And what in God's name had been the meaning of Roger's expression in that last moment? Was it even an expression? Was it peace or calm or understanding, or just a ghost losing his vitality, a ghost giving up the ghost!

Ah! I had been screaming. I realized it. Lots of mortals around me, high up in the night, were telling me to be quiet.

I walked on and on.

I was alone. I cried quietly. There was no one in the empty street to hear.

I crept on, bent nearly double, crying out loud. I never noticed anyone now who saw or heard or stopped or took note. I wanted to reenact it in my mind, but I was terrified it would knock me flat on my back if I did it. And Roger, Roger . . . Oh, God, I wanted in my monstrous selfishness to go to Dora and go down on my knees. I did this, I killed, I. . . .

Midtown. I suppose. Mink coats in a window. The snow was touching my eyelids in the tenderest way. I took off the scarf tie, wiped my face thoroughly so there was no blood from the tears on it.

And then I blundered into a small bright hotel.

I paid for the room in cash, extra tip, don't disturb me for twenty-four hours, went upstairs, bolted the door, pulled the curtains, shut off the bothersome stinking heat, and crawled under the bed and went to sleep.

The last strange thought that passed through my mind before I went into mortal slumber—it was hours before sunrise, and plenty of time for dreaming—was that David was going to be angry about all this somehow, but that Dora, Dora might believe and understand . . .

I must have slept a few hours at least. I could hear the night sounds outside.

When I woke, the sky was lightening. The night was almost up. Now would come oblivion. I was glad. Too late to think. Go back into the deep vampire sleep. Dead with all the other Undead wherever they were, covering themselves against the coming light.

A voice startled me. It spoke to me very distinctly:

"It's not going to be that simple."

I rose up in one motion, overturning the bed, on my feet, staring in the direction from which the voice had come. The little hotel room was like a tawdry trap.

A man stood in the corner, a simple man. Not particularly tall, or small, or beautiful like Roger, or flashy like me, not even very young, not even very old, just a man. A rather nice-looking man, with arms folded and one foot crossed over the other.

The sun had just come up over the buildings. The fire hit the windows. I was blinded. I couldn't see anything.

I went down towards the floor, just a little burnt and hurt, the bed falling down upon me to protect me.

Nothing else. Whoever or whatever it was, I was powerless once the sun had come into the sky, no matter how white and thick the veil of winter morning.

5

VERY well," said David. "Sit down. Stop pacing. And I want
you to go over every detail again. If you need to feed before
you do this, then we'll go out and—"

"I have told you! I am past that. I don't need to feed. I don't need
blood. I crave it. I love it. And I don't want any now! I feasted on
Roger last night like a gluttonous demon. Stop talking about blood."

"Would you take your place there at the table?"

Across from him, he meant.

I was standing at the glass wall, looking right down on the roof of
St. Patrick's.

He'd gotten us perfect rooms in the Olympic Tower and we were
only just above the spires. An immense apartment far in excess of our
needs but a perfect domicile nevertheless. The intimacy with the cathedral seemed essential. I could see the cruciform of the roof, the
high piercing towers. They looked as if they could impale you, they
seemed so sharply pointed at heaven. And heaven as it had been the
night before was a soft soundless drift of snow.

I sighed.

"Look, I'm sorry. But I don't want to go all over it again. I can't.
Either you accept it as I told you, or I . . . I . . . go out of my mind."

He remained sitting calmly at the table. The place had come
"turnkey," or furnished. It was the snazzy substantial style of the corporate world—lots of mahogany and leather and shades of beige and
tan and gold that could offend no one, conceivably. And flowers. He
had seen to flowers. We had the perfume of flowers.

The table and chairs were harmoniously Oriental, the fashionable
infusion of Chinese. I think there was a painted urn or two also.

And below we had the Fifty-first Street side of St. Patrick's, and
people down there on Fifth going and coming on the snowy steps.
The quiet vision of the snow.

"We don't have that much time," I said. "We have to get uptown,
and I have to secure that place or move all of those precious objects.
I'm not allowing some accident to happen to Dora's inheritance."

"We can do that, but before we go, try this for me. Describe the
man again . . . not Roger's ghost, or the living statue, or the winged

one, but the man you saw standing in the corner of the hotel room, when the sun came up."

"Ordinary, I told you, very ordinary. Anglo-Saxon? Yes, probably. Distinctly Irish or Nordic? No. Just a man. Not a Frenchman, I don't think. No, a routine flavor of American. A man of good height, my height, but not overwhelmingly tall like you. I couldn't have seen him for more than five seconds. It was sunrise. He had me trapped there. I couldn't flee. I went blank. The mattress covered me, and when I woke, no man. Gone, as if I'd imagined it. But I didn't imagine it!"

"Thank you. The hair?"

"Ash blond, almost gray. You know how ash blond can fade to where it's really truly a . . . a graying brown color, or colorless almost, just sort of deep gray."

He gave a little gesture that he understood.

Cautiously I leant on the glass. With my strength it would have been a simple thing to have accidentally shattered the wall. The last thing I wanted was a blunder.

Obviously he wanted me to say more, and I was trying. I could recall the man fairly distinctly. "An agreeable face, very agreeable. He was the kind of man who doesn't impress one with size or physicality so much as a sort of alertness, a poise and intelligence, I suppose you'd call it. He looked like an interesting man."

"Clothes."

"Not noticeable. Black I think, maybe even a bit dusty? I think I would remember jet black, or beautiful black, or fancy black."

"Eyes distinctive?"

"Only for the intelligence. They weren't large or deeply colored. He looked normal, smart. Dark eyebrows but not terribly heavy or anything like that. Normal forehead, full hair, nice hair, combed, but nothing dandified like mine. Or yours."

"And you believe he spoke the words?"

"I'm sure he did. I heard him. I jumped up. I was awake, you understand, fully awake. I saw the sun. Look at my hand."

I was not as pale as I had been before I went into the Gobi desert, before I had tempted the sun to kill me in the recent past. But we could both see the burn where the rays of the sun had struck my hand. And I could feel the burn on the right side of my face, though it wasn't visible there because I'd probably turned my head.

"And you woke and you were under the bed, and it was askew, and had been thrown over and had fallen back down."

"No question of it. A lamp was overturned. I had not dreamed it any more than I dreamed Roger or anything else. Look, I want you to come uptown with me. I want you to see this place. Roger's things."

"Oh, I want to," he said. He stood up. "I wouldn't miss this for the world. It's just I wanted you to take your ease a little longer, to try to. . . ."

"What? Get calm? After talking to the ghost of one of my victims? After seeing this man standing in my room! After seeing this thing take Roger, this thing which has been stalking me all over the world, this herald of madness, this—"

"But you didn't really see it take Roger, did you?"

I thought about it for a moment.

"I'm not sure. I'm not sure Roger's image was animated anymore. He looked completely calm. He faded. Then the face of the creature or being or whatever it was—the face was visible for an instant. By that time, I was completely lost—no sense of balance or locality, nothing. I don't know whether Roger was just fading as it took him or whether he accepted it and went along."

"Lestat, you don't know that either thing happened. You only know Roger's ghost disappeared and this thing appeared. That's all you know."

"I suppose that's true."

"Think about it this way. Your Stalker chose to make himself manifest. And he obliterated your ghostly companion."

"No. They were connected. Roger heard him coming! Roger knew he was coming even before I heard the footsteps. Thank God for one thing."

"Which is what?"

"That I can't communicate the fear to you. That I can't make you feel how bad it was. You believe me, which is more than sufficient for the moment, but if you really knew, you wouldn't be calm and collected and the perfect British gentleman."

"I might be. Let's go. I want to see this treasure-house. I believe you're absolutely correct that you can't let all these objects slip out of the possession of the girl."

"Woman, young woman."

"And we should check on her whereabouts, immediately."

"I did that on the way here."

"In the state you were in?"

"Well, I certainly snapped out of it long enough to go into the hotel and make certain she'd left. I had to do that much. A limousine had taken her to La Guardia at nine a.m. this morning. She reached New Orleans this afternoon. As for the convent, I have no idea how to reach her there. I don't even know if she has the wiring in it for a phone. For now, she's as safe as she ever was while Roger was living."

"Agreed. Let's go uptown."

SOMETIMES fear is a warning. It's like someone putting a hand on your shoulder and saying Go No Farther.

As we entered the flat, I felt that for a couple of seconds. Panic. Go No Farther.

But I was too proud to show it and David too curious, proceeding before me into the hallway, and noting, no doubt, as I did, that the place was without life. The recent death? He could smell it as well as I could. I wondered if it was less noxious to him since it had not been his kill.

Roger! The fusion of the mangled corpse and Roger the Ghost in memory was suddenly like a sharp kick in the chest.

David went all the way to the living room while I lingered, looking at the big white marble angel with its shell of holy water and thinking how like the granite statue it was. Blake. William Blake had known. He had seen angels and devils and he'd gotten their proportions right. Roger and I could have talked about Blake. . . .

But that was over. I was here, in the hallway.

The thought that I had to walk forward, put one foot before the other, reach the living room, and look at that granite statue was suddenly a little more than I could accept.

"It's not here," David said. He hadn't read my mind. He was merely stating the obvious. He was standing in the living room some fifty feet away, looking at me, the halogens throwing just a little of their dedicated light on him and he said again, "There is no black granite statue in this room."

I gave a sigh. "I'm going to hell," I whispered.

I could see David very distinctly, but no mortal could have. His image was too shadowy. He looked tall and very strong, standing there, back to the dingy light of the windows, the halogens making sparkles on his brass buttons.

"The blood?"

"Yes, the blood, and your glasses. Your violet glasses. A nice piece of evidence."

"Evidence of what!"

It was too stupid of me to stand here at the back door talking to him over this distance. I walked down the hall as if going cheerfully to the guillotine, and I came into the room.

There was only an empty space where the statue had stood, and I wasn't even sure it was big enough. Clutter. Plaster saints. Icons, some so old and fragile they were under glass. Last night I hadn't noticed so very many, sparkling all over the walls in the splinters of light that escaped the directed lamps.

"Incredible!" David whispered.

"I knew you'd love it," I said dismally. I would have loved it, too, if I were not shaken to the bone.

He was studying the objects, eyes moving back and forth over the icons and then the saints. "Absolutely magnificent objects. This is . . . is an extraordinary collection. You don't know what any of this is, do you?"

"Well, more or less," I said. "I'm not an artistic illiterate."

"The series of pictures on the wall," he said. He gestured to a long row of icons, the most fragile.

"Those? Not really."

"Veronica's veil," he said. "These are early copies of the famous mandilion—the veil itself—which supposedly vanished from history centuries ago. Perhaps during the Fourth Crusade. This one's Russian, flawless. This one? Italian. And look there, on the floor, in stacks, those are the Stations of the Cross."

"He was obsessed with finding relics for Dora. Besides, he loved the stuff himself. That one, the Russian Veil of Veronica—he had just brought that here to New York to Dora. Last night they quarreled over it, but she wouldn't take it."

It was quite fine. How he had tried to describe it to her. God, I felt as if I had known him from my youth and we had talked about all of these objects, and every surface for me was layered with his special appreciation and complex of thoughts.

The Stations of the Cross. Of course I knew the devotion, what

Catholic child did not? We would follow the fourteen different stations of Christ's passion and journey to Calvary through the darkened church, stopping at each on bended knee to say the appropriate prayers. Or the priest and his altar boys would make the procession, while the congregation would recite with them the meditation on Christ's suffering at each point. Hadn't Veronica come up at the sixth station to wipe the face of Jesus with her veil?

David moved from object to object. "Now, this crucifix, this is really early, this could make a stir."

"But couldn't you say that about all the others?"

"Oh, yes, but I'm not speaking of Dora and her religion, or whatever that's about, simply that these are fabulous works of art. No, you're right, we cannot leave all this to fate, not possible. Here, this little statue could be ninth century, Celtic, unbelievably valuable. And this, this probably came from the Kremlin."

He paused, gripped by an icon of a Madonna and Child. Deeply stylized, of course, as are they all, and this one very familiar, for the Christ child was losing one of his sandals as He clung to his mother, and one could see angels tormenting Him with little symbols of his coming passion, and the Mother's head was tenderly inclined to the son. Halo overlapped halo. The child Jesus running from the future, into his Mother's protective arms.

"You understand the fundamental principle of an icon, don't you?" David asked.

"Inspired by God."

"Not made by hands," said David. "Supposedly directly imprinted upon the background material by God Himself."

"You mean like Jesus' face was imprinted on Veronica's veil?"

"Exactly. All icons fundamentally were the work of God. A revelation in material form. And sometimes a new icon could be made from another simply by pressing a new cloth to the original, and a magic transfer would occur."

"I see. Nobody was supposed to have painted it."

"Precisely. Look, this is a jewel-framed relic of the True Cross, and this, this book here . . . my God, these can't be the . . . No, this is a famous Book of the Hours that was lost in Berlin in the Second World War."

"David, we can make our loving inventory later. Okay? The point is, what do we do now?" I had stopped being so afraid, though I did keep looking at the empty place where the granite devil had stood.

And he had been the Devil, I knew he was. I'd start trembling if we did not go into action.

"How do we save all this for Dora, and where?" David said. "Come on, the cabinets and the notebooks, let's put things in order, find the Wynken de Wilde books, let's make a decision and a plan."

"Don't think about bringing your old mortal allies into this," I said suddenly, suspiciously, and unkindly, I have to admit.

"You mean the Talamasca?" he asked. He looked at me. He was holding the precious Book of the Hours in his hand, its cover as fragile as piecrust.

"It all belongs to Dora," I said. "We have to save it for her. And Wynken's mine if she never wants Wynken."

"Of course, I understand that," he said. "Good heavens, Lestat, do you think I still maintain contact with the Talamasca? They could be trusted in that regard, but I don't want any contact with my old mortal allies, as you call them. I never want any contact with them again. I don't want my file in their archive the way you wanted yours, remember. 'The Vampire Lestat.' I don't want to be remembered by them, except as their Superior General who died of old age. Now come on."

There was a bit of disgust in his voice, and grief, also. I recalled that the death of Aaron Lightner, his old friend, had been "the final straw" with him and his Talamasca. Some sort of controversy had surrounded Lightner's death, but I never knew what it was.

The cabinet was in a room before the parlour, along with several other boxes of records. Immediately I found the financial papers, and went through them while David surveyed the rest.

Having vast holdings of my own, I'm no stranger to legal documents and the tricks of international banks. Yes, Dora had a legacy from unimpeachable sources, I could see that, which could not be touched by those seeking retribution for Roger's crimes. It was all connected to her name, Theodora Flynn, which must have been her legal name, as the result of Roger's nuptial alias.

There were too many different documents for me to assess the full value, only that it had been accumulated over time. It seemed Dora might have started a new Crusade to take back Istanbul from the Turks had she wanted to. There were some letters . . . I could pinpoint the exact date two years ago when Dora had refused all further assistance from the two trusts of which she had knowledge. As for the rest, I wondered if she had any idea of the scope.

Scope is everything when it comes to money. Imagination and scope. You lack either of these two things and you can't make moral decisions, or so I've always thought. It sounds contemptible, but think about it. It's not contemptible. Money is power to feed the hungry. To clothe the poor. But you have to know that. Dora had trusts and trusts, and trusts to pay taxes on all the trusts.

I thought in a moment's sorrow of how I had meant to help my beloved Gretchen—Sister Marguerite—and how the mere sight of me had ruined everything, and I'd retreated from her life, with all my gold still in the coffers. Didn't it always turn out like that? I was no saint. I didn't feed the hungry.

But Dora! Quite suddenly it dawned on me—she had become my daughter! She had become my saint just as she'd been Roger's. Now she had another rich father. She had me!

"What is it?" David asked with alarm. He was going through a carton of papers. "You've seen the ghost again?"

For one moment, I almost went into one of my major tremours, but I got a grip. I didn't say anything, but I saw it ever more clearly.

Watch out for Dora! Of course I would watch out for Dora, and somehow I'd convince her to accept everything. Maybe Roger hadn't known the proper arguments. And Roger was now a martyr for all his treasures. Yes, his last angle had been the right angle. He'd ransomed his treasures. Maybe with Dora, if properly explained. . . .

I was distracted. There they were, the twelve books. Each in a neat thin film of plastic, lined up on the top shelf of a small desk, right near the file cabinet. I knew what they were. I knew. And then there were Roger's labels on them, his fancy scribbling on a small white sticker, "W de W."

"Look," David said, rising from his knees and wiping the dust from his pants. "These are all simple legal papers on the purchases, everything here is clean, apparently, or has been laundered; there are dozens of receipts, certificates of authentication. I say we take all of this out of here now."

"Yes, but how, and to where?"

"Think, what's the safest place? Your rooms in New Orleans are certainly not safe. We can't trust these things to a warehouse in a city like New York."

"Exactly. I do have rooms here at a little hotel across from the park but that. . . ."

"Yes, I remember, that's where the Body Thief followed you. You mean you didn't change that address?"

"Doesn't matter. It wouldn't hold all this."

"But you realize that our sizable quarters in the Olympic Tower would hold all this," he said.

"You serious?" I asked.

"Of course I am. What could be more secure? Now we've work to do. We can't have any mortal connections with this. We're going to do all this toiling ourselves."

"Ah!" I gave a disgusted sigh. "You mean wrap all this and move it?"

He laughed. "Yes! Hercules had to do such things, and so have angels. How do you think Michael felt when he had to go from door to door in Egypt slaying the First Born of every house? Come on. You don't realize how simple it is to cushion all these items with modern plastics. I say we move it ourselves. It will be a venture. Why not go over the roofs."

"Ah, there is nothing more irritating than the energy of a fledgling vampire," I said wearily. But I knew he was right. And our strength was incalculably greater than that of any mortal helper. We could have all this cleared out perhaps within the night.

Some night!

I will say in retrospect that labor is an antidote for angst and general misery, and the fear that the Devil is going to grab you by the throat at any moment and bring you down into the fiery pit!

We amassed a huge supply of an insulating material made with bubbles of air trapped in plastic, which could indeed bind the most fragile relic in a harmless embrace. I removed the financial papers and the books of Wynken, carefully examining each to make sure I was right about what I had, and then we proceeded to the heavy labor.

Sack by sack we transported all the smaller objects, going over the rooftops as David had suggested, unnoticed by mortals, two stealthy black figures flying as witches might to the Sabbath.

The larger objects we had to take more lovingly, each of us toting one at a time in our arms. I deliberately avoided the great white marble angel. But David loved it, talking to it all the way until we reached our destination. And all this was slipped into the secure rooms of the Olympic Tower in a rather proper way through the freight stairways, with the obligatory mortal pace.

Our little clocks would wind down as we touched the mortal world, and we would pass into it quickly, gentlemen furnishing their new digs with appropriately and securely wrapped treasures.

Soon the clean, carpeted rooms above St. Patrick's housed a wilderness of ghostly plastic packages, some looking all too much like mummies, or less carefully embalmed dead bodies. The white marble angel with her seashell holy water basin was perhaps the largest. The books of Wynken, wrapped and bound, lay on the Oriental dining table. I hadn't really had a chance to look at them, but now was not the moment.

I sank down in a chair in the front room, panting from sheer boredom and fury that I had had to do anything so utterly menial. David was jubilant.

"The security's perfect here," David said enthusiastically. His young male body seemed inflamed with his own personal spirit. When I looked at him, sometimes I saw both merged—the elderly David, the young strapping Anglo-Indian male form. But most of the time, he was merely starkly perfect. And surely the strongest fledgling I had ever produced.

That wasn't due only to the strength of my blood or my own trials and tribulations before I'd brought him over. I'd given him more blood than I'd ever given the others when I made him. I'd risked my own survival. But no matter—

I sat there loving him, loving my own work. I was full of dust.

I realized that everything had been taken care of. We had even brought the rugs last, in rolls. Even the rug soaked with Roger's blood. Relic of the martyred Roger. Well, I would spare Dora that detail.

"I have to hunt," David said in a whisper, waking me from my calculations.

I didn't reply.

"You coming?"

"You want me to?" I asked.

He stood there regarding me with the strangest expression, dark youthful face without any palpable condemnation or even disgust.

"Why don't you? Don't you enjoy seeing it, even if you don't want it?"

I nodded. I'd never dreamed he would let me watch. Louis hated it when I watched. When we'd been together last year, the three of us,

David had been far too reticent and suspicious to suggest such a thing.

We went down into the thick snowy darkness of Central Park. Everywhere one could hear the park's nighttime occupants, snoring, grumbling, tiny whiffs of conversation, smoke. These are strong individuals, individuals who know how to live in the wild in the midst of a city that is itself notoriously fatal to its unlucky ones.

David found what he wanted quickly—a young male with a skullcap, his bare toes showing through his broken shoes, a walker in the night, lone and drugged and insensible to the cold and talking aloud to people of long ago.

I stood back under the trees, wet with snow and uncaring. David reached out for the young man's shoulder, brought him gently around and embraced him. Classic. As David bent to drink, the young man began to laugh and talk simultaneously. And then went quiet, transfixed, until at last the body was gently laid to rest at the foot of a leafless tree.

The skyscrapers of New York glowed to the south of us, the warmer, smaller lights of the East and the West Side hemmed us in. David stood very still, thinking what, I wondered?

It seemed he'd lost the ability to move. I went towards him. He was no calm, diligent archivist at the moment. He looked to be suffering.

"What?" I asked.

"You know what," he whispered. "I won't survive that long."

"You serious? With the gifts I gave you—"

"Shhhh, we're too much in the habit of saying things to each other which we know are unacceptable to each other. We should stop."

"And speak only the truth? All right. This is the truth. Now, you feel as if you can't survive. Now. When his blood is hot and swirling through you. Of course. But you won't feel that way forever. That's the key. I don't want to talk anymore about survival. I took a good crack at ending my life; it didn't work, and besides, I have something else to think about—this thing that's following me, and how I can help Dora before it closes in on me."

That shut him up.

We started walking, mortal fashion, through the dark park together, my feet crunching deep into the snow. We wandered in and out of the leafless groves, pushing aside the wet black branches, the looming buildings of midtown never quite out of sight.

I was on edge for the sound of the footsteps. I was on edge and a dreary thought had come to me—that the monstrous thing that had been revealed, the Devil himself or whoever it was, had merely been after Roger. . . .

But then what of the man, the anonymous and perfectly ordinary man? That is what he had become in my mind, the man I'd glimpsed before dawn.

We drew near to the lights of Central Park South, the buildings rising higher, with an arrogance that Babylon could not have thrown in the face of heaven. But there were the comforting sounds of the well-heeled, and the committed, coming and going, and the never-ending push and shove of taxis adding to the din.

David was brooding, stricken.

Finally I said, "If you'd seen the thing that I saw, you wouldn't be so eager to jump to the next stage." I gave a sigh. I wasn't going to describe the winged thing to either one of us again.

"I'm quite inspired by it," he confessed. "You can't imagine."

"Going to Hell? With a Devil like that?"

"Did you feel it was hellish? Did you sense evil? I asked you that before. Did you feel evil when the thing took Roger? Did Roger give any indication of pain?"

Those questions seemed to me a bit hairsplitting.

"Don't get overly optimistic about death," I said. "I'm warning you. My views are changing. The atheism and nihilism of my earlier years now seems shallow, and even a bit cocky."

He smiled, dismissively, as he used to do when he was mortal and visibly wore the laurels of venerable age.

"Have you ever read the stories of Hawthorne?" he asked me softly. We had reached the street, crossed, and were slowly skirting the fountain before the Plaza.

"Yes," I said. "At some time or other."

"And you remember Ethan Brand's search for the unpardonable sin?"

"I think so. He went off to search for it and left his fellow man behind."

"Recall this paragraph," he said gently. We made our way down Fifth, a street that is never empty, or dark. He quoted the lines to me:

" 'He had lost his hold of the magnetic chain of humanity. He was no longer a brother-man, opening the chambers or the dungeons of our common nature by the key of holy sympathy, which gave him a right to share in all its secrets; he was now a cold observer, looking on mankind as the subject of his experiment, and, at length, converting man and woman to be his puppets, and pulling the wires that moved them to such degrees of crime as were demanded for his study.' "

I said nothing. I wanted to protest, but it was not an honest thing to do. I wanted to say that I would never, never treat humans like puppets. All I had done was watch Roger, damn it all, and Gretchen in the jungles. I had pulled no strings. Honesty had undone her and me together. But then he wasn't speaking of me with these words. He was talking about himself, the distance he felt now from the human. He had only begun to be Ethan Brand.

"Let me continue a little farther," he asked respectfully, then began to quote again. " 'Thus Ethan Brand became a fiend. He began to be so from the moment that his moral nature had ceased to keep the pace of improvement with his intellect—' " He broke off.

I didn't reply.

"That's our damnation," he whispered. "Our moral improvement has reached its finish, and our intellect grows by leaps and bounds."

Still I said nothing. What was I to say? Despair was so familiar to me; it could be banished by the sight of a beautiful mannikin in the window. It could be dispelled by the spectacle of lights surrounding a tower. It could be lifted by the great ghostly shape of St. Patrick's coming into view. And then despair would come again.

Meaningless, I almost said, aloud, but what came from my lips was completely different.

"I have Dora to think of," I said.

Dora.

"Yes, and thanks to you," he said, "I have Dora too, now don't I?"

6

OW AND when and what to tell Dora? That was the question. The journey we made to New Orleans early the next night.

There was no sign of Louis at the town house in the Rue Royale, but this was by no means unusual. Louis took to wandering more and more often, and he had been seen once by David in the company of Armand in Paris. The town house was spotless, a dream set out of time, full of my favorite Louis XV furnishings, luscious wallpaper, and the finest carpets to be found.

David, of course, was familiar with the place, though he hadn't seen it in over a year. One of the many picture-perfect bedrooms, drenched in saffron silks and outrageous Turkish tables and screens, still held the coffin in which he had slept during his brief and first stay here as one of the Undead.

Of course, this coffin was heavily disguised. He had insisted that it be the real thing—as fledglings almost invariably do, unless they are nomads by nature—but it was cleverly enough concealed within a heavy bronze chest, which Louis had chosen for it afterwards—a great hulking rectangular object as defeating as a square piano, with no perceivable opening in it, though of course, if you knew the right places to touch, the lid rose at once.

I had made my resting place as I had promised myself, when restoring this house in which Claudia and Louis and I had once lived. Not in my old bedroom, which now housed only the de rigueur heavy four-poster and dressing table, but in the attic, beneath the eave, I had made a cell of metal and marble.

In sum, we had a comfortable base immediately, and I was frankly relieved that Louis was not there to tell me he didn't believe me when I described the things that I'd seen. His rooms were in order; new books had been added. There was a vivid and arresting new painting by Matisse. Otherwise, things were the same.

As soon as we had settled in, checked all security, as immortals always do, with a breezy scan and a deep resistance to having to do anything mortals have to do, we decided that I should go uptown and try to catch a glimpse of Dora alone.

I had seen or heard nothing of the Stalker, though not much time had passed, of course, and I had seen nothing of The Ordinary Man.

We agreed that either might appear at any moment.

Nevertheless, I broke from the company of David, leaving him to explore the city as he wished.

Before leaving the Quarter for uptown, I called upon Mojo, my dog. If you are unacquainted with Mojo from *The Tale of the Body Thief*, let me tell you only what you need to know—that he is a giant German shepherd, is kept for me by a gracious mortal woman in a building of which I retain ownership, and that Mojo loves me, which I find irresistible. He is a dog, no more, or less, except that he is immense in size, with an extremely thick coat, and I cannot stay long away from him.

I spent an hour or two with him, wrestling, rolling around with him on the ground in the back garden, and talking to him about everything that happened, then debated as to whether I should take him with me uptown. His dark, long face, wolflike and seemingly evil, was full of the usual gentleness and forbearance. God, why didn't you make us all dogs?

Actually, Mojo created a sense of safety in me. If the Devil came and I had Mojo. . . . But that was the most absurd idea! I'd fend off Hell on account of a flesh-and-blood dog. Well, humans have believed stranger things, I suppose.

Just before I'd left David, I'd asked, "What do you think is happening, I mean with this Stalker and this Ordinary Man?" And David had answered without hesitation, "You're imagining both of them, you punish yourself relentlessly; it's the only way you know how to go on having fun."

I should have been insulted. But I wasn't.

Dora was real.

Finally, I decided I had to take leave of Mojo. I was going to spy upon Dora. And had to be fleet of foot. I kissed Mojo and left him. Later we would walk in our favorite wastelands beneath the River Bridge, amid the grass and the garbage, and be together. That I would have for as long as nature let me have it. For the moment it could wait.

Back to Dora.

Of course Dora didn't know Roger was dead. There was no way that she could know, unless—perhaps—Roger had appeared to her.

But I hadn't gathered from Roger that such was even possible. Appearing to me had apparently consumed all his energy. Indeed, I thought he had been far too protective of Dora to have haunted her in any practical or deliberate way.

But what did I know about ghosts? Except for a few highly mechanical and indifferent apparitions, I'd never spoken to a ghost until I'd spoken to Roger.

And now I would carry with me forever the indelible impression of his love for Dora, and his peculiar mixture of conscience and supreme self-confidence. In retrospect, even his visit seemed to me to exhibit extraordinary self-assurance. That he could haunt, that was not beyond probability since the world is filled with impressive and credible ghost stories. But that he could detain me in conversation—that he could make me his confidant—that had indeed involved an enormous and almost dazzling pride.

I walked uptown in human fashion, breathing the river air, and glad to be back with my black-barked oaks, and the sprawling, dimly lighted houses of New Orleans, the intrusions everywhere of grass and vine and flower; home.

Too soon, I reached the old brick convent building on Napoleon Avenue where Dora was lodged. Napoleon Avenue itself is a rather beautiful street even for New Orleans; it has an extraordinarily wide median where once streetcars used to run. Now there are generous shade trees planted on it, just as there were all around the convent that faced it.

It was the leafy depth of Victorian uptown.

I drew close to the building slowly, eager to imprint its details on my mind. How I'd changed since last I'd spied on Dora.

Second Empire was the style of the convent, due to a mansard roof which covered the central portion of the building and its long wings. Old slates had, here and there, fallen away from the sloping mansard, which was concave on the central part and quite unusual on account of that fact. The brickwork itself, the rounded arched windows, the four corner towers of the building, the two-storey plantation-house porch on the front of the central building—with its white columns and black iron railings—all of this was vaguely New Orleans Italianate, and gracefully proportioned. Old copper gutters clung to the base of the roofs. There were no shutters, but surely there had once been.

The windows were numerous, high, rounded at the tops on the second and third stories, trimmed in faded white.

A great sparse garden covered the front of the building as it looked out over the avenue, and of course I knew of the immense courtyard inside. The entire city block was dominated by this little universe in which nuns and orphans, young girls of all ages, had once dwelt. Great oaks sprawled over the sidewalks. A row of truly ancient crape myrtles lined the side street to the south.

Walking round the building, I surveyed the high stained-glass windows of the two-storey chapel, noted the flickering of a light inside, as though the Blessed Sacrament were present—a fact that I doubted—and then coming to the rear I went over the wall.

The building did have some locked doors, but not very many. It was wrapped in silence, and in the mild but nevertheless real winter of New Orleans, it was chillier within than without.

I entered the lower corridor cautiously, and at once found myself loving the proportions of the place, the loftiness and the breadth of the corridors, the intense smell of the recently bared brick walls, and the good wood scent of the bare yellow pine floors. It was rough, all this, the kind of rough which is fashionable among artists in big cities who live in old warehouses, or call their immense apartments lofts.

But this was no warehouse. This had been a habitation and something of a hallowed one. I could feel it at once. I walked slowly down the long corridor towards the northeast stairs. Above to my right lived Dora in the northeast tower, so to speak, of the building, and her living quarters did not begin until the third floor.

I sensed no one in the building. No scent nor sound of Dora. I heard the rats, the insects, something a little larger than a rat, possibly a raccoon feeding away somewhere up in an attic, and then I felt for the elementals, as David called them—those things which I prefer to call spirits, or poltergeists.

I stood still, eyes closed. I listened. It seemed the silence gave back dim emanations of personalities, but they were far too weak and too mingled to touch my heart or spark a thought in me. Yes, ghosts here, and here . . . but I sensed no spiritual turbulence, no unresolved tragedy or hanging injustice. On the contrary, there seemed a spiritual stillness and firmness.

The building was whole and itself.

I think the building liked having been stripped to its nineteenth-century essentials; even the naked beamed ceilings, though never built for exposure, were nevertheless beautiful without plaster, their wood dark and heavy and level because all the carpentry of those years had been done with such care.

The stairway was original. I had walked up a thousand such built in New Orleans. This building had at least five. I knew the gentle curve to each tread, worn down by the feet of children, the silky feel of the banister which had been waxed countless times for a century. I knew the landing which cut directly against an exterior window, ignoring the shape or existence of the window, and simply bisecting the light which came from the street outside.

When I reached the second floor, I realized I was at the doorway of the chapel. It had not seemed such a large space from outside.

It was in fact as large as many a church I'd seen in my years. Some twenty or so pews were in neat rows on either side of its main aisle. The plastered ceiling was coved and crowned with fancy molding. Old medallions still held firmly in the plaster from which, no doubt, gasoliers had once hung. The stained-glass windows, though without human figures, were nevertheless very well executed, as the street-lamp showed to good advantage. And the names of the patrons were beautifully lettered on the lower panes of each window. There was no sanctuary light, only a bank of candles before a plaster Regina Maria, that is, a Virgin wearing an ornate crown.

The place must have been much as the Sisters had left it when the building was sold. Even the holy water fount was there, though it had no giant angel to hold it. It was only a simple marble basin on a stand.

I passed beneath a choir loft as I entered, somewhat amazed at the purity and symmetry of the entire design. What was it like, living in a building with your own chapel? Two hundred years ago I had knelt more than once in my father's chapel. But that had been no more than a tiny stone room in our castle, and this vast place, with its old oscillating electric fans for breeze in summer, seemed no less authentic than my father's little chapel had been.

This was more the chapel of royalty, and the entire convent seemed suddenly a palazzo—rather than an institutional building. I imagined myself living here, not as Dora would have approved, but in splendour, with miles of polished floors before me as I made my way each night into this great sanctuary to say my prayers.

I liked this place. It flamed into my mind. Buy a convent, make it your palace, live within its safety and grandeur in some forgotten spot of a modern city! I felt covetous, or rather, my respect for Dora deepened.

Countless Europeans still lived in such buildings, multi-storeyed, wings facing each other over expensive private courts. Paris had its share of such mansions, surely. But in America, it presented a lovely picture, the idea of living here in such luxury.

But that had not been Dora's dream. Dora wanted to train her women here, her female preachers who would declare the Word of God with the fire of St. Francis or Bonaventure.

Well, if her faith were suddenly swept away by Roger's death, she could live here in splendour.

And what power had I to affect Dora's dream? Whose wishes would be fulfilled if I somehow positioned her so that she accepted her enormous wealth and made herself a princess in this palace? One happy human being saved from the misery which religion can so effortlessly generate?

It wasn't an altogether worthless idea. Just typical of me. To think in terms of Heaven on Earth, freshly painted in pastel hues, floored in fine stone, and centrally heated.

Awful, Lestat.

Who was I to think such things? Why, we could live here like Beauty and the Beast, Dora and I. I laughed out loud. A shiver ran down my back, but I didn't hear the footsteps.

I was suddenly quite alone. I listened. I bristled.

"Don't you dare come near me now," I whispered to the Stalker who was not there, for all I knew. "I'm in a chapel. I am safe! Safe as if I were in the cathedral."

I wondered if the Stalker was laughing at me. *Lestat, you imagined it all.*

Never mind. Walk up the marble aisle towards the Communion Rail. Yes, there was still a Communion Rail. Look at what is before you, and don't think just now.

Roger's urgent voice was at the ear of my memory. But I loved Dora already, didn't I? I was here. I would do something. I was merely taking my time!

My footsteps echoed throughout the chapel. I let it happen. The Stations of the Cross, small, in deep relief in plaster, were still fixed between the stained-glass windows, making the usual circuit of the church, and the altar was gone from its deep arched niche—and there stood instead a giant Crucified Christ.

Crucifixes always fascinate me. There are numerous ways in which various details can be rendered, and the art of the Crucified Christ alone fills much of the world's museums, and those cathedrals and basilicas that have become museums. But this, even for me, was a rather impressive one. It was huge, old, very realistic in the style of the late nineteenth century, Christ's scant loincloth coiling in the wind, his face hollow-cheeked and profoundly sorrowful.

Surely it was one of Roger's finds. It was too big for the altar niche, for one thing, and of impressive workmanship, whereas the scattered plaster saints who remained on their pedestals—the predictable and pretty St. Therese of Lisieux in her Carmelite robes, with her cross and her bouquet of roses; St. Joseph with his lily; and even the Maria Regina with her crown at her shrine beside the altar—were all more or less routine. They were life-size; they were carefully painted; they were not fine works of art.

The Crucified Christ pushed one to some sort of resolution. Either "I loathe Christianity in all its bloodiness," or some more painful feeling, perhaps for a time in youth when one had imagined one's hands systematically pierced with those particular nails. Lent. Meditations. The Church. The Priest's voice entoning the words. *Our Lord.*

I felt both the loathing and the pain. Hovering near in the shadows, watching outside lights flicker and flare in the stained glass, I felt boyhood memories near me, or maybe I tolerated them. Then I thought of Roger's love for his daughter, and the memories were nothing, and the love was everything. I went up the steps that had once led to the altar and tabernacle. I reached up and touched the foot of the crucified figure. Old wood. Shimmer of hymns, faint and secretive. I looked up into the face and saw not a countenance twisted in agony, but wise and still, perhaps in the final seconds before death.

A loud echoing noise sounded somewhere in the building. I stepped back almost too fast, and lost my footing stupidly and found myself facing the church. Someone moved in the building, someone walking at a moderate pace on the lower floor and towards the same stairway up which I'd come to the chapel door.

I moved swiftly to the entrance of the vestibule. I could hear no voice and detect no scent! No scent. My heart sank. "I won't take any more of this!" I whispered. I was already shaking. But some mortal scents don't come that easily; there is the breeze to consider, or rather the draughts, which in this place were considerable.

The figure was mounting the stairs.

I leant back behind the chapel door so I might see it turn at the landing. And if it was Dora I meant to hide at once.

But it wasn't Dora, and it came walking so fast right up the stairs, lightly and briskly towards me, that I realized who it was as he came to a stop in front of me.

The Ordinary Man.

I stood stock-still, staring at him. Not quite my height; not quite my build; regular in every respect as I remembered. Scentless? No, but the scent was not right. It was mingled with blood and sweat and salt and I could hear a faint heartbeat. . . .

"Don't torment yourself," he said, in a very civil and diplomatic voice. "I'm debating. Should I make my offer now, or before you get mixed up with Dora? I'm not sure what's best."

He was four feet away at the moment.

I slouched arrogantly against the doorframe of the vestibule and folded my arms. The whole flickering chapel was behind me. Did I look frightened? Was I frightened? Was I about to perish of fright?

"Are you going to tell me who you are," I asked, "and what you want, or am I supposed to ask questions and draw this out of you?"

"You know who I am," he said in the same reticent, simple manner.

Something struck me suddenly. What was outstanding were the proportions of his figure and his face. The regularity itself. He was rather a generic man.

He smiled. "Exactly. It's the form I prefer in every age and place, because it doesn't attract very much attention." Again the voice was good-natured. "Going about with black wings and goat's feet, you know—it overwhelms mortals instantly."

"I want you to get the hell out of here before Dora comes!" I said. I was suddenly sputtering crazy.

He turned, slapped his thigh, and laughed.

"You are a brat, Lestat," he said in his simple, unimposing voice. "Your cohorts named you properly. You can't give me orders."

"I don't know why not. What if I throw you out?"

"Would you like to try? Shall I take my other form? Shall I let my wings. . . ." I heard the chatter of voices, and my vision was clouding.

"No!" I shouted.

"All right."

The transformation came to a halt. The dust settled. I felt my heart knock against my chest like it wanted to get out.

"I'll tell you what I'm going to do," he said. "I'll let you handle things with Dora, since you seem obsessed with it. And I won't be able to distract you from it. And then when you've finished with all this, this girl and her dreams and such, we can talk together, you and I."

"About what?"

"Your soul, what else?"

"I'm ready to go to Hell," I said, lying through my teeth. "But I don't believe you're what you claim to be. You're something, something like me for which there aren't scientific explanations, but behind it all, there's a cheap little core of facts that will eventually lay bare everything, even the texture of each black feather of your wings."

He frowned slightly, but he wasn't angry.

"We won't continue at this pace," he said. "I assure you. But for now, I'll let you think about Dora. Dora's on her way home. Her car has just pulled into the courtyard. I'm going, with regular footsteps, the way I came. And I give you one piece of advice, for both of us."

"Which is what?" I demanded.

He turned his back on me and started down the stairway, as quick and spry as he had come up. He didn't turn around till he reached the landing. I had already caught Dora's scent.

"What advice?" I demanded.

"That you leave Dora alone completely. Turn her affairs over to worldly lawyers. Get away from this place. We have more important things to discuss. This is all so distracting."

Then he was gone with a clatter down the lower stairs, and presumably out a side door. I heard it open and close.

And almost immediately following, I heard Dora come through the main rear entrance into the center of the building, the way I had entered, and the way he had entered, and she began her progress down the hall.

She sang to herself as she came, or hummed, I should say. The sweet aroma of womb blood came from her. Her menses. Maddeningly, it amplified the succulent scent of the whole child moving to-wards me.

I slipped back into the shadows of the vestibule. She wouldn't see me or have any knowledge of me as she went by and on up the next stairway to her third-floor room.

She was skipping steps when she reached the second floor. She had a backpack slung over her shoulders and wore a pretty, loose old-fashioned dress of flowered cotton with long, white lace-trimmed sleeves.

She swung round to go up when she suddenly stopped. She turned in my direction. I froze. She could not possibly see me in this light.

Then she came towards me. She reached out. I saw her white fin-gers touch something on the wall; it was a light switch. A simple plas-tic light switch, and suddenly a flood came from the bulb above.

Picture this: the blond male intruder, eyes hidden by the violet sunglasses, now nice and clean, with no more of her father's blood, black wool coat and pants.

I threw up my hands as if to say "I won't hurt you!" I was speech-less.

I disappeared.

That is, I moved past her so swiftly she couldn't see it; I brushed her about like the air would brush her. That's all. I made the two flights to an attic, and went through an open door in the dark spaces above the chapel, where only a few windows in the mansard let in a tiny light from the street. One of the windows was broken out. A quick way to make an exit. But I stopped. I sat down very still in the corner. I shrank up into the corner. I drew up my knees, pushed my glasses up on my nose, and looked across the width of the attic to-wards the door through which I'd come.

I heard no screams. I heard nothing. She had not gone into hys-terics; she was not running madly through the building. She had sounded no alarms. Fearless, quiet, having seen a male intruder. I mean, next to a vampire, what in the world is as dangerous to a lone woman as a young human male?

I realized my teeth were chattering. I put my right hand into a fist and pushed it into my left palm. Devil, man, who the hell are you, waiting for me, telling me not to talk to her, what tricks, don't talk to her, I was never going to talk to her, Roger, what the hell am I to do now? I never meant for her to see me like this!

I should never, never have come without David. I needed the anchor of a witness. And the Ordinary Man, would he have dared to come up if David had been here? I loathed him! I was in a whirlpool. I wasn't going to survive.

Which meant what? What was going to kill me?

Suddenly I realized that she was coming up the stairs. This time she walked slowly, and very quietly. A mortal couldn't have heard her. She had her electric torch with her. I hadn't noticed it before. But now she had it, and the beam came through the open attic door and ran along the sloping dark boards of the inner roof.

She stepped into the attic and switched off the torch. She looked around very cautiously, her eyes filling with the white light coming through the round windows. It was possible to see things fairly distinctly here because of those round windows, and because the streetlamps were so close.

Then she found me with her eyes. She looked right at me in the corner.

"Why are you frightened?" she asked. Her voice was soothing.

I realized I was jammed into the corner, legs crossed, knees beneath my chin, arms locked around my legs, looking up at her.

"I . . . I am sorry. . . ." I said. "I was afraid . . . that I had frightened you. I was ashamed that I had caused you distress. I felt that I'd been unforgivably clumsy."

She stepped towards me, fearlessly. Her scent filled the attic slowly, like the vapor from a pinch of burning incense.

She looked tall and lithesome in the flowered dress, with the lace at her cuffs. Her short black hair covered her head like a little cap with curls against her cheeks. Her eyes were big and dark, and made me think of Roger.

Her gaze was nothing short of spectacular. She could have unnerved a predator with her gaze, the light striking the bones of her cheeks, her mouth quiet and devoid of all emotion.

"I can leave now if you like," I said tremulously. "I can simply get up very slowly and leave without hurting you. I swear it. You must not be alarmed."

"Why you?" she asked.

"I don't understand your question," I said. Was I crying? Was I just shivering and shaking? "What do you mean, why me?"

She came in closer and looked down at me. I could see her very distinctly.

Perhaps she saw a mop of blond hair and the glint of light in my glasses and that I seemed young.

I saw her curling black eyelashes, her small but firm chin, and the way that her shoulders so abruptly sloped beneath her lace and flowered dress that she seemed hardly to have shoulders at all—a long sketch of a girl, a dream lily woman. Her tiny waist beneath the loose fabric of the waistless dress would be nothing in one's arms.

There was something almost chilling about her presence. She seemed neither cold nor wicked, but just as frightening as if she were! Was this sanctity? I wondered if I had ever been in the presence of a true saint. I had my definitions for the word, didn't I?

"Why did *you* come to tell me?" she asked tenderly.

"Tell you what, dearest?" I asked.

"About Roger. That he's dead." She raised her eyebrows very lightly. "That's why you came, wasn't it? I knew it when I saw you. I knew that Roger was dead. But why did *you* come?"

She came down on her knees in front of me.

I let out a long groan. So she'd read it from my mind! My big secret. My big decision. Talk to her? Reason with her? Spy on her? Fool her? Counsel her? And my mind had slapped her abruptly with the good news: Hey, honey, Roger's dead!

She came very close to me. Far too close. She shouldn't. In a moment she'd be screaming. She lifted the dead electric torch.

"Don't turn on your flashlight," I said.

"Why don't you want me to? I won't shine it in your face, I promise. I just want to see you."

"No."

"Look, you don't frighten me, if that's what you're thinking," she said simply, without drama, her thoughts stirring wildly beneath her words, her mind embracing every detail in front of her.

"And why not?"

"Because God wouldn't let something like you hurt me. I know that. You're a devil or an evil spirit. You're a good spirit. I don't know. I can't know. If I make the Sign of the Cross you might vanish. But I don't think so. What I want to know is, why are you so frightened of me? Surely it's not virtue, is it?"

"Wait just a second, back up. You mean you know that I'm not human?"

"Yes. I can see it. I can feel it! I've seen beings like you before. I've seen them in crowds in big cities, just glimpses. I've seen many things. I'm not going to say I feel sorry for you, because that's very stupid, but I'm not afraid of you. You're earthbound, aren't you?"

"Absolutely," I said. "And hoping to stay that way indefinitely. Look, I didn't mean to shock you with the news. I loved your father."

"You did?"

"Yes. And . . . and he loved you very much. There are things he wanted me to tell you. But above all, he wanted me to look out for you."

"You don't seem capable of that. You're like a frightened elf. Look at you."

"You're not the one I'm terrified of, Dora!" I said with sudden impatience. "I don't know what's happening! I am earthbound, yes, that's true. And I . . . and I killed your father. I took his life. I'm the one who did that to him. And he talked to me afterwards. He said, 'Look out for Dora.' He came to me and told me to look out for you. Now there it is. I'm not terrified of you. It's more the situation, never having been in such circumstances, never having faced such questions!"

"I see!" She was stunned. Her whole white face glistened as if she'd broken into a sweat. Her heart was racing. She bowed her head. Her mind was unreadable. Absolutely unreadable to me. But she was full of sorrow, anyone could see that, and the tears were sliding down her cheeks now. This was unbearable.

"Oh, God, I might as well be in Hell," I muttered. "I shouldn't have killed him. I . . . I did it for the simplest reasons. He was just . . . he crossed my path. It was a hideous mistake. But he came to me afterwards. Dora, we spent hours talking together, his ghost and me. He told me all about you and the relics and Wynken."

"Wynken?" She looked at me.

"Yes, Wynken de Wilde, you know, the twelve books. Look, Dora, if I touch your hand just to try to comfort you, perhaps it will work. But I don't want you to scream."

"Why did you kill my father?" she asked. It meant more than that. She was asking, Why did someone who talks the way you do, do such a thing?

"I wanted his blood. I feed on the blood of others. That's how I stay youthful and alive. Believe in angels? Then believe in vampires. Believe in me. There are worse things on earth."

She was appropriately stunned.

"Nosferatu," I said gently. "Verdilak. Vampire. Lamia. Earthbound." I shrugged, shook my head. I felt utterly helpless. "There are other species of things. But Roger, Roger came with his soul as a ghost to talk to me afterwards, about you."

She started to shake and to cry. But this wasn't madness. Her eyes went small with tears and her face crumpled with sadness.

"Dora, I won't hurt you for anything under God, I swear it. I won't hurt you. . . ."

"My father's really dead, isn't he?" she asked, and suddenly she broke down completely, her face in her hands, her little shoulders trembling with sobs. "My God, God help me!" she whispered. "Roger," she cried. "Roger!"

And she did make the Sign of the Cross, and she sat there, sobbing and unafraid.

I waited. Her tears and sorrow fed upon themselves. She was becoming more and more miserable. She leant forward and collapsed on the boards. Again, she had no fear of me. It was as if I weren't there.

Very slowly I slipped out of the corner. It was possible to stand up easily in this attic, once you were out of the corner. I moved around her, and then very gently reached to take her by the shoulders.

She gave no resistance; she was sobbing, and her head rolled as if she were drunk with sorrow; her hands moved but only to rise and grasp for things that weren't there. "God, God, God," she cried. "God . . . Roger!"

I picked her up. She was as light as I had suspected, but nothing like that could matter anyway to one as strong as me. I took her out of the attic. She fell against my chest.

"I knew it, I knew when he kissed me," she said through her sobbing, "I knew I would never lay eyes on him again. I knew it. . . ." This was hardly intelligible. She was so crushably small, I had to be most careful, and when her head fell back, her face was blanched and so helpless as to make a devil weep.

I went down to the door of her room. She lay against me, still like a rag doll tossed into my arms, that without resistance. There was warmth coming from her room. I pushed open the door.

Having once been a classroom perhaps, or even a dormitory, the room was very large, set in the very corner of the building, with lofty windows on two sides and full of the brighter light from the street.

The passing traffic illuminated it.

I saw her bed against the far wall, an old iron bed, rather plain, perhaps once a convent bed, narrow like that, with the high rectangular frame intact for the mosquito netting, though none hung from it now. White paint flaked from the thin iron rods. I saw her bookcases everywhere, stacks of books, books open with markers, propped on makeshift lecterns, and her own relics, hundreds of them perhaps, pictures, and statues, and maybe things Roger had given her before she knew the truth. Words were written in cursive on the wooden frames of doors and windows in black ink.

I took her to the bed and laid her down on it. She sank gratefully, it seemed, into the mattress and the pillow. Things here were clean in the modern way, fresh, and so repeatedly and thoroughly laundered that they looked almost new.

I handed her my silk handkerchief. She took it, then looked at it and said, "But it's too good."

"No, use it, please. It's nothing. I have hundreds."

She regarded me in silence, then began to wipe her face. Her heart was beating more slowly, but the scent of her had been made even stronger by her emotions.

Her menses. It was being neatly collected by a pad of white cotton between her legs. I let myself think of it now because the menses was heavy and the smell was overpoweringly delicious to me. It began to torture me, the thought of licking this blood. This isn't pure blood, you understand, but blood is its vehicle and I felt the normal temptation that vampires do in such circumstances, to lick the blood from her nethermouth between her legs, a way of feeding on her that wouldn't harm her.

Except under the circumstances it was a perfectly outrageous and impossible thought.

There was a long silent interval.

I merely sat there on a wooden straight-backed chair. I knew she was beside me, sitting up, legs crossed, and that she'd found a box of tissue which provided a world of comfort to her, and she was blowing her nose and wiping her eyes. My silk handkerchief was still clutched in her hand.

She was extremely excited by my presence but still unafraid, and far too sunk in sorrow to enjoy this confirmation of thousands of beliefs, a pulsing nonhuman with her, that looked and talked as if it were human. She couldn't let herself embrace this right now. But she couldn't quite get over it. Her fearlessness was true courage. She wasn't stupid. She was someplace so far beyond fear that cowards could never even grasp it.

Fools might have thought her fatalistic. But it wasn't that. It was the ability to think ahead, and thereby banish panic utterly. Some mortals must know this right before they die. When the game's up, and everyone has said farewell. She looked at everything from that fatal, tragic, unerring perspective.

I stared at the floor. No, don't fall in love with her.

The yellow pine boards had been sanded, lacquered, and waxed. The color of amber. Very beautiful. The whole palazzo might have this look one day. Beauty and the Beast. And as Beasts go, I mean, really, I'm quite a stunner.

I hated myself for having such a good time in a miserable moment like this, thinking of dancing with her through the corridors. I thought of Roger, and that brought me back quick enough, and the Ordinary Man, ah, that monster waiting for me!

I looked at her desk, two telephones, the computer, more books in stacks, and somewhere in the corner a little television, merely for study, apparently, the screen no bigger than four or five inches across though it was connected to a long coiling and winding black cable, which I knew connected it to the wide world.

There was lots of other blinking electronic equipment. It was no nun's cell. The words scrawled on the white framework of the doors and windows were actually in phrases, such as "Mystery opposes Theology." And "Commotion Strange." And, of all things, "Darkling, I listen."

Yes, I thought, mystery does oppose theology, that was something Roger was trying to say, that she had not caught on as she should because the mystical and the theological were mixed in her, and it wasn't working with the proper fire or magic. He had kept saying she was a theologian. And he thought of his relics as mysterious, of course. And they were.

Again a dim boyhood memory returned to me, of seeing the crucifix in our church at home in the Auvergne and being awestruck by the sight of the painted blood running from the nails. I must have been very small. I was bedding village girls in the back of that church by the time I was fifteen—something of a prodigy for the times, but then the lord's son was supposed to be a perfect billygoat in our village. Everyone expected it. And my brothers, such a conservative bunch, they had more or less disappointed the local mythology by always behaving themselves. It's a wonder that the crops hadn't suffered from their paltry virtue. I smiled. I had certainly made up for it. But when I had looked at the crucifix I must have been six or seven at most. And I had said, What a horrible way to die! I had blurted it out, and my mother had laughed and laughed. My father had been so humiliated!

The traffic on Napoleon Avenue made small, predictable, and slightly comforting noises.

Well, comforting to me.

I heard Dora sigh. And then I felt her hand on my arm, tight and delicate for only an instant, but fingers pressing through the armour of my clothing, wanting the texture beneath.

I felt her fingers graze my face.

For some reason, mortals do that when they want to be sure of us, they fold their fingers inward and they run their knuckles against our faces. Is that a way of touching someone without seeming to be touched oneself? I suppose the palm of the hand, the soft pad of the fingers, is too intimate.

I didn't move. I let her do it as if she were a blind woman and it was a courtesy. I felt her fingers move to my hair. I knew there was plenty enough light to make it fiery and pretty the way I counted upon it to be, shameless vain preening, selfish, confused, and temporarily disoriented being that I was.

She made the Sign of the Cross again. But she had never been actually afraid. She was just confirming something, I suppose. Though precisely what is really open to question, if you think of it. Silently she prayed.

"I can do that too," I said. I did it. "In the name of the Father, and of the Son, and of the Holy Ghost. Amen." I repeated the entire performance, doing it in Latin.

She regarded me with a still, amazed face, and then she let slip a tiny, gentle laugh.

I smiled. This bed and chair—where we sat so close to each other—were in the corner. There was a window over her shoulder, and one behind me. Windows, windows, it was a palazzo of windows. The dark wood of the ceiling must have been fifteen feet above us. I adored the scale of it. It was European, to say the least, and felt normal. It had not been sacrificed to modern dimensions.

"You know," I said, "the first time I walked into Notre Dame, after I'd been made into this, a vampire, that is, and it wasn't my idea, by the way, I was completely human and younger than you are now, the whole thing was forced, completely, I don't remember specifically if I prayed when it was happening, but I fought, that I vividly remember and have preserved in writing. But . . . as I was saying, the first time I walked into Notre Dame, I thought, well, why doesn't God strike me dead?"

"You must have your place in the scheme of things."

"You think? You really believe that?"

"Yes. I never expected to come upon something like you face to face, but it never seemed impossible or even improbable. I've been waiting all these years for a sign, for some confirmation. I would have lived out my life without it, but there was always the feeling . . . that it was going to come, the sign."

Her voice was small and typically feminine, that is, the pitch was without mistake feminine, but she spoke with terrific self-confidence now, and so her words seemed to have authority, rather like those of a man.

"And now you come, and you bring the news that you've killed my father. And you say that he spoke to you. No, I'm not one for simply dismissing such things out of hand. There's an allure to what you say, there is an ornate quality. Do you know, when I was a young girl, the very first reason I believed in the Holy Bible was because it had an ornate quality! I have perceived other patterns in life. I'll tell you a secret. One time I wished my mother dead, and do you know on that very day, within the very hour, she disappeared out of my life forever? I could tell you other things. What you must understand is I want to learn from you. You walked into Notre Dame Cathedral and God didn't strike you dead."

"I'll tell you something that I found amusing," I said. "This was two hundred years ago. Paris before the Revolution. There were vampires living in Paris then, in Les Innocents, the big cemetery, it's long gone, but they lived there in the catacombs beneath the tombs, and they were afraid to go into Notre Dame. When they saw me do it, they, too, thought God would strike me dead."

She was looking at me rather placidly.

"I destroyed their faith for them," I said. "Their belief in God and the Devil. And they were vampires. They were earthbound creatures like me, half demon, half human, stupid, blundering, and they believed that God would strike them dead."

"And before you, they had really had a faith?"

"Yes, an entire religion, they really did," I said. "They thought themselves servants of the Devil. They thought it was a distinction. They lived as vampires, but their existence was miserable and deliberately penitential. I was, you might say, a prince. I came swaggering through Paris in a red cloak lined with wolf fur. But that was my human life, the cloak. Does that impress you, that vampires would be believers? I changed it all for them. I don't think they've ever forgiven me, that is, those few who survive. There are not, by the way, very many of us."

"Stop a minute," she said. "I want to listen to you, but I must ask you something first."

"Yes?"

"My father, how did it happen, was it quick and. . . ."

"Absolutely painless, I assure you," I said, turning to her, looking at her. "He told me himself. No pain."

She was owl-like with such a white face and big dark eyes, and she was actually slightly scary herself. I mean, she might have scared another mortal in this place, the way she looked, the strength of it.

"It was in a swoon that your father died," I said. "Ecstatic perhaps, and filled with various images, and then a loss of consciousness. His spirit had left his body before the heart ceased to beat. Any physical pain I inflicted he never felt; once the blood is being sucked, once I've . . . no, he didn't suffer."

I turned and looked at her more directly. She'd curled her legs under her, revealing white knees beneath her hem.

"I talked with Roger for two hours afterwards," I said. "Two hours. He came back for one reason, to make certain I'd look out for you. That his enemies didn't get you, and the government didn't get you, and all these people he's connected with, or was. And that, and that his death didn't . . . hurt you more than it had to."

"Why would God do this?" she whispered.

"What has God got to do with it? Listen, darling, I don't know anything about God. I told you. I walked into Notre Dame and nothing happened, and nothing ever has. . . ."

Now, that was a lie, wasn't it? What about *Him*? Coming here in the guise of the Ordinary Man, letting that door slam, arrogant bastard, how dare he?

"How can this be God's plan?" she asked.

"You're perfectly serious, aren't you? Look, I could tell you many stories. I mean, the one about the Paris vampires believing in the Devil is just the beginning! Look, there . . . there. . . ." I broke off.

"What is it?"

That sound. Those slow, measured steps! No sooner had I thought of him, insultingly and angrily, than the steps had begun.

"I . . . was going to say. . . ." I struggled to ignore him.

I could hear them approaching. They were faint, but it was the unmistakable walk of the winged being, letting me know, one heavy footfall after another, as though echoing through a giant chamber in which I existed quite apart from my existence in this room.

"Dora, I've got to leave you."

"What is it?"

The footsteps were coming closer and closer. "You dare come to me while I'm with her!" I shouted. I was on my feet.

"What is it?" she cried. She was up on her knees on the bed. I backed across the room. I reached the door. The footsteps were growing fainter.

"Damn you to hell!" I whispered.

"Tell me what it is," she said. "Will you come back? Are you leaving me now forever?"

"No, absolutely not. I'm here to help you. Listen, Dora, if you need me, call to me." I put my finger to my temple. "Call and call and call! Like prayer, you understand. It won't be idolatry, Dora, I'm no evil god. Do it. I have to go."

"What is your name?"

The footsteps came on, distant but loud, without location in the immense building, only pursuing me.

"Lestat." I pronounced my name carefully for her—Le-'stät— primary stress on the second syllable, sounding the final "t" distinctly. "Listen. Nobody knows about your father. They won't for a while. I did everything he asked of me. I have his relics."

"Wynken's books?"

"All of it, everything he held sacred . . . A fortune for you, and all he possessed that he wanted you to have. I've got to go."

Were the steps fading? I wasn't certain. But I couldn't take the risk of remaining.

"I'll come again as soon as I can. You believe in God? Hang on to it, Dora, because you just might be right about God, absolutely right!"

I was out of there like particles of light, up the stairways, through the broken attic window, and up above the rooftop, moving fast enough that I could hear no footfall, and the city below had become a beguiling swirl of lights.

7

IN MOMENTS, I stood in my own courtyard in the French Quarter behind the town house in the Rue Royale, looking up at my own lighted windows, windows that had been mine for so long, hoping and praying that David was there, and afraid he wasn't.

I hated running from this Thing! I had to stand there a moment and let my usual rage cool. Why had I run? Not to be humiliated in front of Dora, who might have seen nothing more than me terrified by the Thing and thrown backwards onto the floor?

Maybe Dora could have seen *it*!

Every instinct in me told me I'd done the proper thing, gotten away, and kept that thing away from Dora. That thing was after me. I had to protect Dora. I now had a very good reason to fight that thing, for another's sake, not my own.

Only now did the full goodness of Dora take a contained shape in my mind, that is, only now did I get a full impression of her, untangled from the blood smell between her legs and her owl-like face peering at me. Mortals tumble through life, from cradle to grave. Once in a century or two perhaps, one crosses the path of a being like Dora. An elegant intelligence and concept of goodness, precisely, and the other thing Roger had struggled to describe, the magnetism which had not burst free as yet from the tangle of faith and scripture.

The night was warm and receptive.

My courtyard banana trees had not been touched by a freeze this winter, and grew thick and drowsing as ever against the brick walls. The wild impatiens and lantana were glowing in the overgrown beds, and the fountain, the fountain with its cherub, was making its crystalline music as the water splashed from the cherub's horn into the basin.

New Orleans, scents of the Quarter.

I ran up the back steps from the courtyard to the rear door of my flat.

I went inside, pounding down the hall, a man in a state of visible and ostentatious confusion. I saw a shadow cross the living room.

"David!"

"He's not here."

I came to a halt in the doorframe.

It was the Ordinary Man.

He stood with his back to Louis's desk between the two front windows, arms folded loosely, face evincing a patient intellect and a sort of unbreakable poise.

"Don't run again," he said without rancour. "I'll go after you. I asked you to please leave that girl out of it. Didn't I? I was only trying to get you to cut it short."

"I've never run from you!" I said, quite unsure of myself and determined to make that the truth from this moment on. "Well, not really! I didn't want you near Dora. What do you want?"

"What do you think?"

"I told you," I said, gathering all my strength, "if you are here to take me, I am ready to go to Hell."

"You're drenched in blood sweat," he said, "look at you, you're so afraid. You know, this is what it takes for me to get through to someone like you." His voice was reasonable, easy to hear. "Now a mortal?" he asked. "I could have simply appeared once and said what I had to say. But you, no, that's a different matter, you've already transcended too many stages, you've got too much to bargain with, that's why you're worth everything to me just now."

"Bargain? You mean I can get out of this? We are not going to Hell? We can have a trial of some sort? I can find a modern Daniel Webster to plead for me?" There was mockery and impatience in all of this, and yet it was the logical question to which I wanted the logical answer at once.

"Lestat," he said with characteristic forbearance, loosening his folded arms and taking a leisurely step towards me. "It goes back to David and his vision in the café. The little story he told you. I *am* the Devil. And I need you. I am not here to take you by force to Hell, and you don't know the slightest thing about Hell anyway. Hell isn't what you imagine. I am here to ask your help! I'm tired and I need you. And I'm winning the battle, and it's crucial that I don't lose."

I was dumbstruck.

For a long moment he regarded me and then deliberately began to change; his form appeared to swell in size, to darken, the wings to rise once more like smoke curling towards the ceiling, and the din of voices to begin and fast grow deafening, and the light suddenly rose behind him. I saw the hairy goat legs move towards me. My feet had no place to stand, my hands nothing to touch but him as I screamed. I could see the gleam of the black feathers, the arch of the wings rising higher and higher! And the din seemed a mixture of almost exquisite music with the voices!

"No, not this time, no!" I hurled myself right at him. I grabbed for him and saw my fingers wrap around his jet-black wrist. I stared right into his immense face, the face of the granite statue, only fully animate and magnificently expressive, the horrific noise of chant and song and howl swelling and drowning out my words. I saw his mouth open, the great eyebrows scowl, the huge innocent almond-shaped eyes grow immense and fill with light.

I held fast with my left hand clutching at his powerful arm, certain he was trying to get away from me and he couldn't! Aha! He couldn't! And then I slammed my right fist into his face. I felt the hardness, preternatural hardness, as if striking another of my own kind. But this was no solid vampiric form.

The entire figure blinked even in its density and defensiveness; the image recoiled and redressed itself and began to grow again; I gave him one last full shove in the chest with every bit of strength I had in me, my fingers splayed out against his black armour, the shimmering ornamented breastplate, my eyes so close in the first instant that I saw the carvings on it, the writing in the metal, and then the wings flapped above me as if to terrify me. He was far from me, suddenly, gigantic, yes, still, but I'd thrown him back, damn him. One fine blow that had been. I gave a war cry before I could stop myself and flew at him, though propelling myself from what base and by what force I couldn't have said.

There came a swirl of black feathers, sleek and shining, and then I was falling; I wouldn't scream, I didn't give a damn, I wouldn't. Falling.

Plummeting. As if through a depth that only nightmare can fathom. An emptiness so perfect we can't conceive of it. And falling fast.

Only the Light remained. The Light obliterated everything visible and was so beautiful suddenly that I lost all sense of my own limbs or parts or organs or whatever I am created of. I had no shape or weight. Only the momentum of my fall continued to terrify, as though gravity remained to ensure utter ruin. There was one great surge of the voices.

"They *are* singing!" I cried out.

Then I lay still.

Slowly I felt the floor beneath me. The slightly rough surface of the carpet. Scent of dust, wax, my home. I knew we were in the same room.

He had taken Louis's chair at the desk, and I lay there on my back, staring at the ceiling, my chest bursting with pain.

I sat up, crossed my legs, and looked at him defiantly.

He was puzzled. "It makes perfect sense," he said.

"And what's that?"

"You're as strong as one of us."

"No, I don't think so," I said furiously. "I can't grow wings; I can't make music."

"Yes, you can, you've made images before for mortals. You know you can. You've wrapped them in spells. You are as strong as we are. You have achieved a very interesting stage in your development. I knew I was right about you all along. I'm in awe of you."

"In awe of what? My independence? Look, let me tell you something, Satan, or whoever you are."

"Don't use that name, I hate it."

"That's likely to make me pepper my speeches with it."

"My name is Memnoch," he said calmly, with a small pleading gesture. "Memnoch the Devil. I want you to remember it that way."

"Memnoch the Devil."

"Aye." He nodded. "That is how I sign my name when I sign it."

"Well, let me tell you, Your Royal Highness of Darkness. I'm not helping you with anything! I don't serve you!"

"I think I can change your mind," he said calmly. "I think you will come to understand things very well from my point of view."

I felt a sudden sagging, a complete exhaustion, and a despair. Typical.

I rolled over on my face and tucked my arm under my head and started crying like a child. I was perishing from exhaustion. I was worn and miserable and I loved crying. I couldn't do anything else. I gave in to it fully. I felt that profound release of the utterly grief-stricken. I didn't give a damn who saw or heard. I cried and cried.

Do you know what I think about crying? I think some people have to learn to do it. But once you learn, once you know how to really cry, there's nothing quite like it. I feel sorry for those who don't know the trick. It's like whistling or singing.

Whatever the case, I was too miserable to take much consolation just from feeling good for a moment in a welter of shudders and salted, bloodstained tears.

I thought of years and years ago, when I had walked into Notre Dame and those fiendish little vampires had lain in wait for me, Servants of Satan, I thought of my mortal self, I thought of Dora, I thought of Armand in those days, the immortal boy leader of Satan's Elect beneath the cemetery, who had made himself a dark saint, sending forth his ragged blood drinkers to torment mortals, to bring death, to spread fear and death like pestilence. I was choking with sobs.

"It is not true!" I think I said. "There is no God or Devil. It is not true."

He didn't answer. I rolled over and sat up. I wiped my face on my sleeve. No handkerchief. Of course, I'd given it to Dora. A faint perfume of Dora rose from my clothes, my chest against which she'd lain, blood sweetness. Dora. I should never have left Dora in such distress. Dear God, I was bound to look out for the sanity of Dora! Damn.

I looked at him.

He was still sitting there, his arm resting on the back of Louis's chair, and he was simply watching me.

I sighed. "You're not going to leave me alone, are you?"

He was taken aback. He laughed. His face was marvelously friendly, rather than neutral.

"No, of course not," he said in a low voice, as if careful not to unbalance me any further. "Lestat, I've been waiting for someone like you for centuries. I've been watching *you yourself* for centuries. No, I'm afraid I'm not going to leave you alone. But I don't want you to be miserable. What can I do to calm you? Some small miracle, gift, anything, so that we can proceed?"

"And how in hell will we proceed?"

"I'll tell you everything," he said with a slight shrug, his hands open, "and then you'll understand why I have to win."

"The implication . . . it's that I can refuse to cooperate with you, isn't it?"

"Absolutely. Nobody can really help me who doesn't choose to do it. And I'm tired. I'm tired of the job. I need help. That part your friend David heard correctly when he experienced that accidental epiphany."

"Was David's epiphany accidental? What happened to that other word? What had it been . . . I don't remember. David wasn't meant to see you or hear you and God talking together?"

"That's almost impossible to explain."

"Did I upset some plan of yours by taking David, making him one of us?"

"Yes and no. But the point is, David heard that part correctly. My task is hard and I'm tired! Some of the rest of David's ideas about that little vision, well—" He shook his head. "The point is, you are the one I want now and it's terribly important you see everything before you make up your mind."

"I'm that bad, am I?" I whispered, lips trembling. I was going to bawl again. "In all the world, with all the things humans have done, all the unspeakable horrors men have visited on other men, the unthinkable suffering of women and children worldwide at the hands of mankind, and I'm that bad! You want me! David was too good, I suppose. He didn't become as consummately evil as you thought he would. Is that it?"

"No, of course you're not that bad," he said soothingly. "That's the very point." He gave a little sigh again.

I was beginning to notice more distinct details of his appearance, not because they were becoming more vivid as had happened with the apparition of Roger, but because I was growing more calm. His hair was a dark ashen blond, and rather soft and curling. And his eyebrows were the same shade, not distinctly black at all, but very care fully drawn to maintain an expression that contained no closed vanity or arrogance. He didn't look stupid either, of course. The clothes were generic. I don't believe they were really clothes. They were material, but the coat was too plain and without buttons, and the white shirt was too simple.

"You know," he said, "you always have had a conscience! That's precisely what I'm after, don't you see? Conscience, reason, purpose, dedication. Good Lord, I couldn't have overlooked you. And I'll tell you something. It was as though you sent for me."

"Never."

"Come on, think of all the challenges you've flung out to the Devil."

"That was poetry, or doggerel, depending on one's point of view."

"Not so. And then think of all the things you did, waking that ancient one Akasha and almost loosing her on humanity." He gave a short laugh. "As if we don't have enough monsters created by evolution. And then your adventure with the Body Thief. Coming into the flesh again, having that chance, and rejecting it for what you were before. You know your friend Gretchen is a saint in the jungles, don't you?"

"Yes. I've seen mentions of it in the papers. I know."

Gretchen, my nun, my love when I'd been so briefly mortal, had never spoken one word since the night she fled from me into her missionary chapel and fell on her knees before the crucifix. She remained in prayer night and day in that jungle village, taking almost no nourishment, and on Fridays people journeyed miles through the jungle, and sometimes even came from Caracas and Buenos Aires just to see her bleed from her hands and her feet. That had been the end of Gretchen.

Although it suddenly struck me for the very first time, in the middle of all this: maybe Gretchen really was with Christ!

"No, I don't believe it," I said coldly. "Gretchen lost her mind; she's fixed in a state of hysteria and it's my fault. So the world has another mystic who bleeds like Christ. There have been a thousand."

"I didn't place any judgment upon the incident," he said. "If we can go back to what I was saying. I was saying that you did everything but ask me to come! You challenged every form of authority, you sought every experience. You've buried yourself alive twice, and once tried to rise into the very sun to make yourself a cinder. What was left for you—but to call on me? It is as if you yourself said it: 'Memnoch, what more can I do now?' "

"Did you tell God about this?" I asked coldly, refusing to be drawn in. Refusing to be this curious and this excited.

"Yes, of course," he said.

I was too surprised to say anything.

I could think of nothing clever. Certain little theological brain twisters flitted through my mind, and sticky little questions, like "Why didn't God already know?" and so forth. But we were beyond that point, obviously.

I had to think, to concentrate on what my senses were telling me.

"You and Descartes," he said. "You and Kant."

"Don't lump me with others," I said. "I am the Vampire Lestat, the one and only."

"You're telling me," he said.

"How many of us are there now, vampires, I mean, in the whole world? I'm not speaking now of other immortals and monsters and evil spirits and things, whatever you are, for instance, but vampires? There aren't a hundred, and none of them is quite like me. Lestat."

"I completely agree. I want you. I want you for my helper."

"Doesn't it gall you that I don't really respect you, believe in you, or fear you, not even after all this? That we're in my flat and I'm making fun of you? I don't think Satan would put up with this sort of thing. I don't usually put up with it; I've compared myself to you, you know. Lucifer, Son of Morning. I have told my detractors and inquisitors that I was the Devil or that if I ever happened upon Satan himself I'd set him to rout."

"Memnoch," he corrected me. "Don't use the name Satan. Please. Don't use any of the following: Lucifer, Beelzebub, Azazel, Sammael, Marduk, Mephistopheles, et cetera. My name is Memnoch. You'll soon find out for yourself that the others represent various alphabetical or scriptural compromises. Memnoch is for this time and all time. Appropriate and pleasing. Memnoch the Devil. And don't go look it up in a book because you'll never find it."

I didn't answer. I was trying to figure this. He could change shapes, but there had to be an invisible essence. Had I come against the strength of the invisible essence when I'd smashed his face? I'd felt no real contour, only strength resisting me. And were I to grab him now, would this man-form be filled with the invisible essence so that it could fight me off with strength equal to that of the dark angel?

"Yes," he said. "Imagine trying to convince a mortal of these things. But that really isn't why I chose you. I chose you not so much because it would be easier for you to comprehend everything but because you're perfect for the job."

"The job of helping the Devil."

"Yes, of being my right-hand instrument, so to speak, being in my stead when I'm weary. Being my prince."

"How could you be so mistaken? You find the self-inflicted suffering of my conscience amusing? You think I like evil? That I think about evil when I look at something beautiful like Dora's face!"

"No, I don't think you like evil," he said. "Any more than do I."

"You don't like evil," I repeated, narrowing my eyes.

"Loathe it. And if you don't help me, if you let God keep doing things His way, I tell you evil—which is nothing really—just might destroy the world."

"It's God's will," I asked slowly, "that the world be destroyed?"

"Who knows?" he asked coldly. "But I don't think God would lift a finger to stop it from happening. I don't will it, that I know. But my ways are the right ways, and the ways of God are bloody and wasteful and exceedingly dangerous. You know they are. You have to help me. I am winning, I told you. But this century has been damn near unendurable for us all."

"So you are telling me that you're not evil. . . ."

"Exactly. Remember what your friend David asked of you? He asked you if in my presence you had sensed evil, and you had to answer that you had not."

"The Devil is a famous liar."

"My enemies are famous detractors. Neither God nor I tell lies per se. But look, I don't expect for a moment that you should accept me on faith. I didn't come here to convince you of things through conversation. I'll take you to Hell and to Heaven, if you like, you can talk to God for as long as He allows, and you desire. Not God the Father, precisely, not *En Sof*, but . . . well, all of this will become clear to you. Only there's no point if I cannot count upon your willing intent to see the truth, your willing desire to turn your life from aimlessness and meaninglessness into a crucial battle for the fate of the world."

I didn't answer. I wasn't sure what I could say. We were leagues from the point at which we had begun this discussion.

"See Heaven?" I whispered, absorbing all of it slowly. "See Hell?"

"Yes, of course," he said with level patience.

"I want a full night to think it over."

"What!"

"I said I want a night to think it over."

"You don't believe me. You want a sign."

"No, I am beginning to believe you," I said. "That's why I have to think. I have to weigh all of this."

"I'm here to answer any question, to show you anything now."

"Then leave me alone for two nights. Tonight and tomorrow night. That's a simple enough request, isn't it? Leave me alone."

He was obviously disappointed, maybe even a little suspicious. But I meant every word of it. I couldn't say anything but what I had said. I knew the truth as I spoke it, so fast were thought and word wedded in my mind.

"Is it possible to deceive you?" I asked.

"Of course," he asked. "I rely upon my gifts such as they are, just as you rely on yours. I have my limits. You have yours. You can be deceived. So can I."

"What about God?"

"Ach!" he said with disgust. "If you only knew how irrelevant that question is. You cannot imagine how much I need you. I'm tired," he said with a faint rise of emotion. "God is . . . beyond being deceived, that much I can say with charity. I'll give you tonight and tomorrow night. I won't bother you, stalk you, as you put it. But may I ask what you mean to do?"

"Why? Either I have the two nights or I don't!"

"You're known to be unpredictable," he said. He smiled broadly. It was very pleasant. And something else, quite obvious, struck me about him. Not only were his proportions perfect, there were no visible flaws in him anywhere; he was a paragon of the Ordinary Man.

He showed no response to this estimation, whether he could read it from my mind or not. He merely waited on me, courteously.

"Dora," I said. "I have to go back to Dora."

"Why?"

"I refuse to explain further."

Again, he was surprised by my answer.

"Well, aren't you going to try to help her with all this confusion regarding her father? Why not explain something as simple as that? I only meant to ask you how deeply you intended to commit yourself, how much you planned to reveal to this woman. I'm thinking of the fabric of things, to use David's phrase. That is, how will it be with this woman, after you've come with me?"

I said nothing.

He sighed. "All right, I've waited for your like for centuries. What is another two nights, such as the case may be. We are speaking of only tomorrow night, really, aren't we? At the sunset of the following evening, after that I shall come for you."

"Right."

"I'll give you a little gift that will help you believe in me. It's not so simple to me to fix your level of understanding. You're full of paradox and conflict. Let me give you something unusual."

"Agreed."

"So this is the gift. Call it a sign. Ask Dora about Uncle Mickey's eye. Ask her to tell you the truth that Roger never knew."

"This sounds like a Spiritualist parlour game."

"Think so? Ask her."

"All right. The truth about Uncle Mickey's eye. Now let me ask you one last question. You are the Devil. Yes. But you're not evil? Why?"

"Absolutely irrelevant question. Or let me put it a little more mysteriously. It's completely unnecessary for me to be evil. You'll see. Oh, this is so frustrating for me because you have so much to see."

"But you're opposed to God!"

"Oh, absolutely, a total adversary! Lestat, when you see everything that I have to show you, and hear all that I have to say, when you've spoken with God and better see it from His perspective, and from my point of view, you will join me as His adversary. I'm sure you will."

He stood up from the chair. "I'm going now. Should I help you up off the floor?"

"Irrelevant and unnecessary," I said crossly. "I'm going to miss you." The words surprised me as they came out.

"I know," he answered.

"I have all of tomorrow night," I said. "Remember."

"Don't you realize," he answered, "that if you come with me now there is no night and day?"

"Oh, that's very tempting," I said. "But that's what Devils do so well. Tempt. I need to think about this, and consult others for advice."

"Consult others?" He seemed genuinely surprised.

"I'm not going off with the Devil without telling anyone," I said. "You're the Devil! Goddamn it, why should I trust the Devil? That's absurd! You're playing by rules, somebody's rules. Everybody always is. And I don't know the rules. Well. You gave me the choice, and this is my choice. Two full nights, and not before then. Leave me alone all that time! Give me your oath."

"Why?" he asked politely, as if dealing with an ornery child. "So you won't have to fear the sound of my footsteps?"

"Possibly."

"What good is an oath on this if you don't accept the truth of all the rest that I've said?" He shook his head as if I were being foolishly human.

"Can you swear an oath or not?"

"You have my oath," he said, laying his hand on his heart, or where his heart should have been. "With complete sincerity, of course."

"Thank you, I feel much better," I said.

"David won't believe you," he said gently.

"I know," I said.

"On the third night," he said with an emphatic nod, "I shall come back for you here. Or wherever you happen to be at the time."

And with a final smile, as bright as the earlier one, he disappeared.

It was not the way I tended to do it, by making off with such swiftness no human could track it.

He actually vanished on the spot.

8

I STOOD up shakily, brushed off my clothes, and noted without surprise that the room was as perfect as it had been when we entered it. The battle obviously had been fought in some other realm. But what was that realm?

Oh, if only I could find David. I had less than three hours before the winter dawn and set off at once to search.

Now, being unable to read David's mind, or to call to him, I had but one telepathic tool at my command, and that was to scan the minds of mortals at random for some image of David as he passed in some recognizable place.

I hadn't walked three blocks when I realized that not only was I picking up a strong image of David, but that it was coming to me from the mind of another vampire.

I closed my eyes, and tried with my entire soul to make some eloquent contact. Within seconds, the pair acknowledged me, David through the one who stood beside him, and I saw and recognized the wooded place where they were.

In my days, the Bayou Road had led through this area into country, and it had been very near here once that Claudia and Louis, having attempted my murder, had left my remains in the waters of the swamp.

Now the area was a great combed park, filled by day, I supposed, with mothers and children, containing a museum of occasionally very interesting paintings, and providing in the dark of night a dense wood.

Some of the oldest oaks of New Orleans lay within the bounds of this area, and a lovely lagoon, long, serpentine, seemingly endless, wound under a picturesque bridge in the heart of it.

I found them there, the two vampires communing with one another in dense darkness, far from the beaten path. David was as I expected, his usual properly attired self.

But the sight of the other astonished me.

This was Armand.

He sat on the stone park bench, boylike, casual, with one knee crooked, looking up at me with the predictable innocence, dusty all over, naturally, hair a long, tangled mess of auburn curls.

Dressed in heavy denim garments, tight pants, and a zippered jacket, he surely passed for human, a street vagabond maybe, though his face was now parchment white, and even smoother than it had been when last we met.

In a way, he made me think of a child doll, with brilliant faintly red-brown glass eyes—a doll that had been found in an attic. I wanted to polish him with kisses, clean him up, make him even more radiant than he was.

"That's what you always want," he said softly. His voice shocked me. If he had any French or Italian accent left, I couldn't hear it. His tone was melancholy and had no meanness in it at all. "When you found me under Les Innocents," he said, "you wanted to bathe me with perfume and dress me in velvet with great embroidered sleeves."

"Yes," I said, "and comb your hair, your beautiful russet hair." My tone was angry. "You look good to me, you damnable little devil, good to embrace and good to love."

We eyed each other for a moment. And then he surprised me, rising and coming towards me just as I moved to take him in my arms. His gesture wasn't tentative, but it was extremely gentle. I could have backed away. I didn't. We held each other tight for a moment. The cold embracing the cold. The hard embracing the hard.

"Cherub child," I said. I did a bold thing, maybe even a defiant thing. I reached out and mussed his snaggled curls.

He is smaller than me physically, but he didn't seem to mind this gesture.

In fact, he smiled, shook his head, and reclaimed his hair with a few casual strokes of his hand. His cheeks went apple-perfect suddenly, and his mouth softened, and then he lifted his right fist, and teasingly struck me hard on the chest.

Really hard. Show-off. Now it was my turn to smile and I did.

"I can't remember anything bad between us," I said.

"You will," he responded. "And so will I. But what does it matter what we remember?"

"Yes," I said, "we're both still here."

He laughed outright, though it was very low, and he shook his head, flashing a glance on David that implied they knew each other very well, maybe too well. I didn't like it that they knew each other at all. David was my David, and Armand was my Armand.

I sat down on the bench.

"So David's told you the whole story," I said, glancing up at Armand and then over at David.

David gave a negative shake of the head.

"Not without your permission, Brat Prince," David said, a little disdainfully. "I would never have taken the liberty. But the only thing that's brought Armand here is worry for you."

"Is that so?" I said. I raised my eyebrows. "Well?"

"You know damned good and well it is," said Armand. His whole posture was casual; he'd learned, beating about the world, I guess. He didn't look so much like a church ornament anymore. He had his hands in his pockets. Little tough guy.

"You're looking for trouble again," he went on, in the same slow manner, without anger or meanness. "The whole wide world isn't enough for you and never will be. This time I thought I'd try to speak to you before the wheel turns."

"Aren't you the most thoughtful of guardian angels?" I said sarcastically.

"Yes, I am," he said without so much as blinking. "So what are you doing, want to let me know?

"Come, I want to go deeper into the park," I said, and they both followed me as we walked at a mortal pace into a thicket of the oldest oaks, where the grass was high and neglected, and not even the most desperate homeless heart would seek to rest.

We made our own small clearing, among the volcanic black roots and rather cool winter earth. The breeze from the nearby lake was brisk and clean, and for a moment there seemed little scent of New Orleans, of any city; we three were together, and Armand asked again: "Will you tell me what you're doing?" He bent close to me, and suddenly kissed me, in a manner that seemed entirely childlike and also a bit European. "You're in deep trouble. Come on. Everyone knows it." The steel buttons of his denim jacket were icy cold, as though he had come from some far worse winter in a very few moments of time.

We are never entirely sure about each other's powers. It's all a game. I would no more have asked him how he got here, or in what manner, than I would ask a mortal man how precisely he made love to his wife.

I looked at him a long time, conscious that David had settled down on the grass, leaning back on his elbow, and was studying us both.

Finally I spoke: "The Devil has come to me and asked me to go with him, to see Heaven and Hell."

Armand didn't answer. Then he frowned just a little.

"This is the same Devil," said I, "which I told you I didn't believe in, when you did believe in him centuries ago. You were right at least on one point. He exists. I've met him." I looked at David. "He wants me as his assistant. He's given me tonight and tomorrow night to seek advice from others. He will take me to Heaven and then to Hell. He claims he is not evil."

David looked off into the darkness. Armand simply stared at me, rapt and silent.

I went on. I told them everything then. I repeated the story of Roger for Armand, and of Roger's ghost, and then I told them both in detail about my blundering visit to Dora, about my exchanges with her, and how I'd left her, and then how the Devil had come pursuing me and annoying me, and we'd had our brawl.

I put down every detail. I opened my mind, without calculation, letting Armand see whatever he could for himself.

Finally I sat back.

"Don't say things to me that are humiliating," I averred. "Don't ask me why I fled from Dora, or blurted out to her all this about her father. I can't get rid of the presence of Roger, the sense of Roger's friendship for me and love for her. And this Memnoch the Devil, this is a reasonable and mild-mannered individual, and very convincing. As for the battle, I don't know what happened, except I gave him something to think about. In two nights, he's coming back, and if memory serves me correctly, which it invariably does, he said he'd come for me wherever I was at the time."

"Yes, that's clear," Armand said sotto voce.

"You aren't enjoying my misery, are you?" I admitted with a little sigh of defeat.

"No, of course not," Armand said, "only, as usual, you don't really seem miserable. You're on the verge of an adventure, and just a little more cautious this time than when you let that mortal run off with your body and you took his."

"No, not more cautious. Terrified. I think this creature, Memnoch, is the Devil. If you had seen the visions, you would think he was the Devil too. I'm not talking about spellbinding. You can do spellbinding, Armand, you've done it to me. I was battling that thing. It has some essence which can inhabit actual bodies! It's objective and bodiless itself, of that I'm sure. The rest? Maybe all that was spells. He implied he could make spells and so could I."

"You're describing an angel, of course," said David offhandedly, "and this one claims to be a fallen angel."

"The Devil himself," mused Armand. "What are you asking of us, Lestat? You are asking our advice? I would not go with this spirit of my own will, if I were you."

"What makes you say this?" David asked before I could get out a word.

"Look, we know there are earthbound beings," Armand said, "that we ourselves can't classify, or locate, or control. We know there are species of immortals, and types of mammalian creatures which look human but are not. This creature might be anything. And there is something highly suspicious in the manner in which he courts you . . . the visions, and then the politeness."

"Either that," said David, "or it simply makes perfect sense. He is the Devil, he is reasonable, the way you always supposed, Lestat— not a moral idiot, but a true angel, and he wants your cooperation. He doesn't want to keep doing things to you by force. He's used force as his introduction."

"I would *not* believe him," said Armand. "What does this mean— he wants you to help him? That you would begin to exist simultaneously on this earth and in Hell? No, I would shun him for his imagery, if nothing else, for his vocabulary. For his name. Memnoch. It sounds evil."

"Oh, all these are things," I admitted, "that I once said, more or less, to you."

"I've never seen the Prince of Darkness with my own eyes," said Armand. "I've seen centuries of superstition, and the wonders done by demonic beings such as ourselves. You've seen a little more than I have. But you're right. That is what you told me before and I'm telling it to you now. Don't believe in the Devil, or that you are his child. And that is what I told Louis, once when he came to me seeking explanations of God and the universe. I believe in no Devil. So I remind you. Don't believe him. Turn your back."

"As for Dora," said David quietly, "you've acted unwisely, but it's possible that that breach of preternatural decorum can somehow be healed."

"I don't think so."

"Why?" he asked.

"Let me ask you both . . . do you believe what I'm telling you?"

"I know you're telling the truth," said Armand, "but I told you, I don't believe this creature is the Devil himself or that he will take you to Heaven or Hell. And very frankly, if it is true . . . well, that's all the more reason perhaps that you shouldn't go."

I studied him for a long moment, fighting the darkness I had deliberately sought, trying to draw from him some impression of his complete disposition on this, and I realized he was sincere. There was no envy in him, or old grudge against me; there was no hurt, or trickery, or anything. He was past all these things, if ever they had obsessed him. Perhaps they'd been fantasies of mine.

"Perhaps so," he said, answering my thoughts directly. "But you are correct in that I am speaking to you directly and truly, and I tell you, I would not trust this creature, or trust the proposition that you must in some way verbally cooperate."

"A medieval concept of pact," said David.

"Which means what?" I asked. I hadn't meant it to be so rude.

"Making a pact with the Devil," said David, "you know, agreeing to something with him. That's what Armand is telling you not to do. Don't make a pact."

"Precisely," said Armand. "It arouses my deepest suspicions that he makes such a moral issue of your agreement." His young face was sorely troubled, his pretty eyes very vivid for a second in the shadows. "Why do you have to agree?"

"I don't know if that's on the mark or not," I said. I was confused. "But you're right. I said something to him myself, something about this being played by rules."

"I want to talk with you about Dora," said David in a low voice. "You must heal what you've done there very quickly, or at least promise us that you won't. . . ."

"I'm not going to promise you anything about Dora. I can't," I said.

"Lestat, don't destroy this young mortal woman!" said David forcefully. "If we are in a new realm, if the spirits of the dead can plead with us, then maybe they can hurt us, have you ever thought of that?"

David sat up, disconcerted, angry, the lovely British voice straining to maintain decency as he spoke: "Don't hurt the mortal girl. Her father asked you for a species of guardianship, not that you shake her sanity to the foundations."

"David, don't go on with your speech. I know what you're saying. But I tell you right now, I am alone in this. I am alone. I am alone with this being Memnoch, the Devil; and you both have been friends to me. You've been kindred. But I don't think anyone can advise me what to do, except for Dora."

"Dora!" David was aghast.

"You mean to tell her this entire tale?" Armand asked timidly.

"Yes. That's exactly what I mean to do. Dora's the only one who believes in the Devil. Dear God, I need a believer right now, I need a saint, and I may need a theologian, and to Dora I'm going."

"You are perverse, stubborn, and innately destructive!" said David. It had the tone of a curse. "You will do what you will!" He was furious. I could see it. All his reasons for despising me were being heated from within, and there really was nothing I could say in my defense.

"Wait," said Armand with gentleness. "Lestat, this is mad. It's like consulting the Sibyl. You want the girl to act as an oracle for you, to tell you what she, a mortal, thinks you must do?"

"She's no mere mortal, she's different. She has no fear of me whatsoever. None. And she has no fear of anything. It's as though she's a different species, but she's the human species. She's like a saint, Armand. She's like Joan of Arc must have been when she led the army. She knows something about God and the Devil that I don't know."

"You're talking about faith, and it's very alluring," said David, "just as it was with your nun companion, Gretchen, who is now stark raving mad."

"Stark mutely mad," I said. "She doesn't say anything but prayers, or so say the papers. But before I came along, Gretchen didn't really believe in God, keep that in mind. Belief and madness, for Gretchen, are one and the same."

"Do you never learn!" said David.

"Learn what?" I asked. "David, I'm going to Dora. She's the only person I can go to. And besides, I can't leave things with her as I did! I have to go back, and I am going back. Now from you, Armand, a promise, the obvious thing. Around this Dora, I've thrown a protective light. None of us can touch her."

"That goes without saying. I won't hurt your little friend. You wound me." He looked genuinely put out.

"I'm sorry," I said. "I know. But I know what blood is and innocence and how delicious both can be. I know how much the girl tempts me."

"Then you must be the one to give in to that temptation," said Armand crossly. "I never choose my victims anymore, you know this. I can stand before a house as always, and out of the doors will come those who want to be in my arms. Of course I won't hurt her. You do hold old grudges. You think I live in the past. You don't understand that I actually change with every era, I always have as best I can. But what in the world can Dora tell you that will help you?"

"I don't know," I said. "But I'm going directly tomorrow night. If there were time left, I'd go now. I'm going to her. David, if something happens to me, if I vanish, if I . . . you have all Dora's inheritance."

He nodded. "You have my word of honor on the girl's best interests, but you must not go to her!"

"Lestat, if you need me—" Armand said. "If this being tries to take you by force!"

"Why do you care about me?" I asked. "After all the bad things I did to you? Why?"

"Oh, don't be such a fool," he begged gently. "You convinced me long ago that the world was a Savage Garden. Remember your old poetry? You said the only laws that were true were aesthetic laws, that was all you could count on."

"Yes, I remember all that. I fear it's true. I've always feared it was true. I feared it when I was a mortal child. I woke up one morning and I believed in nothing."

"Well, then, in the Savage Garden," said Armand, "you shine beautifully, my friend. You walk as if it is your garden to do with as you please. And in my wanderings, I always return to you. I always return to see the colors of the garden in your shadow, or reflected in your eyes, perhaps, or to hear of your latest follies and mad obsessions. Besides, we are brothers, are we not?"

"Why didn't you help me last time, when I was in all that trouble, having switched bodies with a human being?"

"You won't forgive me if I tell you," he said.

"Tell me."

"Because I hoped and prayed for you, that you would remain in that mortal body and save your soul. I thought you had been granted the greatest gift, that you were human again, my heart ached for your triumph! I couldn't interfere. I couldn't do it."

"You are a child and a fool, you always were."

He shrugged. "Well, it looks like you're being given another chance to do *something* with your soul. You'd best be at your very strongest and most resourceful, Lestat. I distrust this Memnoch, far worse than any human foe you faced when you were trapped in the flesh. This Memnoch sounds very far from Heaven. Why should they let you in with him?"

"Excellent question."

"Lestat," said David, "don't go to Dora. Will you remember that my advice last time might have saved you misery!"

Oh, there was too much to comment on there, for his advice might have prevented him from ever being what he was now, in this fine form, and I could not, I could not regret that he was here, that he had won the Body Thief's fleshly trophy. I couldn't. I just couldn't.

"I can believe the Devil wants you," said Armand.

"Why?" I asked.

"Please don't go to Dora," said David seriously.

"I have to, and it's almost morning now. I love you both."

Both of them were staring at me, perplexed, suspicious, uncertain. I did the only thing I could. I left.

9

THE NEXT night, I rose from my attic hiding place and went directly out in search of Dora. I didn't want to see or hear any more of David or Armand. I knew I couldn't be prevented from what I had to do.

How I meant to do it, that was the question. They had unwittingly confirmed something for me. I was not totally mad. I was not imagining everything that was happening around me. Some of it, perhaps, I was imagining, but not all.

Whatever the case, I decided upon a radical course of action with Dora, and one which neither David nor Armand could conceivably have approved.

Knowing more than a little about her habits and her whereabouts, I caught up with Dora as she was coming out of the television studio on Chartres Street in the Quarter. She'd spent the entire afternoon taping an hour-long show, and then visiting with her audience afterwards. I waited in the doorway of a nearby shop as she said farewell to the last of her "sisters" or seeming worshippers. They were young women, though not girls, and very firm believers in changing the world with Dora, and had about them a careless, nonconformist air.

They hurried off, and Dora went the other way towards the square and towards her car. She wore a slender black wool coat and wool stockings with heels that were very high, her very favorites for dancing on her program, and with her little cap of black hair she looked extremely dramatic and fragile, and horribly vulnerable in a world of mortal males.

I caught her around the waist before she knew what was happening. We were rising so fast, I knew she could not see or understand anything, and I said very close to her ear,

"You're with me, and you're safe." Then I wrapped her totally in my arms, so that no harm at all could come to her from the wind or the speed we were traveling, and I went up just as high as I dared to go with her, uncovered and vulnerable and depending upon me, listening keenly beneath the howl of the wind for the proper functioning of her heart and her lungs.

I felt her relaxing in my arms, or more truly, she simply remained trusting. It was as surprising as everything else about her. She had buried her face in my coat, as though too afraid to try to look around her, but this was really more a practical matter in the cold than anything else. At one point, I opened my coat, and covered her with one side of it, and we went on.

The journey took longer than I had supposed; I simply could not take a fragile human being up that high into the air. But it was nothing as tedious or dangerous as it might have been had we taken a fuming and stinking and highly explosive jet plane.

Within less than an hour, I was standing with her inside the glass doors of the Olympic Tower. She awoke in my arms as if from a deep sleep. I realized this had been inevitable. She'd lost consciousness, for a series of physical and mental reasons, but she came to herself at once, her heels striking the floor, and looked at me with huge owl eyes, and then out at the side of St. Patrick's rising in all its obdurate glory across the street.

"Come on," I said, "I'm taking you to your father's things." We made for the elevators.

She hurried after me, eagerly, the way that vampires dream mortals will do it, which never, never happens, as if all this were wondrous and there was no reason under Heaven to be afraid.

"I don't have much time," I said. We were in the elevator speeding upwards. "There is something chasing me and I don't know what it wants of me. But I had to bring you here. And I'll see that you get home safe."

I explained that I knew of no rooftop entrances to this building; indeed, the whole place was new to me, or I would have brought her in that way, and I explained this now, embarrassed that we would cover a continent in an hour and then take a rattling, sucking, and shimmering elevator that seemed only slightly less marvelous than the gift of vampiric flight.

The doors opened onto the correct floor. I put the key in her hand, and guided her towards the apartment. "You open it, everything inside is yours."

She looked at me for a moment, a slight frown on her forehead, then she stroked carelessly at her wind-torn hair, and put the key in the lock and opened the door.

"Roger's things," she said with the first breath she took.

She knew them by the smell as any antiquarian might have known them, these icons and relics. Then she saw the marble angel, poised in the corridor, with the glass wall way beyond it, and I thought she was going to faint in my arms.

She slumped backwards as if counting upon me to catch her and support her. I held her with the tips of my fingers, as afraid as ever that I might accidentally bruise her.

"Dear God," she said under her breath. Her heart was racing, but it was hearty and very young and capable of tremendous endurance. "We are here, and you've been telling me true things."

She sprang loose from me before I could answer and walked briskly past the angel and into the larger front room of the place. The spires of St. Patrick's were visible just below the level of the window. And everywhere were these cumbersome packages of plastic through which one could detect the shape of a crucifix or saint. The books of Wynken were on the table, of course, but I wasn't going to press her on that just now.

She turned to me, and I could feel her studying me, assessing me. I am so sensitive to this sort of appraisal that I actually think my vanity is rooted in each of my cells.

She murmured some words in Latin, but I didn't catch them, and no automatic translation came up in my mind.

"What did you say?"

"Lucifer, Son of Morning," she whispered, staring at me with frank admiration. Then she plopped down into a large leather chair. It was one of the many tiresome furnishings of the place, meant for businessmen but completely comfortable. Her eyes were still locked on me.

"No, that's not who I am," I said. "I'm only what I told you and nothing more. But that's who's after me."

"The Devil?"

"Yes. Now listen, I'm going to tell you everything, and then you must give me your advice. Meantime—" I turned around, yes, there was the file cabinet. "Your inheritance, everything, money you have now that you don't know about, clean and taxed and proper, it's all explained in black folders in those files. Your father died wanting you to have this for your church. If you turn away from it, don't be so sure it's God's will. Remember, your father is dead. His blood cleansed the money."

Did I believe this? Well, it sure as hell was what Roger wanted me to tell her.

"Roger said to say this," I added, trying to sound extremely sure of myself.

"I understand you," she said. "You're worrying about something that doesn't really matter now. Come here, please, let me hold you. You're shivering."

"I'm shivering!"

"It's warm in here, but you don't seem to feel it. Come."

I knelt down in front of her and suddenly took her in my arms the way I had Armand. I laid my head against hers. She was cold but would never even on the day of her burial be as cold as I was, nothing human could be that cold. I had sopped up the winter's worst as though I were porous marble, which I suppose I was.

"Dora, Dora, Dora," I whispered. "How he loved you, and how much he wanted everything to be right for you, Dora."

Her scent was strong, but so was I.

"Lestat, explain about the Devil," she said.

I sat down on the carpet so that I could look up at her. She was perched on the edge of her chair, knees bare, black coat carelessly open now, and a streak of gold scarf showing, her face pale but very flushed, in a way that made her radiant and at the same time a little enchanted, as though she were no more human than me.

"Even your father couldn't really describe your beauty," I said. "Temple virgin, nymph of the wood."

"My father said that to you?"

"Yes. But the Devil, ah, the Devil told me to ask you a question. To ask you the truth about Uncle Mickey's eye!" I had just remembered it. I had not remembered to tell either David or Armand about this, but what difference could that possibly make?

She was surprised by these words, and very impressed. She sank back a little into the chair. "The Devil told you these words?"

"He gave it to me as a gift. He wants me to help him. He says he's not evil. He says that God is his adversary. I'll tell you everything, but he gave me these words as some sort of little extra gift, what do we call it in New Orleans, lagniappe? To convince me that he is what he says he is."

She gave a little gesture of confusion, hand flying to her temple as she shook her head. "Wait. The truth about Uncle Mickey's eye, you're sure he said that? My father didn't say anything about Uncle Mickey?"

"No, and I never caught any such image from your father's heart or soul, either. The Devil said Roger didn't know the truth. What does it mean?"

"My father *didn't* know the truth," she said. "He never knew. His mother never told him the truth. It was his uncle Mickey, my grandmother's brother. And it was *my* mother's people who told me the real story—Terry's people. It was like this, my father's mother was rich and had a beautiful house on St. Charles Avenue."

"I know the place, I know all about it. Roger met Terry there."

"Yes, exactly, but my grandmother had been poor when she was young. Her mother had been a maid in the Garden District, like many an Irish maid. And Roger's Uncle Mickey was one of those easygoing characters who made nothing of himself in anyone's eyes at all.

"My father never knew about the real life of Uncle Mickey. My mother's mother told me to show me what airs my father put on, and what a fool he was, and how humble his origins had been."

"Yes, I see."

"My father had loved Uncle Mickey. Uncle Mickey had died when my father was a boy. Uncle Mickey had a cleft palate and a glass eye, and I remember my father showing me his picture and telling me the story of how Uncle Mickey lost his eye. Uncle Mickey had loved fireworks, and once he'd been playing with firecrackers and one had gone off in a tin can, and wham, the can hit him in the eye. That's the story I always believed about Uncle Mickey. I knew him only from the picture. My grandmother and my great-uncle were dead before I was born."

"Right. And then your mother's people told you different."

"My mother's father was a cop. He knew all about Roger's family, that Roger's grandfather had been a drunk and so had Uncle Mickey, more or less. Uncle Mickey had also been a tout for a bookie when he was young. And one time, he held back on a bet. In other words, he kept the money rather than placing the bet as he should have, and unfortunately the horse won."

"I follow you."

"Uncle Mickey, very young and very scared I imagine, was in Corona's Bar in the Irish Channel."

"On Magazine Street," I said. "That bar was there for years and years. Maybe a century."

"Yes, and the bookie's henchmen came in and dragged Uncle Mickey to the back of the bar. My mother's father saw it all. He was there, but he couldn't do anything about it. Nobody could. Nobody would. Nobody dared. But this is what my grandfather saw. The men beat and kicked Uncle Mickey. They were the ones who hurt the roof of his mouth so he talked as if something were wrong with him. And they kicked out his eye. They kicked it across the floor. And the way my grandfather said it every time he told it was, 'Dora, they could have saved that eye, except those guys stepped on it. They deliberately stepped on it with those pointed shoes.' "

She stopped.

"And Roger never knew this."

"Nobody knows it who is alive," she said. "Except for me, of course. My grandfather's dead. For all I know, everyone who was ever there is dead. Uncle Mickey died in the early fifties. Roger used to take me out to the cemetery to visit his grave. Roger had always loved him. Uncle Mickey with his hollow voice and his glass eye. Everybody sort of loved him, the way Roger told it. And even my mother's people said that too. He was a sweetheart. He was a night watchman before he died. He rented rooms on Magazine Street right over Baer's Bakery. He died of pneumonia in the hospital before anyone even knew he was ill. And Roger never knew the truth about Uncle Mickey's eye. We would have spoken of it if he had, naturally."

I sat there pondering, or rather picturing what she had described. No images came from her, she was closed tight, but her voice had been effortlessly generous. I knew Corona's. So did anyone who had ever walked Magazine Street in those famous blocks of the Irish heyday. I knew the criminals with their pointed shoes. Crushing the eye.

"They just stepped on it and squashed it," said Dora, as though she could read my thoughts. "My grandfather always said, 'They could have saved it, if they hadn't stepped on it the way they did with those pointed shoes.'"

A silence fell between us.

"This proves nothing," I said.

"It proves your friend, or enemy, knows secrets, that's what it proves."

"But it doesn't prove he's the Devil," I said, "and why would he choose such a story, of all things?"

"Maybe he was there," she said with a bitter smile.

We both gave that a little laugh.

"You said this was the Devil but he wasn't evil," she prompted me. She looked persuasive and trusting and thoroughly in command.

I had the feeling that I had been absolutely correct in seeking her advice. She was regarding me steadily.

"Tell me what this Devil has done," she said.

I told her the whole tale. I had to admit how I stalked her father, and I couldn't remember if I had told her that before. I told her about the Devil stalking me in similar fashion, going through it all, just as I had for David and Armand, and found myself finishing with those puzzling words, "And I'll tell you this about him, whatever he is, he has a sleepless mind in his heart, and an insatiable personality! And that's true. When I first used those words to describe him, they just occurred to me as if from nowhere. I don't know what part of my mind intuited such a thing. But it's true."

"Say again?" she asked.

I did.

She lapsed into total silence. Her eyes became tiny and she sat with one hand curled under her chin.

"Lestat, I'm going to make an absurd request of you. Send for some food. Or get me something to eat and drink. I have to ponder this."

I found myself leaping to my feet. "Anything you wish," I said.

"Doesn't matter at all. Sustenance. I haven't eaten since yesterday. I don't want my thoughts distorted by an accidental fast. You go, get something for nourishment and bring it back here. And I want to be alone here, to pray, to think, and to walk back and forth among Father's things. Now, there is no chance this demon will take you sooner than promised?"

"I don't know any more than I told you. I don't think so. Look, I'll get you good food and drink."

I went on the errand immediately, leaving the building in mortal fashion and seeking out one of those crowded midtown restaurants from which to purchase a whole meal for her that could be packed up and kept hot until I returned. I brought her several bottles of some pure, brand-name water, since that's what mortals seem to crave in these times, and then I took my time going back up, the bundle in my arms.

Only as the elevator opened on our floor did I realize how unusual my actions had been. I, two hundred years old, ferocious and proud by nature, had just gone on an errand for a mortal girl because she asked me very directly to do it.

Of course there were mediating circumstances! I'd kidnapped her and brought her over hundreds of miles! I needed her. Hell, I loved her.

But what I'd learnt from this simple incident was this: She did have a power, which saints often have, to make others obey. Without question, I'd gone to get the food for her. Cheerfully gone myself, as though there were grace in it.

I brought the meal inside the apartment and set it down for her on the table.

The apartment was now flooded with her mingling aromas, including that of her menses, that special, perfumed blood collecting neatly between her legs. The place breathed with her.

I ignored the predictable raging desire to feast on her till she dropped.

She was sitting crouched over in the chair, hands locked together, staring before her. I saw that the black leather folders were open all over the floor. She knew about her inheritance or had some idea of it.

She wasn't looking at that, however, and she seemed absolutely unsurprised by my return.

She drifted towards the table now, as though she couldn't break out of her reverie. Meantime, I stirred about in the kitchen drawers of the apartment for plates and utensils for her, found some mildly inoffensive stainless-steel forks and knives and a china plate. I set these down for her, and laid out the cartons of steaming food—meat and vegetables and such, and some sort of sweet concoction, all of it as alien to me as it had always been, as if I hadn't recently been in a mortal body and tasted real food. I didn't want to think about that experience!

"Thank you," she said absently, without so much as looking at me. "You are a darling for having done it." She opened a bottle of the water and drank it all greedily.

I watched her throat as she did this. I didn't let myself think about her in any way except lovingly, but the scent of her was enough to drive me out of the place.

That's it, I vowed. If you feel you cannot control this desire, then you leave!

She ate the food indifferently, almost mechanically, and then looked up at me.

"Oh, forgive me, do sit down, please. You can't eat, can you? You can't take this kind of nourishment."

"No," I said. "But I can sit down."

I sat next to her, trying not to watch her or breathe her scent any more than I had to. I looked directly across the room, out the glass at the white sky. If snow was falling now, I couldn't tell, but it had to be. Because I couldn't see anything but the whiteness. Yes, that meant that either New York had disappeared without a trace, or that it was snowing outside.

It took her less than six and one half minutes to devour the meal. I've never seen anyone eat so fast. She stacked up everything and took it into the kitchen. I had to draw her away from the chores, and bring her back into the room. This gave me a chance both to hold her warm, fragile hands and to be very close to her.

"What is your advice?"

She sat down and pondered, or drew together her thoughts.

"I think you have little to lose by cooperating with this being. It's perfectly obvious he could destroy you anytime he wanted. He has many ways. You slept in your house, even after you knew that he, the Ordinary Man, as you call him, knew the location. Obviously you aren't afraid of him on any material level. And in his realm, you were able to exert sufficient force to push him away from you. What do you risk by cooperating? Suppose he can take you to Heaven or Hell. The implication is that you can still refuse to help him, can't you? You can still say, to use his own fine language, 'I don't see things from your point of view.'"

"Yes."

"What I'm saying is, if you open yourself to what he wants to show you, that does not mean you have accepted him, does it? On the contrary, the obligation lies with him to make you see from his perspective, or so it seems. Besides, the point is, you break the rules whatever they are."

"He can't be tricking me into Hell, you mean."

"You serious? You think God would let people be tricked into Hell?"

"I'm not people, Dora. I'm what I am. I don't mean to draw any parallels with God in my repetitive epithets. I only mean I'm evil. Very evil. I know I am. I have been since I started to feed on humans. I'm Cain, the slayer of his brothers."

"Then God could put you in Hell anytime he wanted. Why not?"

I shook my head. "I wish I knew. I wish I knew why He hasn't. I wish I knew. But what you're saying is that there is power involved here on both sides."

"Clearly."

"And to believe in some sort of trickery is almost superstitious."

"Precisely. If you go to Heaven, if you speak with God. . . ." She stopped.

"Would you go if he were asking you to help him, if he were telling you he wasn't evil, but that he was the adversary of God, that he could change your mind on things?"

"I don't know," she said. "I might. I would maintain my free will throughout the experience, but I very well might."

"That's just it. Free will. Am I losing my will and my mind?"

"You seem to be in full possession of both and an enormous amount of supernatural strength."

"Do you sense the evil in me?"

"No, you're too beautiful for that, you know it."

"But there must be something rotten and vicious inside me that you can feel and see."

"You're asking for consolation and I can't give that to you," she said. "No, I don't sense it. I believe the things you've told me."

"Why?"

She thought for a long time. Then she stood up and went to the glass wall.

"I have put a question to the supernatural," she said, looking down, perhaps at the roof of the cathedral. I could not see it from where I stood. "I have asked it to give me a vision."

"And you think I might be the answer."

"Possibly," she said, turning and looking at me again. "That is not to say that all of this is happening because of Dora and what Dora wants. It is, after all, happening to you. But I have asked for a vision, and I've been given a series of miraculous incidents, and yes, I believe you, as surely as I believe in the existence of and the goodness of God."

She came towards me, stepping carefully through the scattered folders.

"You know, none of us can say why God allows evil."

"Yes."

"Or whence it came into the world. But the world over, there are millions of us—People of the Book—Moslem, Jew, Catholic, Protestant—descendants of Abraham—and over and over we keep being drawn into tales and schemes in which evil is present, in which there is a Devil, in which there is some element that God allows, some adversary, to use your friend's word."

"Yes. Adversary. That's exactly what he said."

"I trust in God," she said.

"And you're saying I should do that too?"

"What could you possibly lose by doing it?" she said.

I didn't answer.

She walked about, thinking, her black hair falling forward in a curl against her cheek, her long black-clad legs looking painfully thin yet graceful as she paced. She had let go of the black coat a long time ago, and I realized now that she wore only a thin black silk dress. I smelled her blood again, her secret, fragrant, female blood.

I looked away from her.

She said, "I know what I have to lose in such matters. If I believe in God, and there is no God, then I can lose my life. I can end up on a deathbed realizing I've wasted the only real experience of the universe I'll ever be permitted to have."

"Yes, exactly, that's what I thought when I was alive. I wasn't going to waste my life believing in something that was unprovable and out of the question. I wanted to know what I was permitted to see and feel and taste in my life."

"Exactly. But you see, your situation is different. You are a vampire. You are, theologically speaking, a demon. You are powerful in your own way, and you cannot die naturally. You have an edge."

I thought about it.

"Do you know what happened today in the world," she said, "just this one day? We always begin our broadcast with such reports; do you know how many people died in Bosnia? In Russia? In Africa? How many skirmishes were fought or murders committed?"

"I know what you're saying."

"What I'm saying is, it's highly unlikely this thing has the power to trick you into anything. So go with it. Let it show you what it promises. And if I'm wrong . . . if you're tricked into Hell, then I've made a horrible mistake."

"No, you haven't. You've avenged your father's death, that's all. But I agree with you. Trickery is too petty to be involved here. I'm going by instincts. And I'll tell you something else about Memnoch, the Devil, something maybe that will surprise you."

"That you like him? I know that. I understood that all along."

"How is that possible? I don't like myself, you know. I love myself, of course, I'm committed to myself till my dying day. But I don't like myself."

"You told me something last night," she said. "You said that if I needed you I was to call to you with my thoughts, my heart."

"Yes."

"You do the same. If you go with this creature, and you need me, call to me. Let me say it this way: If you cannot pull away of your own volition and you need my intercession, then send out your call! I'll hear you. And I'll cry out to the heavens for you. Not for justice but for mercy. Will you make me that promise?"

"Of course."

"What will you do now?" she asked.

"Spend the remaining hours with you, taking care of your affairs. Making sure, through my numerous mortal alliances, that nothing can hurt you in terms of all these possessions."

"My father's done it," she said. "Believe me. He's covered it very cleverly."

"Are you sure?"

"He did it with his usual brilliance. He left more money to fall into the hands of his enemies than the fortune he left to me. They have no need to go looking for anyone. Once they realize he is dead, they will begin to snatch his available assets right and left."

"You are certain of all this."

"Without question. Put your affairs in order tonight. You don't need to worry about mine. Take care of yourself, that you are ready to embark on this."

I watched her for a long time. I was still seated at the table. She stood with her back to the glass. It struck me that she had been drawn against it in black ink except for her white face.

"Is there a God, Dora?" I whispered. I had spoken these same words so many times! I had asked this question of Gretchen when I was flesh and blood in her arms.

"Yes, there is a God, Lestat," Dora answered. "Be assured of it. Maybe you've been praying to Him so loud and so long that finally He has paid attention. Sometimes I wonder if that isn't the disposition of God, not to hear us when we cry, to deliberately shut His ears!"

"Shall I leave you here or take you home?"

"Leave me. I don't ever want to make a journey like that again. I will spend a good part of the rest of my life trying to remember it precisely and failing to do so. I want to stay here in New York with my father's things. With regard to the money? Your mission has been accomplished."

"And you accept the relics, the fortune."

"Yes, of course, I accept them. I'll keep Roger's precious books until such time as they can be properly offered for others to see—his beloved heretical Wynken de Wilde."

"Do you require anything further of me?" I asked.

"Do you think . . . do you think you love God?"

"Absolutely not."

"Why do you say that?"

"How could I?" I asked. "How could anyone love Him? What did you just tell me yourself about the world? Don't you see, everybody hates God now. It's not that God is dead in the twentieth century. It's that everybody hates Him! At least I think so. Maybe that's what Memnoch is trying to say."

She was amazed. She frowned with disappointment and yearning. She wanted to say something. She gestured, as though trying to take invisible flowers from the air to show me their beauty, who knows?

"No, I hate Him," I said.

She made the Sign of the Cross and put her hands together.

"Are you praying for me?"

"Yes," she said. "If I never lay eyes on you again after tonight, if I never come across a single shred of evidence that you really exist or were here with me, or that any of these things were said, I'll still be transformed by you as I am now. You are my miracle of sorts. You're greater proof than millions of mortals have ever been given. You're proof not only of the supernatural and the mysterious and the wondrous, you're proof of *exactly what I believe*!"

"I see." I smiled. It was all so logical and symmetrical. And true. I smiled, truly smiled, and shook my head. "I hate to leave you," I said.

"Go," she said, and then she clenched her fists. "Ask God what He wants of us!" she said furiously. "You're right. We hate Him!" The anger blazed in her eyes, and then subsided, and she stared at me, her eyes looking larger and brighter because they were wet now with salt and tears.

"Good-bye, my darling," I said. This was so extraordinary and painful.

I went out into the heavy, drifting snow.

The doors of the great cathedral of St. Patrick's were closed and bolted, and I stood at the foot of the stone steps looking up at the high Olympic Tower, wondering if Dora could see me as I stood here, freezing in the cold, and letting the snow strike my face, softly, persistently, harmfully, and with beauty.

"All right, Memnoch," I said aloud. "No need to wait any longer. Come now, please, if you will."

Immediately I heard the footsteps!

It was as though they were echoing in the monstrous hollow of Fifth Avenue, among the hideous Towers of Babel, and I had cast my lot with the whirlwind.

I turned round and round. There was not a mortal in sight!

"Memnoch the Devil!" I shouted. "I'm ready!"

I was perishing with fear.

"Prove your point to me, Memnoch. You have to do that!" I called.

The steps were getting louder. Oh, he was up to his finest tricks.

"Remember, you have to make me see it from your point of view! That's what you promised!"

A wind was collecting, but from where I couldn't tell. All of the great metropolis seemed empty, frozen, my tomb. The snow swirled and thickened before the cathedral. The towers faded.

I heard his voice right beside me, bodiless and intimate. "All right, my beloved one," he said. "We'll begin now."

10

WE WERE in the whirlwind and the whirlwind was a tunnel, but between us there fell a silence in which I could hear my own breath. Memnoch was so close to me, his arm locked around me, that I could see his dark face in profile, and feel the mane of his hair against the side of my own face.

He was not the Ordinary Man now, but indeed the granite angel, the wings rising out of my focus, and folded around us, against the force of the wind.

As we rose, steadily, without the slightest reference to any sort of gravity, two things became apparent to me at once. The first was that we were surrounded by thousands upon thousands of individual souls. I say souls! What did I see? I saw shapes in the whirlwind, some completely anthropomorphic, others merely faces, but surrounding me, everywhere, were distinct spiritual entities or individuals, and very faintly I heard their voices—whispers, cries, and howls—mingling with the wind.

The sound couldn't hurt me now, as it had in the prior apparitions, nevertheless I heard this throng as we shot upwards, turning as if on an axis, the tunnel narrowing suddenly so that the souls seemed to touch us, and then widening, only to narrow again.

The second thing which I instantly realized was that the darkness was fading or being drained utterly from Memnoch's form. His profile was bright and even translucent; so were his shapeless unimportant garments. And the goat legs of the dark Devil were now the legs of a large man. In sum, the entire turbid and smokelike presence had been replaced by something crystalline and reflective, but which felt pliant and warm and alive.

Words came back to me, snatches of scripture, of visions and prophetic claims and poetry; but there was no time to evaluate, to analyze, to seal into memory.

Memnoch spoke to me in a voice that may not have been technically audible, though I heard the familiar accentless speech of the Ordinary Man.

"Now, it is difficult to go to Heaven without the slightest preparation, and you will be stunned and confused by what you see. But if you don't see this first, you'll hunger for it throughout our dialogue, and so I'm taking you to the very gates. Be prepared that the laughter you hear is not laughter. It is joy. It will come through to you as laughter because that is the only way such ecstatic sound can be physically received or perceived."

No sooner had he finished the last syllable than we found ourselves standing in a garden, on a bridge across a stream! For one moment, the light so flooded my eyes that I shut them, thinking the sun of our solar system had found me and was about to burn me the way I should have been burnt: a vampire turned into a torch and then forever extinguished.

But this sourceless light was utterly penetrating and utterly benign. I opened my eyes, and realized that we were once again amid hundreds of other individuals, and on the banks of the stream and in all directions I saw beings greeting each other, embracing, convers-

ing, weeping, and crying out. As before, the shapes were in all degrees of distinctness. One man was as solid as if I'd run into him in
the street of the city; another individual seemed no more than a giant
facial expression; while others seemed whirling bits and pieces of material and light. Others were utterly diaphanous. Some seemed invisible, except that I knew they were there! The number was impossible
to determine.

The place was limitless. The waters of the stream itself were brilliant with the reflected light; the grass so vividly green that it seemed
in the very act of becoming grass, of being born, as if in a painting or
an animated film!

I clung to Memnoch and turned to look at him in this new light
form. He was the direct opposite now of the accumulating dark
angel, yet the face had the very same strong features of the granite
statue, and the eyes had the same tender scowl. Behold the angels and
devils of William Blake and you've seen it. It's beyond innocence.

"Now we're going in," he said.

I realized I was clinging to him with both hands.

"You mean *this* isn't Heaven!" I cried, and my voice came out as
direct speech, intimate, just between us.

"No," he said, smiling and guiding me across this bridge. "When
we get inside, you must be strong. You must realize you are in your
earthbound body, unusual as it is, and your senses will be overwhelmed! You will not be able to endure what you see as you would if
you were dead or an angel or my lieutenant, which is what I want you
to become."

There was no time to argue. We had passed swiftly across the
bridge; giant gates were opening before us. I couldn't see the summit
of the walls.

The sound swelled and enveloped us, and indeed it was like laughter, waves upon waves of shimmering and lucid laughter, only it was
canorous, as though all those who laughed also sang canticles in full
voice at the same time.

What I saw, however, overwhelmed me as much as the sound.

This was very simply the densest, the most intense, the busiest,
and the most profoundly magnificent place I'd ever beheld. Our language needs endless synonyms for beautiful; the eyes could see what
the tongue cannot possibly describe.

Once again, people were everywhere, people filled with light, and of distinct anthropomorphic shape; they had arms, legs, beaming faces, hair, garments of all different kinds, yet no costume of any seemingly great importance, and the people were moving, traveling paths in groups or alone, or coming together in patterns, embracing, clasping, reaching out, and holding hands.

I turned to the right and to the left, and then all around me, and in every direction saw these multitudes of beings, wrapped in conversation or dialogue or some sort of interchange, some of them embracing and kissing, and others dancing, and the clusters and groups of them continuing to shift and grow or shrink and spread out.

Indeed, the combination of seeming disorder and order was the mystery. This was not chaos. This was not confusion. This was not a din. It seemed the hilarity of a great and final gathering, and by final I mean it seemed a perpetually unfolding resolution of something, a marvel of sustained revelation, a gathering and growing understanding shared by all who participated in it, as they hurried or moved languidly (or even in some cases sat about doing very little), amongst hills and valleys, and along pathways, and through wooded areas and into buildings which seemed to grow one out of another like no structure on earth I'd ever seen.

Nowhere did I see anything specifically domestic such as a house, or even a palace. On the contrary, the structures were infinitely larger, filled with as bright a light as the garden, with corridors and staircases branching here and there with perfect fluidity. Yet ornament covered everything. Indeed, the surfaces and textures were so varied that any one of them might have absorbed me forever.

I cannot convey the sense of simultaneous observation that I felt. I have to speak now in sequence. I have to take various parts of this limitless and brilliant environment, in order to shed my own fallible light on the whole.

There were archways, towers, halls, galleries, gardens, great fields, forests, streams. One area flowed into another, and through them all I was traveling, with Memnoch beside me, securely holding me in a solid grip. Again and again, my eyes were drawn to some spectacularly beautiful sculpture or cascade of flowers or a giant tree reaching out into the cloudless blue, only to have my body turned back around by him as if I were being kept to a tightrope from which I might fatally fall.

I laughed; I wept; I did both, and my body was convulsing with the emotions. I clung to him and tried to see over his shoulder and around him, and spun in his grip like an infant, turning to lock eyes with this or that person who happened to glance at me, or to look for a steady moment as the groups and the parliaments and congregations shifted and moved.

We were in a vast hall suddenly. "God, if David could see this!" I cried; the books and scrolls were endless, and there seemed nothing illogical or confusing in the manner in which all these documents lay open and ready to be examined.

"Don't look, because you won't remember it," Memnoch said. He snatched at my hand as if I were a toddler. I had tried to catch hold of a scroll that was filled with an absolutely astonishing explanation of something to do with atoms and photons and neutrinos. But he was right. The knowledge was gone immediately, and the unfolding garden surrounded us as I lost my balance and fell against him.

I looked down at the ground and saw flowers of complete perfection; flowers that were the flowers that our flowers of the world might become! I don't know any other way to describe how well realized were the petals and the centers and the colors. The colors themselves were so distinct and so finely delineated that I was unsure suddenly that our spectrum was even involved.

I mean, I don't think our spectrum of color was the limit! I think there was some other set of rules. Or it was merely an expansion, a gift of being able to see combinations of color which are not visible chemically on earth.

The waves of laughter, of singing, of conversation, became so loud as to overwhelm my other senses; I felt blinded by sound suddenly; and yet the light was laying bare every precious detail.

"Sapphirine!" I cried out suddenly, trying to identify the greenish blue of the great leaves surrounding us and gently waving to and fro, and Memnoch smiled and nodded as if in approval, reaching again to stop me from touching Heaven, from trying to grab some of the magnificence I saw.

"But I can't hurt it if I touch, can I?" It seemed unthinkable suddenly that anyone could bruise anything here, from the walls of quartz and crystal with their ever-rising spires and belfries, to the sweet, soft vines twining upwards in the branches of trees dripping with magnificent fruits and flowers. "No, no, I wouldn't want to hurt it!" I said.

My own voice was distinct to me, though the voices of all those around me seemed to overpower it.

"Look!" said Memnoch. "Look at them. Look!" And he turned my head as if to force me not to cower against his chest but to stare right into the multitudes. And I perceived that these were alliances I was witnessing, clans that were gathering, families, groups of kindred, or true friends, beings whose knowledge of each other was profound, creatures who shared similar physical and material manifestations! And for one brave moment, one brave instant, I saw that all these beings from one end of this limitless place to the other were connected, by hand or fingertip or arm or the touch of a foot. That, indeed, clan slipped within the womb of clan, and tribe spread out to intersperse amongst countless families, and families joined to form nations, and that the entire congregation was in fact a palpable and visible and interconnected configuration! Everyone impinged upon everyone else. Everyone drew, in his or her separateness, upon the separateness of everyone else!

I blinked, dizzy, near to collapsing. Memnoch held me.

"Look again!" he whispered, holding me up.

But I covered my eyes; because I knew that if I saw the interconnections again, I would collapse! I would perish inside my own sense of separateness! Yet each and every being I saw was separate.

"They are all themselves!" I cried. My hands were clapped on my eyes. I could hear the raging and soaring songs more intensely; the long riffs and cascades of voices. And beneath all there came such a sequence of flowing rhythms, lapping one over the other, that *I* began to sing.

I sang with everyone! I stood still, free of Memnoch for a moment, opened my eyes, and heard my voice come out of me and rise as if into the universe itself.

I sang and I sang; but my song was full of longing and immense curiosity and frustration as well as celebration. And it came home to me, thudded into me, that nowhere around me was there anyone who was unsafe or unsatisfied, was there anything approximating stasis or boredom; yet the word "frenzy" was in no way applicable to the constant movement and shifting of faces and forms that I saw.

My song was the only sad note in Heaven, and yet the sadness was transfigured immediately into harmony, into a form of psalm or canticle, into a hymn of praise and wonder and gratitude.

I cried out. I think I cried the single word "God." This was not a prayer or an admission, or a plea, but simply a great exclamation.

We stood in a doorway. Beyond appeared vista upon vista, and I was vaguely sensible suddenly that over the nearby balustrade there lay below the world.

The world as I had never seen it in all its ages, with all its secrets of the past revealed. I had only to rush to the railing and I could peer down into the time of Eden or Ancient Mesopotamia, or a moment when Roman legions had marched through the woods of my earthly home. I would see the great eruption of Vesuvius spill its horrid deadly ash down upon the ancient living city of Pompeii.

Everything there to be known and finally comprehended, all questions settled, the smell of another time, the taste of it—

I ran towards the balustrade, which seemed to be farther and farther away. Faster and faster I headed towards it. Yet still the distance was impossible, and suddenly I became intensely aware that this vision of Earth would be mingled with smoke and fire and suffering, and that it might utterly demolish in me the overflowing sense of joy. I had to see, however. I was not dead. I was not here to stay.

Memnoch reached out for me. But I ran faster than he could.

An immense light rose suddenly, a direct source infinitely hotter and more illuminating than the splendid light that already fell without prejudice on everything I could see. This great gathering magnetic light grew larger and larger until the world down below, the great dim landscape of smoke and horror and suffering, was turned white by this light, and rendered like an abstraction of itself, on the verge of combusting.

Memnoch pulled me back, throwing up his arms to cover my eyes. I did the same. I realized he had bowed his head and was hiding his own eyes behind me.

I heard him sigh, or was it a moan? I couldn't tell. For one second the sound filled the universe; all the cries and laughter and singing; and something mournful from the depths of Earth—all this sound— was caught in Memnoch's sigh.

Suddenly I felt his strong arms relaxed and releasing me.

I looked up, and in the midst of the flood of light I saw again the balustrade, and against it stood a single form.

It was a tall figure who stood with his hands on the railing, looking over it and down. This appeared to be a man. He turned around and looked at me and reached out to receive me.

His hair and eyes were dark, brownish, his face perfectly symmetrical and flawless, his gaze intense; and the grasp of his fingers very tight.

I drew in my breath. I felt my body in all its solidity and fragility as his fingers clung to me. I was on the verge of death. I might have ceased to breathe at that moment, or ceased to move with the commitment to life and might have died!

The being drew me towards himself, a light flooding from him that mingled with the light behind him and all around him, so his face grew brighter yet more distinct and more detailed. I saw the pores of his darkening golden skin, I saw the cracks in his lips, the shadow of the hair that had been shaved from his face.

And then he spoke loudly, pleadingly to me, in a heartbroken voice, a voice strong and masculine and perhaps even young.

"You would never be my adversary, would you? You wouldn't, would you? Not you, Lestat, no, not you!"

My God.

In utter agony, I was torn out of His grip, out of His midst, and out of His milieu.

The whirlwind once again surrounded us. I sobbed and beat on Memnoch's chest. Heaven was gone!

"Memnoch, let go of me! God, it was God!"

Memnoch tightened his grip, straining with all his force to carry me downwards, to make me submit, to force me to begin the descent.

We plummeted, that awful falling, which struck such fear in me that I couldn't protest or cling to Memnoch or do anything except watch the swift currents of souls all around us ascending, watching, descending, the darkness coming again, everything growing dark, until suddenly we traveled through moist air, full of familiar and natural scents, and then came to a soft and soundless pause.

It was a garden again. It was still and beautiful. But it was Earth. I knew it. My earth; and it was no disappointment in its intricacy or scents or substance. On the contrary, I fell on the grass and let my fingers dig into the earth itself. I felt it soft and gritted under my fingernails. I sobbed. I could taste the mud.

The sun was shining down on us, both of us. Memnoch sat looking at me, his wings immense and then slowly fading, until we became two manlike figures; one prone and crying like a child, and the other a great Angel, musing and waiting, his hair a mane of gradually settling light.

"You heard what He said to me!" I cried. I sat up. My voice should have been deafening. But it seemed only loud enough to be perfectly understood. "He said, 'You wouldn't ever be my adversary!' You heard Him! He called me by name."

Memnoch was completely calm, and of course infinitely more seductive and enchanting in this pale angelic shape than ever he could have been as the Ordinary Man.

"Of course he called you by name," he said, his eyes widening with emphasis. "He doesn't want you to help me. I told you. I'm winning."

"But what were we doing there! How could we get into Heaven and yet be his adversaries!"

"Come with me, Lestat, and be my lieutenant, and you can come and go there whenever you like."

I stared at him in astonished silence.

"You mean this? Come and go there?"

"Yes. Anytime. As I told you. Don't you know the Scriptures? I'm not claiming an authenticity for the fragments that remain, or even the original poetry, but of course you can come and go. You won't be of that place until you are redeemed and in it. But you can certainly get in and out, once you're on my side."

I tried to realize what he was saying. I tried to picture again the galleries, the libraries, the long, long rows of books, and realized suddenly it had become insubstantial; the details were disappearing. I was retaining a tenth of what I'd beheld; perhaps even less. What I have described here in this book is what I could remember then and now. And there had been so much more!

"How is that possible, that He would let us into Heaven!" I said. I tried to concentrate on the Scriptures, something David had said once a long time ago, about the Book of Job, something about Satan flying around and God saying, almost casually, Where have you been? Some explanation of the *bene ha elohim* or the court of heaven—

"We are his children," said Memnoch. "Do you want to hear how it all started, the entire true story of Creation and the Fall, or do you want to go back and just throw yourself into His arms?"

"What more is there!" I asked. But I knew. There was understanding of what Memnoch was saying. And there was also something required to get in there! I couldn't just go, and Memnoch knew

it. I had choices, yes, and they were these, either to go with Memnoch or return to the earth. But admission to Heaven was hardly automatic. The remark had been sarcastic. I couldn't go back and throw
myself in His arms.

"You're right," he said. "And you're also very wrong."

"I don't want to see Hell!" I said suddenly. I drew myself up. I
recoiled. I looked around us. This was a wild garden, this was my
Savage Garden, of thorny vines and hunkering trees, of wild grass,
and orchids clinging to the mossy knuckles of branches, of birds
streaking high above through webs of leaves. "I don't want to see
Hell!" I cried. "I don't want to, I don't! . . ."

Memnoch didn't answer. He seemed to be considering things.
And then he said, "Do you want to know the why of all of it, or not?
I was so sure you would want to know, you of all creatures. I thought
you would want every little bit of information!"

"I do!" I cried. "Of course I want to know," I said. "But I . . . I
don't think I can."

"I can tell you as much as I know," he said gently, with a little
shrug of his powerful shoulders.

His hair was smoother and stronger than human hair, the strands
were perhaps thicker, and certainly more incandescent. I could see
the roots of his hair at the top of his smooth forehead. His hair was
tumbling soundlessly into some sort of order, or just becoming less
disheveled. The flesh of his face was equally smooth and apparently
pliant all over, the long, well-formed nose, the full and broad mouth,
the firm line of the jaw.

I realized his wings were still there, but they had become almost
impossible to see. The pattern of the feathers, layer after layer of
feathers, was visible, but only if I squinted my eyes and tried to make
out the details against something dark behind him, like the bark of
the tree.

"I can't think," I said. "I see what you think of me, you think
you've chosen a coward! You think you've made a terrible mistake.
But I tell you, I can't reason. I . . . I saw Him. He said, 'You wouldn't
be my adversary!' You're asking me to do it! You took me to Him and
away from Him."

"As He Himself has allowed!" Memnoch said with a little rise to
his eyebrows.

"Is that so?"

"Of course!" he answered.

"Then why did He plead with me! Why did He look that way!"

"Because He was God Incarnate, and God Incarnate suffers and feels things with His human form, and so He gave you that much of Himself, that's all! Suffering! Ah, suffering!"

He looked to heaven and shook his head. He frowned a little, thoughtfully. His face in this form could not appear wrathful or twisted with any ugly emotion. Blake had seen into Heaven.

"But it was God," I said.

He nodded, with his head to the side. "Ah, yes," he said wearily, "the Living Lord."

He looked off into the trees. He didn't seem angry or impatient or even weary. Again, I didn't know if he could. I realized he was listening to sounds in the soft garden, and I could hear them too.

I could smell things—animals, insects, the heady perfume of jungle flowers, those overheated, mutated blooms that a rain forest can nourish either in the depths or in its leafy heights. I caught the scent of humans suddenly!

There were people in this forest. We were in an actual place.

"There are others here," I said.

"Yes," he said. And now he smiled at me very tenderly. "You are not a coward. Shall I tell you everything, or simply let you go? You know now more than millions ever glimpse in their lifetimes. You don't know what to do with that knowledge, or how to go on existing, or being what you are . . . but you have had your glimpse of Heaven. Shall I let you go? Or don't you want to know why I need you so badly?"

"Yes, I do want to know," I said. "But above all, more than anything else, I want to know how you and I can stand there side by side, adversaries, and how you can look as you look and be the Devil, and how . . . and how . . ." I laughed. ". . . and how I can look like I look and be the Devil I've been! That's what I want to know. I have never in my whole existence seen the aesthetic laws of the world broken. Beauty, rhythm, symmetry, those are the only laws I've ever witnessed that seemed natural.

"And I've always called them the Savage Garden! Because they seemed ruthless and indifferent to suffering—to the beauty of the butterfly snared in the spiderweb! To the wildebeast lying on the veldt with its heart still beating as the lions come to lap at the wound in its throat."

"Yes, how well I understand and respect your philosophy," he said. "Your words are my words."

"But I saw something more up there!" I said. "I saw Heaven. I saw the perfected Garden that was no longer Savage. I saw it!" I began to weep again.

"I know, I know," he said, consoling me.

"All right." I drew myself up again, ashamed. I searched in my pockets, found a linen handkerchief, pulled it out and wiped my face. The linen smelled like my house in New Orleans, where jacket and handkerchief both had been kept until sunset this night, when I'd taken them out of the closet and gone to kidnap Dora from the streets.

Or was it the same night?

I had no idea.

I pressed the handkerchief to my mouth. I could smell the scent of New Orleans dust and mold and warmth.

I wiped my mouth.

"All right!" I declared breathlessly. "If you haven't become completely disgusted with me—"

"Hardly!" he said, as politely as David might have said.

"Then tell me the Story of Creation. Tell me everything. Just go on! Tell me! I. . . ."

"Yes . . . ?"

"I *have* to know!"

He rose to his feet, shook the grass from his loose robe, and said:

"That's what I've been waiting for. Now, we can truly begin."

11

"LET'S move through the forest as we talk," he said. "If you don't mind the walking."

"No, not at all," I said.

He brushed a little more of the grass from his garment, a fine spun robe that seemed neutral and simple, a garment that might have been worn either yesterday or a million years ago. His entire form was slightly bigger all over than mine, and bigger perhaps than that of most humans; he fulfilled every mythic promise of an angel, except that the white wings remained diaphanous, retaining their shape under some sort of cloak of invisibility, more it seemed for convenience than anything else.

"We're not in Time," he said. "Don't worry about the men and the women in the forest. They can't see us. No one here can see us, and for that reason I can keep my present form. I don't have to resort to the dark devilish body which He thinks is appropriate for earthly maneuvers, or to the Ordinary Man, which is my own unobtrusive choice."

"You mean you couldn't have appeared to me on Earth in your angelic form?"

"Not without a lot of argument and pleading, and frankly I didn't want to do it," he said. "It's too overwhelming. It would have weighted everything too much in my favor. In this form, I look too inherently good. I can't enter Heaven without this form; He doesn't want to see the other form, and I don't blame Him. And frankly, on Earth, it's easiest to go about as the Ordinary Man."

I stood up shakily, accepting his hand, which was firm and warm. In fact, his body seemed as solid as Roger's body had seemed near the very end of Roger's visitation. My body felt complete and entire and my own.

It didn't surprise me to discover my hair was badly tangled. I ran a comb through it hastily for comfort, and brushed off my own clothes—the dark suit I had put on in New Orleans, which was full of tiny specks of dust, and some grass from the garden, but otherwise unharmed. My shirt was torn at the collar, as if I myself had ripped it open hastily in an effort to breathe. Otherwise, I was the usual dandy, standing amid a thick and verdant forest garden, which was not like anything I'd ever seen.

Even a casual inspection indicated that this was no rain forest, but something considerably less dense, yet as primitive.

"Not in Time," I said.

"Well, moving through it as we please," he said, "we are only a few thousand years before your time, if you must know it. But again, the men and women roaming here won't see us. So don't worry. And the animals can't harm us. We are watchers here but we affect nothing. Come, I know this terrain by heart, and if you follow me, you'll see we have an easy path through this wilderness. I have much to tell you. Things around us will begin to change."

"And this body of yours? It's not an illusion? It's complete."

"Angels are invisible, by nature," he said. "That is, we are immaterial in terms of earth material, or the material of the physical universe, or however you would like to describe matter for yourself. But you were right in your early speculation that we have an essential body; and we can gather to ourselves sufficient matter from a whole variety of sources to create for ourselves a complete and functioning body, which we can later shatter and disperse as we see fit."

We walked slowly and easily through the grass. My boots, heavy enough for the New York winter, found the uneven ground no problem at all.

"What I'm saying," Memnoch continued, looking down at me—he was perhaps three inches taller—with his huge almond-shaped eyes—"is that this isn't a borrowed body, nor is it strictly speaking a contrived body. It's my body when surrounded and permeated with matter. In other words, it's the logical result of my essence drawing to it all the various materials it needs."

"You mean you look this way because you look this way."

"Precisely. The Devilish body is a penance. The Ordinary Man is a subterfuge. But this is what I look like. There were angels like me throughout Heaven. Your focus was mainly on human souls in Heaven. But the angels were there."

I tried to remember. Had there been taller beings, winged beings? I thought so, and yet I wasn't certain. The beatific thunder of Heaven beat in my ears suddenly. I felt the joy, the safety, and above all the satisfaction of all those thriving in it. But angels, no, I had not noticed.

"I take my accurate form," Memnoch continued, "when I am in Heaven, or outside of Time. When I am on my own, so to speak, and not bound to the earth. Other angels, Michael, Gabriel, any of those can appear in their glorified form on earth if they want to. Again, it would be natural. Matter being drawn to them by their magnetic force shapes them to look their most beautiful, the way God created them. But most of the time they don't let this happen. They go about as Ordinary Men or Ordinary Women, because it's simply much easier to do so. Continuously overwhelming human beings do not serve our purposes—neither our Lord's nor mine."

"And that is the question. What is the purpose? What are you doing, if you're not evil?"

"Let me start with the Creation. And let me tell you right now that I know nothing of where God came from, or why, or how. No one knows this. The mystic writers, the prophets of Earth, Hindu, Zoroastrian, Hebrew, Egyptian—all recognized the impossibility of understanding the origin of God. That's not really the question for me and never has been, though I suspect that at the end of Time we will know."

"You mean God hasn't promised that we will know where He came from."

"You know what?" he said, smiling. "I don't think God knows. I think that's the whole purpose of the physical universe. He thinks through watching the universe evolve, He's going to find out. What He has set in motion, you see, *is* a giant Savage Garden, a giant experiment, to see if the end result produces beings like Himself. We are made in His image, all of us—He is anthropomorphic, without question, but again He is not material."

"And when the light came, when you covered your eyes in Heaven, that was God."

He nodded. "God, the Father, God, the Essence, Brahma, the Aten, the Good God, *En Sof,* Yahweh, God!"

"Then how can He be anthropomorphic?"

"His essence has a shape, just as does mine. We, His first creations, were made in His image. He told us so. He has two legs, two arms, a head. He made us invisible images of the same. And then set the universe into motion to explore the development of that shape through matter, do you see?"

"Not quite."

"I believe God worked backwards from the blueprint of Himself. He created a physical universe whose laws would result in the evolution of creatures who resembled Him. They would be made of matter. Except for one striking and important difference. Oh, but then there were so many surprises. You know my opinion already. Your friend David hit upon it when he was a man. I think God's plan went horribly wrong."

"Yes, David did say that, that he thought angels felt God's plan for Creation was all wrong."

"Yes. I think He did it originally to find out what it would have been like had He been Matter. And I think He was looking for a clue as to how He got where He is. And why He is shaped like He is, which is shaped like me or you. In watching man evolve, He hopes to understand His own evolution, if such a thing in fact occurred. And whether this has worked or not to His satisfaction, well, only you can judge that for yourself."

"Wait a minute," I said. "But if He is spiritual and made of light, or made of nothing—then what gave Him the idea for matter in the first place?"

"Ah, now that is the cosmic mystery. In my opinion, His imagination created Matter, or foresaw it, or longed for it. And I think the longing for it was a most important aspect of His mind. You see, Lestat, if He Himself did originate in Matter . . . then all this is an experiment to see when Matter can evolve into God again.

"If He didn't originate Matter, if He proceeded and it is something He imagined and desired and longed for, well, the effects upon Him are basically the same. He wanted Matter. He wasn't satisfied without it. Or He wouldn't have made it. It was no accident, I can assure it.

"But let me caution you, not all the angels agree on this interpretation, some feel the need for no interpretation, and some have completely different theories. This is my theory, and since I am the Devil, and have been for centuries, since I am the Adversary, the Prince of Darkness, the Ruler of the World of Men and of Hell, I think my opinion is worth stating. I think it's worth believing in. So you have my article of faith.

"The design of the universe is immense, to use a feeble word, but the whole process of evolution was His calculated experiment, and we, the angels, were created long before it began."

"What was it like before Matter began?"

"I can't tell you. I know, but I don't, strictly speaking, remember. The reason for this is simple: When Matter was created, so was Time. All angels began to exist not only in heavenly perfection with God but to witness and be drawn into Time.

"Now we can step out of it, and I can to some extent recall when there was no lure of Matter or Time; but I can't really tell you what that early stage was like anymore. Matter and Time changed everything totally. They obliterated not only the pure state that preceded them, they upstaged it; they overshadowed it; they, how shall I say . . . ?"

"Eclipsed it."

"Exactly. Matter and Time eclipsed the Time before Time."

"But can you remember being happy?"

"Interesting question. Dare I say this?" he asked himself as he continued to speculate. "Dare I say, I remember the longing, the incompleteness, more than I remember complete happiness? Dare I say there was less to understand?

"You cannot underestimate the effect upon us of the creation of the physical universe. Think for one moment, if you can, what Time means, and how miserable you might be without it. No, that's not right. What I mean is, without Time you could not be conscious of yourself, either in terms of failure or achievement, or in terms of any motion backwards or forwards, or any effect."

"I see it. Rather like the old people who've lost so much intelligence that they have no memory moment to moment. They're vegetative, wide-eyed, but they are no longer human with the rest of the race because they have no sense of anything . . . themselves or anyone else."

"A perfect analogy. Though let me assure you such aged and wounded individuals still have souls, which will at some point cease to be dependent upon their crippled brains."

"Souls!" I said.

We walked slowly but steadily, and I tried not to be distracted by the greenery, and the flowers; but I have always been seduced by flowers; and here I saw flowers of a size which our world would surely find impractical and impossible to support. Yet these were species of trees I knew. This was the world as it had once been.

"Yes, you're correct on that. Can you feel the warmth around you? This is a time of lovely evolutionary development on the planet. When men speak of Eden or Paradise, they 'remember' this time."

"The Ice Age is yet to come."

"The second Ice Age is coming. Definitely. And then the world will renew itself, and Eden will come again. All through the Ice Age, men and women will develop. But realize of course that even by this point, life as we know it had existed for millions of years!"

I stopped. I put my hands to my face. I tried to think it through again. (If you want to do this, just reread the last two pages.)

"But He knew what Matter was!" I said.

"No, I'm not sure He did," said Memnoch. "He took that seed, that egg, that essence and He cast it in a form which became Matter! But I don't know how truly He foresaw what that would mean. You see, that's our big dispute. I don't think He sees the consequences of

His actions! I don't think He pays attention! That's what the big fight is about!"

"So He created Matter perhaps by discovering what it was as He did it."

"Yes, Matter and energy, which are interchangeable as you know, yes, He created them, and I suspect that the key to Him lies within the word 'energy,' that if human anatomy ever reaches the point where angels and God can be satisfactorily explained in human language, energy will be the key."

"So He was energy," I said, "and in making the universe, He caused some of that energy to be changed into Matter."

"Yes, and to create a circular interchange independent of himself. But of course nobody said all this to us at the beginning. He didn't say it. I don't think He knew it. We certainly didn't know it. All we knew was that we were dazzled by His creations. We were absolutely astonished by the feel and taste and heat and solidity and gravitational pull of Matter in its battle with energy. We knew only what we saw."

"Ah, and you saw the universe unfolding. You saw the Big Bang."

"Use that term with skepticism. Yes, we saw the universe come into existence; we saw everything set into motion, as it were. And we were overawed! That's why almost every early religion on earth celebrates the majesty, the grandeur, the greatness and genius of the Creator; why the earliest anthems ever put into words on Earth sing the glories of God. We were impressed, just as humans later would come to be impressed, and in our angelic minds, God was Almighty and Wondrous and Beyond Comprehension before man came into being.

"But let me remind you, especially as we walk through this magnificent garden, that we witnessed millions of explosions and chemical transformations, upheavals, all of which involved nonorganic molecules before 'life' as we call it ever came to exist."

"The mountain ranges were here."

"Yes."

"And the rains?"

"Torrents upon torrents of rain."

"Volcanos erupted."

"Continuously. You can't conceive of how enthralled we were. We watched the atmosphere thicken and develop, watching it change in composition.

"And then, and then, came what I will call for you the Thirteen

Revelations of Physical Evolution. And by revelation, I mean what was revealed in the process to the angels, to those of us who Watched, to *us*.

"I could tell you in greater detail, take you inside every basic species of organism that ever thrived in this world. But you wouldn't remember it. I'm going to tell you what you can remember so that you can make your decision while you're still alive."

"Am I alive?"

"Of course. Your soul has never suffered physical death; it's never left the earth, except with me by special dispensation for this journey. You know you are alive. You're Lestat de Lioncourt, even though your body has been mutated by the invasion of an alien and alchemic spirit, whose history and woes you have recorded yourself."

"To come with you . . . to decide to follow you . . . I have to die then, don't I?"

"Of course," he said.

I found myself stopped still again, hands locked to the side of my head. I stared down at the grass underneath my boots. I sensed the swarm of insectile light gathered in the sun falling on us. I looked at the reflection of radiance and verdant forest in Memnoch's eyes.

He lifted his hand very slowly, as if giving me full opportunity to move away from him, and then he laid his hand on my shoulder. I loved this sort of gesture, the respectful gesture. I tried so often to make this sort of gesture myself.

"You have the choice, remember? You can return to being exactly what you are now."

I couldn't answer. I knew what I was thinking. *Immortal, material, earthbound, vampire.* But I didn't speak the words. How could anyone return from this? And again, I saw His face and heard His words. *You would never be my adversary, would you?*

"You are responding very well to what I tell you," he said warmly. "I knew you would, for several reasons."

"Why?" I asked. "Tell me why. I need a little reassurance. I'm too shattered by all my past weeping and stammering, though I have to confess, I'm not too interested in talking about myself."

"What you are is part of what we are doing," he said. We had come to an enormous spiderweb, suspended over our broad path by thick, shimmering threads. Respectfully, he ducked beneath it rather than destroy it, drawing his wings downward around him, and I followed his lead.

"You're curious, that's your virtue," he said. "You want to know. This is what your ancient Marius said to you, that he, having survived thousands of years, or well, nearly . . . would answer your questions as a young vampiric creature, because your questions were truly being asked! You wanted to know. And this is what drew me to you also.

"Through all your insolence, you wanted to know! You have been horribly insulting to me and to God continuously, but then so is everyone in your time. That's nothing unusual, except with you there was tremendous genuine curiosity and wonder behind it. You saw the Savage Garden, rather than simply assuming a role there. So this has to do with why I have picked you."

"All right," I said with a sigh. It made sense. Of course I remembered Marius revealing himself to me. I remembered him saying the very things to which Memnoch referred. And I knew, too, that my intense love of David, and of Dora, revolved around very similar traits in both beings: an inquisitiveness which was fearless and willing to take the consequence of the answers!

"God, my Dora, is she all right?"

"Ah, it's that sort of thing which surprises me, the ease with which you can be distracted. Just when I think I've really astonished you and I have you locked in, you step back and demand to be answered on your own terms. It's not a violation of your curiosity, but it is a means of controlling the inquiry, so to speak."

"Are you telling me that I must, for the moment, forget about Dora?"

"I'll go you one better. There is nothing for you to worry about. Your friends, Armand and David, have found Dora, and are looking out for her, without revealing themselves to her."

He smiled reassuringly, and gave a little doubtful, maybe scolding, shake of the head.

"And," he said, "you must remember your precious Dora has tremendous physical and mental resources of her own. You may well have fulfilled what Roger asked of you. Her belief in God set her apart from others years ago; now what you've shown her has only intensified her commitment to all that she believes. I don't want to talk anymore about Dora. I want to go on describing Creation."

"Yes, please."

"Now, where were we? There was God; and we were with Him. We had anthropomorphic shapes but we didn't call them that because we had never seen our shapes in material form. We knew our limbs, our heads, our faces, our forms, and a species of movement which is purely celestial, but which organizes all parts of us in concert, fluidly. But we knew nothing of Matter or material form. Then God created the Universe and Time.

"Well, we were astonished, and we were also enthralled! Absolutely enthralled.

"God said to us, 'Watch this, because this will be beautiful and will exceed your conceptions and expectations, as it will Mine.' "

"God said this."

"Yes, to me and the other angels. Watch. And if you go back to scripture in various forms, you will find that one of the earliest terms used for us, the angels, is the Watchers."

"Oh, yes, in Enoch and in many Hebrew texts."

"Right. And look to the other religions of the world, whose symbols and language are less familiar to you, and you will see a cosmology of similar beings, an early race of godlike creatures who looked over or preceded human beings. It's all garbled, but in a way—it's all there. We were the witnesses of God's Creation. We preceded it, and therefore did not witness our own. But we were there when He made the stars!"

"Are you saying that these other religions, that they contain the same validity as the religion to which we are obviously referring? We are speaking of God and Our Lord as though we were European Catholics—"

"It's all garbled, in countless texts throughout the world. There are texts which are irretrievable now which contained amazingly accurate information about cosmology; and there are texts that men know; and there are texts that have been forgotten but which can be rediscovered in time."

"Ah, in time."

"It's all essentially the same story. But listen to my point of view on it and you will have no difficulty reconciling it with your own points of reference, and the symbology which speaks more clearly to you."

"But the validity of other religions! You're saying that the being I saw in Heaven wasn't Christ."

"I *didn't* say that. As a matter of fact, I said that He was God Incarnate. Wait till we get to that point!"

We had come out of the forest and stood now on what seemed the edge of a veldt. For the first time I caught sight of the humans whose scent had been distracting me—a very distant band of scantily clothed nomads moving steadily through the grass. There must have been thirty of them, perhaps less.

"And the Ice Age is yet to come," I repeated. I turned round and round, trying to absorb and memorize the details of the enormous trees. But even as I did so, I realized the forest had changed.

"But look carefully at the human beings," he said. "Look." He pointed. "What do you see?"

I narrowed my eyes and called upon my vampiric powers to observe more closely. "Men and women, who look very similar to those of today. Yes, I would say this is *Homo sapiens sapiens*. I would say, they are our species."

"Exactly. What do you notice about their faces?"

"That they have distinct expressions that seem entirely modern, at least readable to a modern mind. Some are frowning; some are talking; one or two seem deep in thought. The shaggy-haired man lagging behind, he seems unhappy. And the woman, the woman with the huge breasts—are you sure she can't see us?"

"She can't. She's merely looking in this direction. What differentiates her from the men?"

"Well, her breasts, clearly, and the fact that she is beardless. The men have beards. Her hair is longer of course, and well, she's pretty; she's delicate of bone; she's feminine. She isn't carrying an infant, but the others are. She must be the youngest, or one who hasn't given birth."

He nodded.

It did seem that she could see us. She was narrowing her gaze as I did mine. Her face was longish, oval, what an archaeologist would call Cro-Magnon; there was nothing apelike about her, or about her kin. She wasn't fair, however, her skin was dark golden, rather like that of the Semitic or Arab peoples, like His skin in Heaven Above. Her dark hair lifted exquisitely in the wind as she turned and moved forward.

"These people are all naked."

Memnoch gave a short laugh.

We moved back into the forest; the veldt vanished. The air was thick and moist and fragrant around us.

Towering over us were immense conifers and ferns. Never had I seen ferns of this size, their monstrous fronds bigger by far than the blades of banana trees, and as for the conifers, I could only compare them to the great, barbaric redwoods of the western California forests, trees which have always made me feel alone and afraid.

He continued to lead us, oblivious to this swarming tropical jungle through which we made our way. Things slithered past us; there were muted roars in the distance. The earth itself was layered over with green growth, velvety, ruckled, and sometimes seemingly with living rocks!

I was aware of a rather cool breeze suddenly, and glanced over my shoulder. The veldt and the humans were long gone. The shadowy ferns rose so thickly behind us that it took me a moment to realize that rain was falling from the sky, high above, striking the topmost greenery and only touching us with its soft, soothing sound.

There had been no humans in this forest ever, that was certain, but what manner of monsters were there, which might step from the shadows?

"Now," Memnoch said, easily moving aside the dense foliage with his right arm as we continued to walk. "Let me get to the specifics, or what I have organized into the Thirteen Revelations of Evolution as the angels perceived them and discussed them with God. Understand, throughout we will speak of this world only—planets, stars, other galaxies, these have nothing to do with our discussion."

"You mean, we are the only life in the entire universe."

"I mean my world and my heaven and my God are all that I know."

"I see."

"As I told you, we witnessed complex geological processes; we saw the mountains rise, we saw the seas created, we saw the continents shift. Our anthems of praise and wonder were endless. You cannot imagine the singing in Heaven; you heard a mere taste of it in a Heaven filled with human souls. Then we were only the celestial choirs, and each new development prompted its psalms and canticles. The sound was different. Not better, no, but not the same.

"Meantime, we were very busy, descending into the atmosphere of earth, oblivious to its composition, and losing ourselves in contemplation of various details. The minutiae of life involved a demand on our focus which did not exist in the celestial realm."

"You mean everything there was large and clear."

"Precisely and fully illuminated, the Love of God was in no way enhanced or enlarged or complicated by any question of tiny details."

We had come now to a waterfall, thin, fierce, and descending into a bubbling pool. I stood for a moment, refreshed by the mist of water on my face and hands. Memnoch seemed to enjoy the same.

For the first time I realized his feet were bare. He let his foot slip into the water itself, and watched the water swirl around his toes. The nails of his toes were ivory, perfectly trimmed.

As he looked down into the churning, bubbling water, his wings became visible, rising straight up suddenly to great peaks above him, and I could see the moisture glittering as it coated the feathers. There was a commotion; the wings appeared to close, exactly like those of a bird, and to fold back behind him, and then to disappear.

"Imagine now," he said, "the legions of angels, the multitudes of all ranks—and there are ranks—coming down to this earth to fall in love with something as simple as the bubbling water we see before us or the changing color of sunlight as it pierces the gases surrounding the planet itself."

"Was it more interesting than Heaven?"

"Yes. One has to say yes. Of course, on reentry, one feels complete satisfaction in Heaven, especially if God is pleased; but the longing returns, the innate curiosity, thoughts seemed to collect inside our minds. We became aware of having a mind in this fashion, but let me move on to the Thirteen Revelations.

"The First Revelation was the change of inorganic molecules to organic molecules . . . from rock to tiny living molecule, so to speak. Forget this forest. It didn't exist then. But look to the pool. It was in pools such as this, caught in the hands of the mountain, warm, and busy, and full of gases from the furnaces of the earth, that such things started—the first organic molecules appeared.

"A clamour rose to Heaven. 'Lord, look what Matter has done.' And the Almighty gave His usual beaming smile of approval. 'Wait and Watch,' He said again, and as we watched, there came the Second Revelation: Molecules commenced to organize themselves into three forms of Material: cells, enzymes, and genes. Indeed, no sooner had the one-celled form of such things appeared than the multicellular forms began to appear; and what we had divined with the first organic molecules was now fully apparent; some spark of life animated these things; they had a crude form of purpose, and it was as if we could see that spark of life and recognize it as a tiny, tiny evidence of the essence of life which we in abundance possessed!

"In sum, the world was full of commotion of a new kind altogether; and as we watched these tiny multicelled beings drift through water, collecting to form the most primitive algae, or fungi, we saw these green living things then take hold upon the land itself! Out of the water climbed the slime which had clung for millions of years to its shores. And from these creeping green things sprang the ferns and the conifers which you see around us, rising finally until they attained massive size.

"Now angels have size. We could walk beneath these things on the green-covered world. Again, listen, if you will, in your imagination, to the anthems of praise that rose to heaven; listen if you will to the joy of God, perceiving all this through His own Intellect and through the choruses and tales and prayers of his angels!

"Angels began to spread out all over the earth; they began to delight in certain places; some preferred the mountains; others the deep valleys, some the waters, some the forest of green shadow and shade."

"So they became like the water spirits," I said, "or the spirits of the woods—all the spirits that men later came to worship."

"Precisely. But you jump way ahead!

"My response to these very first Two Revelations was like that of many of my legions; as quickly as we sensed a spark of life emanating from these multicelled plant organisms, we also began to sense the death of that spark, as one organism devoured another, or overran it and took its food from it; indeed we saw multiplicity and destruction!

"What had been mere change before—exchange of energy and matter—now took on a new dimension. We began to see the beginning of the Third Revelation. Only it did not come home to us until the first animal organisms distinguished themselves from plants.

"As we watched their sharp, determined movement, with their seemingly greater variety of choices, we sensed that the spark of life they evinced was *indeed very similar* to the life inside ourselves. And what was happening to these creatures? To these tiny animals and to plants?

"They died, that's what was happening. They were born, lived and died, and began to decay. And that was the Third Revelation of Evolution: Death and Decay."

Memnoch's face became the darkest I'd ever seen it. It retained the innocence, and the wonder, but it was clouded with something terrible that seemed a mixture of fear and disappointment; maybe it was only the naive wonder that perceives a horrible conclusion.

"The Third Revelation was Death and Decay," I said. "And you found yourself repelled by it."

"Not repelled! I just assumed it had to be a mistake! I went soaring to heaven! 'Look,' I said to God, 'these tiny things can cease to live, the spark can go out—as it could never go out of You or us, and then what is left behind them in matter rots.' I wasn't the only angel who went flying into the face of God with this great cry.

"But I think my anthems of wonder were more colored by suspicion and fear. Fear had been born in my heart. I didn't know it, but it had come to me with the perception of decay and death; and the perception felt punitive to my mind."

He looked at me. "Remember, we are angels. Until this time, there had been nothing punitive to our minds; nothing that made suffering in our thoughts! You grasp? And I suffered; and fear was a tiny component of it."

"And what did God say?"

"What do you think He said?"

"That it was all part of the plan."

"Exactly. 'Watch. Watch, and look, and you will see that essentially nothing new is happening; there is the same interchange of energy and matter.'"

"But what about the spark?" I cried.

"'You are living creatures,' said God. 'It is a credit to your fine intellect that you perceive such a thing. Now watch. More is to come.'"

"But suffering, the punitive quality. . . . "

"It was all resolved in a Great Discussion. Discussion with God involves not only coherent words but immense love of God, the light you saw, surrounding and permeating us all. What God gave us was reassurance, and perhaps the reassurance that this inkling of suffering in me required—that there was Nothing To Fear."

"I see."

"Now comes the Fourth Revelation, and remember my organization of these revelations is arbitrary. I cannot take you through the minutiae, as I've said. The Fourth Revelation I call the Revelation of

Color, and it began with flowering plants. The creation of flowers; the introduction of an entirely more extravagant and visibly beautiful means of mating between organisms. Now understand mating had always taken place. Even in the one-celled animals there had been a mating.

"But flowers! Flowers introduced in profusion colors which had never been before in nature, except in the rainbow! Colors we had known in Heaven and thought to be purely celestial and now we saw they were not purely celestial but could develop in this great laboratory called earth for natural reasons.

"Let me say at this time that spectacular colors were also developing in sea creatures, in fishes in warm waters. But the flowers struck me in particular as exquisitely beautiful, and when it became obvious that the species would be numberless, that the patterns of petals should be endless, our anthems again rose to Heaven in such music that everything before seemed lesser, or not so deep.

"This music had of course already been tinged with something dark . . . dare I say it—the hesitation or the shadow produced in us by the Revelation of Death and Decay. And now with the flowers, this dark element grew even stronger in our songs and exclamations of wonder and gratitude, for when the flowers died, when they lost their petals, when they fell to the earth, it seemed a terrible loss.

"The spark of life had emanated most powerfully from these flowers, and from the larger trees and plants that were growing everywhere in profusion; and so the song took on its sombre notes.

"But we were more than ever enthralled with the earth. In fact, I would say at this time that the character of Heaven had been changed utterly. All of Heaven, God, the angels in all ranks, were now focused on the Earth. It was impossible to be in Heaven merely singing to God as before. The song would have to have something in it about Matter and process and beauty. And of course those angels who make the most complex songs did wind together these elements—death, decay, beauty—into more coherent anthems than those which came from me.

"I was troubled. I had a sleepless mind in my soul, I think. I had something in me which had already become insatiable. . . . "

"Those words, I spoke those words to David when I spoke of you, when you first stalked me," I said.

"They come from an old poem that was sung of me, written in

Hebrew and now rarely found in translation anywhere in the world. Those were the words of the Sibylline Oracle when she described the Watchers . . . we angels whom God had sent to observe. She was right. I liked her poetry, so I remember it. I adopted it in my definition of myself. God only knows why other angels are more nearly content."

Memnoch's whole manner had become sombre. I wondered if the music of Heaven which *I* had heard included this sombre quality he was describing to me, or whether its pure joy had been restored.

"No, you hear now the music of human souls in heaven as well as angels. The sounds are completely different. But let me go on quickly through the Revelations, because I know that they aren't easy to grasp except as a whole.

"The Fifth Revelation was that of Encephalization. Animals had differentiated themselves in the water from plants some time ago, and now these gelatinous creatures were beginning to form nervous systems and skeletons and with this formation came the process of encephalization. Creatures began to develop heads!

"And it did not escape our notice for one divine instant that we, as angels, had heads! The thinking processes of these evolving organisms were centered in the head. So it was with us, obviously! No one had to tell us. Our angelic intelligence knew how we were organized. The eyes were the giveway. We had eyes, and these eyes were part of our brains and sight led us in our movements, and in our responses, and in our search for knowledge more than any other sense.

"'There was a tumult in heaven. 'Lord,' I said, 'what is happening? These creatures are developing shapes . . . limbs . . . heads.' And once again the anthems rose, but this time mingled with confusion as well as ecstasy, fear of God that such things could happen, that from Matter things could spring which had heads.

"Then even before the reptiles began to crawl out of the sea into the land, even before that happened, there came the Sixth Revelation, which struck nothing short of horror in me. These creatures, with their heads and their limbs, no matter how bizarre, or various in their structures, these things had faces! Faces like ours. I mean the simplest anthropoid had two eyes, a nose, and a mouth. This is a face, such as I have! First the head, now the face, the expression of intelligence within the mind!

"I was aghast! I raised the worst arguments. 'Is this something you want to happen? Where will this end? What are these creatures? The spark of life from them grows stronger, flares hotter, and dies hard! Are you paying attention!' Some of my fellow angels were horrified.

"They said, 'Memnoch, you are pushing God too far! Obviously there is a kinship between us, magnificent as we are, the Sons of God, the inhabitants of the *bene ha elohim*, and these creatures. The head, the face, yes, it's evident. But how dare you challenge the plan of God?'

"I couldn't be comforted. I was too full of suspicion, and so were those who agreed with me. We were puzzled, and back down to Earth we went, persuaded by the earth to wander, to walk. I could now measure myself in size by the scale of things as I earlier mentioned, and I could lie amongst soft bowers of plants, listening to them grow and thinking about them, and letting their colors fill my eyes.

"Yet, still the promise of disaster haunted me. Then an exceptional thing happened. God came to me.

"God doesn't leave Heaven when He does this. He merely extends Himself, so to speak; His light came down and took me in where I was, rolled me up into it and against Him, and He began to talk to me.

"Of course this was immediately comforting. I had denied myself the bliss of Heaven for long periods, and now to have this bliss come down and enfold me in perfect love and quiet, I was satisfied. All my arguments and doubts left me. Pain left me. The punitive effect upon my mind of death and decay was eased.

"God spoke. I was of course fused with Him and had no sense of my form in this moment; we had been so close many a time in the past, and we were this close when I had been made, and came forth out of God. But nevertheless it was a profound, merciful gift for it to happen now.

" 'You see more than other angels,' He said. 'You think in terms of the future, a concept which they are just beginning to learn. They are as mirrors reflecting the magnificence of each step; whereas you have your suspicions. You do not trust in me.'

"These words filled me with sorrow. 'You do not trust in me.' I had not thought of it as distrust, my fears. And no sooner had I realized this than that realization was sufficient for God, and He called me back to Heaven and said that now I should watch more often from that vantage point and not go so deep into the foliage of the world."

I could only stare at Memnoch as he explained all these things. We stood on the bank of the stream still. He didn't seem comforted now as he told me about this comfort. Only eager to go on with his tale.

"I did go back to Heaven, but as I told you, the entire composition of Heaven was now changed. Heaven was focused on Earth. Earth was the Heavenly Discourse. And never was I so aware of it as on this return. I went to God, I knelt in adoration, I poured out my heart, my doubts, above all my gratitude that He had come to me as He had. I asked if I was free again to return to the World below.

"He gave one of His sublime noncommittal answers, meaning, 'You are not forbidden. You are a Watcher and your duty is to Watch.' So I went down—"

"Wait," I said. "I want to ask you a question."

"Yes," he answered patiently. "But come, let's continue on our journey. You can step on the rocks as you cross the stream."

I followed him this way easily enough, and within minutes we had left the sound of the water behind us, and we were in an even denser forest alive, I think, with creatures, though I couldn't tell.

"My question," I pressed, "was this. Was Heaven boring compared to Earth?"

"Oh, never, it's just that the Earth was the focus. One could not be in Heaven and forget about Earth because everybody in Heaven was watching Earth and singing about it. That's all. No, Heaven was as fascinating and blissful as ever; in fact, the sombre note which had been introduced, the solemn acknowledgment of decay and death had added to the infinite variation of things which might be said and sung and dwelt upon in Heaven."

"I see. Heaven expanded with these revelations."

"Always! And remember the music, never, never think that that is a cliché of religion. The music was reaching new heights all the time in its celebration of wonder. It would be millennia before physical instruments would reach a level where they could make even a pale imitation of the sounds of the music of the angels—their voices, mingling with the beat of their wings, and some interplay with the winds that rose from Earth."

I nodded.

"What is it?" he asked. "What do you want to say?"

"I can't put it in words! Only that our understanding of Heaven fails again and again because we are not taught this, that Heaven is focused upon the earth. Why, all my life, I've heard nothing but the contrary, the denigration of matter, and that it is a prison for the soul."

"Well, you saw Heaven for yourself," he said. "But let me continue:

"The Seventh Revelation was that the animals came out of the sea. That they came into the forests which now covered the land and they found ways to live in it. The Reptiles were born. They became great lizards, monsters, things of such size that even the strength of angels couldn't have stopped them. And these things had heads and faces, and now they not only swam with their legs—legs like ours—but they walked upon them, and some walked on two legs instead of four, holding against their chests two tiny legs like our arms.

"I watched this happen as someone watches a fire grow. From the tiny blaze, giving warmth, I now saw a conflagration!

"Insects in all forms developed. Some took to the air with a form of flight very different and monstrous compared to our own. The world swarmed with all these new species of the living and mobile and the hungry, for creature fed upon creature just as it had always been, but now with the animals, the feasting and killing was far more obvious and happened not merely in minuscule but with giant skirmishes amongst lizards who tore each other to pieces, and great reptilian birds who could glide down upon the lesser crawling things and carry them away to their nests.

"The form of propagation began to change. Things were born in eggs. Then some spawn came live from the mother.

"For millions of years I studied these things, talking to God about them, more or less absently, singing when I was overwhelmed with beauty, going up to the heavens, and generally finding my questions disturbing to everyone as before. Great debates happened. Should we question nothing? Look, the spark of life flares monstrous and hot from the giant lizard as he dies! And again and again into the womb of God I was taken, just when I thought my agitation would give me no peace.

" 'Look at the scheme more closely. You are deliberately seeing only parts of it,' He said to me. He pointed out as He had from the beginning that waste was unheard of in the universe, that decay became food for others, that the means of interchange was now Kill and Devour, Digest and Excrete.

" 'When I'm with you,' I told Him, 'I see the beauty of it. But when I go down there, when I roll in the high grass, I see differently.'

" 'You are my angel and my Watcher. Overcome that contradiction,' He said.

"I went back down to the Earth. And then came the Eighth Revelation of Evolution: the appearance of warm-blooded birds with *feathered wings*!"

I smiled. It was partly the expression on his face, the knowing, patient expression, and the emphasis with which he had described the wings.

"Feathered wings!" he said. "First we see our faces on the heads of insects, of lizards and monsters! And now behold, there is a warm-blooded creature, a creature completely more fragile and pulsing with precarious life and it has feathered wings! It flies as we fly. It rises, it spreads its wings, it soars.

"Well, for once mine was not the only outcry in heaven. Angels by the thousands were astonished to discover that little beings of matter had wings so like our own. Feathers, such as the feathers that covered ours, made them soft and made them move through the wind . . . all this now had its corollary in the material world!

"Heaven was stormy with songs, exclamations, outcries. Angels took flight after birds, surrounding them in the air, and then following them and imitating them and following them to their nests and watching as chicks were born from these eggs and grew to full size.

"Now, you know we had seen this entire question of birth, growth, maturity in other creatures, but in nothing that so resembled ourselves."

"God was silent?" I asked.

"No. But this time He called us all together and He asked us why we had not learnt enough by now that we were not insulated from such horror and pride. Pride, he said, is what we suffered; we were outraged that such puny, tiny-headed things, things that had really very limited faces, actually, had feathered wings. He gave us a stern lesson and warning: 'Once again, I tell you, this process will continue and you will see things that will astonish you, and you are my angels and you belong to me, and your trust is mine!'

"The Ninth Revelation of Evolution was painful for all angels. It was filled with horror for some, and fear for others; indeed it was as if the Ninth Revelation mirrored for us the very emotions it produced in our hearts. This was the coming of mammals upon the earth, mammals whose hideous cries of pain rose higher to Heaven than any noise of suffering and death that any other animal had ever made! Ooooh, the promise of fear that we had seen in death and decay was now hideously fulfilled.

"The music rising from Earth was transformed; and all we could do in our fear and suffering was sing in even greater amazement, and the song darkened, and became more complex. The countenance of God, the light of God, remained undisturbed.

"At last the Tenth Revelation of Evolution. The apes walked upright! Was not God Himself mocked! There it was, in hairy, brutal form, the two-legged, two-armed upright creature in whose image we had been made! It lacked our wings, for the love of Heaven; indeed the winged creatures never even came close to it in development. But there it lumbered upon the earth, club in hand, brutal, savage, tearing the flesh of enemies with its teeth, beating, biting, stabbing to death all that resisted it—the image of God and the proud Sons of God, his angels—in hairy material form and wielding tools!

"Thunderstruck, we examined its hands. Had it thumbs? Almost. Thunderstruck, we surrounded its gatherings. Was speech coming from its mouth, the audible eloquent expression of thoughts? Almost! What could be God's plan? Why had He done this? Would this not rouse His anger?

"But the light of God flowed eternal and unceasingly, as if the scream of the dying ape could not reach it, as if the monkey torn to pieces by its larger assailants had no witness to the great flaring spark that sputtered before it died.

" 'No, no, this is unthinkable, this is unimaginable,' I said. I flew in the face of Heaven again, and God said, very simply, and without consolation, 'Memnoch, if I am not mocked by this being, if it is my creation, how can you be mocked? Be satisfied, Memnoch, and enjoy amazement in your satisfaction, and trouble me no more! Anthems rise all around you which tell me of every detail my Creation has accomplished. You come with questions that are *accusations*, Memnoch! No more!'

"I was humbled. The word 'accusations' frightened or caused a long pause in my thoughts. Do you know that Satan means in Hebrew 'the accuser'?"

"Yes," I said.

"Let me continue. To me this was a wholly new concept and yet I realized that I had been flinging accusations at God all along. I had insisted that this evolutionary process could not be what He wanted or intended.

"Now He told me plainly to stop, and to examine further. And He also gave me to know again, in wide perspective, the immensity and diversity of the developments I witnessed. In sum, He visited upon me a flash of His perspective, which mine could never be.

"As I said, I was humbled. 'May I join with you, Lord?' I asked. And He said, 'But of course.' We were reconciled, and slumbering in the divine light, yet I kept waking as an animal might wake, ever on alert for its lurking enemy, waking and fearing, *But what is happening now down there!*

"Lo and behold! Are those the words I should use, or shall I speak like J, the author of the book of Genesis, and say 'Look!' with all its fierce power. The hairy upright ones had begun a strange ritual. The hairy upright ones had begun all kinds of different patterns of complex behavior. Allow me for the moment to skip over to the most significant. The hairy upright ones had begun to bury their dead."

I narrowed my eyes, looking at Memnoch, puzzled. He was so deeply invested in this tale that he looked for the first time convincingly unhappy, and yet his face retained its beauty. You couldn't say unhappiness distorted him. Nothing could.

"Was this then the Eleventh Revelation of Evolution?" I asked. "That they should bury their dead?"

He studied me a long time, and I sensed his frustration, that he couldn't begin to get across to me all that he wanted me to know.

"What did it mean?" I pressed, impatient and eager to know. "What did it mean, they buried their dead?"

"Many things," he whispered, shaking his finger emphatically, "for this ritual of burying came along with a kinship we had seldom if ever witnessed in any other species for more than a moment—the caring for the weak by the strong, the helping and the nourishing of the crippled by the whole, and finally the burial with flowers. Lestat, *flowers*! Flowers were laid from one end to the other of the body softly deposited in the earth, so that the Eleventh Revelation of Evolution was that Modern Man had commenced to exist. Shaggy, stooped, awkward, covered with apelike hair, but with faces more than ever like our faces, modern man walked on the earth! And modern man knew affection such as only angels had known in the universe, angels and God who made them, and modern man showered that affection upon his kindred, and modern man loved flowers as we had, and *grieved* as—with flowers—he buried his dead."

I was silent for a long time, considering it, and considering above all Memnoch's starting point—that he and God and the angels represented the ideal towards which this human form was evolving before their very eyes. I had not considered it from such a perspective. And again came the image of Him, turning from the balustrade, and the voice asking me with such conviction, *You would never be my adversary, would you?*

Memnoch watched me. I looked away. I felt the strongest loyalty to him already, rising out of the tale he was telling me and the emotions invested in it, and I was confused by the words of God Incarnate.

"And well you should be," said Memnoch. "For the question you must ask yourself is this: Knowing you, Lestat, as surely He must, why He does not already consider you His adversary? Can you guess?"

Stunned.

Quiet.

He waited until I was ready for him to continue, and there were moments there when I thought that point might never come. Drawn to him as I was, totally enthralled as I was, I felt a sheer mortal desire to flee from something overwhelming, something that threatened the structure of my reasoning mind.

"When I was with God," Memnoch continued, "I saw as God sees—I saw the humans with their families; I saw the humans gathered to witness and assist the birth; I saw the humans cover the graves with ceremonial stones. I saw as God sees, and I saw as if Forever and in All Directions, and the sheer complexity of every aspect of creation, every molecule of moisture, and every syllable of sound issuing from the mouths of birds or humans, all seemed to be nothing more than the product of the utter Greatness of God. Songs came from my heart which I have never equaled.

"And God told me again, 'Memnoch, stay close to me in Heaven. Watch now from afar.'

" 'Must I, Lord?' I asked. 'I want so badly to watch them and over them. I want with my invisible hands to feel their softening skin.'

" 'You are my angel, Memnoch. Go then and watch, and remember that all you see is made and willed by me.'

"I looked down once before leaving Heaven, and I do speak now in metaphor, we both know this, I looked down and I saw the Creation teeming with Watcher angels, I saw them everywhere engaged in their various fascinations as I have described, from forest to valley to sea.

"But there seemed something in the atmosphere of Earth that had changed it; call it a new element; a thin swirl of tiny particles? No, that suggests something greater than what it was. But it was there.

"I went to Earth, and immediately the other angels confirmed for me that they, too, had sensed this new element in the atmosphere of Earth, though it was not dependent upon the air as was every other living thing.

" 'How can this be?' I asked.

" 'Listen,' said the Angel Michael. 'Just listen. You can hear it.'

"And Raphael said, 'This is something invisible but living! And what is there under Heaven that is invisible and lives but us!'

"Hundreds of other angels gathered to discuss this thing, to speak of their own experience of this new element, this new presence of invisibility which seemed to swarm about us, unaware of our presence yet making some vibration, or that is, inaudible sound, which we struggled to hear.

" 'You've done it!' said one of the angels to me, and let him remain nameless. 'You've disappointed God with all your accusing and all your rages, and He has made something else other than us that is invisible and has our powers! Memnoch, you have to go to Him and find out if He means to do away with us, and let this new invisible thing rule.'

" 'How can that be so?' asked Michael. Michael is, of all the angels, one of the most calm and reasonable. Legend tells you this; so does Angelology, folklore, the whole kit and caboodle. It's true. He is reasonable. And he pointed out now to the distressed angels that these tiny invisible presences of which we were aware could not conceivably equal our power. They could scarcely make themselves known to us, and we were angels, from whom nothing on earth could possibly hide!

" 'We have to find out what this is,' I said. 'This is bound to the earth and part of it. This is not celestial. It is here, dwelling close to the forests and hills.'

"Everyone agreed. We were beings from whom the composition of nothing was secret. You might take thousands of years to understand cynobacteria, or nitrogen, but we understood them! But we didn't understand this. Or let me say, we could not recognize this for what it was."

"Yes, I understand."

"We listened; we reached out our arms. We perceived that it was bodiless and invisible, yes, but that it had to it a continuity, an individuality, indeed, what we perceived were a multitude of individualities. And they were weeping, and very gradually, that sound was heard within our own realm of invisibility, and by our own spiritual ears."

He paused again.

"You see the distinction I make?" he asked.

"They were spiritual individuals," I said.

"And as we pondered, as we opened our arms and sang and tried to comfort them, while stepping invisibly and artfully through the material of Earth, something momentous made itself known to us, shocking us out of our explorations. Before our very eyes, the Twelfth Revelation of Physical Evolution was upon us! It struck us like the light from Heaven; it distracted us from the cries of the covert invisible! It shattered our reason. It caused our songs to become laughter and wails.

"The Twelfth Revelation of Evolution was that the female of the human species had begun to look more distinctly different from the male of the human species by a margin so great that no other anthropoid could compare! The female grew pretty in our eyes, and seductive; the hair left her face, and her limbs grew graceful; her manner transcended the necessities of survival; and she became beautiful as flowers are beautiful, as the wings of birds are beautiful! Out of the couplings of the hairy ape had risen a female tender-skinned and radiant of face. And though we had no breasts and she had no wings, she looked like US!!!!"

We stood facing each other in the stillness.

Not for one second did I fail to grasp.

Not for one second did I seek to understand. I knew. I looked at him, at his large beautiful face and streaming hair, at his smooth limbs, and his tender expression, and I knew that he was right, of course. One need not have been a student of evolution to realize that such a moment had surely come to pass with the refinement of the species, and he did embody the empowered feminine if ever a creature could. He was as marble angels, as the statues of Michelangelo; the absolute preciseness and harmony of the feminine was in his physique.

He was agitated. He was on the verge it seemed of wringing his hands. He looked at me intently, as if he would look into me and through me.

"And in short order," he said, "the Thirteenth Revelation of Evolution made itself known. Males mated with the loveliest of the females, and those who were most lithe, and smooth to touch, and tender of voice. And from those matings came males themselves who were as beautiful as the females. There came humans of different complexions; there came red hair and yellow hair as well as black hair and locks of brown and startling white; there came eyes of infinite variety—gray, brown, green, or blue. Gone was the man's brooding brow and hairy face and apish gait, and he, too, shone with the beauty of an angel just as did his female mate."

I was silent.

He turned away from me, but it seemed impersonal. It seemed he required of himself a pause, and a renewal of his own strength. I found myself staring at the high arched wings, drawn close together, their lower tips just above the ground where we stood, each feather still faintly iridescent. He turned around to face me, and unfolding out of the angelic shape, his face was a graceful shock.

"There they stood, male and female, He created them, and except for that, Lestat, except for—that one was male and one was female, they were made in the Image of God and of His Angels! It had come to this! To this! God split in Two! Angels split in Two!

"I don't know how long the other angels held me but finally they could no longer, and I went up to Heaven, ablaze with thoughts and doubts and speculations. I knew wrath. The cries of suffering mammals had taught me wrath. The screams and roars of wars amongst apelike beings had taught me wrath. Decay and death had taught me fear. Indeed all of God's Creation had taught all I needed to speed before him and say, " 'Is this what you wanted! Your own image divided into male and female! The spark of life now blazing huge when either dies, male or female! This grotesquerie; this impossible division; this monster! Was this the plan?'

"I was outraged. I considered it a disaster! I was in a fury. I flung out my arms, calling on God to reason with me, to forgive me, and save me with reassurance and wisdom, but nothing came from God. Nothing. Not light. Not words. Not punishment. Not judgment.

"I realized I stood in Heaven surrounded by angels. All of them were watching and waiting.

"Nothing came from Almighty God but the most tranquil light. I was weeping. 'Look, tears such as their tears,' I said to the others, though of course my tears were nonmaterial. And as I wept, and as they watched me, I realized I wasn't weeping alone.

"Who was with me? I turned round and round looking at them: I saw all the choruses of angels, the Watchers, the Cherubim, the Seraphim, the Ophanim, all. Their faces were rapt and mysterious, and yet I heard a weeping!

" 'Where is the weeping coming from!' I cried.

"And then I knew. And they knew. We came together, wings folded, heads bowed, and we listened, and rising from the earth we heard the voices of those invisible spirits, those invisible individualities; it was they—the immaterial ones—who wept! And their crying reached to Heaven as the Light of God Shone on Eternal, without change upon us all.

" 'Come now and witness,' said Raphael. 'Come watch as we have been directed.'

" 'Yes, I have to see what this is!' I said, and down I went into the earth's air, and so did all of us, driving in a whirlwind these tiny wailing, weeping things that we could not even see!

"Then human cries distracted us! Human cries mingled with the cries of the invisible!

"Together, we drew in, condensed and still a multitude, invisibly surrounding a small camp of smooth and beautiful human beings.

"In their midst one young man lay dying, twisting in his last pain on the bed they'd made for him of grass and flowers. It was the bite of some deadly insect which had made his fever, all part of the cycle, as God would have told us had we asked.

"But the wailing of the invisible ones hovered over this dying victim. And the lamentations of the human beings rose more terrible than I could endure.

"Again I wept.

" 'Be still, listen,' said Michael, the patient one.

"He directed us to look beyond the tiny camp, and the thrashing body of the feverish man, and to see in thin air the spirit voices gathering and crying!

"And with our eyes we saw these spirits for the first time! We saw them clustering and dispersing, wandering, rolling in and falling back, each retaining the vague shape in essence of a human being. Feeble, fuddled, lost, unsure of themselves, they swam in the very atmosphere, opening their arms now to the man who lay on the bier about to die. And die that man did."

Hush. Stillness.

Memnoch looked at me as if I must finish it.

"And a spirit rose from the dying man," I said. "The spark of life flared and did not go out, but became an invisible spirit with all the rest. The spirit of the man rose in the shape of the man and joined those spirits who had come to take it away."

"Yes!"

He gave a deep sigh and then threw out his arms. He sucked in his breath as if he meant to roar. He looked heavenward through the giant trees.

I stood paralyzed.

The forest sighed in its fullness around us. I could feel his trembling, I could feel the cry that hovered just inside him and might burst forth in some terrible clarion. But it only died away as he bowed his head.

The forest had changed again. The forest was our forest. These were oaks and the dark trees of our times; and the wildflowers, and the moss I knew, and the birds and tiny rodents who darted through the shadows.

I waited.

"The air was thick with these spirits," he said, "for once having seen them, once having detected their faint outline and their ceaseless voices, we could never again not see them, and like a wreath they surrounded the earth! The spirits of the dead, Lestat! The spirits of the human dead."

"Souls, Memnoch?"

"Souls."

"Souls had evolved from matter?"

"Yes. In His image. Souls, essences, invisible individualities, souls!"

I waited again in silence.

He gathered himself together.

"Come with me," he said. He wiped his face with the back of his hand. As he reached for mine, I felt his wing, distinctly for the first time, brush the length of my body, and it sent a shiver through me akin to fear, but not fear at all.

"Souls had come out of these human beings," he said. "They were whole and living, and hovered about the material bodies of the humans from whose tribe they had come.

"They could not see us; they could not see Heaven. Whom could they see but those who had buried them, those who had loved them in life, and were their progeny, and those who sprinkled the red ochre over their bodies before laying them carefully, to face the east, in graves lined with ornaments that had been their own!"

"And those humans who believed in them," I said, "those who worshipped the ancestors, did they feel their presence? Did they sense it? Did they suspect the ancestors were still there in spirit form?"

"Yes," he answered me.

I was too absorbed to say anything else.

It seemed my consciousness was flooded with the smell of the wood and all its dark colors, the endlessly rich variations of brown and gold and deep red that surrounded us. I peered up at the sky, at the shining light fractured and gray and sullen yet grand.

Yet all I could think and consider was the whirlwind, and the souls who had surrounded us in the whirlwind as though the air from the earth to Heaven were filled with human souls. Souls drifting forever and ever. Where does one go in such darkness? What does one seek? What can one know?

Was Memnoch laughing? It sounded small and mournful, private and full of pain. He was perhaps singing softly, as if the melody were a natural emanation of his thoughts. It came from his thinking as scent rises from flowers; song, the sound of angels.

"Memnoch," I said. I knew he was suffering but I couldn't stand it any longer. "Did God know it?" I asked. "Did God know that men and women had evolved spiritual essences? Did he know, Memnoch, about their souls?"

He didn't answer.

Again I heard the faint sound, his song. He, too, was looking up at the sky, and he was singing more clearly now, a sombre and humbling canticle, it seemed, alien to our own more measured and organized music, yet full of eloquence and pain.

He watched the clouds moving above us, as heavy and white as any clouds I'd ever beheld.

Did this beauty of the forest rival what I had seen in Heaven? Impossible to answer. But what I knew with perfect truth is that heaven had not made this beauty dim by comparison! And that was the wonder. This Savage Garden, this possible Eden, this ancient place was miraculous in its own right and in its own splendid limitations. I suddenly couldn't bear to look on it, to see the small leaves flutter downwards, to fall into loving it, without the answer to my question. Nothing in the whole of my life seemed as essential.

"Did God know about the souls, Memnoch!" I said. "Did He know!"

He turned to me.

"How could He not have known, Lestat!" he answered. "How could He not have known! And who do you think flew to the very heights of Heaven to tell Him? And had He ever been surprised, or caught unawares, or increased or decreased, or enlightened, or darkened, by anything I had ever brought to His Eternal and Omniscient attention?"

He sighed again, and seemed on the verge of a tremendous outburst, one that would make all his others look small. But then he was calm again and musing.

We walked on. The forest shifted, mammoth trees giving way to slender, more gracefully branching species, and here and there were patches of high, waving grass.

The breeze had the smell of water in it. I saw it lift his blond hair, heavy as this hair was, and smooth it back from the side of his face. I felt it cool my head and my hands, but not my heart.

We peered into an open place, a deep, wild valley. I could see distant mountains, and green slopes, a ragged and rambling wood breaking here and there for spaces of blowing wheat or some other form of wild grain. The woods crept up into the hills and into the mountains, sending its roots deep into the rock; and as we grew closer to the valley, through the branches I would see the glitter and twinkling light of a river or sea.

We emerged from the older forest. This was a marvelous and fertile land. Flowers of yellow and blue grew in profusion, caught this way and that in dancing gusts of color. The trees were olive trees and fruit trees, and had the low, twisted branches of trees from which food has been gathered for many generations. The sunlight poured down upon all.

We walked through tall grasses—the wild wheat perhaps—to the edge of the water, where it lapped very gently without a tide, I think, and it was clear and shimmering as it shrank back, exposing the extraordinary array of pebbles and stones.

I could see no end to this water either to the right or to the left, but I could see the far bank and the rocky hills growing down towards it as if they were as alive as the roots of the straggling green trees.

I turned around. The landscape behind us now was the same. The rocky hills, rising eventually to mountains, with miles upon miles of scalable slopes, copses of fruit trees, black, open mouths of caves.

Memnoch said nothing.

He was stricken and sad and staring down at the waters, and to the far horizon where the mountains came as if to close in the waters, only to be forced to let the waters flow out and beyond our sight.

"Where are we?" I asked gently.

He took his time to answer. Then he said, "The Revelations of Evolution are, for the time being, finished. I've told you what I saw— the thin outline of all you'll know once you die.

"Now what is left is the heart of my story, and I should like to tell it here. Here in this beautiful place, though the rivers themselves are long gone from the earth and so are the men and women who roamed at this time. And to answer your question, 'Where are we?' Let me say: Here is where He finally flung me down from Heaven. Here is where I Fell."

12

GOD SAID: 'Wait!' So I found myself stopped at the gates of Heaven, along with all my companions, the angels who generally went and did what I did, and Michael and Gabriel and Uriel, though not among my companions, were there too.

" 'Memnoch, my accuser,' said God, and the words were spoken with the characteristic gentleness and a great effulgence of light. 'Before you come into Heaven, and you begin your diatribe, go back down to the Earth and study all you have seen thoroughly and with respect—by this I mean humankind—so that when you come to me, you have given yourself every chance to understand and to behold all I have done. I tell you now that Humankind is part of Nature, and subject to the Laws of Nature which you have seen unfold all along. No one should understand better than you, save I.

" 'But go, see again for yourself. Then, and only then, will I call together a convocation in Heaven, of all angels, of all ranks and all endowments, and I will listen to what you have to say. Take with you those who seek the same answers you seek and leave me those angels who have never cared, nor taken notice, nor thought of anything but to live in My Light.' "

Memnoch paused.

We walked slowly along the bank of the narrow sea until we came to a place where several boulders made a natural place to sit and to rest. I wasn't feeling weariness in any real physical sense, but the change of posture seemed to sharpen all my fears, and concentration, and eagerness to hear what he said. He sat beside me, turned to me slightly on his left, and his wings once again faded. But first they rose, and stretched out, the left far above my head and the whole wingspan startling me. But then they disappeared. There simply wasn't room for them when Memnoch was seated, at least not for them to be folded behind him, so they were gone.

He continued: "Immediately following these words," he said, "there was a great commotion in Heaven over who wanted to go down and examine the Creation with me and who did not. Now understand, angels were all over Creation as it was, as I've told you, and many had already been years on Earth, and fallen in love with creeks, and valleys, and even the deserts which had begun to appear. But this was a special message the Lord had given me—Go and Learn All You Can About Mankind—and there was some question as to who was as interested or as passionate about the mysteries of the human race as was I."

"Wait a minute," I interrupted. "If you forgive me. How many angels are there? You quoted God as saying 'all ranks,' and 'all endowments.'"

"Surely you've heard some of the truth," he answered, "from the lore. God created us first—the archangels—Memnoch, Michael, Gabriel, Uriel, and many others whose names have never been discovered—either inadvertently or deliberately—so I would rather not say. The whole number of archangels? Fifty. And we were the First Made as I said, though who exactly came before whom has become a hysterical subject of argument in Heaven, and one in which I lost interest a long time ago. Besides, I'm convinced I am the first anyway. But it doesn't matter.

"We are those who communicate in the most direct way with God, and also with Earth. That's why we have been labeled Guardian Angels, as well as Archangels, and sometimes in the religious literature we are given a low rank. We don't have a low rank. What we have is the greatest personality and the greatest flexibility, between God and man."

"I see. And Raziel? And Metatron? And Remiel?"

He smiled. "I knew these names would be familiar to you," he said. "They all have their place among the Archangels, but I cannot possibly explain all of this to you now. You'll know when you're dead. And also it's almost too much for a human mind, even a vampiric mind, such as your own, to comprehend."

"Very well," I said. "But what you're saying is the names refer to actual entities. Sariel is an entity."

"Yes."

"Zagzagel."

"Yes, an entity. Now let me continue. Let me stick with the schemes. We, as I told you, are God's Messengers, and Most Powerful Angels, and I was fast becoming God's Accuser, as you can see!"

"And Satan means accuser," I said. "And all those other dreadful names you don't like are in some way connected with that idea. Accuser."

"Exactly," he replied. "And the early religious writers, knowing only bits and pieces of the truth, thought it was man whom I accused, not God; but there are reasons for this, as you'll soon see. You might say I have become the Great Accuser of everybody." He seemed mildly exasperated, but then his voice resumed, very calm and measured. "But my name is Memnoch," he reminded me, "and there is no angel more powerful or clever than I am and there never was."

"I see," I said, meaning this to be polite. And also because I actually didn't question this statement at all. Why should I?

"The Nine Choirs?" I asked.

"All there," he said. "The Nine Choirs, of course, making up the *bene ha elohim*. And very well described by Hebrew and Christian scholars, thanks to times of revelation and perhaps disaster, though one would be hard put to determine the nature of each event. The First Triad is made of Three Choirs, the Seraphim, Cherubim, and Thrones or Ophanim, as I prefer to call them. And this First Triad is in general locked to the glory of God. They are in His thrall, thrive in the light which can blind or dazzle others, and almost never get very far from the light at all.

"At times when I am angry and making speeches to all of Heaven, I accuse them . . . if you'll pardon the expression again—of being held to God as if by a magnet and not having a free will or personality such as we possess. But they have these things, they do, even the Ophanim, who are in general the least articulate or eloquent—in fact, Ophanim are likely to say nothing for eons—and any of these First Triad can be sent by God to do this and that, and have appeared on Earth, and some of the Seraphim have made rather spectacular appearances to men and women as well. To their credit, they adore God utterly, they experience without reserve the ecstasy of His presence, and He fills them completely so that they do not ask questions of Him and they are more docile, or more truly aware of God, depending on one's point of view.

"The Second Triad has Three Choirs which have been given the names by men of Dominations, Virtues, and Powers. But to tell the truth, there is very little difference between these angels and the First Triad. The Second Triad is a little farther from the Light of God and perhaps as close as it can come, given its endowments, and perhaps it is not so clever when it comes to logic or questions. Who knows? Certainly the Second is more docile altogether; but then there is more coming and going from the Second Triad, from Earth to Heaven, than from the devoted and magnetized and sometimes arrogant Seraphim. You can see how this could lead to much discussion."

"I think I understand it."

"Both triads sing continuously when they are in Heaven, and most of the time when they are on Earth; their songs rise to Heaven spontaneously and continuously; they don't erupt with the deliberate jubilation of my song or the songs of those like me. Nor do they fall silent for long periods as my kind—Archangels—are apt to do.

"When you're dead you'll be able to hear the song of all these triads. It would destroy you now if you did. I've let you hear part of the Din of Heaven, but that's all it can be to you, a din—the sound of song and mingled laughter, and seemingly erratic eruptions of beautiful sound."

I nodded. It had been both painful and gorgeous to hear it.

"The Lowest Triad is supposed to include Principalities, Archangels, and Angels," he continued, "but this is misleading, as I said. For we, the Archangels, are in fact the most powerful and the most important, have the most personality, and are the most questioning and concerned.

"The other angels think we are flawed on that account. It does not occur to the average Seraph to plead for mercy for mankind.

"But here you have the rough scheme of things. The angels are innumerable. And there is mobility among angels, some drifting closer to God than others, and then away when the majesty is too great for them, and they choose to slip back and sing a softer song. It's continuous.

"Now, the important thing is that the Guardian Angels of Earth, the Watchers, those who became intent upon the Creation, came from all these ranks! Even from the very Seraphim there have come Guardians who have spent millions of years on Earth and then gone Home. Going and coming is common. The disposition I describe is innate but not fixed.

"Angels aren't perfect. You can see that already. They are Created Beings. They don't know everything God knows, that's obvious to you and everyone else. But they know a great deal; they know all that can be known in Time *if they wish to know it*; and that is where angels differ, you see. Some wish to know everything in Time, and some care only for God and God's reflection in those of His most devoted souls."

"I see, then. What you're saying is everybody's right about it, and everybody's sort of wrong."

"More right than wrong. Angels are individuals, that is the key. We Who Fell are no single species, unless being the brightest, the most clever, and the most comprehending makes us a species, which I don't think it does."

"Go on."

He laughed. "You think I'm going to stop now?"

"I don't know," I said. "Where do I fit in? I don't mean me, Lestat de Lioncourt, I mean what I am . . . the vampire I am."

"You're an earthbound phenomenon, just like a ghost. We'll get to that in a moment. When God sent us down to Earth to Watch, specifically to observe all Mankind, we were as curious about the dead as the living—this wreath of souls we could see and hear, gathered about the world, and which we called Sheol immediately because it seemed to us that the realm of these weeping souls was the realm of pure gloom. 'Sheol' means gloom."

"And the spirit that made the vampires—"

"Wait. It's very simple. Let me present it, however, *as it came to me*. If I don't do that, how can you understand my position? What I ask of you—to be my lieutenant—is so personal and so total that you can't fully grasp it unless you listen."

"Please go on."

"All right. A gathering of Angels decided to go with me, to draw as close as possible to Matter in order to pull together for ourselves our entire knowledge, to better comprehend, as God had asked us to do. Michael came with me. And so did a host of other archangels. There were a few Seraphim. There were a few Ophanim. And some of the lower orders which are the least intelligent angels, but nevertheless angels, and much in love with Creation and curious as to what was making me so angry with God.

"I can't give you the number of how many we were. But when we reached the earth, we went our separate ways to perceive things, and came together often and instantly and agreed upon what we had seen.

"What united us was our interest in the statement of God that Humankind was part of Nature. We just couldn't see how this was true. We went exploring.

"Very quickly, I learnt that men and women lived now in large groups, very unlike the other primates, that they built shelters for themselves, that they painted their bodies with various colors, that the women often lived separate from the men, and that they believed in something invisible. Now what was that? Was it the souls of the ancestors, the dearly departed who were still locked in the air of Earth, disembodied and confused?

"Yes, it was the souls of ancestors, but the humans worshipped other entities as well. They imagined a God who had made the Wild Beasts and to him they made blood sacrifice on Altars, thinking this aspect of Almighty God to be a personality of very distinct limits and rather easy to please or displease.

"Now, I can't say all this was a big surprise to me. I'd seen the early signs of it. After all, I telescoped millions of years for you in my Revelations. But when I drew near to these altars, when I heard the specific prayer to the God of the Wild Animals; when I began to see the care and deliberation of the sacrifice—the slaying of a ram or a deer—I was much struck by the fact that not only had these humans come to look like Angels, but they had guessed at the truth.

"They had come upon it instinctively! There was a God. They knew. They didn't know what He was like but they knew. And this instinctive knowledge seemed to spring from the same essence as did their surviving spiritual souls. Let me be even clearer.

"Self-consciousness, and the awareness of one's own death—this had created a sense of distinct individuality in humans, and this individuality feared death; feared annihilation! Saw it, knew what it was, saw it happening. And prayed for a God that He would not let such a thing have no meaning in the world.

"And it was this very same tenacity—the tenacity of this individuality—that made the human soul stay alive after it left the body, imitating the shape of the body, holding itself together, so to speak, clinging to life, as it were, perpetuating itself, by shaping itself according to the only world it knew."

I didn't speak. I was wound up in the story and only wanted for him to continue. But naturally I thought of Roger. I thought very distinctly of Roger because Roger was the only ghost I'd ever known. And what Memnoch had just described was a highly organized and very willful version of Roger.

"Oh, yes, precisely," said Memnoch, "which is probably why it is just as well that he came to you, though at the time I regarded it as one of the greatest annoyances in the world."

"You didn't want Roger to come to me?"

"I watched. I listened. I was amazed, as you were, but I have been amazed by other ghosts before him. It wasn't that extraordinary, but no, it certainly wasn't something orchestrated by me, if that's what you mean."

"But it happened so close to your coming! It seems connected."

"Does it? What's the connection? Look for it inside yourself. Don't you think the dead have tried to speak before? Don't you think the ghosts of your victims have come howling after you? Admittedly, the ghosts of your victims usually pass in total bliss and confusion, unaware of you as the instrument of their death. But that's not always the case. Maybe what has changed is you! And as we know, you loved this mortal man, Roger, you admired him, you understood his vanity and love of the sacred and the mysterious and the costly, because you have these traits within yourself."

"Yes, all of that's true, without doubt," I said. "I still think you had something to do with his coming."

He was shocked. He looked at me for a long moment as if he were going to become angry, and then he laughed.

"Why?" he asked. "Why would I bother with such an apparition? You know what I'm asking of you! You know what it means! You're no stranger to the mystical or the theological revelation. You knew when you were a living man—the boy back in France who realized he might die without knowing the meaning of the universe and ran to the village priest to demand of the poor fellow, 'Do you believe in God?' "

"Yes, but it just all happened at the same time. And when you claim there's no connection, I just . . . I don't believe it," I said.

"You are the damnedest creature! You really are!" he said. His exasperation was mild and patient but still there. "Lestat, don't you see that what impelled you towards the complexity of Roger and his daughter, Dora, was the same thing that compelled me to come to you? You had come to a point where you were reaching out for the supernatural. You were crying to Heaven to be laid waste! Your taking David, that was perhaps your first real step towards utter moral peril! You could forgive yourself for having made the child vampire Claudia, because you were young and stupid.

"But to bring David over, against his will! To take the soul of David and make it vampiric? That was a crime of crimes. That was a crime that cries to Heaven, for the love of God. David, whom we had allowed to glimpse us once, so much did we feel an interest in him and whatever path he might take."

"Ah, so the appearance to David was deliberate."

"I thought I said so."

"But Roger and Dora, they were simply in the way."

"Yes. Of course, you chose the brightest and most alluring victim! You chose a man who was as good at what he did—his criminality, his racketeering, his thieving—as you are good at what you are. It was a bolder step. Your hunger is growing. It becomes ever more dangerous to you and those around you. You don't take the downfallen and the bereft and the cutthroats any longer. When you reached for Roger, you reached for the power and the glory, but so what?"

"I'm torn," I whispered.

"Why?"

"Because I feel love for you," I said, "and that's something I always pay attention to, as we both know. I feel drawn into you. I want to know what else you have to tell me! And yet I think you're lying about Roger. And about Dora. I think it is all connected. And when I think of God Incarnate—" I broke off, unable to continue.

I was flooded by the sensations of Heaven, or what I could still remember, what I could still feel, and the breath did leave me in a sorrow that was far greater than any I ever expressed in tears.

I must have closed my eyes. Because when I opened them, I realized Memnoch was holding both my hands in his. His hands felt warm and very strong and uncommonly smooth. How cold my own must have felt to him. His hands were larger; flawless. My hands were . . . my strange white, slender, glittering hands. My fingernails flashed like ice in the sun as they always do.

He drew away, and it was excruciating. My hands remained rigid, clasped, and utterly alone.

He was standing yards away from me, his back to me, looking out over the narrow sea. His wings were apparent, huge, and moving uneasily, as if an inner tension caused him to work the invisible muscular apparatus to which they were attached. He looked perfect, irresistible, and desperate.

"Maybe God is right!" he said with rage in his low voice, staring not at me but at the sea.

"Right about what?" I stood up.

He wouldn't look at me.

"Memnoch," I said, "please go on. There are moments when I feel I'll collapse beneath the things being made known to me. But go on. Please, please go on."

"That's your way of apologizing, isn't it?" he asked gently. He turned around, towards me. The wings vanished. He walked slowly up to me, and past me, and sat down again on my right. His robe was hemmed in dust from the ground. I absorbed the detail before I actually thought about it. There was a tiny bit of leaf, green leaf, caught in the long flowing tangles of his hair.

"No, not really," I said. "It wasn't an apology. I usually say exactly what I mean."

I studied his face—the sculpted profile, the utter absence of hair on otherwise magnificently human-looking skin. Indescribable. If you turn and look at a statue in a Renaissance church, and you see it is bigger all over than you are, that it is perfect, you don't get frightened because it's stone. But this was alive.

He turned as if he'd just noticed I was looking at him. He stared down into my eyes. Then he bent forwards, his eyes very clear, and filled with myriad colors, and I felt his lips, smooth, evenly and modestly moist, touch my cheek. I felt a burn of life through the hard coldness of my self. I felt a raging flame that caught every particle of me, as only blood can do it, living blood. I felt a pain in my heart. I might have laid my finger on my chest in the very place.

"What do *you* feel!" I asked, refusing to be ravaged.

"I feel the blood of hundreds," he whispered. "I feel a soul who has known a thousand souls."

"Known? Or merely destroyed?"

"Will you send me away out of hatred for yourself?" he asked. "Or shall I continue with my story?"

"Please, please go on."

"Man had invented or discovered God," he said. His voice was calm now and back to the same polite and almost humble instructive manner. "And in some instances, tribes worshipped more than one such deity who was perceived to have created this or that part of the world. And yes, humans knew of the souls of the dead surviving; and they did reach out to these souls and make offerings to them. They brought offerings to their graves. They cried out to these dead souls. They begged for their help in the hunt, and in the birthing of a child, in all things.

"And as we angels peered into Sheol, as we passed into it, invisible, our essence causing no disturbance in a realm that was purely souls at that point . . . souls and nothing but souls . . . we realized these souls were strengthened in their survival by the attentions of those living on earth, by the love being sent to them by humans, by the thoughts of them in human minds. It was a process.

"And just as with angels, these souls were individuals with varying degrees of intellect, interest, or curiosity. They were hosts as well to all human emotions, though in many, mercifully, all emotion was on the wane.

"Some souls, for example, knew they were dead, and sought to respond to the prayers of their children, and actively attempted to advise, speaking with all the power they could muster in a spiritual voice. They struggled to appear to their children. Sometimes they broke through for fleeting seconds, gathering to themselves swirling particles of matter by the sheer force of their invisible essence. Other times they made themselves visible in dreams, when the soul of the sleeping human was opened to other souls. They told their children of the bitterness and darkness of death, and that they must be brave and strong in life. They gave their children advice.

"And they seemed, in some instances at least, to know that the belief and attention of their sons and daughters strengthened them. They requested offerings and prayers, they reminded the children of their duty. These souls were to some extent the least confused, except for one thing. They thought they had seen all there was to be seen."

"No hint of Heaven?" I asked.

"No, and no light from Heaven penetrated Sheol, nor any music. From Sheol one saw the darkness and the stars, and the people of Earth."

"Unbearable."

"Not if you think you are a god to your children and can still derive strength from the mere sight of the libations they pour on your grave. Not if you feel pleasure in those who hearken to your advice and anger at those who don't, and not if you can communicate occasionally, sometimes with spectacular results."

"I see, of course. And gods they seemed to their children."

"Ancestral gods of a certain kind. Not the Creator of All. Human beings had distinct ideas on both questions, as I've said.

"I became greatly absorbed with this whole question of Sheol. I traveled the length and breadth of Sheol. Some of these souls didn't know they were dead. They knew only they were lost and blind and miserable and they cried all the time like infant humans. They were so weak I don't even think they felt the presence of other souls.

"Other souls were clearly deluded. They thought they were still alive! They chased after their kindred, trying vainly to get the oblivious son or daughter to listen, when of course the kindred could not hear or see them; and these, these who thought they were still living, well, these had no presence of mind to gather matter to make themselves appear or to come to the living in a dream, because they didn't know they were dead."

"Yes."

"To continue, some souls knew they were ghosts when they came to mortals. Others thought they were alive and the whole world had turned against them. Others simply drifted, seeing and hearing the sounds of other living beings but remote from this as if in a stupor or dream. And some souls died.

"Before my very eyes, some died. And soon I realized many were dying. The dying soul would last a week, perhaps a month in human time, after its separation from the human body, retaining its shape, and then begin to fade. The essence would gradually disperse, just as did the essence inside an animal upon its death. Gone into the air, returned perhaps to the energy and essence of God."

"That's what happened?" I asked desperately. "Their energy went back into the Creator; the light of a candle returned to the eternal fire?"

"I don't know. And that I didn't see, little flames wafted to Heaven, drawn aloft by a mighty and loving blaze. No, I saw nothing of the kind.

"From Sheol the Light of God was not visible. For Sheol, the consolation of God did not exist. Yet these were spiritual beings, made in our image and His image, and clinging to that image and hungering for a life beyond death. That was the agony. The hunger for the life beyond death."

"If that was absent at the time of the death, would the soul simply be extinguished?" I asked.

"No, not at all. The hunger seemed innate. The hunger had to die out in Sheol before the soul would disintegrate. Indeed, souls went through many, many experiences in Sheol, and those who had become the strongest were those who perceived themselves as gods, or humans passed into the realm of the good God, and attentive to humans; and these souls gained power even to sway the others and strengthen them sometimes and keep them from fading away."

He paused as if not sure how to proceed. Then, he went on:

"There were some souls who understood things in a different way. They knew they weren't gods. They knew they were dead humans. They knew they didn't really have the right to change the destiny of those who prayed to them; they knew that the libations essentially were symbolic. These souls understood the meaning of the concept symbolic. They knew. And they knew they were dead and they perceived themselves to be lost. They would have reentered the flesh if they could have. For there in the flesh was all the light and warmth and comfort that they had ever known and could still see. And sometimes these souls managed to do exactly that!

"I witnessed it in various different fashions. I saw these souls deliberately descend and take possession of a stupefied mortal, take over his limbs and brain and live in him until the man gained the strength to throw the soul off. You know these things. All men do—what is involved in possession. You have possessed a body that wasn't yours, and your body has been possessed by another soul."

"Yes."

"But this was the dawn of such invention. And to watch these clever souls learn the rules of it, to see them grow ever more powerful, was something to behold.

"And what I could not fail to be frightened by, being the Accuser as I am, and horrified by Nature, as God calls it, what I could not ignore was that these souls did have an effect on living women and men! There were those living humans already who had become oracles. They would smoke or drink some potion to render their own minds passive, so that a dead soul might speak with their voice!

"And because these powerful spirits—for I should call them spirits now—because these powerful spirits knew only what Earth and Sheol could teach them, they might urge human beings on to terrible mistakes. I saw them order men into battle; I saw them order executions. I saw them demand blood sacrifice of human beings."

"You saw the Creation of Religion out of Man," I said.

"Yes, insofar as Man can Create anything. Let us not forget Who Created us all."

"The other angels, how did they fare with these revelations?"

"We gathered, exchanged stories in amazement, then went off again on our own explorations; we were more entangled with the earth than we had ever been. But essentially, the reactions of angels varied. Some, the Seraphim mainly, thought the whole process was downright marvelous; that God deserved a thousand anthems in praise that his Creation should lead to a being who could evolve an invisible deity from itself who would then command it to ever greater efforts at survival or war.

"Then there were those who thought, 'This is an error, this is an abomination! These are the souls of humans pretending to be Gods! This is unspeakable and must be stopped immediately.'

"And then there was my passionate reaction: 'This is really ghastly and it is headed for worse and worse disasters! This is the beginning of an entirely new stage of human life, bodiless, yet purposeful and ignorant, which is gaining momentum every second, and filling the atmosphere of the world with potent interfering entities as ignorant as the humans round whom they swirled.' "

"Surely some of the other angels agreed with you."

"Yes, some were as vehement, but as Michael said, 'Trust in God, Memnoch, Who has done this. God knows the Divine Scheme.'

"Michael and I had the most extensive dialogues. Raphael and Gabriel and Uriel had not come down, by the way, as part of this mission. And the reason for that is fairly simple. Almost never do all of those four go the same way. It's a law with them, a custom, a . . . a vocation, that two are always on hand in heaven for the call of God; and never do all four leave at once. In this instance, Michael was the only one who wanted to come.

"Does this Archangel Michael still exist now?"

"Of course he exists! You'll meet him. You could meet him now if you wish, but no, he wouldn't come now. He wouldn't. He's on the side of God. But you'll be no stranger to him if you join with me. In fact, you might be surprised by how sympathetic Michael can be to my endeavors. But my endeavors are not unreconcilable to heaven, surely, or I would not be allowed to do what I do."

He looked sharply at me.

"All those of the *bene ha elohim* whom I describe to you are alive now. They are immortal. How could you think it would be any other way? Now, there were souls in Sheol at that time who no longer exist, not in any form I know of, but perhaps they do in some form known to God."

"I understand. It was a stupid-sounding question," I admitted. "As you watched all this, as it filled you with fear, how did you relate it to God's statement about nature? That you would see humankind were part of nature."

"I couldn't except in terms of the endless exchange of energy and Matter. The souls were energy; yet they retained a knowledge from Matter. Beyond that, I could not reconcile it. But for Michael, there was another view. We were on a stairway, were we not? The lowest molecules of inorganic matter constituted the lowest steps. These disembodied souls occupied the step above man yet below angels. It was all one flowing procession to Michael, but then again, Michael trusted that God was doing all this deliberately and wanted it this way.

"I could not believe this! Because the *suffering* of the souls horrified me. It hurt Michael too. He covered his ears. And the *death* of the souls horrified me. If souls could live, then why not let all know! And were they doomed forever to exist in this gloom? What else in nature remained so static? Had they become as sentient asteroids forever orbiting the planet, moons that could scream and cry and weep?

"I asked Michael, 'What will happen? Tribes pray to different souls. These souls become their gods. Some are stronger than others. Look at the war everywhere, the battle.'

" 'But Memnoch,' he said, 'primates did this before they had souls. Everything in Nature eats and is eaten. This is what God has been trying to tell you since you first began to cry out in protest at the sound of suffering from the Earth. These soul-god-spirits are expressions of humans, and part of humankind, born of humans and sustained by humans, and even if these spirits grow in strength to where they can manipulate living people exquisitely, they are nevertheless born out of Matter and part of Nature as God said.'

" 'So nature is this unspeakable unfolding horror,' I said. 'It is not enough that a shark swallows whole the infant dolphin and that the butterfly is crushed in the teeth of the wolf who chews it up, oblivious to its beauty. It's not enough. Nature must go further, and spin from matter these spirits in torment. Nature comes this close to Heaven, but is so far short of it that only Sheol will do for the name of this place.'

"This speech was too much for Michael. One cannot speak this way to the Archangel Michael. Just doesn't work. So at once he turned away from me, not angrily, not in cowardice that God's thunderbolt might miss me by a fraction and shatter his left wing. But he turned away in silence, as if to say, Memnoch you are impatient and unwise. Then he turned and mercifully said, 'Memnoch, you do not look deep enough. These souls have only begun their evolution. Who knows how strong they may become? Man has stepped into the invisible. What if he is meant to become as we are?'

" 'But how is that to happen, Michael?' I demanded. 'How are these souls to know what are angels and what is Heaven? Do you think if we made ourselves visible to them and told them that they . . . ' I stopped. Even I knew this was unthinkable. I wouldn't have dared. Not in millions of years would I have dared.

"But no sooner had this thought occurred to us, had we begun brooding over it, than other angels gathered with us, and said, 'Look, living people know that we are here.'

" 'How so?' I demanded. As sorry as I felt for humanity, I didn't consider mortal men and women very smart. But these angels explained immediately.

" 'Some have sensed our presence. They sense it as they sense the presence of a dead soul. It is the same part of the brain which perceives other things invisible; I tell you we have been glimpsed and we shall now be imagined by these people. You will see.'

" 'This can't be God's wish,' said Michael. 'I say we return to Heaven at once.'

"The majority agreed with him instantly, the way angels agree, without a sound. I stood alone looking at the entire multitude.

" 'Well?' I said. 'God has given me my mission. I cannot go back until I understand,' I insisted. 'And I don't understand.'

"There ensued a huge argument. But finally Michael kissed me as angels always kiss, tenderly on the lips and cheeks, and went up to Heaven, and the whole league ascended with him.

"And I remained, standing on the earth alone. I did not pray to God; I did not look to men; I looked into myself and I thought, What shall I do? I do not wish to be seen as an angel. I do not wish to be worshipped like these surviving souls. I do not wish to anger God; but I have to fulfill His commandment to me. I have to understand. Now, I am invisible. But what if I can do what these clever souls do—

that is, gather matter to me to make for myself a body—gather sufficient tiny particles from all the world—and who knows better than I do what a man is made of, having seen him evolve from his earliest stages, who knows better the makeup of tissue and cell and bone and fiber and brain matter than I know? Except God?

"So I did it. I focused my entire will and strength upon constructing for myself a living sheath of human flesh, complete in all parts, and I chose—without even thinking about it—to be male. Does this require an explanation?"

"Not really," I said. "I would imagine you had seen enough of rape, childbirth, and helpless struggle to make the wiser choice. I know I have."

"Correct. But sometimes I wonder. Sometimes I wonder if things would have been entirely different if I had chosen to be female. I could have. The females resemble us more, truly. But if we are both, then surely we are more male than female. It is not in equal parts."

"From what you've shown me of yourself, I tend to agree."

"So. I became sheathed in flesh. It took a little longer than one might suppose. I had to consciously evoke every bit of knowledge in my angelic memory; I had to construct the body, and then insert my essence in it exactly in the manner in which the natural life essence would have been inside it; and I had to surrender, that is, encase myself within this body, really go into it, and fill out its limits and not panic. Then I had to look through its eyes."

I nodded quietly with a trace of a smile. Having given up my vampire body for a human one, I could perhaps imagine a small particle of what Memnoch had experienced. I wasn't about to boast that I understood.

"The process involved no pain," he said. "Only submission. And for no good reason, really, or I should say from simple Nature, to use God's favorite word, I sheathed my own self, my own essence in flesh. Only the wings did I leave out of the scheme altogether, and so I stood as tall as an angel, and as I walked to the water of a clear pool near me and looked down in it, I saw Memnoch for the first time in material form. I saw exactly myself, my fair hair, my eyes, my skin, all the gifts God had given me in invisible form made manifest in flesh.

"I realized immediately that this was too much! I was too large all over; I was blazing with the essence inside me! This would not work. And so instantly I began to reshape and scale down the entire body until it resembled more myself the size of a man.

"You'll know how to do all this once you're with me," he said, "if you choose to come, and die, and be my lieutenant. But let me say for now that this is neither impossible nor terribly simple. It is not like pressing the keys of a complex computer program and sitting back and watching the machine execute the commands one by one. On the other hand, it is not cumbersome and overly conscious. It merely takes angelic knowledge, angelic patience, and angelic will.

"Now a man stood beside the pool, naked, blond of hair and light of eye, very similar to many of those who inhabited the region, though perhaps more nearly perfect, and endowed with physical organs of reasonable but not splendid size.

"Now as my essence went into these organs, into the scrotum and the penis, to be specific, I felt something which had been utterly unknown to me as an angel. Utterly unknown. It was compounded of many realizations. I knew gender, I knew maleness; I knew a certain human vulnerability firsthand now rather than from watching and sensing; and I was very surprised at how powerful I felt.

"I had expected to be quaking with humility in this form! To be shivering with indignity at the mere smallness of myself, and my immobility and a host of other things—things you felt when you swapped your vampire body for that of a man."

"I remember vividly."

"But I didn't feel this. I had never been material. I had never, never thought about doing it. I had never, never even thought of wanting to see what I might look like in an earthly mirror. I knew my image from its reflection in the eyes of other angels. I knew my parts because I could see them with my angelic eyes.

"But now I was a man. I felt the brain inside my skull. I felt its wet, intricate, and near-chaotic mechanics; its layers and layers of tissue, involving as it does the earliest stages of evolution, and wedding them to a wealth of higher cells in the cortex in a manner that seemed utterly illogical and yet totally natural—natural if you knew what I, as an angel, knew."

"Such as what?" I asked, making it as polite as I could.

"Such as that emotions stirred in the limbic part of my brain could take hold of me without having first made themselves known to my consciousness," he said. "That can't happen with an angel. Our emotions cannot slip by our conscious minds. We cannot feel irrational terror. At least I don't think so. And whatever the case, I certainly didn't think so then when I stood on the earth, in the flesh of a man."

"Could you have been wounded, or killed, in this form?" I asked.

"No. I'll get to that in a minute, as a matter of fact. But as I was in a wild, wooded area, as I was in this very valley which is Palestine, if you would know it, before it was ever called Palestine, as I was here, I was aware that this body was food for wild animals, and so I did create around myself, of angelic essence, an extremely strong shield. It behaved electrically. That is, when an animal approached me, which happened almost immediately, it was repulsed by this shield.

"And thus shielded, I decided to start walking all through the nearby settlements of men and to look at things, knowing full well no one could hurt me or push me or attack me or anything else. Yet I would not appear miraculous. On the contrary, I would seem to dodge the blows if any were dealt, and I would seek to behave in such a matter that nobody noticed me at all.

"I waited for nightfall, and went to the nearest encampment, which was the largest in the area and had grown so in strength that it now exacted tribute from other encampments nearby. This was a huge circular walled gathering place, full of individual huts in which men and women lived. Fires burnt in each hut. There was a central place where everyone gathered. There were gates to be locked at night.

"I slipped inside, slumped down beside a hut, and watched for hours what the people of this encampment did in the twilight and then by dark. I crept from place to place. I peered inside the little doorways. I watched many things.

"The next day, I watched from the forest. I tracked a band of hunters, so that they did not see me, but I could see them. When I was glimpsed, I ran, which seemed the acceptable and predictable behavior. Nobody chased me.

"I hung around the thriving life of these humans for three days and three nights, and during this time, I knew their limits, I knew their bodily needs and aches, and I had gradually come to know their lust, because all of a sudden, I discovered it flaming inside of me.

"This is how it happened. Twilight. The third day. I had come to an entire score of conclusions as to why these people were not part of Nature. I had an entire case to make to God. I was almost about to leave.

"But one thing which has always fascinated angels, and which I had not experienced in the flesh, was sexual union. Now as an invisible angel one can come quite close to those coupled, and see into their half-shut eyes, and hear their cries, and touch the flushed flesh of the woman's breast and feel her heart race.

"Countless times I'd done this. And I realized now that passionate union—a true experience of it—could be crucial to my case. I knew thirst, I knew hunger, I knew pain, I knew weariness, I knew about how these people lived and felt and thought and talked to each other. But I really didn't know what happened in sexual union.

"And at twilight on the third day, as I stood by this very sea, here, far, far from the encampment, looking towards it miles to our right, there came towards me as if out of nowhere a beautiful woman—a daughter of man.

"Now, I had seen scores of beautiful women! As I told you, when I first beheld the beauty of women . . . before men had become quite so smooth and hairless . . . it had been one of the shocks of Physical Evolution for me. And of course during these three days, I had from afar studied many beautiful women. But, in my subterfuge, I hadn't dared to go very close. After all, I was in the flesh and trying to go unnoticed.

"But three days, mark me, I had had this body. And the organs of this body, being perfectly made, responded at once to the sight of this woman, who came walking boldly along the banks of the sea, a rebel woman, without a guardian male or other females, a young, bold, slightly angry, longhaired and beautiful girl.

"Her garment was no more than a coarse animal skin, with a chewed leather belt around it, and she was barefoot and her legs were naked from the knee down. Her hair was long and dark, and her eyes blue—a beguiling combination. And her face very youthful yet full of the character imparted to a face by anger and rebellion—a girl filled with pain and recklessness and some desire to do herself harm.

"She saw me.

"She stopped, realizing her vulnerability. And I, never having bothered with garments, stood naked, looking at her. And the organ in me wanted her, wanted her immediately and violently; and I felt the first promise of what that union might be like. That is, the first stirring of real desire. For three days, I had lived by the mind as an angel. Now the body spoke and I listened with an angel's ears.

"She meantime did not run from me, but took several steps closer; and in her reckless heart made a resolution, based upon what experience I couldn't know, but she made it; that she would open her arms to me if I wanted her. And with the smoothest, most graceful movement of her hips, and with a gesture of her right hand, lifting her hair and then dropping it, she let me know.

"I went to her and she took my hand and led me up those rocks, there, to where the cave is, you can see it, just over your left shoulder and up the slope. She took me there, and by the time we reached the entrance, I realized that she was flaming for me as I was flaming for her.

"She was no virgin, this girl. Whatever her story, she was not ignorant of passion. She knew what it was, and she wanted it, and the lunge of her hips towards me was deliberate, and when she kissed me and put her tongue into my mouth, she knew what she sought.

"I was overcome. For one instant I held her back, merely to look at her, in her mysterious material beauty, a thing of flesh and decay that nevertheless rivaled any angel I'd ever seen, and then I gave her back her kisses, brutally, making her laugh and push her breasts against me.

"Within seconds, we had fallen down together on the mossy floor of the cave as I had seen mortals do a thousand times. And when my organ went inside of her, when I felt the passion, I knew then what no angel could possibly know! It had nothing to do with reason, or observation, or sympathy, or listening, or learning, or trying to grasp. I was in her flesh and consumed with lust, and so was she, and the tender muscles of her hairy little vaginal mouth clamped down upon me as if she meant to devour me, and as I thrust inside of her, again and again, she went blood red in her consummation, and her eyes rolled back into her head and her heart stood still.

"I came at the same moment. I felt the ejaculate shoot from my body into her. I felt it fill the warm, tight cavity. My body continued to writhe with the same rhythm, and then the feeling, the indescribable and wholly new feeling, slowly ebbed and went away.

"I lay exhausted beside her, my arm over her, and my mouth sought the side of her face and kissed her, and I said in her language, in a rush of words, 'I love you, I love you, I love you, sweet and beautiful creature, I love you!'

"And to this she gave a yielding and respectful smile, and snuggled close to me, and then seemed about to weep. Her carelessness had led her to a tenderness! Her soul suffered inside her, and I felt it through the palms of her hands!

"But in me there was a tumult of knowledge! I had felt the orgasm! I had felt the highly developed physical sensations that come to fulfillment when humans sexually mate! I stared at the ceiling of the cave, unable to move, unable to speak.

"Then very gradually, I realized something had startled her. She clung to me, then she rose on her knees, and she ran away.

"I sat up. The light had come down from Heaven! It was coming down from Heaven and it was God's light and it was looking for me! I rushed to my knees and to my feet and ran out into the light.

" 'Here I am, Lord!' I cried. 'Lord, I am full of joy! Lord, God, what I have felt, Lord!' And I let out a great anthem, and as I did so the material particles of my body dissolved about me, shorn off by me, almost as if by the power of my angel voice, and I rose to my full height and spread my wings and sang in thanks to Heaven, for what I had known in this woman's arms.

"The voice of God came quiet yet full of wrath.

" 'Memnoch!' He said. 'You are an Angel! What is an Angel, a Son of God, doing with a Daughter of Men!'

"Before I could answer, the light had withdrawn and left me with the whirlwind, and turning, my wings caught in it, I saw the mortal woman was only there, at the bank of the sea, and that she had seen and heard something inexplicable to her, and now in terror she fled.

"She ran and I was carried upwards to the very gates of Heaven, and then those gates for the first time took on height and shape for me as they had for you, and they were slammed shut against me, and the Light struck me and down I went, forced down, plummeting as you plummeted in my arms, only I was alone, alone as I was slammed again, invisible, but bruised and broken and crying, against the wet earth.

" 'You, my Watcher, what have you done!' said the voice of God, small and certain by my ear.

"I started to weep, uncontrollably. 'Lord, God, this is a terrible misunderstanding. Let me . . . let me lay my case before you . . .'

" 'Stay with the mortals you love so much!' He said. 'Let them minister to you, for I will not listen until my anger is cooled. Embrace the flesh you crave, and with which you are polluted. You won't come into my sight again until I send for you, and that shall be by my choice.'

"The wind rose again, swirling, and as I turned over on my back, I realized I was wingless, and in the flesh once more and the size of a man.

"I was in the body I had created for myself, generously reassembled for me by the Almighty, down to the last cell, and I lay hurting and aching and weak on the ground, moaning, and sad.

"I had never heard myself cry before with a human voice. I was not loud. I was not full of challenge or desperation. I was too sure of myself still as an Angel. I was too sure God loved me. I knew He was angry, yes, but He'd been angry with me many, many times before.

"What I felt was the agony of separation from Him! I could not at will ascend to Heaven! I could not leave this flesh. And as I sat up and lifted my arms, I realized I was trying to do this with my whole being, and I couldn't do it, and then sadness came over me, so great, so lonely, and so total that I could only bow my head.

"The night had begun. The stars filled the firmament and were as distant from me as if I had never known Heaven at all. I closed my eyes, and I heard the souls of Sheol wailing. I heard them pressing near me, asking me what I was, what had they witnessed, whence had I been thrown to the earth? Before I had gone unnoticed, my transformation having been quiet and secret, but when God had thrust me downwards, I had fallen spectacularly as an angel and immediately into the shape of a man.

"All Sheol was crying in curiosity and foment.

" 'Lord, what do I say to them? Help me!' I prayed.

"And then came the perfume of the woman near me. I turned and I saw her creeping towards me cautiously, and, when she saw my face, when she saw my tears and my distress, she came boldly towards me, slipping her warm breasts against my chest again, and clasping in her trembling hands my head."

13

SHE TOOK me back to the encampment. She brought me inside the gates. Men and women rose from the campfires and children ran towards me. I knew that I possessed angelic beauty, and their admiring glances didn't surprise me. But I did wonder what in the name of Heaven they meant to do.

"I was seated, and given food and drink. This I needed. For three days I'd drunk nothing but water, and eaten only a few berries gathered here and there in the woods.

"I sat down cross-legged with them and ate the cooked meat they gave me, and she, my woman, my Daughter of Men, crushed up against me, as if daring anyone to challenge the pair of us, and then she spoke.

"She stood up, threw up her arms, and in a loud voice told them what she had seen. Her language was simple. But she had plenty enough words to describe it—how she had come upon me on the banks of the sea and seen that I was naked and she had given herself to me in sanctity and worship, knowing I could not be a man of the earth.

"No sooner had my seed come into her than a magnificent light from above had filled the cave. She had rushed in fear from it, but I had walked out into it, fearless, knowing it, and before her eyes I changed so that she could see through me, yet still she saw me. And I was grown tall, with immense white feathered wings! This vision—this creature through whom she could see as if through water—she saw only for an instant. Then I vanished. I was gone as surely as I sit here now. She had hovered, shivering, watching, praying to the ancestors, to the Creator, to the Demons of the Desert, to all powers for protection, when suddenly she had seen me again—transparent, to summarize her simple words, but visible, falling—winged and enormous—smashing towards earth in a fall that would have killed a man, though that is what I became—a man, solid as everyone could see, sitting in the dust.

" 'God,' I prayed. 'What do I do? What this woman has said is true! But I am no God. You are God. What do I do?'

"No answer came from Heaven, not to my ears, not to my heart, not to my cumbersome and elaborate brain.

"As for the crowd of listeners, whom I judged to be about thirty-five, exclusive of all the children, no one spoke. Everyone was considering this. No one was quick to accept it. No one was going to jump forward and challenge it either. Something in my manner and posture held them aloof.

"No surprise. I certainly didn't cower or shiver or evince what I was suffering. I had not learnt to express angelic suffering through flesh. I merely sat there, aware that by their measure I was young, comely, and a mystery; and they were not brave enough to try to hurt me as they so often hurt others, to stab, or pierce, or burn me as I had seen them do enough times to their enemies, and to their own despised.

"Suddenly the whole group burst into murmuring. A very old man rose to his feet. His words were even simpler than hers. I would say he had perhaps half of her working vocabulary. But this was enough to express himself and he asked of me simply: 'What do you have to say for yourself?'

"The others reacted as if this question were an expression of sheer genius. Maybe it was. The woman pulled very close to me at that moment. She sat down beside me and with an imploring look, she embraced me.

"I realized something—that her fate was connected to mine. She was slightly afraid of all these people, her kindred. And she wasn't afraid of me! Interesting. That is what tenderness and love can do, and marvels also, I thought. And God says these people are part of Nature!

"I hung my head, but not for long. Finally, I rose to my feet, bringing her up with me, my mate, as it were, and, using all the words known in her language, some even that the children had been adding already in this generation that the adults didn't yet know, I said:

"'I mean you no harm. I came from Heaven. I came to learn about you and to love you. And I wish you only all good things under God!'

"There was a great clamour, a happy clamour, with people clapping their hands, and rising to their feet, and the little ones jumping up and down. It seemed a consensus emerged that Lilia, the woman I had been with, could now return to the group. She had been cast out to die when she had come upon me. But she was now surely upheld. And she had returned with a god, a deity, a sky being . . . they aimed for it with many syllables and combinations of syllables.

" 'No!' I declared. 'I am not a god. I did not make the world. I worship, just as you do, the God who did.'

"This, too, was accepted in jubilation. Indeed, the frenzy began to alarm me. I felt the limits of my body keenly with all these others dancing and screaming and shouting and kicking at the wood in the fire, and this lovely Lilia clinging to me.

" 'I must sleep now!' I said suddenly. And this was no more or less than the perfect truth. I had scarce slept an hour or more at any one time in my three days in the flesh and was bone weary and bruised and cast out of Heaven. I wanted to turn to this woman, and bury my sorrow in her arms.

"Everyone gave their approval. A hut was prepared for us. People ran hither and thither gathering the finest skins and furs for us, and the softest chewed leather, and we were ushered into this place in silence, and I lay back down on the fur beneath me, the skin of a mountain goat, long and soft.

" 'God, what do you want me to do!' I asked aloud. There came no answer. There was only the silence and the darkness in the hut, and then the arms of a Daughter of Men around me, luscious and loving and full of tenderness and passion, that mystery, that combination, that purely living miracle, tenderness and lust rolling and rolling into one."

Memnoch stopped. He seemed exhausted suddenly. He rose and again walked to the bank of the sea. He stood in the soft sand and pebbles. I saw the outline of his wings flash for a moment, perhaps exactly the way the woman had seen it, and then he was merely the large figure, with his shoulders hunched as he stood with his back to me, his face apparently buried in his hands.

"Memnoch, what happened!" I said. "Surely God didn't leave you there! What did you do? What happened the next morning when you woke up?"

He gave a sigh and turned around finally. He walked slowly back to the boulder, and sat down again.

"By morning, I had known her a half dozen times and lay half dead, and that in itself was another lesson. But I had no thought whatsoever on what I might do. While she'd slept, I had prayed to God, I had prayed to Michael and to the other angels. I had prayed and prayed, asking what I should do.

"Can you guess who answered me?" he asked.

"The souls in Sheol," I said.

"*Yes*, precisely! Those are the spirits who answered. How could you know? Those are the spirits—the strongest souls of Sheol who heard my prayers to the Creator and heard the impetus and essence of my cries and my excuses and my pleas for mercy and forgiveness and understanding—heard all of it, absorbed it, drank it up, as they did the spiritual yearnings of their human and living children. And by the time the sun rose, by the time all the men of the group had started to gather, I knew one thing only:

"Whatever happened to me, whatever was the will of God, the souls of Sheol would never be the same! They had learnt too much from the voice of this Angel fallen into Matter who had thoughtlessly cried to Heaven and to God.

"Of course the full impact didn't hit me. I didn't sit there reasoning it out. The strongest souls had had their first glimpse of Paradise. They knew now of a Light which made an Angel weep and beg in desperation, because he was afraid he would never see that Light again. I didn't think of it. No.

"God had left me here. That is what I thought. God had left me. I went out into the crowd. The encampment was overflowing. In fact, men and women were coming from all the nearby encampments to see me.

"And we had to leave the enclosure and go out into the open, into one of the fields. Look down to the right, where the land slopes? You see down there where the field spreads out and the water turns. . . ."

"Yes."

"That's where we gathered. And it was soon clear that all of these men and women were expecting something of me, that I speak, that I work marvels, that I sprout wings, something, but what I didn't know. As for Lilia, she clung to me as ever, enticing and beautiful, and filled with vague wonder.

"Together we climbed onto that rock . . . you see there, the boulders left there by the glaciers millions of years ago. There. We climbed up and she sat down and I stood before these people, and then I looked to Heaven and I opened my arms.

"With all my heart, I begged God to forgive me, to take me back, to climax this intrusion with my merciful disappearance, that is, to let me take my angelic shape, invisible, and rise. I willed it, I pictured it, I tried in every conceivable way to assume my former nature. No luck.

"In the heavens above I saw what men saw. I saw the blue of the sky, and the willowy white clouds blowing eastward, and I saw the faint daytime moon. The sun hurt my shoulders. It hurt the top of my head. And something became known to me then in all its horror: that I was probably going to die in this body! That I had forfeited my immortality! God had made me mortal and turned his back.

"I thought this over a long time. I'd suspected it from the first moment, but now with the haste of a man I became convinced of it. And in me a deep anger rose. I looked at all these men and women. I thought of God's words to me, to go with those I had chosen, with the flesh I preferred to Heaven. And a decision came into my head.

"If this was to be my finish, if I was to die in this mortal body as all men die, if some days or weeks or even years were left to me—whatever this body could hope to survive amid the perils of life—then I must do with it the very finest thing that I knew. I must offer to God my finest. I must go out like an Angel, if going out is what I had to do!

" 'I love you, my Lord,' I said aloud. And I racked my brain for the greatest acts I could perform.

"What came to me was immediate and logical, and perhaps obvious. I would teach these people everything I knew! I wouldn't just tell them about Heaven and God and Angels, because what good would that do? Though of course I would tell them, and tell them to look for a peaceful death and peace in Sheol, for that they could attain.

"But that would be the least of what I would do. For that was nothing! What was better was this—I'd teach them everything about *their world* that I could perceive logically but which had not yet become known to them.

"Immediately I started speaking to them. I led them to the mountains and took them into the caves and showed them the veins of ore, and told them that when this metal was hot it bubbled forth from the earth in liquid, and that if they could heat it again they could make it soft and make things out of it.

"Returning to the sea, I picked up the soft earth and shaped it into little people to show them how simple this was to do! Picking up a stick, I drew a circle in the sand, and spoke to them of symbols. How we might make a symbol for Lilia that resembled the flower for which she was named which they called the lily. And how we might make a symbol for what I was . . . a man with wings. I drew pictures everywhere, showing them how easy it was to do it, to connect an image with a concept or a concrete thing.

"By evening, I had gathered around me all the women, and was showing them ways to tie their thongs of chewed leather, which had never occurred to them, elaborate ways of plaiting it, and making it into big pieces of one fabric. All logical. All simply what I inferred from what I knew as an Angel about the whole world.

"Now, these people already knew the seasons of the moon, but they didn't know the calendar of the sun. I told them all this. How many days to a year there should be according to how the sun and the planets moved, and I told them how they could write all this down with symbols. And soon we took the clay from the banks of the sea and we made flat plates of it, and on these plates with sticks I made little pictures of stars and heaven and Angels. And these plates or tablets were then allowed to dry in the sun.

"For days and nights, I remained with my people. I began to teach them more and more and more. When one group was tired and could take no more lessons, I turned to another, and examined what they were doing, and tried to improve their ways.

"Many things they would figure out for themselves, I knew. Weaving was very soon to occur to them, and then they would make better garments. That was all well and good. I showed them pigments similar to the red ochre they already used. I took things out of the raw earth that would make different colors for them. Every thought that occurred to me, every advance of which I could conceive, I imparted to them, greatly expanding their language in the process, obviously teaching them writing, and then I also taught them music of a wholly new kind. I taught them songs. And the women came to me, over and over again, the women—and Lilia stepped back—that the seed of the Angel might go into many, many women, 'the comely Daughters of Men.' "

He paused again. His heart seemed broken, remembering. His eyes were distant and totally reflecting the pale blue of the sea.

I spoke up very softly, cautiously, and from memory and ready at any sign from him to break off. I quoted from the Book of Enoch:

" 'And Azazel . . . made known to them the metals, and the art of working them, and bracelets and ornaments, and the use of antimony, and the beautifying of eyelids, and all kinds of costly stones, and all colored tinctures.' "

He turned to look at me. He seemed almost unable to speak. His voice came softly, almost as softly as mine had as he spoke the next lines of the book of Enoch, " 'And there arose much godlessness, and they committed fornication, and they were led astray. . . . ' " Again he paused and then resumed, " 'And as men perished, they cried, and their cry went up to heaven.' " He stopped again, smiling slowly and bitterly. "And what is the rest of it, Lestat, and what lies in between the lines you've spoken and the lines I've spoken! Lies! I taught them civilization. I taught them knowledge of Heaven and Angels! *That's all I taught them.* There was no blood, no lawlessness, no monstrous giants in the earth. It's lies and lies, fragments and fragments buried in lies!"

I nodded, fearlessly, and rather certain of it, and seeing it perfectly, and seeing it from the point of view of the Hebrews who later believed so firmly in the purification and law, and had seen it as uncleanness and evil . . . and told again and again of these Watchers, these teachers, these Angels who had fallen in love with the Daughters of Men.

"There was no magic," Memnoch said quietly. "There were no enchantments. I didn't teach them to make swords! I didn't teach them war. If there was knowledge amongst another people on Earth, and I knew of that, I told them. That in the valley of another river, men knew how to gather wheat with scythes! That there were Ophanim in Heaven, Angels who were round, Angels who were wheels, and that if this shape was imitated in matter, if a simple piece of wood connected two rounded pieces, one could make an object which would roll upon these wheels!"

He gave a sigh. "I was sleepless, I was crazed. As the knowledge poured forth from me, as they were worn down by it, and struggled under the burden of it, I went to the caves and carved my symbols on the walls. I carved pictures of Heaven and Earth and angels. I carved the light of God. I worked tirelessly until every mortal muscle in me ached.

"And then, unable to endure their company anymore, satiated with beautiful women, and clinging to Lilia for comfort, I went off into the forest, claiming I needed to talk to my God in silence, and there I collapsed.

"I lay in perfect stillness, comforted by the silent presence of Lilia, and I thought of all that had taken place. I thought of the case I had meant to lay before God, and how what I had learnt since had only fitted neatly into the case I had meant to make! Nothing I had seen in men could incline me to think differently. That I had offended God, that I had lost Him forever, that I had Sheol to look forward to, for all eternity, these things were real and I knew them, and they beat on my soul and heart. But I couldn't change my mind!

"The case I had meant to lay before the Almighty was that these people were above Nature and beyond Nature and demanded more of Him, and all that I had seen only upheld me in what I believed. How they had taken to celestial secrets. How they suffered, and sought for some meaning to justify that suffering! If only there were a Maker and the Maker had his reasons . . . Oh, it was agony. And at the heart of it blazed the secret of lust.

"In the orgasm, as my seed had gone into the woman, I had felt an ecstasy that was like the joy of Heaven, I had felt it and felt it only in connection with the body that lay beneath me, and for one split second or less than that I had known, known, known that men were not part of Nature, no, they were better, they belonged with God and with us!

"When they came to me with their few confused beliefs—were there not invisible monsters everywhere?—I told them no. Only God and the Heavenly Court which ordained everything, and the souls of their own in Sheol.

"When they asked if bad men and women—who did not obey their laws—were not thrown at death into fire forever—an idea very current amongst them and others—I was horrified, and told them that God would never allow such a thing. A wee newborn soul to be punished in fire forever? Atrocity, I told them. Once again, I said to them that they should venerate the souls of the Dead to ease their own pain and the pain of those Souls, and that when death came they should not be afraid but go easily in the gloom and keep their eyes on the brilliant light of Life on Earth.

"I said most of these things because I simply didn't know what to say.

"Oh, blasphemy. I had done it, I had really done it. And now what would be my fate? I would grow old and die, a venerated teacher, and before I did—or before some pestilence or wild beast cut off my life sooner—I would engrave into stone and clay everything I could. And then into Sheol I would go, and I would begin to draw the souls to me, and I would say: 'Cry, cry to Heaven!' I would teach them to look upwards. I would say the Light is there!"

He took a breath, as if each word burnt him with pain.

I spoke again softly from the Book of Enoch. " 'And now, behold the souls of those who have died are crying and making suit to the gates of heaven.' "

"Yes, you know your scriptures like a good Devil," he said bitterly, but his face was so stricken with sadness and compassion, and this mockery was said with such feeling, that it had no sting. "And who knew what might happen?" he asked. "Who knew! Yes, yes, I would strengthen Sheol until those cries battered Heaven's gates and brought them down. If you have souls and your souls can grow, then you can be as angels! That was the only hope I had, to rule amongst the forgotten of God."

"But God didn't let this happen, did he? He didn't let you die in that body."

"No. And he didn't send the Flood either. And all that I had taught was not washed in a Deluge. What remained, what worked its way into myth and scripture was that I had been there, and that those things had been taught, and it was within the compass of a man to have done it; it was within logic, and not magic, and even the secrets of Heaven were what the souls would on their own perhaps have come to see. Sooner or later, the souls would have seen."

"But how did you get out of it? What happened to Lilia?"

"Lilia? Ah, Lilia. She died venerated, the wife of a god. Lilia." His whole face brightened and he laughed. "Lilia," he said again, memory lifting her out of the story and bringing her close, obviously. "My Lilia. Cast out, and casting her lot with a god."

"God had taken you by that time?" I asked. "He had put a stop to what you were doing?"

We gazed at each other for a moment. "Not quite so simple. I'd been there three months perhaps when I woke up and discovered Michael and Raphael had come for me, and said very distinctly: 'God wants you now.'

"And I being Memnoch, the unredeemable, said, 'Oh? Why then doesn't He pick me up and take me out of here, or do what He wishes?'

"At this point, Michael looked miserable on my behalf and he said, 'Memnoch, for the love of God, go willingly back into your proper form. Feel your body grow in stature; let your wings carry you to Heaven. He wants you only if you want to come! Now, Memnoch, think before you. . . .'

" 'No, you don't have to caution me, beloved,' I said to Michael. 'I'm coming, with tears in my eyes, I come.' I knelt down and kissed the sleeping Lilia. She looked up at me. 'This is farewell, my mate, my teacher,' I said. I kissed her, and then, turning, became the Angel, visible to her, letting the matter define me so that she, sitting up on her elbows and crying, would see this last vision and hold it to her heart perhaps when she needed it.

"And then, invisible, I joined Michael and Raphael and went Home.

"In the first moments I could scarce believe it; when I passed through Sheol, the souls screamed in agony and I threw my hands out in consolation. 'I will not forget you! I swear it. I take your suit to Heaven,' and then on and up I went, the light coming down to meet me and envelop me, and the warm love of God—whether prelude to judgment or punishment or forgiveness, I did not know—surrounded me and upheld me. The cries of joy in Heaven were deafening even to my ears.

"All the angels of the *bene ha elohim* were gathered. The Light of God pulsed from the center.

" 'Am I to be punished?' And all I could feel was thanks that I had seen this light, if only for moments, once again.

"I couldn't look into the light. I had to put my hands up. And as always happens at a meeting of all of Heaven, the Seraphim and the Cherubim closed around God so that the light came in rays from behind them, glorious, and a brightness that we could bear.

"The voice of God was immediate and total.

" 'I have a word for you, my brave one, my arrogant one,' He said. 'I have a concept for you to ponder in your angelic wisdom. It is the concept of Gehenna, of hell.' This word unfolded to me in all its implications. 'Fire and torment eternal,' said God, 'the inverse of Heaven. Tell me, Memnoch, from your heart. Would that be the appropriate punishment for you—the very opposite of the glory you forsook for the Daughters of Men? Would it be the appropriate sentence—suffering everlasting or until Time is no more?' "

14

"IT DIDN'T take a second to answer," Memnoch said. He raised his eyebrows slightly as he looked at me. "I said, 'No, Lord, you wouldn't do that to anyone. We are all your creatures. That is a horror too terrible for anyone or anything that has been deliberately made. No, Lord. When the men and the women of earth told me they had dreamed of such torments for those who had been bad and caused them pain and misery, I assured them no such place existed or ever would.'

"Laughter rang out in heaven. Laughter from one end of the skies to the other. Every single angel was laughing, and of course the laughing was melodic and filled with delight and wonder as always, but laughter it was, and not song.

"Only one being wasn't laughing. Memnoch. I. I stood there, having spoken with perfect seriousness and utter amazement that they were laughing at what I had said.

"But the strangest phenomenon had occurred. God, too, had laughed, and was laughing, softly, with them, in unison, or in a leading rhythm, and only as His laughter slowly died away, so did theirs.

" 'So you told them that, Memnoch. That there would never be a Hell of Eternal Punishment of the Bad; never; that such a place would never exist.'

" 'Yes, Lord, I did,' I said. 'I couldn't imagine why they had thought of it. Except they get so angry sometimes with their enemies. . . .'

"The laughter began again, but God silenced it.

"God said, 'Memnoch, have you left all your mortal cells on earth? You are in possession of all your angelic faculties? You are not still acting the simpleton out of habit?'

"I spoke loud over the continuing laughter. 'No, Lord. I dreamt of this moment. Separation from you was agony. I did what I did out of love, isn't it so? Surely you know better than I.'

" 'I fear you did,' He answered. 'It was love, yes, that much is true.'

" 'Lord, I dreamt you would let me come before you and explain the entire thing, make the case I had meant to make when I first saw a Daughter of Men and went to her. Is this to be granted?'

"Silence.

"I could hear nothing from the Divine Presence, but I realized suddenly that some among the *bene ha elohim* had drawn close to me. At first I thought no, they are merely shifting and spreading their wings in the light, but I realized now that close behind me stood a small legion or group of angels, and that they had been at the edges of the crowd all the time and were now being pushed towards me.

"These angels I knew of course, some much more intimately through debate and argument than others, and they came from all ranks. I looked at them in confusion and then towards the Divine Presence.

" 'Memnoch,' said the Lord suddenly. 'These behind you, your cohorts, are also asking that you be granted your wish, to make your case, in the hopes that you can make it for them too.'

" 'I don't understand, Lord.' But in a twinkling I did. I saw now the sorrow on their faces, and the way they cleaved to me as if I were their protector. I knew in an instant what had happened, that ranging over the whole earth, these angels had done as I had done.

" 'Not with such a flourish or with such invention,' said the Lord God. 'But they, too, saw the heat and mystery between the coupled man and woman; and they, too, found the Daughters of Men to be fair, and took them as wives.'

"There came again a great uproar. Some were laughing still in that light gay manner as if all of this was splendid and novel entertainment and others were amazed, and those Watchers who clung to me, who seemed in comparison to the *bene ha elohim* a small number, looked to me desperately, and some even accusingly, and there came a whisper from their midst.

" 'Memnoch, we saw you do it.'

"Was God laughing? I couldn't hear it. The light poured out in its immense rays beyond the heads and shoulders and shaded forms of the Seraphim and Cherubim, and the wealth of love seemed eternal and constant as it had always been.

" 'In tribes throughout the world, my Sons of Heaven have gone down to know the flesh as you would know it, Memnoch, though as I have already said, with far less flair and desire to stir the thick atmosphere of Nature and so deliberately disturb my Divine Plan.'

" 'Lord, God, forgive me,' I whispered. And from the legion with me came the same hushed and respectful chorus.

" 'But tell me, you who stand behind Memnoch, what do you have to say for yourselves as to why you did this and what you discovered, and what case would you put before the Heavenly Court?'

"The answer was silence. These angels fell prostrate before the Lord, asking only forgiveness with such total abandon that no eloquence was required. I alone stood there.

" 'Ah,' I said, 'it seems, Lord, that I stand alone.'

" 'Haven't you always? My Son of Heaven, my angel who does not trust the Lord.'

" 'Lord, God, I do trust you!' I said at once, angry suddenly. 'I do! But I don't understand these things, and I cannot still my mind or my personality, it's impossible for me. No, not impossible, but it does not . . . it does not seem right to be silent. It seems right to make the case. It seems that the greatest thing I can do is to make the case, and the greatest thing I can do is to please God.'

"There seemed great divisions amongst the others—not the Watchers, who didn't dare to climb to their invisible feet, and had their wings folded over them as if they were birds afraid in the nest— but among the entire Court. There were murmurings, and little songs, and riffs of melody and laughter, and deep, soft questions, and many faces turned on me with eyes full of curiosity and even tinged with anger so that their eyebrows made a scowl.

" 'Make your case!' said the Lord. 'But before you begin, remind yourself, for my sake and the sake of everyone present, that I know all things. I know humankind as you can never know it. I have seen its bloody altars, and its rain dances, and its reeking sacrifices, and I have heard the cries of the wounded, the afflicted, the slowly annihilated. I see Nature in Humankind as I see it in the savagery of the seas or the forests. Don't waste my Time, Memnoch. Or to put it more clearly so that you will understand it, don't waste the Time you have with me.'

"So the moment had come. I stood quietly preparing myself. Never in all my existence had I felt the importance or significance of an event as I felt the meaning of this one now. It is what you would call excitement, perhaps, or exhilaration. I had my audience. And I did not know how to doubt myself! But I was already furious with all the legion behind me lying on their faces and saying nothing! And suddenly in my fury I realized that as long as they lay there, leaving me alone in the open before God and his court, I wasn't going to speak a word. I folded my arms and stood there.

"God started to laugh, a slow, gentle rising laugh, and then all of

Heaven joined in it irresistibly. And God said to the Fallen ones, the Watchers, 'Stand up, my sons, or we will all be here until the End of Time.'

" 'Mockery, Lord, I deserve it,' I said. 'But I thank you.'

"In a great shuffling of wings and gowns, I heard them rising behind me to stand at least as tall and as straight as brave humans could stand on the earth below.

" 'Lord, my case is simple,' I said, 'but surely you cannot ignore it. And I shall state it as simply and as finely as I can.

" 'Up until a point in his development, the primate below was part of Nature, and bound by all its laws. And with his larger brain, he grew ever more cunning, and his battles with other animals became as fierce and bloody as the Heavenly Court has ever seen. This is all true. And with this intelligence there came also an increase in the ways and means that Humankind could inflict upon its own great pain.

" 'But never in all that I have Watched in war, and execution, and even the laying waste of whole settlements and villages have I seen anything to surpass the sheer violence of the insect Kingdom or the Kingdom of the Reptiles, or of the Lower Mammals, who blindly and senselessly struggle to do only two things—survive and make more of their own kind.'

"I stopped, out of courtesy and also for effect. The Lord said nothing. I went on.

" 'Then there came a point, however, when these primates, who had, by then, come to strongly resemble Your Own Image as we perceive it in Ourselves, diverged from the rest of Nature, in a marked way. And it was no mere moment of Self Awareness, Lord, when the logic of Life and Death became apparent to them. It was nothing as simple as that. On the contrary, the Self Awareness grew from a new and totally unnatural capacity to love.

" 'And it was then that humankind broke itself into tight families and clans and tribes, bound together by intimate knowledge of the individuality of each other, rather than sheer recognition of species, and were held together, through suffering and happiness, by the bond of love.

" 'Lord, the human family is beyond Nature. If you were to go down and—'

" 'Memnoch, take care!' God whispered.

" 'Yes, Lord,' I said, nodding, and clasped my hands behind me so as not to make ferocious gestures. 'What I should have said was that when I went down and I looked into the family, here and there and all over the World which you have Created, which you have allowed to unfold magnificently, I saw the family as a new and unprecedented flower, Lord, a blossom of emotion and intellect that in its tenderness was cut loose from the stems of Nature from which it had taken its nourishment, and was now at the mercy of the wind. Love, Lord, I saw it, I felt Love of Men and Women for one another and for their Children, and the willingness to sacrifice for one another, and to grieve for those who were dead, and to seek for their souls in the hereafter, and to think, Lord, of a hereafter where they might be reconciled with those souls again.

" 'It was out of this love and the family, it was out of this rare and unprecedented bloom—so Creative, Lord, that it seemed in your Image of your Creations—that the souls of these beings remained alive after death! What else in Nature can do this, Lord? All gives back to the Earth what it has taken. Your Wisdom is Manifest throughout; and all those that suffer and die beneath the canopy of your heavens are mercifully bathed in brutal ignorance of the scheme which ultimately involved their own deaths.

" 'Man, not so! Woman, not so! And in their hearts, loving one another as they do, mate with mate, and family with family, they have imagined Heaven, Lord. They have imagined it; the time of the reunion of souls when their kin will be restored to them and to each other, and all will sing in bliss! They have imagined eternity because their love demands it, Lord. They have conceived of these ideas as they conceive of fleshly children! This I, the Watcher, have seen.'

"Another silence. All of heaven was so still that the only sounds came from the earth below, the purring of the wind, and the dim stirring of the seas, and the cries, the pale faraway cries of souls on earth as well as souls in Sheol.

" 'Lord,' I said, 'they long for Heaven. And imagining eternity, or immortality, I know not which, they suffer injustice, separation, disease, and death, as no other animal could possibly suffer it. And their souls are great. And in Sheol they reach out beyond the love of self and the service of self in the name of Love. Love goes back and forth between Earth and Sheol eternally. Lord, they have made a lower tier of the invisible court! Lord, they seek to propitiate your wrath, be-

cause they know You are Here! And Lord, they want to know everything about You. And about themselves. They know and they want to
know!'

"This was the heart of my case, and I knew it. But again, there
came from God no response or interruption.

" 'I couldn't see this,' I said, 'as anything less than Your greatest
accomplishment, the self-aware human, conceiving of Time, with a
brain vast enough already for learning that is coming so fast we
Watchers could scarce keep track of all of it. But the suffering, the
torment, the curiosity—it was a lamentation seemingly made for the
ears of Angels, and of God, if I may dare to say.

" 'The case I came to make was, Lord, can these souls, either in
the flesh, or in Sheol, not be given some part of our light? Can they
not be given Light as animals are given water when they thirst? And
will not these souls, once taken into Divine Confidence, be worthy
perhaps to take some small place in this Court which is without End?'

"The quiet seemed dreamy and eternal, like the Time before
Time.

" 'Could it be tried, Lord? For if it is not tried, what is to be the
fate of these invisible surviving souls except to grow stronger and
more entangled with the flesh in ways that give rise not to revelations
of the true Nature of things, but corrupted ideas based on fragmentary evidence and instinctive fear?'

"This time, I gave up on the idea of a polite pause and immediately forged ahead.

" 'Lord, when I went into the flesh; when I went with the woman,
it was because she was fair, yes, and resembled us, and offered a species of pleasure in the flesh which to us is unknown. Granted, Lord,
that pleasure is immeasurably small compared to your magnificence,
but Lord, I tell you, in the moment when I lay with her, and she with
me, and we knew that pleasure together, that small flame did roar
with a sound very like the songs of the Most High!

" 'Our hearts stopped together, Lord. We knew in the flesh eternity, the man in me knew that the woman knew it. We knew something that rises above all earthly expectations, something that is
purely Divine.'

"I fell silent. What more could I say? I would be embroidering my
case with examples, for Someone Who knew all things. I folded my
arms and looked down, respectfully, musing and listening to the souls

in Sheol, and for one second their faint faraway cries distracted me, drew me right out of the heavenly presence for an instant of realization that they were calling on me and reminding me of my promise and hoping for my return.

" 'Lord God, forgive me,' I said. 'Your wonders have snared me. And I am wrong if that was not your plan.'

"Once again the silence was thunderous and soft and utterly empty. It was an emptiness of which those on Earth cannot conceive. I stood my ground because I could do nothing but what I had done, and I felt in my heart that every word I'd spoken had been true and untainted by fear. It occurred to me very clearly that if the Lord threw me out of Heaven, that whatever He did, really, I would deserve it. I was His Created Angel, and His to Command. And His to destroy if He wished it. And once again, I heard the cries of Sheol in my memory, and I wondered, as a human might, if He would send me there soon or do something far more fearful, for in Nature there were countless examples of excruciating destruction and catastrophe, and I as an Angel could be made by God to suffer whatever He wanted me to suffer, I knew.

" 'I trust in you, Lord,' I said suddenly, thinking and speaking simultaneously. 'Or else I would have fallen on my face as have the other Watchers. And that is not to say that they do not trust. But only to say that I believe you want me to understand Goodness, that your essence is Goodness, and you will not suffer these souls to cry in gloom and ignorance. You will not suffer the ingenious Humankind to continue without any inkling of the Divine.'

"For the first time, he spoke very softly and offhandedly.

" 'Memnoch, you've given them more than an inkling.'

" 'Yes, Lord, it is so. But Lord, the souls of the dead have given them much inspiration, and encouragement, and those souls are out of Nature, as we have beheld it, and growing stronger by the day. If there is a species of energy, Lord, natural and complicated beyond my understanding, then I am totally taken by surprise. For it seems they are made of what we are made of, Lord, the invisible, and each is individual and has its own will.'

"Silence again. Then the Lord spoke:

" 'Very well. I have heard your case. Now I have for you a question. For all that you gave Humankind, Memnoch, what precisely did they give you?'

"I was startled by the question.

" 'And don't speak to me of love now, Memnoch,' He added. 'Of their capacity to love one another. On this the Heavenly Court is well informed and totally agreed. But what did they give you, Memnoch? What did you get in return for the risks you took by entering into their realm?'

" 'Confirmation, Lord,' I said hastily, reaching for the deepest truth without distortion. 'They knew an Angel when they saw one. Just as I supposed they would.'

" 'Ah!' A great roar of laughter came from the Heavenly Throne and once again it swept up Heaven, so loud I'm sure that it must have reached the weak and struggling ears of Sheol. The Whole Heavens were rocking with laughing and singing.

"At first I didn't dare to speak or do anything, and then suddenly, angrily perhaps, or should I say, willfully, I raised my hand. 'But I mean this in all seriousness, Lord! I was not some being beyond their dreams! Lord, did you plant the seed for this when you Created the Universe, that these beings would raise their voices to you? Will you tell me? One way or the other, can I know?'

"The angels quieted down in little groups and pockets at first and then the laughter tapered off altogether, and something else replaced it, a soft singing of tribute to God in his patience, a soft acknowledgment of his patience with me.

"I didn't join in this song. I looked to the great outer stretches of the rays of Light that came from God, and the mystery of my own stubbornness and my own anger and my own curiosity subdued me somewhat, but did not throw me for one second into despair.

" 'I trust in you, Lord. You know what you're doing. You have to. Otherwise we are . . . lost.'

"I broke off, stunned at what I had just said. It far exceeded any challenge I'd thrown at God so far, it far exceeded any suggestion that I had made. And in horror, I looked at the Light, and thought, What if He doesn't know what He's doing and never has!

"My hands went to my face to stop my lips from saying something rash and thereby tell my brain to stop with its rash and blasphemous thoughts. I knew God! God was There. And I stood before Him. How dare I think such a thing, and yet He had said, 'You do not trust me,' and that was exactly what He had meant.

"It seemed the Light of God grew infinitely brighter; it expanded;

the shapes of the Seraphim and Cherubim grew small and utterly transparent, and the light filled me and filled the recesses of all angels, and I felt in communion with them that all of us were so totally loved by God that we could never long for or imagine anything more.

"Then the Lord spoke, the words wholly different now, for they competed with this effulgence of Love which overpowered the thinking mind. Nevertheless, I heard them and they penetrated to my heart.

"And everyone else heard them too.

" 'Memnoch, go into Sheol,' He said, 'and find there but ten souls who are worthy, of all those millions, to join us in Heaven. Say what you will to them as you examine them; but find Ten whom you believe are worthy to live with us. Then bring those souls back to me, and we will continue from there on.'

"I was ecstatic. 'Lord, I can do it, I know I can!' I cried out.

"And suddenly I saw the faces of Michael and Raphael and Uriel, who had been almost obscured by the light of God, which was now receding within more endurable bounds. Michael looked frightened for me and Raphael was weeping. Uriel seemed merely to watch, without emotion, neither on my side or for me, or for the souls, or for anyone. It was the face that Angels used to have before Time began.

" 'I can go now?' I said. 'And when must I return?'

" 'When you will,' said the Lord, 'and when you can.'

"Ah, I understood it. If I didn't find those ten souls I wasn't coming back.

"I nodded, lovely logic. I understood it. I accepted it.

" 'Years pass on Earth as we speak, Memnoch. Your settlement and those visited by others have grown into cities; the world spins in the Light of Heaven. What can I say to you, my beloved one, except that you should go now to Sheol and return with those Ten Souls as soon as you possibly can.'

"I was about to speak, to ask, What of the Watchers, this little legion of meek, flesh-educated angels behind me, when the Lord answered.

" 'They will wait in the proper place in Heaven for your return. They will not know my decision, nor their fate, until you bring these souls to me, Memnoch, souls that I shall find worthy to be in my Heavenly Home.'

" 'I understand, Lord, I'm leaving with your permission!'

"And asking nothing further, broaching no questions as to restrictions or limitations, I, Memnoch, the Archangel and the Accuser of God, left Heaven immediately and descended into the great airy mists of Sheol."

15

BUT, MEMNOCH," I interrupted. "He gave you no criteria! How were you to evaluate these souls? How could you know?"

Memnoch smiled. "Yes, Lestat, that's exactly what He did and how He did it, and believe me, I knew, and no sooner had I entered Sheol than the question of the Criteria for Entrance into Heaven became my full focus and desperate obsession. It is exactly the way He does things, no?"

"I would have asked," I said.

"No, no. I had no intention of it. I got out of there and started to work! As I said, this was His way and I knew that my only hope was to come up with a Criterion of my own and make a case for it, don't you see?"

"I think I do."

"You know you do," he said. "All right. Picture this. The population of the world has swelled to millions, and cities have risen though not in very many places, and mostly in that very valley where I had descended and left my marks on the walls of caves. Humankind had wandered north and south as far as it could on the planet; settlements and towns and forts existed in various stages of development. The land of the cities is called Mesopotamia now, I think, or is it Sumer, or will it be Ur? Your scholars uncover more with every passing day.

"Man's wild imaginings of immortality and reunion with the dead had everywhere given rise to religion. In the Nile Valley, a civilization of astonishing stability had developed, while war was waged all the time in the land we call the Holy Land.

"So I come to Sheol, which I have only observed from outside before, and which is now enormous, containing still some of the first souls that ever sputtered with enduring life, and now millions of souls whose creeds and yearnings for the eternal have brought them to this place with great ferocity. Mad expectations have pitched countless ones into confusion. Others have grown so strong they exert a sort of rulership amongst the others. And some have learnt the trick of going down to Earth, escaping from the pull of other invisible souls altogether, and for wandering close to the flesh they would possess again, or influence, or harm, or love as the case might be.

"The world is populated by spirits! And some, having no memory anymore at all of being human, have become what men and women will for eternity call demons, prowling about, eager to possess, wreak havoc, or make mischief, as their developments allow."

"And one of those," I said, "passed into the vampiric mother and father of our kind."

"Yes, precisely. Amel created that mutation. But it was not the only one. There are other monsters on earth, existing twixt the visible and the invisible; but the great thrust of the world was and always has been the fate of its millions of Humankind."

"The mutations have never influenced history."

"Well, yes, and no. Is a mad soul screaming from the mouth of a flesh-and-blood prophet an influence, if this prophet's words are recorded in five different languages and for sale today on the shelves of stores in New York? Let's say that the process which I had seen and described to God had continued; some souls died; some grew strong; some managed to actually return in new bodies, though by what knack I did not at that time know."

"Do you know now?"

"Reincarnation isn't by any stretch common. Don't think of it. And it gains very little for the souls involved. You can imagine the situations that make it possible. Whether it always involves the extinction of an infant soul when it happens—that is, whether it always involves a replacement in the new body—this varies with individual cases. Those who persistently reincarnate are certainly something that cannot be ignored. But that, like the evolution of vampires and other earthbound immortals, falls into a small realm. Once again, we are talking now about the fate of Humankind as a whole. We are talking about the Whole Human World."

"Yes, I really do understand, perhaps better than you know."

"All right. I have no criteria, but I go into Sheol and I find there a great sprawling replica of earth! Souls have imagined and projected into their invisible existence all manner of jumbled buildings and creatures and monsters; it is a riot of imagination without Heavenly guidance, and as I suspected, there is still an enormous majority of souls who don't know that they are dead.

"Now, I plunge into the very middle of this, trying to make myself as invisible as I possibly can; to conceive of myself as utterly without any discernible form; but this is hard. For this is a realm of the invisible; everything here is invisible. And so there I begin to wander on the dreary roads in semidarkness, among the malformed, the half-formed, the unformed, the moaning and dying, and I am in my angelic form.

"Nevertheless, these confused souls don't take very much notice of me! It's as if many can't see clearly at all. Now, you know this state has been described by human shamans, by saints, by those who have come close to death, passed through it, and then been revived and continued to live."

"Yes."

"Well, what human souls see of this is a fragment. I saw the whole. I roamed extensively and fearlessly and regardless of Time, or out of it, though Time always continues to pass, of course, and I went where I chose."

"A madhouse of souls."

"Very nearly, but within this great madhouse were many, many mansions, to use the Scriptural words. Souls believing in like faiths had come together in desperation and sought to reinforce each other's beliefs and still each other's fears. But the light of Earth was too dim to warm anyone here! And the Light of Heaven simply did not penetrate at all.

"So yes, you are right, a madhouse of sorts, the Valley of the Shadow of Death, the terrible river of monsters over which souls dread to cross to Paradise. And of course, none had ever crossed up to that point.

"The first thing I did was listen: I listened to the song of any soul who would sing to me, that is, speak, in my language; I caught up any coherent declaration or question or supposition that struck my ears. What did these souls know? What had become of them?

"And in short order I discovered that there were tiers to this awful, gloom-filled place, tiers created out of the will of souls to seek others like themselves. The place had become stratified, rather loosely and grimly, but there was an order born out of the degree of of each soul's awareness, acceptance, confusion, or wrath.

"Closest to earth lay the damnedest, those who kept struggling to eat or drink or possess others, or could not accept what had happened or did not understand.

"Just beyond them came a layer of souls who did nothing but fight each other, scream, yell, push, shove, strive to harm or overcome or invade or escape in hopeless confusion. These souls never even saw me. But again, your humans have seen this and described it in many, many manuscripts over the centuries. Nothing I say surely is a surprise.

"And farther from this struggle, nearest to the calm of Heaven— though I don't speak really of literal directions here—were those who had come to understand that they had passed out of Nature, and were somewhere else. And these souls, some of them having been there since the Beginning, had grown patient in their attitudes, and patient in their watching of Earth, and patient with others around them, whom they sought to help in Love to accept their death."

"You found the souls who loved."

"Oh, they all love," Memnoch said. "All of them. There is no such thing as a soul who loves nothing. He or she loves something, even if it exists only in memory or as an ideal. But yes, I found those most peacefully and serenely expressing love in immense amounts to one another, and to the living below. Some I found who had turned their eyes entirely to earth, and sought nothing but to answer the prayers that rose from the desperate, the needy, and the sick.

"And Earth by this time, as you know, had seen wars unspeakable, and whole civilizations dissolved by volcanic disaster. The variety and possibilities of suffering increased all the time. It wasn't only in proportion to learning, either, or cultural development. It had become a scheme beyond an angel's comprehension. When I looked at Earth, I didn't even try to figure out what ruled the passions of those in one jungle as opposed to the groups in another, or why one population spent generations piling stones upon stones. I knew, of course, more or less everything, but I was not now on an earthly mission.

"The dead had become my realm.

"I drew near to these souls who looked down with mercy and

compassion, who sought by thought to influence others for the good. Ten, twenty, thirty, I saw thousands. Thousands, I tell you, in whom all hope of rebirth or great reward was gone; souls in which existed total acceptance; that this was death; this was eternity; souls enamored with the flesh and blood they could see just as we Angels had been enamored and still were.

"I sat amongst these souls and started to talk with them, here and there, where I could get their attention, and it soon became obvious that they were rather indifferent to my form, because they assumed that I had chosen it as they had chosen theirs, and some of them resembled men and women, and some didn't bother. So I suspect they actually thought me rather new to Sheol in that I had to make such ferocious displays with arms and legs and wings. But they could be distracted from earth, if approached very politely, and I began to question them, remembering to strike for the truth only, but not to be rude.

"I must have talked to millions. I roamed Sheol, talking to souls. And the hardest thing in each instance was to get the attention of the individual either off the earth, or off some phantasm of lost existence, or out of a state of airy contemplation in which concentration was now so alien and required such an effort that it couldn't be induced.

"The wisest, the most loving souls did not want to bother with my questions. And only gradually would they realize that I was not a mortal man but something of much different substance, and that there was a point to my questions that had to do with a place of reference beyond Earth. You see, this was the dilemma. They had been in Sheol so long that they no longer speculated about the reason for Life or Creation; they no longer cursed a God they didn't know, or sought a God who hid from them. And when I began to ask my questions, they thought I was way down there with the new souls, dreaming of punishments and rewards which were never to come.

"These wise souls contemplated their past lives in a long wrathless reverie, and sought to answer prayers from below as I have said. They watched over their kindred, their clansmen, their own nations; they watched over those who attracted their attention with accomplished and spectacular displays of religiosity; they watched with sadness the suffering of humans and wished they could help and tried to help by thought when they could.

"Almost none of these very strong and patient souls sought the flesh again. But some of them had in the past. They had gone down and been reborn and discovered in the final analysis that they could not remember from one fleshly life to another, so there was no real reason to keep being born! Better to linger here, in the eternity that was known to them, and to watch the Beauty of Creation, and it did seem very beautiful to them, as it had seemed to us.

"Well, it was out of these questions, these endless and thoughtful conversations with the dead, that my criteria evolved.

"First, to be worthy of Heaven—to have a ghost of a chance with God, I could say—the Soul had to understand life and death in the simplest sense. I found many souls who did. Next there had to be in this understanding an appreciation of the Beauty of God's work, the harmony of Creation from God's point of view, a vision of Nature wrapped in endless and overlapping cycles of survival and reproduction and evolution and growth.

"Many souls had come to understand this. Many had. But many who thought life was beautiful, felt that death was sad and endless and terrible and they would have chosen never to have been born, had they been given the choice!

"I didn't know what to do in the face of that conviction, but it was very widespread. Why did He make us, Whoever He is, if we are to be here like this forever, out of it and never part of it again, unless we wish to dip down and suffer all that torment all over again, for a few moments of glory, which we won't appreciate any more next time than last time, because we can't take our knowledge with us if we are reborn!

"Indeed, it was at this point which many souls had ceased to develop or change. They felt great concern and mercy for those who were alive, but they knew sorrow, and joy was not something that they could even imagine anymore. They moved towards peace; and peace indeed seemed about the finest state which they could achieve. Peace, broken by the struggle to answer prayers, was particularly difficult, but to me, as an angel, very attractive. And I stayed in the company of these souls for a long, long time.

"Now, if I could only tell them, I thought, if I could begin to instruct them, maybe I could bring them around, prepare them, make them ready for Heaven, but in this state they are not ready, and I don't know if they will believe what I say. And what if they do believe and are filled suddenly with the hunger for Heaven and then God doesn't let them in.

"No, I had to be very careful. I could not proclaim knowledge from atop boulders as I had done in my short time on earth. If I was to intrude on the progress of one of these dead ones, there had to be a very good chance that that soul would follow me to God's Throne.

"Understanding of life and death? That wasn't enough. Acceptance of death? That wasn't enough. Indifference to life and death, that wasn't good enough surely. Quiet confusion and drifting. No. That sort of soul had lost its character. It was as far from an Angel as was the rain that fell on Earth.

"At last I came into a region smaller than the others, and peopled with only a few souls. Now I speak comparatively. Remember, I'm the Devil. I spend a lot of time in Heaven and Hell. So when I say a few, that is to make a picture that is manageable to your mind. For the sake of exposition, let's say a few thousand or more. But I speak of great numbers. Don't doubt."

"I follow you."

"And these souls absolutely astonished me by their radiance, their tranquility, and the degrees of knowledge which they had attained and retained. First of all, almost every one of them had a full human shape. That is, they had realized their original forms or perhaps ideal forms in the invisible. They looked like angels! They were invisible men, women, and children, and they had about them accoutrements that had been dear in life. Some of them were brand new and had come from death thoughtful and seeking and ready for the mysterious. Others had learned all in Sheol over centuries of watching and fearing to lose their individuality, no matter how terrible things did appear. But all were intensely visible! And anthropomorphic, though of course they were diaphanous, as all spirits are; and some were paler than others; but all essentially could be seen clearly by others and themselves.

"I went amongst them, expecting to be snubbed, but I realized immediately that these souls saw me differently than the others. They saw everything differently. They were more attuned to the subtleties of the invisible because they had accepted its conditions totally. If I wished to be what I was, let me be it, they thought, and they judged me very seriously on how well I succeeded in being this tall creature, winged and longhaired and dressed in flowing robes. Within moments of my arrival, I felt happiness around me. I felt acceptance. I felt a total lack of resistance and a daring curiosity. They knew I was not a human soul. They knew because they had reached a point where they could see this! They could see a lot about every other soul they looked at. And they could see a great deal of the world below.

"One of these souls was in the shape of a woman, and it was not my Lilia at all, by the way, for I never did see her in any form again. But it was a woman who had died I think in midlife having had numerous children, some of whom were with her now, and some of whom were still below. This soul existed in a serenity that was almost becoming bright. That is, its evolution was so high on the invisible level that it was beginning to generate something like the Light of God!

" 'What makes you so different?' I asked this woman. 'What makes all of you here, clustered together in this place, so very different?'

"With an acuity that astonished me, this woman asked me who I was. Dead souls just usually don't ask that question. They plunge right into their helpless preoccupations and obsessions. But she said, 'Who are you and what are you? I have never seen one like you before here. Only when I was alive.'

" 'I don't want to tell you yet,' I said. 'But I want to learn from you. Will you tell me why you seem happy? You are happy, aren't you?'

" 'Yes,' she said, 'I'm with those I love, and look below, look at all of it.'

" 'Then you harbour no questions about all of it?' I pushed. 'You don't long to know why you were born or why you suffered or what happened to you when you died or why you're here?'

"To my further amazement, she laughed. Laughter I had never heard in Sheol. It was soft, soothing, merry laughter, sweet laughter, laughter like the laughter of angels, and I think I sang to her softly in response, rather naturally, and at this her soul exploded like a blossom, the way fleshly souls had exploded below when they had learnt to love each other! She warmed to me and opened. 'You are beautiful,' she whispered respectfully.

" 'But why, why are all these others in this place so unhappy, and why are you few here filled with peace and joy? Yes, I know, I have looked below. And you are with those you love. But so are all these others.'

" 'We don't resent God anymore,' she said. 'Any of us here. We don't hate Him.'

" 'The others do?'

" 'It's not that they hate Him,' she said gently, being very careful with me, as if I were easy to bruise. 'It's that they can't forgive Him for all this . . . for the world, for what's happened, and for this state of Sheol in which we languish. But we can. We have forgiven Him. And all of us have done it for various reasons, but forgiveness of God, that we have attained. We accept that our lives have been wondrous experiences, and worth the pain and the suffering, and we cherish now the joy we knew, and the moments of harmony, and we have forgiven Him for not ever explaining it all to us, for not justifying it, not punishing the bad or rewarding the good, or whatever else it is that all these souls, living and dead, expect of Him. We forgive Him. We don't know, but we suspect that maybe He knows a great secret about how all this pain could come to pass and still be good. And if He doesn't want to tell, well, He is God. But whatever, we forgive Him and we Love Him in our forgiveness, even though we know He may never care about any of us, any more than He cares for the pebbles on a beach below.'

"I was speechless. I sat very still, letting these souls of their own volition gather around me. Then one very young soul, the soul of a child, said:

" 'It seemed a terrible thing at first that God would bring us into the world to be murdered as we were, all of us—for you see, we three here died in war—but we have forgiven Him, because we know that if He could make something as beautiful as Life and Death, then he must Understand.'

" 'You see,' said another soul to me, 'it comes to this. We would suffer it all again, if we had to. And we would try to be better to each other and more loving. But it was worth it.'

" 'Yes,' said another. 'It took me all my life on Earth to Forgive God for the world, but I did it before I died, and came to dwell here with these others. And look, if you try hard, you'll see that we have made this something of a garden. It's hard for us. We work only with our minds and wills and memories, and imaginations, but we are making a place where we can remember what was good. And we forgive Him and we love Him that He gave us this much.'

" 'Yes,' said another, 'that He gave us anything at all. We are grateful and full of love for Him. For surely out there in the darkness is a great Nothing, and we have seen so many below who were obsessed with Nothing and with Misery, and they never knew the joys that we knew or know now.'

" 'This isn't easy,' said another soul. 'It's been a great struggle. But to make love was good, and to drink was good, and to dance and sing was beautiful, and to run drunk through the rain was joyous; and beyond there lies a chaos, an absence, and I am grateful that my eyes opened upon the world below and that I can remember it and see it from here.'

"I thought for a long time without answering any of them, and they continued to talk to me, drawn to me, as if the light in me, if there was any visible light, was attracting them. In fact, the more I responded to their questions, the more they opened and seemed to understand their own answers more meaningfully, the denser and more intense the declarations became.

"I soon saw these people had come from all nations and all walks of life. And though kinship bound many of them tightly together, that was not true with them all. In fact, many had lost sight of their dead kin entirely in other realms of Sheol. Others had never even laid eyes on them. While some had been greeted at the moment of death by their lost ones! And these were people of the world and all its beliefs gathered here in this place where light was beginning to shine forth.

" 'Your lives on earth, was there one common thread?' I asked finally. They couldn't answer. They really didn't know. They had not questioned each other about their lives, and as I asked them quick, random questions, it became clear that there had been no thread! Some of these people had been very rich, others poor, some had suffered unspeakably, some had suffered nothing but had known a golden prosperity and leisure in which they had grown to love Creation before they were even dead. But I began to sense that if I wanted to, I could start to count these responses and evaluate them in some way. In other words, all these souls had learnt to forgive God in various ways. But very possibly one way was better for this than another, infinitely more efficient. Perhaps. I couldn't be sure. And for now I couldn't know.

"I wrapped my arms around these souls. I drew them to me. 'I want you to come on a journey with me,' I said to them, having spoken now to each and every one and being completely certain of where we stood. 'I want you to come to Heaven and stand before God. Now it may be brief, and you may see Him for no more than an instant, and possibly He will not allow Himself to be seen by you at all. You may find yourselves returned here, having learnt nothing, but also having suffered nothing. The truth is, I can't guarantee what will happen! No one knows God.

" 'We know,' they answered.

" 'But I invite you to come to God and tell Him what you've told me. And now I'll answer your question to me: I am his Archangel Memnoch, of the very mold of other Angels of whom you heard when you were alive! Will you come?'

"Several were astonished and hesitated. But the majority said in one voice, a mingling of answers that was this answer: 'We will come. One glimpse of God, the chance of it even, is worth anything. If that's not so then I don't remember the smell of the sweet olive tree, or how the fresh grass felt beneath me when I laid on it. I never tasted wine, and I never bedded the ones I loved. We will come.'

"Several refused. It took a few moments before we all realized it but several had totally withdrawn. They saw me now for what I was, an Angel, and they understood what had been withheld from them, and they had lost their peace and lost their power to forgive in that instant. They stared at me in horror or anger or both. The other souls hastened to change their minds, but they wouldn't be changed. No, they did not want to see this God who had deserted His Creation and left it to rear up gods on altars all over the planet and pray in vain for intervention or final judgment! No, no, no!

" 'Come,' I said to the others, 'Let's try to enter Heaven. Let's give it all our strength! How many are we? A thousand times ten? A million? What does it matter? God said ten but not ten only. God meant at least ten. Come, let's go!' "

16

IN A FLASH, I shall have my answer, I thought. He will either admit us or cast us back down with His Might the way He once threw me to Earth. He might even dissolve the lot of us, for surely He can make His judgment on my success or failure before I ever reach the gates of Heaven. What had He said in His Infinite Wisdom? He had said, 'Come back as soon as you *can*.'

"I drew these souls to me, tight as I drew you when I took you upwards, and out of Sheol we rose, into the full blasting light of Heaven as it came pouring over the walls and the gates. And once again, those gates, which I had never seen in my early eons, were thrown open, and we found ourselves, one Archangel and a few million human souls, standing once more in the very midst of Heaven before amazed and laughing and pointing and startled and flabbergasted angels who gathered around us in a great circle, crying to get the attention of everyone until Heaven finally fell quiet.

"Well, I thought, so far so good. We're inside. And the human souls! The human souls could see the angels and the human souls were overjoyed. Oh, I can't even remember this moment without dancing. I can't remember it without singing. The souls were jubilant, and when the angels began their great potentially cacophonous singing of questions and exclamations, the human souls began to sing!

"Indeed, Heaven was never going to be the same. I knew it. I knew it instantly. Because this is what took place. These souls brought with them the same powers of projection which they had learnt in Sheol, that is to create around them out of the invisible something of an environment that they wanted, longed for, and to which they were able to give their full wills.

"And the geography of Heaven was changed dramatically and instantly and in an infinite capacity. There rose the towers and castles and mansions which you saw when I took you there, the domed palaces and libraries, and the gardens, oh, the breathtaking projections of flowers in all directions, things that angels simply never thought to bring to Heaven . . . well, it was all there. Trees rose in their mature fullness; rain came in whispering gusts, full of fragrance. The sky warmed and colors everywhere expanded or deepened. These souls took the invisible fabric of Heaven, whatever it is—energy, essence, the light of God, the Creative Power of God—and in a twinkling surrounded us all with wondrous constructions representing their curiosity, their concepts of beauty and their desires!

"All that they had learnt on Earth they had brought into Heaven, creating it irresistibly in its most cherished form!

"The commotion was beyond anything I had ever witnessed since the Creation of the Universe itself.

"And nobody appeared more astonished than the Archangel Michael, who was staring at me as if to say, 'Memnoch, you've brought them into Heaven!'

"But before he could get those words out, and as the souls still stood together, only beginning to realize that they could shift and touch the angels and touch the things they envisioned, there came the light of God Himself—*En Sof*—rising and spreading out from behind the figures of the Seraphim and Cherubim, and very gently and considerately falling down upon these human souls, filling each and laying all secrets of each totally open, as angels are open.

"The human souls cried with joy. Anthems rose from the Angels. I began to sing with my arms outstretched, 'Lord, Lord, I have your souls, worthy of Heaven, and look what they have brought to Heaven, Lord, look on your Creation, look on the Souls of those you evolved from the tiniest cells through flesh and blood and Sheol to your very Throne. Lord, we are here! Lord, it's done, it's done. It's happened. I have come back and you have allowed it.'

"And having said more than enough, I fell down on my knees.

"The songs had reached a frenzy, a sound no flesh-and-blood human could endure. Anthems rose from all quarters. The human souls were growing denser, more visible, until they appeared as clearly to us as we did to them and to each other. Some of them were locking hands and jumping up and down like little children. Others were merely crying and screaming and the tears were flooding down their faces.

"And then the light swelled. We knew God was about to speak. We fell silent, en masse. We were all the *bene ha elohim*. And God said:

" 'My Children. My beloved Children. Memnoch stands with his Millions, and they are worthy of Heaven.'

"And the voice of God ceased, and the light grew stronger and warmer, and all of Heaven became pure acceptance and pure love.

"I lay down upon the floor of Heaven in weariness, staring upwards into the great firmament of beautiful blue sky and ever-twinkling stars. I heard the souls of the humans rushing hither and thither. I heard the welcoming hymns and incantations of the angels. I heard everything, and then, in imitation of a mortal, I closed my eyes.

"Did God ever sleep? I don't know. I closed my eyes, and I lay still in the Light of God, and after all those years and years in Sheol I was safe again, and I was warm.

"Finally, I realized that the Seraphim had come to me, three or four of them, I didn't really notice, and they were standing over me, and looking down on me, their faces almost unendurably bright with reflected light.

" 'Memnoch, God wants to speak to you alone,' they said.

" 'Yes, at once!' I sprang to my feet.

"And far from the jubilant throngs, I found myself standing in silence, in quiet, without companions, my arm up over my eyes, my eyes down, and near as I could possibly be to the presence of the Lord."

17

UNCOVER your eyes and look at me,' said the Lord.

"Instantly, aware that this might mean my total obliteration, that all might have been folly and misunderstanding, I obeyed.

"The radiance had become uniform, glorious yet tolerable, and in the very midst of it, broadcast in it, I saw distinctly a countenance such as my own. I cannot say that it was a human face. Countenance, person, expression—this is what I beheld, and this Highly Personal Countenance was regarding me directly and fully.

"It was so beautiful that I couldn't imagine moving or ever turning away from it, but then it began to brighten, it began to force me to blink and to struggle not to cover my eyes rather than imperil my vision forever.

"The light then became muted; it contracted; it became bearable and engulfing, but not blinding to me. And I stood, trembling, very glad I had not reached to cover my face.

" 'Memnoch,' God said. 'You have done well. You have brought souls from Sheol who are worthy of Heaven; you have increased the joy and the bliss of Heaven; you have done well.'

"I uttered a thanks which was in fact an anthem of adoration, repeating the obvious, that God had made all these souls and that in His mercy He had allowed them to come to Him.

" 'This makes you very happy, does it not?' He asked.

" 'Only if it makes you happy, Lord,' I said, which was a bit of a lie.

" 'Rejoin the angels, Memnoch,' He said. 'You are forgiven for becoming flesh and blood without my permission, and forgiven for having slept with the Daughters of Men. You are upheld in your hopes for the souls of Sheol. Leave me now and do whatever it is you wish, but interfere no more with Nature, or with humankind, since you insist they are not part of Nature, and on which point you are wrong.'

" 'Lord—' I started timidly.

" 'Yes???'

" 'Lord, these souls I brought from Sheol, why, they are less than one one-hundredth of the souls in Sheol; they probably are less than one one-hundredth of souls who have disintegrated or vanished since the beginning of the world. Lord, Sheol is filled with confusion and misunderstanding. These were but the elect.'

" 'I am supposed to be surprised by this information? How could I not know it?' He asked.

" 'Surely, Lord, you'll let me go back to Sheol and to try to advance those souls who haven't reached the level of Heaven. Surely you'll let me try to purge them of whatever keeps them unworthy of heavenly bliss.'

" 'Why?'

" 'Lord, there are millions lost to you for every million saved.'

" 'You know that I know this, do you not?'

" 'Lord, have mercy on them! Have mercy on the humans of the Earth who seek through countless rituals to reach you, know you, and appease you.'

" 'Why?'

"I didn't answer. I was dumbstruck. I thought. And then I said, 'Lord, do you not care for these souls who are drifting in confusion? Who suffer so in darkness?'

" 'Why should I?' He asked.

"Again, I took my time. It was imperative that this answer count. But in the interval he spoke:

" 'Memnoch, can you count for me all of the stars? Do you know their names, their orbits, their destinies in Nature? Can you give me a rough calculation, Memnoch, of the number of grains of sand in the sea?'

" 'No, Lord, I can't.'

" 'Throughout my Creation, there are creatures whose spawn numbers in the thousands, of which only a tiny portion survive—fishes of the sea, turtles of the sea, winged insects of the air. A hundred, a million even, of one species may be born under the arc of one day's sun, with only a handful to survive and reproduce. Don't you know this?'

" 'Yes, Lord, I know. I knew in ages past. I knew when the animals were evolved. I knew.'

" 'So what is it to me that only a handful of souls come to the Gates of Heaven? Maybe I will send you to Sheol again, in Time. I will not say.'

" 'Lord, humankind is sentient and suffering!'

" 'Must we argue again about Nature? Humankind is my creation, Memnoch, and its development whether you know it or not follows my Laws.'

" 'But, Lord, everything under the sun dies eventually, and these souls have the potential to live forever! *They are outside the cycle!* They are made of invisible will and knowledge. Lord, surely they were meant within the Laws to come to Heaven, how could it not be? I am asking you, Lord, I am asking you to tell me, because as much as I love you, I don't understand.'

" 'Memnoch, the invisible and the willful are embodied in my angels and they obey my laws.'

" 'Yes, Lord, but they don't die. And you talk to us, and you reveal yourself to us, and you love us, and you let us see things.'

" 'You don't think the beauty of Creation reveals my light to Humankind? You don't think these souls, which you yourself have brought here, have not developed out of a perception of the glory of all that has been made?'

" 'Many more could come, Lord, with just a little help. The number here now is so small. Lord, the lower animals, what can they conceive of that they cannot have? I mean, the lion conceives of the meat of the gazelle and he gets it, does he not? Human souls have conceived of Almighty God and are longing for Him.'

" 'You've proved that to me already,' he said. 'You've proved it to all of Heaven.'

" 'But these were a few! Lord, if you were only flesh and blood, if you had only gone down as I did—'

" 'Caution, Memnoch.'

" 'No, Lord, forgive me, but I can't deny you my finest efforts, and my finest efforts at logic tell me that if you went down and became flesh and blood as I did, you would better know these Creatures whom you think you know but you don't!'

"No answer.

" 'Lord, your light doesn't penetrate human flesh. It mistakes it for animal flesh and always has! Lord, you may know all but you don't know every tiny thing! You can't, or you couldn't leave these souls languishing in Sheol in agony. And you could not allow the suffering of men and women on Earth to go without context. I don't believe it! I don't believe you would do it! I don't believe it.'

" 'Memnoch, for me it is only necessary to say something once.'

"I didn't answer.

" 'I'm being gentle with you,' He said.

" 'Yes, you are, but you are wrong, and in that, too, you are wrong, for you would hear your anthems of praise sung over and over without end and forever, and Lord! These souls could come to you and sing those anthems.'

" 'I don't need the anthems, Memnoch,' He said.

" 'Then why do we sing?'

" 'You of all my angels are the only one who accuses me! Who does not trust in me. Why, these souls you brought from Sheol trust in me as you do not! That was your standard for selecting them! That they trusted in the Wisdom of God.'

"I couldn't be silenced:

" 'I knew something when I was flesh and blood, Lord, which upheld all that I had suspected before, and which confirms all I have seen since. What can I do, Lord, tell you lies? Speak things with my tongue that are flat-out falsehoods? Lord, in humankind you have made something that even you do not fully comprehend! There can be no other explanation, for if there is, then there is no Nature and there are no Laws.'

" 'Get out of my sight, Memnoch. Go down to Earth and get away from me and interfere with Nothing, do you hear?'

" 'Put it to the test, Lord. Become flesh and blood as I did. You who can do anything, sheath yourself in flesh—'

" 'Silence, Memnoch.'

" 'Or if you do not dare to do that, if it is unworthy of the Creator to understand in every cell his Creation, then silence all the anthems of Angels and Men! Silence them, since you say you do not need them, and observe then what your Creation means to you!'

" 'I cast you out, Memnoch!' He declared, and in an instant all of Heaven had reappeared around me, the entire *bene ha elohim* and with it the millions of souls of the saved, and Michael and Raphael were standing before me, watching in horror as I was forced backwards right out of the gates and into the whirlwind.

" 'You are merciless to your Creations, my Lord!' I roared as loud as I could over the din of distressful singing. 'Those men and women made in your own image are right to despise you, for nine-tenths of them would be better off if they had never been born!' "

Memnoch stopped.

He made a little frown, just a tiny very perfectly symmetrical scowl for a moment, and then lowered his head as if listening to something. Then slowly he turned to me.

I held his gaze. "It's just what you would have done, isn't it?" he asked.

"God help me," I said, "I really don't know."

The landscape was changing. As we looked at each other, the world around us was filled with new sounds. I realized there were humans in the vicinity, men with flocks of goats and sheep, and far off in the distance I could see the walls of a town, and above on a hill, yet another small settlement. Indeed, we were in a populated world now, ancient, but not that far from our own.

I knew these people couldn't see us, or hear us. I didn't have to be told.

Memnoch continued to stare at me, as if asking me something, and I didn't know what it was. The sun was beating down full on both of us. I realized my hands were moist with blood sweat and I reached up and wiped the sweat from my forehead, and looked at the blood on my hand. He was covered with a faint shimmer, but nothing more than that. He continued to stare at me.

"What happened!" I asked. "Why don't you tell me! What happened? Why don't you go on?"

"You know damned good and well what happened," he said. "Look down at your clothes now. They're robes, and better suited for the desert. I want you to come there, just over those hills . . . with me."

He stood up, and I at once followed him. We were in the Holy Land, there was no question. We passed dozens upon dozens of small groups of people, fishermen near a small town on the edge of the sea, others tending sheep or goats, or driving small flocks towards nearby settlements or walled enclosures.

Everything looked distinctly familiar. Disturbingly familiar, quite beyond déjà vu or intimations of having lived here before. Familiar as if hardwired into my brain. And I refer to everything now—even a naked man with crooked legs, hollering and raving, as he passed us, not seeing us, one hand bent on a stick of a cane.

Beneath the layers of grit that covered all, I was surrounded by forms and styles and manners of behavior I knew intimately—from Scripture, from engraving, from embellished illustration, and from film enactment. This was—in all its stripped-down, burning-hot glory—a sacred as well as familiar terrain.

We could see people standing before caves in which they lived high on the hills. Here and there little groups sat in the shade beneath a copse, dozing, talking. A distant pulse came from the walled cities. The air was filled with sand. Sand blew into my nostrils and clung to my lips and my hair.

Memnoch had no wings. His robes were soiled and so were mine. I think we wore linen; it was light and the air passed through it. Our robes were long and unimportant. Our skin, our forms, were unchanged.

The sky was vividly blue, and the sun glared down upon me as it might on any being. The sweat felt alternately good and unbearable. And I thought, fleetingly, how at any other time I might wonder at the sun alone, the marvel of the sun denied to the Children of Night—but all this time I had not even thought of it, not once, because having seen the Light of God, the Sun had ceased to be that Light for me.

We walked up into the rocky hills, climbing steep paths, and crossing over outcroppings of rock and ragged tree, and finally there appeared below and before us a great patch of unwatered sand, burning and shifting slowly in comfortless wind.

Memnoch came to a halt at the very threshold of this desert, so to speak, the place where we would leave the firm ground, rocky and uncomfortable as it was, and pass into the soft drudgery of the sand.

I caught up with him, having fallen a little behind. He put his left arm around me, and his fingers spread out firm and large against my shoulder. I was very glad he did, because I was feeling a predictable apprehension; in fact, a dread was building in me, a premonition as bad as any I'd ever known.

"After He cast me out," Memnoch said, "I wandered." His eyes were on the desert and what seemed the barren, blazing rocky cliffs in the distance, hostile as the desert itself.

"I roamed the way you have often roamed, Lestat. Wingless, and brokenhearted, I drifted along through the cities and nations of the earth, over continents and wastes. Sometime or other I can tell you all of it, if you wish. It's of no consequence now.

"Let me say only what is of consequence, that I did not dare to make myself visible or known to Humankind but rather hid amongst them, invisible, not daring to assume flesh for fear of angering God again; and not daring to join the human struggle under any disguise, for fear of God, and fear of what evil I might bring on humans. On account of the same fears . . . I didn't return to Sheol. I wanted in no way to increase the sufferings of Sheol. God alone could free those souls. What hope could I give them?

"But I could see Sheol, I could see its immensity, and I felt the pain of the souls there, and wondered at the new and intricate and ever-changing patterns of confusion created by mortals as they departed one faith or sect or creed after another for that miserable margin of gloom.

"Once a proud thought did come to me—that if I did penetrate Sheol, I might instruct the souls there so thoroughly that they themselves might transform it, create in it forms invented by hope rather than hopelessness, and some garden might be made of it in time. Certainly the elect, the millions I had taken to Heaven, they had transformed their portion of the place. But then what if I failed at this, and only added to the chaos? I didn't dare. I didn't dare, out of fear of God and fear of my own inability to accomplish such a dream.

"I formulated many theories in my wanderings but I did not change my mind on anything which I believed or felt or had spoken to God. In fact, I prayed to Him often, though He was utterly silent, telling Him how much I continued to believe that He had deserted His finest creation. And sometimes out of weariness I only sung His praises. Sometimes I was silent. Looking, hearing . . . watching. . . .

"Memnoch, the Watcher, the Fallen Angel.

"Little did I know my argument with Almighty God was only begun. But at a certain time, I found myself wandering back to the very valleys which I had first visited, and where the first cities of men had been built.

"This land for me was the land of beginnings, for though great peoples had sprung up in many nations, it was here that I had lain with the Daughters of Men. And here that I had learnt something in the flesh which I still held that God did not Himself know.

"Now, as I came to this place, I came into Jerusalem, which by the way is only six or seven miles west of here, where we now stand.

"And the times were immediately known to me, that the Romans governed the land, that the Hebrews had suffered a long and terrible captivity, and that those tribes going back to the very first settlements here—who had believed in the One God—were now under the foot of the polytheists who did not take their legends with any seriousness.

"And the Tribes of Monotheists, themselves, were divided on many issues, with some Hebrews being strict Pharisees, and others Sadducees, and still others having sought to make pure communities in caves in those hills beyond.

"If there was one feature which made the times remarkable to me—that is, truly different from any other—it was the might of the Roman Empire, which stretched farther than any empire of the West which I had ever witnessed, and remained somehow in ignorance of the Great Empire of China, as if that were not of the same world.

"Something drew me to this spot, however, and I knew it. I sensed a presence here that was not as strong as a summons; but it was as if someone were crying out to me to come here, and yet would not use the full power of his voice. I must search, I must wander. Maybe this thing stalked and seduced me as I did you. I don't know.

"But I came here, and wandered Jerusalem, listening to what the tongues of men had to say.

"They spoke of the prophets and holy men of the wilderness, of arguments over the law and purification and the will of God. They spoke of Holy Books and Holy Traditions. They spoke of men going out to be 'baptized' in water so as to be 'saved' in the eyes of God.

"And they spoke of a man who had only lately gone into the wilderness after his baptism, because at the moment that he had stepped into the River Jordan and the water had been poured over him, the skies had opened above this man, and Light had been seen from God.

"Of course one could hear stories like this all over the world. It was not unusual, except that it drew me. That this was my country; and I found myself as if directed, wandering out of Jerusalem to the east, into the wasteland, my keen angelic senses telling me that I was near to the presence of something mysterious, something that partook of the sacred in a way that an angel would know upon seeing, and a man might not. My reason rejected it, yet I walked on and on, in the heat of the day, wingless and invisible into the very wastes."

Memnoch drew me with him and we walked into the sand, which was not as deep as I had imagined, but was hot and full of little stones. We moved on into canyons and up slopes and finally came to a little clearing of sorts where rocks had been gathered, as if others were wont to come here from time to time. It was as natural as the other place we had chosen to remain for so long.

A landmark in the desert, so to speak, a monument to something, perhaps.

I waited on tenterhooks for Memnoch to begin again. My uneasiness was growing. He slowed his pace until we stood well over a stone's throw from this little gathering of rocks.

"Closer and closer I came," he said, "to those markers there that you see, and with my angelic eyes, powerful as are yours, I spied from a long way off a single human man. But my eyes told me this was no human, that on the contrary this man was filled with the fire of God.

"I didn't believe it, and yet I walked on, closer and closer, unable to stop myself, and then stopped where we are now, staring at the figure who sat on that rock before me, looking up at me here.

"It was God! There was no question. He was sheathed in flesh, dark-skinned from the sun, dark-haired, and had the dark eyes of the desert people, but it was God! My God!

"And there he sat in this fleshly body, looking at me with human eyes, and the eyes of God, and I could see the Light totally filling Him and contained within Him and concealed from the outside world by His flesh as if it were the strongest membrane betwixt Heaven and Earth.

"If there was anything more terrible than this revelation, it was that He was looking at me and that He knew me and had been waiting for me, and that all I felt for Him, as I looked at Him, was love.

"We sing over and over again the songs of love. Is that the one song intended for all Creation?

"I looked at Him in terror for His mortal parts, His sunburnt flesh, His thirst, the emptiness of His stomach and the suffering of His eyes in the heat, for the presence of Almighty God inside Him, and I felt overwhelming love.

" 'So, Memnoch,' He said in a man's tongue and with a man's voice. 'I have come.'

"I fell on my face before Him. This was instinctive. I just lay there, reaching out and touching the very tip of the latchet of His sandal. I sighed and my body shook with the relief of loneliness, the attraction to God and the satisfaction of it, and I began a giddy weeping just to be near Him and see Him and I marveled at what this must mean.

" 'Stand up, come sit near me,' He said. 'I am a man now and I am God, but I am afraid.' His voice was indescribably moving to me, human yet filled with the wisdom of the divine. He spoke with the language and accents of Jerusalem.

" 'Oh, Lord, what can I do to ease your pain?' I said, for the pain was obvious. I stood up. 'What have you done and why?'

" 'I have done exactly what you tempted me to do, Memnoch,' He answered, and His face wore the most dreamlike and engaging smile. 'I have come into the flesh. Only I have done you one better. I was born of a mortal woman, planting the seed myself in her, and for thirty years, I have lived on this Earth as a child and as a man, and for long periods doubting—no, even forgetting and ceasing to believe altogether—that I was really God!'

" 'I see you, I know you. You are the Lord my God,' I said. I was so struck by His face; by the recognition of Him in the mask of skin that covered the bones of His skull. In a shivering instant I recovered the exact feeling of when I'd glimpsed His countenance in the light, and I saw now the same expression in this human face. I went down on my knees. 'You are my God,' I said.

" 'I know that now, Memnoch, but you understand that I allowed myself to be submerged in the flesh utterly, to forget it, so that I could know what it means, as you said, to be human, and what humans suffer, and what they fear and what they long for, and what they are capable of learning either here or above. I did what you told me to do, and I did it better than you ever did it, Memnoch, I did it as God must do it, to the very extremity!'

" 'Lord, I can scarcely bear the sight of you suffering,' I said quickly, unable to rip my eyes off Him and yet dreaming of water and food for Him. 'Let me wipe the sweat from you. Let me get you water. Let me take you to it in an angelic instant. Let me comfort you and wash you and clothe you in a finery fit for God on Earth.'

" 'No,' He said. 'In those days when I thought myself mad, when I could scarce remember that I was God, when I knew I had yielded my omniscience deliberately in order to suffer and to know limitations, you might have persuaded me that that was the path. I might have seized upon your offer. Yes, make me a King. Let that be my way of revealing myself to them. But not now. I know Who I am and What I am, and I know What Will Happen. And you are right, Memnoch, there are souls in Sheol ready for Heaven and I myself will take them there. I have learnt what you tempted me to learn.'

" 'Lord, you're starving. You're suffering from terrible thirst. Here, turn these stones into bread by your power, that you can eat. Or let me get you food.'

" 'For once will you listen to me!' He said, smiling. 'Stop talking of food and drink. Who is human here? I am! You impossible adversary, you argumentative devil! Hush for now and listen. I am in the flesh. Have pity at least and let me speak my piece.' He laughed at me, His face full of kindness and sympathy.

" 'Here, come into the flesh, too, with me,' He said. 'Be my brother and sit beside me, Son of God and Son of God, and let us talk.'

"I did as He said at once, creating a body thoughtlessly that matched what you see now, as that was as natural to me as thinking was natural, and I gave myself a similar robe, and I realized that I was sitting on that rock there by His side. I was bigger than He was, and had not thought to reduce the scale of my limbs, and now I did it hastily until we were men of equal proportion, more or less. I was fully angelic in my form, and not hungry or thirsty or tired.

" 'How long have you been in this wilderness?' I asked. 'The people in Jerusalem say almost forty days.'

"He nodded. 'That's about the right number,' He answered me. 'And it's time now for me to begin my ministry, which will last three years. I will teach the great lessons that must be learnt for admission to Heaven—awareness of Creation and the Understanding of its deliberate unfolding; an appreciation of its beauty and laws which makes possible an acceptance of suffering and seeming injustice and all forms of pain; I will promise a final glory to those who can attain understanding; to those who can surrender their souls to the understanding of God and what He has done. I will give that to Men and Women, which is precisely, I think, what you wanted me to do.'

"I didn't dare to answer him.

" 'Love, Memnoch, I have learnt to love them as you told me I would. I have learnt to love and cherish as men and women do, and I have lain with women and I have known that ecstasy, that spark of jubilation of which you spoke so eloquently when I could not conceive of wanting such a tiny thing.'

" 'I will talk more of love than any other subject. I will say things that men and women can twist and misunderstand. But love, that shall be the message. You convinced me and I have convinced myself that that is what elevates Human above animal, though animal is what Humankind is.'

" 'Do you mean to leave them with specific guidance as to how to love? As to how to stop war and come together in one form of worship—'

" 'No, not at all. That would be an absurd intervention and would undo the entire grand scheme which I have put into motion. It would stop the dynamics of the unfolding of the universe.

" 'Memnoch, to me we human beings are all still part of Nature, as I said, only Humans are better than animals. It's a matter of degrees. Yes, humans cry out against suffering and they are conscious of it when they suffer, but in a sense they behave exactly like the lower animals, in that suffering improves them and drives them towards evolutionary advance. They are quick-witted enough to see its value, where the animals only learn to avoid suffering by instinct. Humans can actually be improved within one lifetime by suffering. But they are part of Nature still. The world will unfold as it always has, full of surprises. Some of those surprises will be horrid, and others wondrous, and some beautiful. But what is known for certain is that the world will continue to grow and Creation will continue to unfold.'

" 'Yes, Lord,' I said, 'but surely suffering is an evil thing.'

" 'What did I teach you, Memnoch, when you first came to me saying that decay was wrong, that death was wrong? Don't you understand the magnificence in human suffering?'

" 'No,' I said. 'I see the ruin of hope and love and family; the destruction of peace of mind; I see pain beyond endurance; I see man buckle under this, and fall into bitterness and hate.'

" 'You haven't looked deep enough, Memnoch. You are only an angel. You refuse to understand Nature, and that has been your way since the start.

" 'I will bring my light into Nature, through the flesh for three years. I will teach the wisest things I can know and say in this flesh-and-blood body and brain; and then I will die.'

" 'Die? Why do that? I mean, what do you mean, die? Your soul will leave—' I broke off, uncertain.

"He smiled.

" 'You do have a soul, don't you, Lord? I mean, you are my God inside this Son of Man, and the light fills every particle of you, but you . . . you don't have a soul, do you? You don't have a human soul!'

" 'Memnoch, these distinctions don't matter. I am God Incarnate. How could I have a human soul? What is important is that I will remain in this body as it is tortured and slain; and my death will be evidence of my Love for those whom I have created and allowed to suffer so much. I will share their pain and know their pain.'

" 'Please, Lord, forgive me, but there seems to be something wrong with this whole idea.'

"Again, he seemed amused. His dark eyes were filled with a sympathetic and silent laughter. 'Wrong? What is wrong, Memnoch, that I shall take the form of the Dying God of the Wood, whom men and women have imagined and dreamed of and sung of since time immemorial, a dying god who symbolizes the very cycle of nature itself in which all that is born must die.

" 'I shall die, and I shall rise from the Dead, as that god has risen in every myth of the eternal return of the spring after winter in nations all over the world. I shall be the god destroyed and the god uplifted, only here it will happen literally in Jerusalem, not in ceremony, or with human substitutes. The Son of God himself shall fulfill the myths. I have chosen to sanctify those legends with my literal death.

" 'I shall walk out of the Tomb. My resurrection will confirm the eternal return of the spring after winter. It will confirm that in Nature all things that have evolved have their place.

" 'But Memnoch, it will be for my death that I am remembered. My death. It's going to be terrible. It won't be for my resurrection they'll remember me, you can be sure of it, for that is something many simply will never see or believe. But my death, my death will spring full blown into a confirmation of mythology, underscored by all the myths which have preceded it, and my death will be a sacrifice *by* God to know His own Creation. Just what you told me to do.'

" 'No, no, wait, Lord, there's something wrong with this!'

" 'You always forget yourself and to whom you are speaking,' He said kindly, the mixture of human and divine continuing to obsess me as I looked at Him, falling into His beauty and staggered by His divinity, and overcome again and again by my own sure belief that this was all wrong.

" 'Memnoch, I've just told you what no one knows but Me,' He said. 'Don't speak to me as if I can be wrong. Don't waste these moments with the Son of God! Can't you learn from me in the flesh as you learn from humans in flesh? Have I nothing to teach you, my beloved Archangel? Why do you sit here questioning me? What could possibly be the meaning of your word, *wrong*?'

" 'I don't know, Lord, I don't know how to answer. I can't find all the words. I just know this is not going to work. First of all, who will do this torturing and killing?'

" 'The people of Jerusalem,' He said. 'I will succeed in offending everyone, the traditional Hebrews, the callous Romans, everyone will be offended by the blinding message of pure love and what love demands of humans. I will show contempt for the ways of others, for their rituals and their laws. And into the machinery of their justice I will fall.

" 'I will be condemned on charges of treason when I speak of my Divinity, that I am the Son of God, God Incarnate . . . and for my very message I will be tortured with such embellishment that it will never be forgotten; my death, by crucifixion, is going to be the same.'

" 'By crucifixion? Lord, have you see men die in this way? Do you know how they suffer? They are nailed to the wood and they suffocate, hanging as they do, weakening, unable to lift their own weight on their nailed feet, and finally strangling in blood and in pain?'

" 'Of course I've seen it. It's a common form of execution. It's filthy and it's very human.'

" 'Oh, no, no,' I cried out. 'This can't be. You don't mean to climax your teachings with such spectacular failure and execution, with such cruelty and death itself!'

" 'This is not failure,' he said. 'Memnoch, I shall be a martyr to what I teach! Blood offerings of the innocent lamb to the good God have been made since Humans began! They instinctively render to God what is of great value to them to show their love. Who knows better than you who spied on their altars and listened to their prayers and insisted that I listen! Sacrifice and love are connected in them.'

" 'Lord, they sacrifice out of fear! It has nothing to do with love of God, does it? All the sacrifices? The children sacrificed to Baal, and a hundred other hideous rituals the world over. They do it out of fear! Why would love demand sacrifice?'

"I had clamped my hands over my mouth. I couldn't reason further. I was horrified. I could not sort out the thread of my horror from the overall stifling weave. Then I spoke, thinking aloud:

" 'It's all wrong, Lord. That God should be so degraded in human form, that in itself is unspeakable; but that men should be allowed to do this to God . . . But will they know what they're doing, that you are God? I mean, they couldn't . . . Lord, it will have to be done in confusion and misunderstanding. That spells chaos, Lord! Darkness!'

" 'Naturally,' He said. 'Who in his right mind would crucify the Son of God?'

" 'Then what does it mean?'

" 'Memnoch, it means I subjected myself to the human for the love of those whom I have made. I am in the flesh, Memnoch. I have been in it for thirty years. Would you explain yourself to me?'

" 'To die like that, it's wrong, Lord. It's a filthy killing, Lord, it's a bloody horrible exemplum to lay before the human race! And you say yourself they will remember you for this? More than for your rising from the death, from the light of God exploding out of your human body and making this suffering fall away?'

" 'The Light won't burst out of this body,' He said. 'This body shall die. I shall know death. I shall pass into Sheol and there for three days remain with those who are dead, and then I shall return to this body and raise it from the Dead. And yes, it will be my Death they will remember, for how can I Rise if I do not Die?'

" 'Just don't do either one,' I pleaded. 'Really, I'm begging you. Don't make yourself this sacrifice. Don't dip down into their most misguided blood rituals. Lord, have you ever drawn near to the stench of their sacrificial altars? Yes, I used to say to you, listen to their prayers, but I never meant that you would dip down from your great height to smell the stink of the blood and the dead animal, or to see the dumb fear in its eyes as its throat is slit! Have you seen the babies heaved into the fiery God Baal?'

" 'Memnoch, this is the way to God which man himself has evolved. All over the world the myths sing the same song.'

" 'Yes, but that's because you never interfered to stop it, you let it happen, you let this humankind evolve and they looked back in horror on their animal ancestors, they beheld their mortality, and they seek to propitiate a god who has abandoned them to all this. Lord, they look for meaning, but they find none in this. None.'

"He looked at me as if I were mad, truly. He stared at me in silence. 'You disappoint me,' He said softly and gently. 'You wound me, Memnoch, you wound my human heart.' He reached out and put His roughened hands against my face, hands of a man who had worked in this world, labored as I had never labored in my brief visit.

"I shut my eyes. I didn't speak. But something had come to me! A revelation, an insight, a sudden grasping of everything here that was in error, but could I reason it out? Could I speak?

"I opened my eyes again, letting him hold me, feeling the callouses on his fingers, looking into his gaunt face. How he had starved himself; how he had suffered in this desert, and how he had labored these thirty years! Oh, no, this was wrong!

" 'What, my Archangel, what is wrong!' He demanded of me with infinite patience and human consternation.

" 'Lord, they chose these rituals which involve suffering because they cannot avoid suffering in the Natural World. The natural world is what must be overcome! Why must anyone suffer what humans suffer? Lord, their souls come to Sheol distorted, twisted by pain, black as cinders from the heat of loss and misery and violence which they have witnessed. Suffering is evil in this world. Suffering is decay and death. It's terrible. Lord, You can't believe that to suffer like this would do any good to anyone. This suffering, this unspeakable capacity to bleed and to know pain and to know annihilation, is what has to be overcome in this world if anyone is to reach God!'

"He didn't answer. He lowered his hands.

" 'My angel,' He said, 'you draw from me even more affection now that I have a human heart. How simple you are! How alien you are to the vast Material Creation.'

" 'But it was I who urged you to come down! How am I alien? I am the Watcher! I see what other angels don't dare to look at for fear they'll weep, and it will make you angry with them.'

" 'Memnoch, you simply don't know the flesh. The concept is too complex for you. What do you think taught your souls in Sheol their perfection? Was it not suffering? Yes, they enter perhaps twisted and burnt if they have failed to see beyond suffering on Earth, and some may despair and disappear. But in Sheol, over the centuries of suffering and longing, others are purged and purified.

" 'Memnoch, Life and Death are part of the cycle, and suffering is its by-product. And the human capacity to know it exempts no one! Memnoch, that the illuminated souls you brought from Sheol knew it, that they had learnt to accept its beauty, is what made them worthy to come through the heavenly gates!'

" 'No, Lord, that's not true!' I said. 'You've gotten it wrong. Utterly. Oh, I see what's happened.'

" 'You do? What are you trying to say to me? That I the Lord God, having spent thirty years in this human body, have not struck the truth?'

" 'But that's just it! You've known all along you were God. You mentioned times when you thought you were mad or almost forgot, but those were brief! Too brief! And now as you plot your death, you know Who you are and You won't forget it, will you?'

" 'No, I won't. I must be the Son of God Incarnate to fulfill my ministry, to work my miracles, of course. That's the whole point.'

" 'Then, Lord, you don't know what it means to be flesh!'

" 'How dare you assume that you do, Memnoch.'

" 'When you left me in that fleshly body, when you cast me down for the Daughters of Men to heal and care for, in the early centuries of this very land, I had no promise you would take me back to Heaven. Lord, you're not playing fair in this experiment. You've known all along you're going back, you're going back to be God!'

" 'And who better than I can understand what this flesh feels!' He demanded.

" 'Somebody who doesn't fully rest assured that He is the immortal Creator of the Universe,' I said. 'Any mortal man hanging on a cross now on Golgotha outside Jerusalem would know better than you!'

"His eyes grew wide as He stared at me. But He didn't challenge me. His silence unnerved me. And once again, the power of His expression, the radiance of God in man dazzled me, and drew upon the angel in me to simply shut up and fall at His feet. But I wouldn't do it!

" 'Lord, even when I went to Sheol,' I said, 'I didn't know whether or not I'd ever come back to Heaven. Don't you see? I don't claim to have your understanding of anything. We wouldn't be talking here if I did. But I didn't have any promise I would be allowed back into Heaven, don't you see? So the suffering and the darkness spoke to me and taught me, because I took the risk that I might never overcome it. Don't you see?'

"He considered this a long time and then He shook His head sadly. 'Memnoch, you are the one who has failed to understand. When is Humankind closest to God than when they suffer for the love of another, when they die so that another might live, when they plunge towards certain death for the protection of those they leave behind or those truths about Life which Creation has taught them?'

" 'But the world doesn't need all that, Lord! No, no, no. It doesn't need the blood, the suffering, the war. That wasn't what taught Humans to love! Animals already did all that bloody, horrible catastrophe to one another. What taught Humans was the warmth and affection of another, the love for a child, the love in a mate's arms, the capacity to understand another's suffering and want to protect that other, to rise above savagery into the formation of family and clan and tribe that would mean peace and security for all!'

"There came a long silence. And then very tenderly He laughed. 'Memnoch, my angel. What you learnt of life you learnt in bed.'

"I didn't answer for a moment. The comment was charged with contempt and humour, of course. Then I spoke:

" 'That's true, Lord. And suffering is so terrible for humans, injustice is so terrible for the balance of their minds that it can destroy those lessons learnt in bed, magnificent as they are!'

" 'Oh, but when love is reached through suffering, Memnoch, it has a power it can never gain through innocence.'

" 'Why do you say that? I don't believe it! I don't think you grasp it. Lord, listen to me. There's one chance for this to be proven my way. One chance.'

" 'If you think for one moment you will interfere with my ministry and my sacrifice, if you think you can turn the tide of the vast forces already moving towards this event, then you are no more an angel, but a demon!' He said.

" 'I don't ask that,' I said. 'Go through with it. Minister, outrage them; be arrested, tried, and executed on the cross, yes, do all of it. But do it as a man!'

" 'I intend to.'

" 'No, you'll know the whole time you're God. I'm saying Forget that you are God! Bury your divinity in the flesh the way it's been buried intermittently. Bury it, Lord, leaving yourself only your faith and your belief in Heaven, as if it had come to you through Revelation immense and undeniable.

" 'But bury in this desert the true certainty that you are God. Then, you'll suffer it all as a man suffers it. Then you'll know what this suffering is at its heart. Then will all the glory be stripped from agony! And you will see what men see when flesh is ripped, and torn, and blood flows, and it is your own. It's filth!'

" 'Memnoch, men die on Golgotha every day. What is important is that the Son of God knowingly dies on Golgotha in the body of a man.'

" 'Oh, no, no!' I cried out. 'This is disaster.'

"He seemed so sad suddenly that I thought he might weep for me. His lips were parched and cracked from the desert. His hands were so thin I could see the veins. He was not even a great specimen of a man, only an ordinary one, worn down by years of toil.

" 'Look at you,' I said, 'starving, thirsting, suffering, tired, lost in all the darknesses of life, the true spontaneous evils of nature, and dreaming of glory when you exit this body! What kind of lesson can such suffering be? And who will you leave with the guilt for your murder? What will become of all those mere mortals who denied you? No, please, Lord, listen to me. If you won't leave your Divinity, then don't do it. Change this plan.

" 'Don't die. Above all, don't be murdered! Don't hang from a tree like the God of the Wood in the Greek stories. Come with me into Jerusalem; and know women and wine and singing and dancing and the birth of little ones, and all the joy the human heart can contain and express!

" 'Lord, there are times when the hardest men hold infants in their arms, their own children, and the happiness and satisfaction of those moments is so sublime that there is no horror on earth that can destroy the peace they feel! That is the human capacity for love and understanding! When one can achieve harmony in spite of everything, and men and women do this, Lord. They do. Come, dance with your people. Sing with them. Feast with them. Throw your arms around the women and the men and know them in the flesh!'

" 'I feel pity for you, Memnoch,' He said. 'I pity you as I pity the mortals who will kill me, and those who will inevitably misunderstand my laws. But I dream of those who will be touched to the core by my suffering, and who will never forget it, and will know what love I felt for mortals that I would let myself die among them before opening the gates of Sheol. I pity you. Feeling as you do, your guilt will become too terrible to bear.'

" 'My guilt? What guilt?'

" 'You're the cause of all this, Memnoch. You're the one who said I should come down in the flesh. You're the one who urged me on to do it, who challenged me, and now you fail to see the miracle of my sacrifice.

" 'And when you do see it, when you do see souls perfected by suffering ascending to Heaven, what will you think then of your paltry little discoveries made in the arms of the Daughters of Men? What will you think? Don't you see? I will redeem suffering, Memnoch! I will give it its greatest and fullest potential within the cycle! I will bring it to fruition. I will allow it to sing its own magnificent song!'

" 'No, no, no!' I stood up and railed at Him. 'Lord, just do as I ask. Go through with it, yes, if you must, found this miracle upon a murder, do it that way, if that is your will, but bury your certainty of Divinity, so that you really, really do die, Lord, so that when they drive the nails through your hands and feet you know what a man feels and no more, and when you enter the gloom of Sheol yours is a human soul! Please, Lord, please, I'm begging you. For all humanity, I'm begging you. I can't see the future but I have never been more frightened of it than I am now.' "

Memnoch broke off.

We stood alone in the sands, Memnoch looking into the distance and me beside him, shaken.

"He didn't do it, did he?" I asked. "Memnoch, God died knowing He was God. He died and rose knowing the whole time. The world argues over it and debates and wonders, but He knew. When they drove the nails, He knew He was God."

"Yes," said Memnoch. "He was man, but that man was never without the power of God."

Suddenly I was distracted.

Memnoch seemed too shaken to say any more just yet.

Something changed in the landscape. I looked towards the circle of stones, and realized a figure was sitting there, the figure of a dark-skinned, dark-eyed man, emaciated and covered with the sand of the desert, and he was looking at us. And without one fiber of his flesh being other than human, He was obviously God.

I was petrified.

I had lost the map. I didn't know the way back or the way forward, or what lay to left or to right.

I was petrified, yet I wasn't frightened, and this man, this dark-eyed one, was merely looking at us with the softest sympathy in his face, and the same unbounded acceptance of us that I had seen in Him in Heaven when He'd turned and taken me by the arms.

The Son of God.

"Come here, Lestat," he called now softly, over the desert wind, in a human voice. "Come closer."

I looked at Memnoch. Memnoch was looking at him, too, now and he gave a bitter smile. "Lestat, it is always a good idea, no matter how He is behaving, to do exactly what He says."

Blasphemy. I turned, shivering.

I went directly towards the figure, conscious of each shuffling step through the boiling sand, the dark thin form coming ever more clear to me, a tired and suffering man. I sank down on my knees in front of Him, looking up into His face.

"The Living Lord," I whispered.

"I want you to come into Jerusalem," He said. He reached out and brushed back my hair, and the hand was as Memnoch described it, dry, calloused, darkened from the sun as his brow was darkened. But the voice hovered somewhere between natural and sublime, it struck a timbre beyond the angelic. It was the voice that had spoken to me in Heaven, only confined to human sounds.

I couldn't answer. I couldn't do anything. I knew that I would do nothing until I was told. Memnoch stood off, arms folded, watching. And I knelt, looking into the eyes of God Incarnate and I knelt before Him completely alone.

"Come into Jerusalem," He said. "It won't take you long, no more perhaps than a few moments, but come into Jerusalem with Memnoch, on the day of my death, and glimpse my Passion—see me crowned with thorns and carrying my cross. Do this for Me before you make your decision whether or not to serve Memnoch or the Lord God."

Every part of me knew I couldn't do it. I couldn't stand it! I

couldn't watch it. I couldn't. I was paralyzed. Disobedience, blasphemy, those weren't the issues. I couldn't endure the thought of it! I
stared at Him, at His sunburnt face, at His soft and loving eyes, at the
sand clinging to the edge of His cheek. His dark hair was neglected,
wind-torn, swept back from His face.

No! I can't do it! I can't bear it!

"Oh, yes, you can," He said reassuringly. "Lestat, my brave
bringer of death to so many. Would you really return to Earth without this glimpse of what I offer? Would you really give up this chance
to glimpse me crowned with thorns? When have you ever passed up a
challenge, and think what I am offering to you now. No, you
wouldn't back off from it, even if Memnoch urged you to do it."

I knew He was right. Yet, I knew I couldn't stand it. I could not go
into Jerusalem and see the actual Christ carrying His Cross. I
couldn't. I couldn't. I didn't have the strength, I would— I was silent.
A riot of thought within me condemned me to utter confusion and
continued paralysis. "Can I look at this?" I said. I closed my eyes!
Then I opened them and looked at Him again and at Memnoch, who
had come near and looked down with a near, cold expression at me,
cold as his face could be, which wasn't cold at all so much as serene.

"Memnoch," said God Incarnate. "Bring him, show him the way,
let him but glimpse it. You be his guide, and then go on with your
examination and your appeal."

He looked at me. He smiled. How frail a vessel He seemed for His
own magnificence. A man with lines around his eyes from the hot
sun, with worn teeth, a man.

"Remember, Lestat," God said to me. "This is only the world.
And you know the world. Sheol awaits. You have seen the World and
Heaven but you have not seen Hell."

18

WE WERE in the city, a city of deep brown and faded yellow stones and clay. Three years had passed. It had to be so. All I knew was that we were in a huge crowd of people, robed and veiled and ragged—that I could smell the human sweat, and the heat of stagnant breath, and stench of human waste and camel dung overpoweringly, and that though no one took notice of us, I could feel the press around us, I could feel unwashed men shoving against me, and brushing in front of me, and the sand salted the air here within the walls of the city, within these narrow streets, just as it had salted the air of the desert.

People clustered in small rounded doorways, peeped from windows above. Soot mingled with the everlasting sand. Women drawing their veils around their faces cleaved to one another, pushing past us. Up ahead I could hear screams and shouting. Suddenly, I realized that the crowd was pressed so tight around us, I couldn't move. Desperately I looked for Memnoch.

He was right beside me, watching all calmly, neither of us shining with any preternatural gleam among these drab and soiled humans, these everyday creatures of this early and harsh time.

"I don't want to do it!" I said, digging in my heels, shoved along by the crowd, yet resisting. "I don't think I can do it! I can't look, Memnoch, no, this is not required of me. No . . . I don't want to go any farther. Memnoch, let me go!"

"Quiet," he said dourly. "We are almost to the place where He will pass."

With his left arm around me, clutching me protectively, he divided the crowd in front of us, effortlessly it seemed, until we emerged in the front line of those who waited at a broader thoroughfare as the procession advanced. The shouts were deafening. Roman soldiers moved past us, the garments soiled with grit, faces tired, bored even, dreary. Across the way, on the other side of the procession, a beautiful woman, her hair covered by a long white veil, threw up her hands and screamed.

She was looking at the Son of God. He had come into view. I saw the big crossbar of the crucifix first, on his shoulders sticking out on either side of Him, and then His hands, bound to the beam, dangling from the ropes, already dripping with blood. His head was bowed; the brown hair was matted and dirty and covered over with the crude black crown of spiking thorns; spectators were pressed to walls on either side of Him, some taunting Him, others silent.

There was barely room for Him to walk with his burden, His robes torn, His knees bruised and bleeding, but walk He did. The stench of urine was overpowering from the nearby walls.

He trudged towards us, face hidden, then fell, one knee going down into the stones of the street. Behind Him I saw others carrying the long post of the cross which would be planted in the ground.

At once the soldiers beside Him pulled Him up. They steadied the crossbar on his shoulders. His face was visible, not three feet from where we stood, and He looked at us both. Sunburnt, cheeks hollow, mouth open and shuddering, dark eyes wide and fixed on us, He looked, without expression, without appeal. The blood poured down from the black thorns sticking into His forehead; it ran in tiny streams into His eyelids and down His cheeks. His chest was naked under the open rag of robe which He wore, and it was covered with the ripe, red stripes of the lash!

"My God!" Again I had lost all volition; Memnoch held me upright as we both stared into God's face. And the crowd, the crowd went on screaming and cursing, and shouting and pushing; little children peeped through; women wailed. Others laughed; a great horrid stinking multitude beneath the relentless sun that sent its rays amongst the close urine-stained walls!

Closer He came! Did He know us? He shuddered in His agony, the blood ran down his face into his shivering lips. He gave a gasp as if He would strangle, and I saw that the robe over His shoulders, beneath the rough wood of the beam, was soaked with blood from the scourging. He could not endure another instant, and yet they pushed Him, and He stood directly before us, eyes down, face wet with sweat and the blood swimming in it, and then slowly He turned and looked at me.

I was weeping uncontrollably. What did I witness? A brutality unspeakable in any time and place, but the legends and prayers of my childhood fired with grotesque vitality; I could smell the blood. I could smell it. The vampire in me smelled it. I could hear my sobs, I threw out my arms. "My God!"

Silence fell over the whole world. People shouted and pushed, but not in the realm in which we stood. He stood there staring at me and at Memnoch, stepped out of time and holding the moment in its fullness, in its agony, as He looked at us both.

"Lestat," He said, His voice so feeble and torn I could scarce hear it. "You want to taste it, don't you?"

"Lord, what are you saying?" I cried, my words so full of tears I could scarce control them.

"The blood. Taste it. Taste the Blood of Christ." And a terrible smile of resignation came over him, almost a grimace, his body convulsing beneath the immense beam, and the blood trickling freshly as if with each breath He took the thorns tore deeper into his face and the stripes on His chest began to swell into seams through which the blood leaked.

"No, my God!" I cried out, and I reached for Him and felt His fragile arms, bound to the huge crossbar, His aching, thin arms beneath the torn sleeves, and the blood blazed in front of me.

"The Blood of God, Lestat," He whispered. "Think of all the human blood that has flowed into your lips. Is my blood not worthy? Are you afraid?"

Sobbing, I cupped His neck with both hands, my knuckles against the crossbar, and I kissed His throat, and then my mouth opened without will or struggle and my teeth pierced the flesh. I heard Him moan, a long echoing moan that seemed to rise up and fill the world with its sound, and the blood flooded into my mouth.

The cross, the nails driven through His wrists, not His hands, His body twisting and turning as if in the last moments, He would escape, and His head bashed down on the crossbar, so that the thorns went into His scalp, and then the nails through His feet, and His eyes rolling, the pound and the pound of the hammer, and then the Light, the immense Light rising as it had risen over the balustrade of Heaven, and filling the world, and obliterating even this warm, solid, luscious glut of blood that sank into me. The Light, the light itself and the being within it, *In His Image!* The light receded, swift, soundless, and leaving behind a long tunnel or path, and I knew the path was straight from Earth to the Light.

Pain! The Light was disappearing. The separation was unspeakable! A swift blow struck my entire body with full force.

I was flung back into the crowd. Sand stung my eyes. The screams rose all around me. The blood was on my tongue. It flowed from my lips. Time pressed in with suffocating heat. And He was before us, staring at us, and tears spilled down out of His eyes, through the blood that already covered Him.

"My God, my God, my God!" I cried, swallowing the last of the blood; I sobbed.

The woman across the way blazed into visibility. Suddenly her voice rose above the babble and the cursing, the horrid cacophony of coarse and feelingless humans everywhere struggling to witness.

"My God!" she screamed, and her voice was like a trumpet. She stepped into his path.

She stood before Him and drew the fine white veil from her hair, and put it up with both hands before His face.

"Lord, God, this is Veronica," she cried. "Remember Veronica. Twelve years I suffered a flow of blood, and when I touched the hem of your garment, I was healed."

"Unclean, filth!" came the cries.

"Lawbreaker, blasphemer!"

"Son of God, you dare!"

"Unclean, unclean, unclean!"

The cries grew frantic. People reached out for her, yet seemed loath to touch her. Pebbles and stones rained in the air towards her. The soldiers were undecided, baffled, and belligerent.

But God Incarnate, shoulders bent under the beam, only looked at her, and then He said, "Yes, Veronica, gently, your veil, my beloved, your veil."

The white cloth, virgin and fine, she spread over His face, to blot the blood, the sweat, to soothe, to comfort, His profile clear beneath its whiteness for an instant, and then, as she meant to wipe gently, the soldiers drew her back and she stood, holding up the veil for all to see in both hands.

His Face was on it!

"Memnoch, look!" I cried. "Look at the veil of Veronica!"

The face had been transferred, flawlessly and perfectly, sealed into the cloth as no painter could have rendered it, as if the veil had taken the perfect print of Christ's countenance like a modern camera, only even more vivid, as if a thin layer of flesh had made the flesh in the picture, and blood had made the blood, and the eyes had blazed into the cloth their duplicates, and the lips had left their incarnate imprint as well.

Everyone nearest it saw the likeness. People shoved and pushed against us to see it. Screams rose.

The hand of Christ slipped loose from the rope that bound it to the crossbar, and reached out and took the veil from her, and she fell on her knees crying, her hands to her face. The soldiers were stupefied, confused, shoving at the crowd with their elbows, snarling at those who pressed in.

Christ turned and handed the veil to me.

"Take it, keep it! Hide it, take it with you!" He whispered.

I grasped the cloth, terrified that I might damage or smear the image. Hands reached for it. I closed it tight against my chest.

"He's got the veil," someone shouted. I was shoved backwards.

"Get the veil!" An arm struggled to snatch it from me.

Those who lunged towards us were blocked suddenly by those who came from behind to see the spectacle and shoved us thoughtlessly out of their path. We were pushed backwards by the sheer swell, tumbling through the filthy ragged bodies, through the din and the shouts and the curses.

All sight of the procession was gone; the cries of "the veil" were hopelessly distant.

I folded it, tight, and turned and ran.

I didn't know where Memnoch was; I didn't know where I was going. I ran down the narrow street and through another and another and another, people streaming by me, indifferent to me, on the way to the crucifixion, or simply trudging their accustomed path.

My chest burnt from my running, my feet were bruised and torn, I tasted His blood again and saw the Light in a blinding flash. Unable to see, I clutched the cloth. I lifted it and shoved it inside my robe and clutched it tight there. No one would get it. No one.

A terrible wailing came from my lips. I looked upwards. The sky shifted; the blue sky over Jerusalem, the sand-filled air shifted; the whirlwind had mercifully surrounded me, and the Blood of Christ sank into my chest and my heart, circling my heart, the Light filling my eyes, both my hands pressed tight to the folded veil.

The whirlwind carried me in silence and stillness. With all my will I forced myself to look down, to reach inside my robe, which was not my robe now, but my coat and my shirt—the suit I'd worn in the snows of New York, and under the cloth of my vest, next to my shirt, I felt the folded veil! It seemed the wind would tear off my clothes! It would rip the hair from my head. But I clutched tight to the folded cloth that lay safe against my heart.

Smoke rose from the earth. Cries and screams again. Were they more terrible than the cries surrounding Christ on the road to Calvary?

With a hard, shattering blow, I struck a wall and a floor. Horses went by, the hooves barely missing my head, sparks flying from the stones. A woman lay bleeding and dying before me, her neck obviously broken, blood pouring out of her nose and ears. People fled in all directions. Again the smell of excrement mixed with blood.

It was a city at war, the soldiers looting and dragging the innocents from out of archways, screams echoing as if off endless ceilings, the flames coming so close they singed my hair.

"The veil, the veil!" I said, and felt it with my hand, secure, still tucked between my vest and shirt. A soldier's foot came up and kicked the side of my face hard. And I went sprawling on the stones.

I looked up. I wasn't in a street at all. I was in a huge domed church, with gallery upon gallery of Roman arches and columns. All around me, against the glitter of gold mosaics, men and women were being cut down. Horses were trampling them. The body of a child struck the wall above me, the skull crushed and the tiny limbs dropping like debris at my feet. Horsemen slashed at those fleeing, with broadswords hacking through shoulders and arms. A violent explosion of flames made it as light as midday. Through the portals men and women fled. But the soldiers went after them. Blood soaked the ground. Blood soaked the world.

All around and high above, the golden mosaics blazed with faces which seemed now transfixed in horror as they beheld this slaughter. Saints and saints and saints. Flames rose and danced. Piles of books were burning! Icons were smashed into pieces, and statuary lay in heaps, smoldering and blackened, the gold gleaming as it was eaten by the flames.

"Where are we!" I cried out.

Memnoch's voice was right beside me. He was sitting, collected, against the stone wall.

"Hagia Sophia, my friend," he said. "It's nothing, really. It's only the Fourth Crusade."

I reached out with my left hand for him, unwilling to let go of the veil with my right.

"What you see is the Roman Christians slaughtering the Greek Christians. That's all there is to it. Egypt and the Holy Land have for the moment been forgotten. The Venetians have been given three days to loot the city. It was a political decision. Of course they were all here to win back the Holy Land, where you and I have lately been, but the battle wasn't in the cards, and so the authorities have let the troops loose on the town. Christian slaughters Christian. Roman against Greek. Do you want to walk outside? Would you like to see more of it? Books by the millions are being lost now forever. Manuscripts in Greek and Syriac and Ethiopian and Latin. Books of God and books of men. Do you want to walk among the convents where the nuns are being dragged out of their cells by fellow Christians and raped? Constantinople is being looted. It's nothing, believe me, nothing at all."

I lay against the ground, crying, trying to close my eyes and not see, but unable not to see—flinching at the clang of the horses' hooves so perilously close, choking on the reek of the blood of the dead baby who lay against my leg heavy and limp like something wet from the sea. I cried and cried. Near me lay the body of a man with his head half severed from his neck, the blood pooling on the stones. Another figure tumbled over him, knee twisted, bloody hand grasping for anything that would give him purchase, and finding only the naked pink child's body which he threw aside. Its little head was now nearly broken off.

"The veil," I whispered.

"Oh, yes, the precious veil," he said. "Would you like a change of scenery? We can move on. We can go to Madrid and treat ourselves to an auto-da-fé, do you know what that is, when they torture and burn alive the Jews who won't convert to Christ? Perhaps we should go back to France and see the Cathars being slaughtered in the Languedoc? You must have heard those legends when you were growing up. The heresy was wiped out, you know, the whole heresy. Very successful mission on the part of the Dominican Fathers, who will then start on the witches, naturally. There are so many choices. Suppose we go to Germany and see the martyrdom of the Anabaptists. Or to England to watch Queen Mary burn those who had turned against the Pope during the reign of her father, Henry. I'll tell you an extraordinary scene that I have often revisited. Strasbourg, 1349. Two thousand Jews will be burned there in February of that year, blamed for the Black Death. Things like that will happen all over Europe. . . ."

"I know the history," I cried, trying to catch my breath. "I know!"

"Yes, but seeing it is a little different, isn't it? As I said, this is small potatoes. All this will do is divide Greek and Roman Catholics forever.

"And as Constantinople weakens, then the new People of the Book, the Moslems, will pour past the weakened defenses into Europe. Do you want to see one of those battles? We can go directly to the twentieth century if you like. We can go to Bosnia or Herzegovina, where Moslems and Christians are fighting now. Those countries, Bosnia and Herzegovina, are names on the lips of people today in the streets of New York.

"And while we are considering all the People of the Book—Moslems, Jews, Christians—why not go to southern Iraq and listen to the cry of the starving Kurds whose marshes have been drained and whose people are being exterminated? If you want, we could just concentrate on the sack of holy places—mosques, cathedrals, churches. We could use that method to travel right up to the present time.

"Mind you, not one suggestion I've made has involved people who don't believe in God or Christ. People of the Book, that's what we're talking about, the Book which starts with the One God and keeps changing and growing.

"And today and tonight, documents of inestimable value go up in flames. It is the unfolding of Creation; it is Evolution; it is sanctified suffering on somebody's part surely, because all these people you see here worship the same God."

I made no answer.

Mercifully his voice stopped, but the battle didn't. There was an explosion. The flames roared so high that I could see the saints on the very dome. In one flash the entire magnificent scope of the basilica blazed around me—its great oval, its rows upon rows of columns, the great half-arches supporting the dome above. The light dimmed, exploded again, as cries rang out with renewed vigor.

Then I closed my eyes and lay still, ignoring the kicks and the feet that even ran over me, crushing down on my back for a moment as they moved on. I had the veil and I was lying there, still.

"Can hell be worse than this?" I asked. My voice was small and I didn't think he could hear me over the noise of battle.

"I actually don't know," he said, in the same intimate tone as if whatever bound us together carried our messages between each other effortlessly.

"Is it Sheol?" I asked. "Can souls get out?"

He didn't answer.

"Do you think I would wage this battle with Him on any terms if souls couldn't?" he asked, as if the very idea of an eternal hell offended him.

"Get me out of here, please," I whispered. My cheek was resting on the stone floor. The stench of the manure of the horses was mingled with urine and blood. But the cries were the worst. The cries and the incessant clatter of metal!

"Memnoch, get me out of here! Tell me what this battle is about between you and Him! Tell me the rules!"

I struggled to sit up, drawing my legs in, wiping at my eyes with my left hand, the right still clutching the veil. I began to choke on the smoke. My eyes burned.

"Tell me, what did you mean when you said you needed me, that you were winning the battle? What *is* the battle between you and Him! What do you want me to do? How are you his adversary! What in the name of God am I supposed to do!"

I looked up. He sat relaxed, one knee up, arms folded, face clear one moment in a flash of flame and pale the next. He was soiled all over, and seemed rather limp and in a strange misery of ease. His expression was neither bitter nor sarcastic, only thoughtful—fixed with an enduring expression just as the faces on the mosaics were fixed as they bore lifeless witness to the same events.

"So we pass so many wars? We leave behind so many massacres? We have passed over so much martyrdom," he said. "But then you do not lack imagination, Lestat."

"Let me rest, Memnoch. Answer my questions. I am not an angel, only a monster. Please let's go."

"All right," he said. "We'll go now. You've been brave, actually, just as I thought you would be. Your tears are plentiful and they come from the heart."

I didn't answer. My chest was heaving. I held on to the veil. I put my left hand over my ear. How could I move? Did I expect him to take us in the whirlwind? Had I limbs any longer that would obey commands?

"We'll go, Lestat," he said again. I heard the wind rising. It was the whirlwind, and the walls had already flown backwards. I pressed my hand against the veil. I heard his voice in my ear:

"Rest now."

The souls whirled around us in the dimness. I felt my head against his shoulder, the wind ripping at my hair. I closed my eyes and I saw the Son of God enter a great vast dark and gloomy place. The rays of Light emanated from his small distinct figure in all directions, illuminating hundreds of struggling human forms, soul forms, ghost forms.

"Sheol," I struggled to say. But we were in the whirlwind, and this was an image against the blackness of my closed eyes only. Again the Light grew brighter, the rays merging in one great blaze as if I were in its very presence, and songs rose, louder and clearer, drowning out the wailing souls around us, until the mingling of wail and song became the nature of the vision and the nature of the whirlwind. And they were one.

19

I WAS lying still somewhere, in an open place, on the rocky ground. I had the veil. I could feel the bulk of it, but I didn't dare to reach inside and draw it out or examine it.

I saw Memnoch standing some distance away, in full glorified form, his wings high and stiffly drawn down behind him, and I saw God Incarnate, risen, the wounds still red on His ankles and on His wrists, but He had been bathed and cleaned, and His body was on the same scale as that of Memnoch, that is, greater than human. His robes were white and fresh and His dark hair still richly colored with dried blood, but beautifully combed. It seemed more light seeped through the epidermal cells of His body than it had before His crucifixion, and He gave off a powerful radiance, which rendered the radiance of Memnoch slightly dim by comparison. But the two did not fight each other, and were basically the same kind of light.

I lay there, looking up, and listening to them argue. And only out of the corner of my eye—before their voices became distinct to me—did I see this was a battlefield littered with the dead. It wasn't the same time as the Fourth Crusade. No one had to tell me. This was an earlier epic, and the bodies wore the armour and the clothes that I might connect, if asked, to the third century perhaps, though I could not be certain. These were early, early times.

The dead stank. The air was filled with feasting insects, and even some lowering, awkward vultures, which had come to tear at the swollen hideous flesh of the soldiers, and far off, I heard the nasty argument, in growls and barking—of contending wolves.

"Yes, I see!" declared Memnoch angrily. He was speaking in a tongue that wasn't English or French, but I understood him perfectly. "The gateway is open to Heaven for all those who die with Understanding and Acceptance of the Harmony of Creation and the Goodness of God! But what about the others! What about the millions of others!"

"And once again, I ask you," said the Son of God, "why I should care about the others! Those who die without understanding and acceptance and knowledge of God. Why? What are they to me?"

"Your Created children, that's what they are! With the capacity for Heaven if only they could find the way! And the number of the lost exceeds by billions those few who have the wisdom, the guidance, the experience, the insight, the gift. And you know it! How can you let so many vanish into the shadows of Sheol once more, or disintegrate, or hug the earth becoming evil spirits? Didn't you come to save them all?"

"I came to save those who would be saved!" He said. "Again, I tell you it is a cycle, it is Natural, and for each soul that goes now unimpeded into the Light of Heaven, thousands of others must fail. Of what value is it to Understand, to Accept, to Know, to See the Beauty? What would you have me do?"

"Help the souls who are lost! Help them. Don't leave them in the whirlwind, don't leave them in Sheol struggling for millennia to gain understanding by what they can still see on Earth! You've made things worse, that's what you've done!"

"How dare you!"

"You've made it worse! Look at this battlefield, and Your Cross appeared in the sky before this battle, and now Your Cross becomes the emblem of the empire! Since the death of the witnesses who saw your Risen Body, only a trickle of the dead has gone into the Light from Earth, and multitudes have been lost in argument, and battle, and misunderstanding, languishing in darkness!"

"My Light is for those who would receive it."

"That's not good enough!"

God Incarnate struck Memnoch hard across the face. Memnoch staggered back, wings unfolding, as if reflexively so that he could take flight. But they settled once again, a few graceful white feathers swirling in the air, and Memnoch raised his hand to the imprint of God's hand which blazed on the side of his face. I could see the imprint of the hand distinctly, blood-red as the wounds in the ankles and in the hands of Christ.

"Very well," said God Incarnate. "Since you care more for those lost souls than for your God, let your lot be to collect them! Let Sheol be your Kingdom! Gather them there by the millions and tutor them for the Light. I say none shall dissolve or disintegrate beyond your power to draw them back into being; I say none shall be lost, but all shall be your responsibility, your students, your followers, your servants.

"And until such a day as Sheol is empty! Until such a day as all souls go directly to the Heavenly Gates, you are my Adversary, you are my Devil, you are Damned to spend no less than one third of your existence on Earth which you love so much, and no less than one third in Sheol or Hell, whichever you choose to call it, your Kingdom. And only now and then by my grace may you come into Heaven, and see to it that when you do you have your angelic form!

"On the Earth, let them see you as the demon! The Beast God— the God of the dance and the drink and the feast and the flesh and all the things *you* love enough to challenge *Me*. Let them see you as that, if you would have power, and your wings shall be the color of soot and ashes, and your legs shall be as a goat's legs, as if you were Pan himself! Or as a man only, yes, I give you that mercy, that you may be a man among them, since you think it is such a worthy enterprise to be human. But an Angel among them, no! Never!

"You will not use your Angelic form to confuse and mislead them, to dazzle them or humble them. You and your Watchers did that enough. But see that when you come through my gates, you are attired properly for me, that your wings are like snow, and so are your robes. Remember to be yourself in my realm!"

"I can do it!" Memnoch said. "I can teach them; I can guide them. You let me run Hell as I choose to run it and I can reclaim them for Heaven; I can undo all that your Natural Cycle has done to them on Earth."

"Fine, then, I should like to see you do it!" said the Son of God. "Send me more souls then, through your purgation. Go ahead. Increase my Glory. Increase the *bene ha elohim*. Heaven is endless and welcomes your efforts.

"But you don't come home forever until the task is finished, until the passage from Earth to Heaven includes all those who die, or until the world itself is destroyed—until evolution has unfolded to the point where Sheol, for one reason or another, is empty, and mark my words, Memnoch, that time may never come! I have promised no ending to the unfolding of the universe! So you have a long tenure among the Damned."

"And on earth? What are my powers? Goat God or Man, what can I do?"

"What you should do! Warn humans. Warn them so that they come to me and not to Sheol."

"And I can do that my way? By telling them what a merciless God you are, and that to kill in your name is wicked, and that suffering warps and twists and damns its victims more often than redeems them? I can tell them the truth? That if they would go to you, they would abandon your religions and your holy wars and your magnificent martyrdom? They would seek to understand what the mystery of the flesh tells them, the ecstasy of love tells them? You give me permission? You give me permission to tell them the truth?"

"Tell them what you will! And in each case that you draw them away from my churches, my revelations, misunderstood and garbled though they may be—in every case that you turn them away, you risk another pupil in your hellish school, another soul which you must reform. Your hell will be crammed to overflowing!"

"Not through my doings, Lord," Memnoch said. "It will be full to overflowing, but that will be thanks to you!"

"You dare!"

"Let it unfold, My Lord, as you have said it always should. Only now I am part of it, and Hell is part of it. And will you give to me those angels who believe as I do and will work for me, and endure the same darkness with me?"

"No! I will not give you one angelic spirit! Recruit your helpers from the earthbound souls themselves. Make those your demons! The Watchers who fell with you are contrite. I will not give you anyone. You are an Angel. Stand alone."

"Very well, I stand alone. Hobble me in my earthly form if you will, but still I will triumph. I will bring more souls through Sheol to Heaven than you will bring by your direct Gate. I will bring more reformed souls singing of Paradise than you will ever gather through your narrow tunnel. It is I who will fill Heaven and magnify your glory. You will see."

They fell silent, Memnoch in a fury, and God Incarnate in a fury or so it seemed, the two figures facing each other, both of equal size, except that Memnoch's wings spread back and out in the semblance of a form of power, and from God Incarnate came the more powerful, heartrendingly beautiful Light.

Suddenly, God Incarnate smiled.

"Either way I triumph, don't I?" God asked.

"I curse you!" said Memnoch.

"No, you don't," said God sadly and gently. He reached out and He touched Memnoch's face and the imprint of His angry hand vanished off the angelic skin. God Incarnate leant forward and kissed Memnoch on the mouth.

"I love you, my brave adversary!" He said. "It is good that I made you, as good as all else I've made. Bring souls to me. You are only part of the cycle, part of Nature, as wondrous as a bolt of lightning or the eruption of a great volcano, as a star exploding suddenly, miles and miles out in the galaxies so that thousands of years pass before those on earth see its light."

"You're a merciless God," Memnoch said, refusing to give an inch. "I shall teach them to forgive you what you are—Majestic, Infinitely Creative, and Imperfect."

God Incarnate laughed softly and kissed Memnoch again on the forehead.

"I am a wise God and a patient God," He said. "I am the One who made you."

The images vanished. They did not even fade. They simply disappeared.

I lay on the battlefield alone.

The stench was a layer of gases hanging over me, poisoning every breath I drew.

For as far as I could see were dead men.

A noise startled me. The thin, panting figure of a wolf drew near to me, bearing down on me with its lowered head. I stiffened. I saw its narrow uptilted eyes as it pushed its snout arrogantly at me. I smelt its hot, rank breath. I turned my face away. I heard it sniff at my ear, my hair. I heard a deep growl come out of it. I just shut my eyes and with my right hand in my coat, I felt the veil.

Its teeth grazed my neck. Instantly, I turned, rose and knocked the wolf backwards, and sent it tumbling and yelping and finally scuttling away from me. Off it ran over the bodies of the dead.

I took a deep breath. I realized the sky overhead was the daytime sky of Earth and I looked at the white clouds, the simple white clouds and the dim faraway horizon beneath them, and I listened to the storm of the insects—the gnats and the flies rising and swirling here and there over the bodies—and the big humpish ugly vultures, tiptoeing through the feast.

From far away came the sound of human weeping.

But the sky was magnificently clear. The clouds moved so that they released the sun in all its power, and down came the warmth on my hands and face, on the gaseous and exploding bodies around me.

I think I must have lost consciousness. I wanted to. I wanted to fall backwards again on the earth and roll over and lie with my forehead against it, and slip my hand into my coat and feel that the veil was there.

20

THE GARDEN of Waiting. The tranquil and radiant place before the Heavenly Gates. A place from which souls return from time to time, when death brings them into it, and they are then told that it is not the moment, and they can go home again.

In the distance, beneath the shining cobalt sky, I saw the Newly Dead greet the Older Dead. Gathering after gathering. I saw the embraces, heard the exclamations. Out of the corner of my eyes, I saw the dizzyingly high walls of Heaven, and Heaven's gates. This time I saw the angels, less solid than all the rest, chorus after chorus, moving through the skies, unbound and dipping down at will into the little crowds of mortals crossing the bridge. Shifting between visibility and invisibility, the angels moved, watched, drifted upwards to fade into the inexhaustible blue of the sky.

The sounds of Heaven were faint and achingly seductive as they came from beyond the walls. I could close my eyes and almost see the sapphirine colors! All songs sang the same refrain: "Come in, come here, come inside, be with us. Chaos is no more. This is Heaven."

But I was far from all this, in a little valley. I sat amid wildflowers, tiny white and yellow wildflowers, on the grass bank of the stream which all souls cross to get into Heaven, only here it seemed no more than any magnificent rushing stream. Or rather, it sang a song that said—after smoke and war, after soot and blood, after stench and pain—All streams are as magnificent as this stream.

Water sings in multiple voices as it slides over rocks and down through tiny gullies and rushes abruptly over rises in the earth so that it may again tumble in a mingling of fugue and canon. While the grass bends its head to watch.

I rested against the trunk of a tree, what the peach tree might be if she bloomed forever, both blossoms and fruit, so that she was never bare of either, and her limbs hung down not in submission, but with this richness, this fragrance, this offering, this fusion of two cycles into one eternal abundance. Above, amid fluttering petals, the supply of which seemed inexhaustible and never alarming, I saw the fleeting movement of tiny birds. And beyond that, angels, and angels, and angels, as if they were made of air, the light luminous glittering spirits so faint as to vanish at times in one brilliant breath of the sky.

The Paradise of murals; the Paradise of mosaics. Only no form of art can touch this. Question those who have come and gone. Those whose hearts have stopped on an operating table, so that their souls flew to this garden, and then were brought back down into articulate flesh. Nothing can touch it.

The cool, sweet air surrounded me, slowly removing, layer by layer, the soot and filth that clung to my coat and my shirt.

Suddenly, as if waking to life again from nightmare, I reached inside my shirt and drew out the veil. I unfolded it and held it by its two edges.

The face burned in it, the dark eyes staring at me, the blood as brilliantly red as before, the skin the perfect hue, the depth almost holographic, though the whole expression moved very faintly as the veil moved on the breeze. Nothing had been smeared, torn, or lost.

I felt myself gasp, and my heart speeded dangerously. The heat flooded to my own face.

The brown eyes were steady in their gaze as they had been at that moment, not closing for the soft finely woven fabric. I drew the whole veil close to me, then folded it up again, almost in a panic, and shoved it tight against my skin this time, inside my shirt. I struggled to restore all the buttons to their proper holes. My shirt was all right. My coat was filthy though intact, but all its buttons were gone, even the buttons that had graced the sleeves and had been no longer of any use and were merely decorative. I looked down at my shoes; they were broken and tattered and barely held together anymore. How strange they looked, how unlike anything I had seen of late, made as they were of such fancy leather.

Petals fell in my hair. I reached up and brushed loose a small shower of them, pink and white, as they fell on my pants and shoes.

"Memnoch!" I said suddenly. I looked around me. Where was he? Was I here alone? Far, far away moved the procession of happy souls across the bridge. Did the gates open and close or was that an illusion?

I looked to the left, to a copse of olive trees, and saw standing beneath it first a figure I didn't recognize, and then realized it was Memnoch as the Ordinary Man. He stood collected, looking at me, face grim and set; then the image began to grow and spread, to sprout its huge black wings, and twisted goat legs, and cloven feet, and the angel face gleamed as if in living black granite. Memnoch, my Memnoch, the Memnoch I knew once again clothed as the demon.

I made no resistance. I didn't cover my face. I studied the details of his robed torso, the way the cloth came down over the hideous fur-covered legs. The cloven feet dug into the ground beneath him, but his hands and arms were his own beautiful hands and arms. His hair was the flowing mane, only jet black. And in all the Garden he was the only pure absence of color, opaque, or at least visible to me, seemingly solid.

"The argument is simple," he said. "Do you have any trouble now understanding it?"

His black wings came in close, hugging the body, lower tips curved forward, near his feet, so that they did not scrape the ground.

He walked towards me, a horrid animalian advance carrying the overwhelmingly perfect torso and head, a hobbled being, thrust into a human conception of evil.

"Right you are," he said, and slowly, almost painfully, seated himself, the wings once more fading because they could never have allowed it; and there he sat, the goat god glaring at me, hair tangled, but face as serene as always, no harsher, no sweeter, no wiser or more cruel, because it was graven out of blackness instead of the shimmering image of flesh.

He began to talk:

"You see, what He actually did was this. He said over and over to me, 'Memnoch, everything in the universe is used . . . made use of . . . you understand?' And He came down, suffered, died, and rose from the Dead to consecrate human suffering, to enshrine it as a means to an end; the end was illumination, superiority of the soul.

"But the myth of the suffering and Dying God—whether we speak of Tammuz of Sumer or Dionysus of Greece, or any other deity the world over, whose death and dismemberment preceded Creation—this was a Human idea! An idea conceived by Humans who could not imagine a Creation from nothing, one which did not involve a sacrifice. The Dying God who gives birth to Man was a young idea in the minds of those too primitive to conceive of anything absolute and perfect. So He grafted himself—God Incarnate—upon human myths that try to explain things as if they had meaning, when perhaps they don't."

"Yes."

"Where was His sacrifice in making the world?" Memnoch asked. "He was not Tiamat slain by Marduk. He is not Osiris chopped into pieces! What did He, Almighty God, give up to make the material universe? I do not remember seeing anything taken from Him. That it came out of Him, this is true, but I do not remember Him being lessened, or decimated, or maimed, or decreased by the act of Physical Creation! He was after the Creation of the planets and the stars, the same God! If anything He was increased, or seemed to be in the eyes of His angels, as they sang of new and varying aspects of His Creation. His very nature as Creator grew and expanded in our perceptions, as evolution took His path.

"But when He came as God Incarnate, He imitated myths that men had made to try to sanctify all suffering, to try to say that history is not horror, but has meaning. He plunged down into man-made religion and brought His Divine Grace to those images, and He sanctified suffering by His death, whereas it had *not* been sanctified in His Creation, you understand?"

"It was a bloodless Creation and without sacrifice," I said. My voice was dull but my mind had never been more alert. "That is what you're saying. But He does believe suffering is sacrosanct or can be. Nothing is wasted. All things are used."

"Yes. But my position is that He took the awful flaw in His cosmos—human pain, misery, the capacity to suffer unspeakable injustice—and He found a place for it, using the worst superstitious beliefs of Men."

"But when people die—what happens? Do His believers find the tunnel and the Light and Loved ones?"

"In the places where they have lived in peace and prosperity, generally, yes. They rise without hate or resentment directly into Heaven. And so do some who have no belief in Him whatsoever or His teachings.

"Because they too are Illuminated."

"Yes. And this gratifies Him and expands His Heaven, and Heaven is ever enhanced and enriched by these new souls from all quarters of the world."

"But Hell is also full of souls."

"Hell so far exceeds the size of Heaven as to be laughable. Where on the planet has He ruled where there has not been self-sacrifice, injustice, persecution, torment, war! Every day my confused and embittered pupils are increased in number. There are times of such privation and horror that few souls ascend to Him in peace at all."

"And He does not care."

"Precisely. He says that suffering of sentient beings is like decay; it fertilizes the growth of their souls! He looks from His lofty height upon a massacre and He sees magnificence. He sees men and women never loving so much as when they lose their loved ones, never loving so much as when they sacrifice for others for some abstract notion of Him, never loving so much as when the conquering army comes down to lay waste the hearth, divide the flock, and catch up the bodies of infants on their spears.

"His justification? It's in Nature. It's what He created. And if battered and embittered souls must fall into my hands first and suffer my tutelage in Hell, so much the greater will they become!"

"And your job grows heavier all the time."

"Yes and no. I am winning. But I have to win on His terms. Hell is a place of suffering. But let's go over it carefully. Look at it; what He did:

"When He threw open the gates of Sheol, when He went down into the gloom of Sheol, like the god Tammuz into the Sumerian hell, the souls flocked to Him and saw His redemption and saw the wounds in His Hands and Feet, and that He should die for them gave a focus to their confusion, and of course they flooded with Him into the Gates of Heaven—for everything they had suffered seemed suddenly to have a meaning.

"But *did* it have a meaning? Can you give a sacred meaning to the cycle of Nature simply by immersing your Divine Self in it? Is that enough?

"What about the souls who shrink in bitterness, who never flower as the heels of warriors walk over them, what about the souls warped and twisted by unspeakable injustice, who go into eternity cursing, what about a whole modern world which is personally angry with God, angry enough to curse Jesus Christ and God Himself as Luther did, as Dora did, as you have done, as all have done.

"People in your modern world of the late twentieth century have never stopped believing in Him. It's that they hate Him; they resent Him; they are furious with Him. They feel . . . they feel. . . ."

"Superior to Him," I said quietly, keenly aware that he was saying now some of the very words I myself had said to Dora. We hate God. We hate Him.

"Yes," he said. "Yes, you feel superior to Him."

"And *you* feel superior."

"Yes. I can't show them His wounds in Hell. That isn't going to win them over, these victims, these grieving, furious sufferers of pain beyond His imagining. I can just tell them that it was the Dominican Fathers in His Name who burnt their bodies alive, thinking them witches. Or that when their families and clans and villages were annihilated by Spanish soldiers, it was all right because His bleeding Hands and Feet were on the banner which the men carried to the New World. You think that would get somebody out of Hell, finding out that He let it happen? And lets other souls ascend without suffering one drop of pain?

"If I were to begin their education with that image—Christ has Died for You—how long do you think the Hellish education of a soul would take?"

"You haven't told me what Hell is or how you do teach there."

"I run it my way, of that I can assure you.

"I have put my throne above His throne—as the poets and the redactors of Scripture say it—because I know that for souls to attain Heaven, suffering was never necessary, that full understanding and receptivity to God never required a fast, a scourging, a crucifixion, a death. I know that the human soul transcended Nature, and needed no more than an eye for beauty to do this! Job was Job before he suffered! Just as after! What did the suffering teach Job that he didn't know before?"

"But how do you make up for it in Hell?"

"I don't begin by telling them that for Him, the human eye expresses the perfection of creation when it looks with horror upon a maimed body, just as it expresses the perfection of Creation when it looks in peace upon a garden.

"And He persists that it's all there. Your Savage Garden, Lestat, *is* His version of Perfection. It all evolved from the same seed, and I, Memnoch, the Devil, fail to see it. I have an angel's simple mind."

"How do you fight Him in Hell and still win Heaven for the damned, then? How?"

"What do you think Hell is?" he asked. "You must have a surmise by now."

"First of all, it is what we call purgatory," I said. "No one is beyond redemption. I understood from your argument on the battlefield. So what must the souls of Hell suffer to be fully qualified for Heaven?"

"What do you think they should suffer?"

"I don't know. I'm frightened. We're about to go there, aren't we?"

"Yes, but I'd like to know what you expect."

"I don't know what to expect. I know that creatures who have robbed others of life—as I have—should suffer for it."

"Suffer or pay for it?"

"What would be the difference?"

"Well, suppose you had a chance to forgive Magnus, the vampire who brought you into this, suppose he stood before you and said, 'Lestat, forgive me for taking you out of your mortal life and putting you outside Nature, and making you drink blood to live. Do with me what you will so that you can forgive me.' What would you do?"

"You chose a bad example," I said. "I don't know that I haven't

forgiven him. I don't think he knew what he was doing. I don't care
about him. He was mad. He was an Old World monster. He started
me on the Devil's Road on some warped, impersonal impulse. I don't
even think about him. I don't care about him. If he has to seek forgiveness from someone, then let it be from the mortals he killed
when he was in existence.

"In his tower was a dungeon filled with slain mortal men—young
men who resembled me, men he'd brought there to test, apparently,
and then killed rather than initiated. I remember them still. But it's
just one form of massacre—heaps of bodies of young men, all with
blond hair and blue eyes. Young beings robbed of potential and of
life itself. His forgiveness would have to come from all those whom
he robbed of life in any fashion—he would have to gain the forgiveness of each one."

I was beginning to tremble again. My anger was so familiar to me.
And how angry I had become many a time when others had accused
me of my various flamboyant attacks upon mortal men and women.
And children. Helpless children.

"And you?" he said to me. "For you to get into Heaven, what do
you think would be necessary?"

"Well, apparently working for you will do it," I said defiantly. "At
least I think it would from what you've said to me. But you haven't
really told me precisely what you do! You've told me the story of
Creation and the Passion, of Your Way and His Way, you've described how you oppose Him on Earth, and I can imagine the ramifi-
cations of that opposition—we are both sensualists, we are both
believers in the wisdom of the flesh."

"Amen to that."

"But you have not gotten to a full explanation of what you do in
Hell. And how can you be winning? Are you sending them speedily to
His arms?"

"Speedily and with powerful acceptance," he said. "But I am not
speaking to you now about my offer to you, or my Earthly opposition
to Him; I'm asking you this: Given all that you have seen—*What do
you think Hell should be!*"

"I'm afraid to answer. Because I belong there."

"You're never really that afraid of anything. Go on. Make a statement. What do you think Hell ought to be, what should a soul have
to endure to be worthy of Heaven? Is it enough to say 'I believe in
God'; Jesus, 'I believe in Your Suffering'? Is it enough to say, 'I'm

sorry for all my sins because they offend thee, my God?' Or to say, 'I'm sorry because when I was on Earth, I really didn't believe in You and now I know it's true, and wham, bang, one look at this infernal place, and I'm ready! I wouldn't do anything the same way, and please let me into Heaven quick.'"

I didn't answer.

"Should everyone just go to Heaven?" he asked. "I mean, should everyone go?"

"No. That can't be," I said. "Not creatures like me, not creatures who have tortured and killed other creatures, not people who have deliberately duplicated through their actions punishments as severe as disease, or fire, or earthquake—that is, not people who have done wrongs that hurt others just as much or worse than natural disasters. It can't be right for them to go to Heaven, not if they don't know, not if they don't understand, not if they haven't begun to comprehend what they've done! Heaven would be Hell in no time if every cruel, selfish, vicious soul went to Heaven. I don't want to meet the un-reformed monsters of Earth in Heaven! If it's that easy, then the suffering of this world is damned near...."

"Damn near what?

"Unforgivable," I whispered.

"What *would* be forgivable—from the point of view of a soul who died in pain and confusion? A soul who knew that God didn't care?"

"I don't know," I said. "When you described the elect of Sheol, the first million souls you took through the Heavenly Gates, you didn't speak of reformed monsters; you spoke of people who had forgiven God for an unjust world, didn't you?"

"That's right, I did. That's what I found. That's what I took with me with certainty to Heaven's Gates, yes."

"But you spoke entirely as if these people had been victims of God's injustice. You didn't touch upon the souls of the guilty? Those like me—the transgressors, those who were the doers of injustice?"

"Don't you think they have their story?"

"Some may have their excuses, engrained in their stupidity and their simplicity and their fear of authority. I don't know. But many, many evildoers must be just like me. They know how bad they are. They don't care. They do what they do because ... because they love it. I love making vampires. I love drinking blood. I love taking life. I always have."

"Is that really why you drink blood? Just because you love it? Or isn't it because you were made into a perfect preternatural mechanism for craving blood eternally, and thriving only on blood—snatched out of life and made a gleaming Child of the Night by an unjust world that cared no more for you and your destiny than it cared for any infant who starved that night in Paris?"

"I don't justify what I do or what I am. If you think I do, if that's why you want me to run Hell with you, or accuse God . . . then you picked the wrong person. I deserve to pay for what I've taken from people. Where are their souls, those I've slain? Were they ready for Heaven? Have they gone to Hell? Did those souls loosen in their identity and are they still in the whirlwind between Hell and Heaven? Souls are there, I know, I saw them, souls who have yet to find either place."

"Yes, true."

"I could have sent souls into the whirlwind. I am the embodiment of greed and cruelty. I devoured the mortals I've killed like so much food and drink. I cannot justify it."

"Do you think I want you to justify it?" Memnoch asked. "What violence have I justified so far? What makes you think I would like you if you justified or defended your actions? Have I ever defended anyone who made anyone else suffer?"

"No, you haven't."

"Well, then?"

"What is Hell, and how can you run it? You don't want people to suffer. You don't even seem to want me to suffer. You can't point to God and say He makes it all Good and Meaningful! You can't. You're His opposition. So what is Hell?"

"What do you think it is?" he asked me again. "What would you morally settle for . . . before rejecting me out of hand! Before fleeing from me. What sort of Hell could you believe in and would you—if you were in my place—create?"

"A place where people realize what they've done to others; where they face every detail of it, and realize every particle of it, so that they would *never, never* do the same thing again; a place where souls are reformed, literally, by knowledge of what they'd done wrong and how they could have avoided it, and what they should have done. When they *understand*, as you said of the Elect of Sheol, when they can *forgive* not only God for this big mess, but themselves for their own failures, their own horrible angry reactions, their own spite and meanness, when they love everyone totally in complete forgiveness, then they would be worthy of Heaven. *Hell would have to be where they see the consequences of their actions, but with a full merciful comprehension of how little they themselves knew.*"

"Precisely. To know what has hurt others, to realize that you didn't know, that nobody gave you the knowledge, yet still you had the power! And to forgive that, and forgive your victims, and forgive God and forgive yourself."

"Yes. That would be it. That would terminate my anger, my outrage. I couldn't shake my fist anymore, if only I could forgive God and others and myself."

He didn't say anything. He sat with his arms folded, eyes wide, his dark smooth brow barely touched with the moisture of the air.

"That's what it is, isn't it?" I asked fearfully. "It's . . . it's a place where you learn to understand what you've done to another being . . . where you come to realize the suffering you've inflicted on others!"

"Yes, and it is terrible. I created it and I run it to make whole again the souls of the just and the unjust, those who had suffered and those who had done cruelty. And the only lesson of that Hell is Love."

I was frightened, as frightened as I had been when we went into Jerusalem.

"He loves my souls when they come to Him," said Memnoch. "And He sees each one as a justification of His Way!"

I smiled bitterly.

"War is magnificent to Him, and disease is like the color purple in His eyes, and self-sacrifice seems to Him a personal magnification of His Glory! As if He's ever done it! He tries to overwhelm me with numbers. In the name of the cross, more injustice has been perpetrated than for any other single cause or emblem or philosophy or creed on Earth.

"And I empty Hell so fast, soul by soul, by speaking truth about what humans suffer and humans know and what humans can do that my souls go flooding through His gates.

"And who do you think comes into Hell feeling most cheated? Most angry and unforgiving? The child who died in a gas chamber in an extermination camp? Or a warrior with blood up to his elbows who was told that if he exterminated the enemies of the state he would find his place in Valhalla, Paradise, or Heaven?"

I didn't answer. I was quiet, listening to him, watching him.

He sat forward, commanding my attention even more deliberately, and as he did he changed, changed before my eyes from the Devil, goat-legged, cloven-hoofed beast-man, to the angel, Memnoch, Memnoch in his loose and unimportant robe, his fair eyes beaming at me beneath his golden scowling brows.

"Hell is where I straighten things out that He has made wrong," he said. "Hell is where I reintroduce a frame of mind that might have existed had suffering never destroyed it! Hell is where I teach men and women that they can be better than He is.

"But that's my punishment, Hell—for arguing with Him, that I must go there and help the souls to fulfill their cycle as He sees it, that I must live there with them! And that if I don't help them, if I don't school them, they may be there forever!

"But Hell is not my battlefield.

"The earth is my battlefield. Lestat, I fight Him not in Hell but on Earth. I roam the world seeking to tear down every edifice He has erected to sanctify self-sacrifice and suffering, to sanctify aggression and cruelty and destruction. I lead men and women from churches and temples to dance, to sing, to drink, to embrace one another with license and love. I do everything I can to show up the lie at the heart of His religions! I try to destroy the lies He's allowed to grow as the Universe Unfolds Itself.

"He is the only one who can enjoy suffering with impunity! And that's because He's God and He doesn't know what it means and He never has known. He's created beings more conscientious and loving than Himself. And the final victory over all human evil will come only when He is dethroned, once and for all, demystified, ignored, repudiated, thrown aside, and men and women seek for the good and the just and the ethical and the loving in each other and for all."

"They're trying to do that, Memnoch! They are!" I said. "That's what they mean when they say they hate Him. That's what Dora meant when she said 'Ask Him why He allows all this!' When she made her hands into fists!"

"I know. Now, do you want to help me fight Him and his Cross or not?

"Will you go with me from Earth to Heaven to that filthy Hell of painful recognition, filthy with its obsession with His suffering! You will not serve me in one place or the other or the other. But in all three. And like me, you may soon come to find Heaven just about as unbearable in its pitch as Hell. Its bliss will make you eager to heal the evil He has done, you will seek Hell to work on those tortured confused souls, to help them up from the morass and into the Light. When you're in the Light you can't forget them! That's what it means to serve me."

He paused, then he asked:

"Do you have the courage to see it?"

"I want to see it."

"I warn you, it's Hell."

"I am just beginning to imagine. . . . "

"It won't exist forever. The day will come when either the world itself is blown to pieces by His human worshippers or when all who die are Illuminated and surrender to Him, and go straight into His arms.

"A perfect world, or a world destroyed, one or the other—someday will come the end of Hell. And then I shall go back to Heaven, content to stay there for the first moment of my existence, since the beginning of Time."

"Take me with you into Hell, please. I want to see it now."

He reached out and stroked my hair, put his two hands on the sides of my face. They felt evenly warm and caressing. A sense of tranquility came over me.

"So many times in the past," he said, "I almost had your soul! I saw it almost spring loose from your body, and then the strong preternatural flesh, the preternatural brain, the hero's courage, would hold together the entire monster and the soul would flicker and blaze inside, beyond my grasp. And now, now I risk plunging you into it before you need to go, plunging you into it when you can choose to go or come, in the hope that you can endure what you see and hear and return and be with me and help me."

"Was there ever a time when my soul would have soared to Heaven, past you, past the whirlwind?"

"What do you think?"

"I remember . . . once, when I was alive. . . . "

"Yes?"

"A golden moment, when I was drinking and talking with my good friend, Nicolas, and we were in an inn together in my village in France. And there came this golden moment when everything seemed tolerable and independently beautiful of any horror that could be or ever had been done. Just a moment, a drunken moment. I described it once in writing; I tried to reinvoke it. It was a moment in which I could have forgiven anything, and given anything, and perhaps when I didn't even exist: when all I saw was beyond me, outside me. I don't know. Maybe if death had come at that very moment—"

"But fear came, fear when you realized that even if you died you might not understand anything, that there might be nothing. . . ."

". . . yes. And now I fear something worse. That there is something, certainly, and it may be worse than nothing at all."

"You're right to think so. It doesn't take much of a thumbscrew or the nails or the fire to make men and women wish for oblivion. Not much at all. Imagine, to wish that you had never lived."

"I know the concept. I fear knowing the feeling again."

"You're wise to fear, but you've never been more ready for what I have to reveal."

21

THE WIND swept the rocky field, the great centrifugal force dissolving and releasing those souls who struggled to be free of it at last as they assumed distinct human shape and pounded on the Gates of Hell, or wandered along the impossibly high walls, amid the flicker of fires within, reaching out for and imploring each other.

All voices were lost in the sound of the wind. Souls in human shape fought and struggled, others roamed as if in search of something small and lost and then lifted their arms and let the whirlwind once again take hold of them.

The shape of a woman, thin and pale, reached out to gather a wandering, weeping flock of baby souls, some not old enough yet to walk on two legs. The spirits of children wandered, crying piteously.

We drew near the gates, near narrow broken arches rising as black and fine as onyx worked by medieval craftsmen. The air was filled with soft and bleating cries. Everywhere spirit hands reached to take hold of us; whispers covered us like the gnats and flies of the battlefield. Ghosts tore at my hair and coat.

Help us, let us in, damn you, curse you, cursed, take me back, free me, I curse you forever, damn you, help me, help . . . a rising roar of opprobrium.

I struggled to clear the way for my eyes. Tender faces drifted before me, mouths issuing hot and mournful gasps against my skin.

The gates weren't solid gates at all but gateways.

And beyond stood the Helpful Dead, seemingly more solid, only more vividly colored and distinct, but diaphanous still, beckoning to the lost souls, calling to them by name, howling over the fierce wind that they must find the way inside, that this was not Perdition.

Torches were held high; lamps burnt atop the walls. The sky was torn with streaks of lightning, and the great mystic shower of sparks that comes from cannons both modern and ancient. The smell of gunpowder and blood filled the air. Again and again the lights flared as if in some magical display to enchant a Chinese court of old, and then the blackness rolled back, thin and substanceless and cold all around us.

"Come inside," sang the Helpful Dead, the well-formed, well-proportioned ghosts—ghosts as determined as Roger had been, in garbs of all times and all nations, men and women, children, old ones, no body opaque, yet none weak, all reaching past us into the valley beyond, trying to assist the struggling, the cursing, the foundering. The Helpful Dead of India in their silk saris, of Egypt in cotton robes, of kingdoms long gone bequeathing jeweled and magnificent courtly garments; costumes of all the world, the feathered confections we call savage, the dark robes of priests, self-conceptions of all the world, from the crudest to the most magnificent.

I clung to Memnoch. Was this beautiful, or was it not hideous, this throng of all nations and times? The naked, the black, the white, the Asian, those of all races, reaching out, moving with confidence through the lost and confused souls!

The ground itself hurt my feet; blackened, rocky marl strewn with shells. Why this? Why?

In all directions slopes rose or gently fell away, to run into sheer cliffs rising beyond or opening into chasms so deep and filled with smoky dissolving gloom they seemed the abyss itself.

Doorways flickered and flashed with light; stairways wound precipitously up and down the stark, steep walls, leading out of sight, to vales I could only glimpse, or to gushing streams golden and steaming and red with blood.

"Memnoch, help me!" I whispered. I dared not let go of the veil.

I couldn't cover both ears. The howls were picking at my soul as if they were axes that could tear away pieces of it. "Memnoch, this is unbearable!"

"We will all help you," cried the Helpful Ghosts, a cluster of them closing in on all sides to kiss and to embrace me, their eyes wide with concern. "Lestat has come. Lestat is here. Memnoch's brought him back. Come into Hell."

Voices rose and fell and overlapped, as if a multitude said the Rosary, each from a different starting point, voices having become chant.

"We love you."

"Don't be afraid. We need you."

"Stay with us."

"Shorten our time."

I felt their soft sweet soothing touch even as the lurid light terrified me, and the explosions blazed across the sky and the smell of smoke rose in my nostrils.

"Memnoch!" I clung to his blackened hand as he pulled me along, his profile remote, his eyes seeming to sternly survey his kingdom.

And there below us, as the mountain was cleft, lay the plains without end, covered with wandering and arguing dead, with the weeping and lost, and seeking, and afraid, with those being led and gathered and comforted by the Helpful Ghosts, and others running headlong as if they could escape, only to find themselves tumbling through the spirit multitudes, in hopeless circles.

From where did this hellish light come, this magnificent and relentless illumination? Showers of sparks, sudden bursts of burning red, flames, comets arching over the peaks.

Howls rose, echoing off the cliffs. Souls wailed and sang. The Helpful Dead rushed to aid the fallen to their feet, to usher those who would at last come to this or that stairs or gate or cave mouth or pathway.

"I curse Him, I curse Him, I curse Him!" It echoed off the mountains and through the valleys.

"No justice, not after what was done!"

"You cannot tell me. . . ."

". . . someone has to make right. . . ."

"Come, I have your hand," Memnoch said, and on he walked, the same stern look on his face as he led me quickly down an echoing stairs, steep, dangerously narrow, and winding about the cliff.

"I can't bear this!" I cried out. But my voice was snatched away. My right hand plunged into my coat again to feel the bulk of the veil, and then I reached out for the pitted and crumbling wall. Were these carvings in the rocks? Were these places where other hands had clawed or tried to climb? The screaming and the wails blotted out my reason. We had come again to yet another valley.

Or was it a world, as vast and complex in its own right as Heaven? For here were myriad palaces and towers and arches as before, in colors of sombre brown, and burnt sienna, and ochre, and burnished if not blackened gold, and rooms filled with spirits of all ages and nations again, engaged in argument, discourse, struggle, or even song, some holding each other like newfound friends in the midst of woe, uniformed soldiers of ancient wars and modern wars, women in the shapeless draped black of the Holy Land, the souls of the modern world in their store-made finery now covered with dust and soot, so that all that blazed was muted in the blaze, as if no color could shine forth itself in its more baleful glory. They wept and patted each other's faces, and others nodded as they screamed their wrath, fists clenched.

Souls in ragged monks' habits of coarse brown, nuns with the stiff white wimples intact, princes in puffed sleeves of velvet, naked men who walked as though they had never known clothes, dresses of gingham and old lace, of modern glittering silks and chemical fabrics sheer and thick, soldiers' olive green coats, or armour of gleaming bronze, peasants' tunics of crude cloth, or fine tailored wool suits of modern fashion, gowns of silver; hair of all colors tangled and mingled in the wind; faces of all colors; the old knelt with hands clasped, bald heads pink and tenderly wrinkled at the neck, and the thin white soulbodies of those who had starved in life drank out of the streams as dogs might do it, with their mouths, and others lay back, eyes half shut against the rocks and gnarled trees, singing and dreaming, and praying.

My eyes grew more accustomed to the gloom with every second. More details leapt into my vision, more comprehension clarified each square inch or foot of what I beheld! For around each true soul, a dozen figures that danced or sang or wailed were no more than images projected from that soul and to that soul for it to commune with.

The horrid figure of a woman consumed in flames was no more than a chimera for the howling souls who plunged into the fire, seeking to free her from the stake, to stamp out the flames that ate her hair, to rescue her from her unspeakable agony! It was the Witches Place. They were all burning! Save them! Oh, God, her hair is on fire!

Indeed the soldiers stoking the cannon and covering their ears now as they made the shot were but an illusion for those true legions weeping on their knees, and a hulk of a giant wielding an ax was but a phantom for those who stared at him in recognition and stupification, seeing in him themselves.

"I cannot . . . I cannot look!"

Monstrous images of murder, torture, flashed before me so hot they burnt my face. Phantoms were dragged to their deaths in pots of boiling pitch, solders sank on their knees, eyes wide, a prince of some lost Persian kingdom screamed and leapt into the air, his arms out, his black eyes full of reflected fire.

The wails, the whispers, took on the urgency of protest, and question, and discovery. All around were particular voices if only one had the courage to hear, to pick the themes fine as steel thread from the raging dirge.

"Yes, yes, and I thought, and I knew . . ."

". . . my darlings, my little ones . . ."

". . . into your arms, because you didn't, you never . . ."

". . . and I all the time I thought and you . . ."

"Love you, love you, love you, yes, and always . . . and no, you didn't know. You didn't know, you didn't know."

". . . and always thought that it was what I should, but I knew, I felt . . ."

". . . the courage to turn and say that it wasn't . . ."

"We didn't know! We didn't know."

It was blended finally into that one incessant cry.

We Did Not Know!

Before me the wall of a mosque rose, crowded with those screaming and covering their heads as the plaster came down upon them, the roar of the artillery deafening. Phantoms all.

We didn't know, we didn't know, the voices of the souls wailed. The Helpful Dead gathered on their knees, tears streaming down their faces . . . "Yes, we understand, you understand."

"And that year, just to go home then and be with . . ."

"Yes . . ."

I fell forward, my foot striking a rock, and pitching me into the middle of a swarm of soldiers on their hands and knees, weeping as they clutched at one another and the wraithlike phantoms of the conquered, the slain, the starved, all rocking and crying together in one voice.

There came a chain of explosions, each more violent than the one before, such as only the modern world can make. The sky was light as day if day could be colorless and merciless and then dissolve into flickering darkness.

Darkness Visible.

"Help, help me out of this," I cried, but they didn't seem to hear or notice my screams, and when I looked for Memnoch, I saw only a pair of elevator doors slide open suddenly, and before me loomed a great modern room full of elaborate chandeliers and buffed floors and carpets without end. The hard polished glitter of our machine-made world. Roger came running towards me.

Roger, in all his dandified finery of purple silk jacket and tightly tailored pants, of perfumed hair, and manicured hands.

"Lestat," he cried. "Terry is here, they are here. Lestat." He clung to my coat, the very eyes I'd seen in the ghost and in the human in my arms, staring at me, breath on my face, the room dissolving into smoke, the dim spirit of Terry with her bright bottle-blond hair, throwing her arms about his neck, her face open with amazement, her pink lips speechless, Memnoch's wing touching down, shutting me off from them, the floor cracking open.

"I wanted to tell him about the veil. . . ." I insisted. I struggled. Memnoch held me.

"This way!"

The heavens opened with another fiery shower of sparks and the clouds burst above, clashing together, the lightning touching down over our heads, and on came a thunderous deluge of cold and chilling rain.

"Oh God, oh, God, oh God!" I cried. "This cannot be your school! God! I say no!"

"Look, *look*!"

He pointed to the figure of Roger on his hands and knees, turning like a dog, amongst those he'd slain, men imploring him with outstretched arms, women tearing open the cloth of their dresses to show the wounds, the chatter of voices rising perilously as if the sound of Hell itself would suddenly explode, and Terry—the very same Terry—with her arms still around his neck. Roger lay on the ground, his shirt torn open, his feet naked, the jungle rising around him. Shots rang out in the dark. Crack of automatic guns spitting their numberless fatal bullets in unstinted fury. The lights of a house flickered among vines, amid monstrous trees. Roger turned to me, trying to rise, sinking back on his leg, crying, the tears streaming down his face.

". . . and each and every act, in its own way, Lestat, and I didn't know . . . I didn't know. . . ."

Distinct and ghastly and demanding, he rose before me only to recede into the countless others.

In all directions I saw them. The others.

Scenario lapping into scenario, ashen colors brightening, or dying in a murky haze, and rising here and there from the horrid furious turbulent fields of Hell, the Purified Souls. There came the beat of drums, there came the piercing shrieks of some unendurable torture; a mass of men in crude white robes shoved into the blazing logs, their arms appealing to the souls who shrank and howled and screamed in remorse, in awful recognition.

"My God, my God, we are both forgiven!"

What was this sudden whirl of the filthy, stinking wind?

Upward souls went with arms out, garments suddenly stripped or faded away into the indistinguishable robes of the Saved, the Tunnel opening.

I saw the Light, saw the myriad spirits flying loose up the Tunnel towards the celestial blaze, the Tunnel perfectly round, and widening as they rose and for one blessed moment, one blessed tiny instant, the songs of Heaven resounded down the tunnel as if its curves were not made of wind but of something solid that could echo these ethereal songs, and their organized rhythm, their heartbreaking beauty piercing the catastrophic suffering of this place.

"I didn't know, I didn't know!" The voices rose. The Tunnel closed.

I stumbled, turning this way and that. Here soldiers tortured a young woman with their spears, while others wept and sought to throw themselves between her writhing form and her tormentors. Here babies ran on chubby legs with little hands outstretched to be gathered in the arms of weeping fathers, mothers, murderers.

And pinned to the ground, his body covered in armour, his beard long and red, his mouth open in a howl, lay one cursing God cursing the Devil and cursing all Fate. *"I will not, I will not, I will not!"*

"And who stands behind those doors," said a sombre Helpful Ghost, her beautiful hair shimmering around her in ethereal whiteness, her soft hand on my face. "See there—" The double doors about to open, the walls lined with books. "Your dead, my beloved, your dead, all those you've killed!"

I stared at the soldier on his back, roaring from his red-bearded mouth, "Never, never will I say it was right, never, never. . . ."

"Not my dead," I cried. I turned and ran. I stumbled and fell again on my face in the soft press of bodies. Beyond, the ruins of a city withered in fire; walls crumbled on all sides, the cannon exploded again, and once more, a noxious gas filled the air, people fell coughing and choking for breath, the chorus of I DID NOT KNOW blended all in one instant of order that was worse than none!

"HELP ME!" I cried and cried. I never knew such release in screaming, such pure and abandoned cowardice, to shout to High Heaven in this Godforsaken place where cries were the very air itself, and no one heard, no one but the smiling Helpful Dead.

"Learn, my dearest."

"Learn." Whispers like kisses. A wraith, an Indian man, turbaned head, darkened face. "Learn, my young one."

"Look up, see the blossoms, see the sky. . . ." A Helpful Ghost danced in circles, her white dress passing in and out of the clouds and spurts of soot and filth, her feet sinking into the marl but turning still with certainty.

"Don't fool me, there is no garden here!" I shouted. I was on my knees. My clothes were torn, but in my shirt I had the veil! I *had* it.

"Take my hands. . . ."

"No, let me go!" I slipped my hand in my coat to cover the veil. Staggering towards me a dim figure rose, hand outstretched, "You, you cursed boy, you filthy boy, you in the Paris streets, like Lucifer Himself full of golden light, you! Think what you did to me!"

The tavern took form, the boy falling backwards from the blow of my mortal fist, the barrels going over and the growl of the disheveled and drunken men who closed in on me.

"No, stop it," I roared. "Get him away from me. I don't remember him. I never killed him. I don't remember, I tell you, I can't. . . .

"Claudia, where are you? Where are *you*, the one I wronged! Claudia! Nicolas, help me!"

But were they here, lost in this torrent, or gone, long gone through the Tunnel to the blazing glory above, to the blessed songs that wove the silence into their very chords and melodies? Pray gone, pray there, above.

My own cries had lost all dignity and yet how defiant they sounded in my own ears. "Help me, someone! Help!"

"Must you die first to serve me?" Memnoch asked. He rose before me, the granite angel of darkness, wings outstretched. Oh yes, blot out the horrors of Hell, please, even in this most monstrous of forms! "You scream in Hell as you sang in Heaven. This is my kingdom, this is our work. Remember the Light!"

I fell back on my shoulder, hurting my left arm, but refusing to pull my right hand free of the veil. I saw the blue sky above in a flash and the peach blossoms blowing from the green leaves of the tree even as the luscious fruit itself clung to the branches.

Smoke stung my eyes. A woman on her knees said to me:

"I know now that no one can forgive me but myself, but how could I have done those things to her, and she so small, how could I. . . ."

"I thought it was the other things," whispered a young girl who had hold of my neck, her nose touching mine as she spoke, "but you know that kindness, that just holding his hand and he. . . ."

"Forgive!" Memnoch said, and parted the way, gently pushing the souls aside. But the crowd crushed in; pale figures raced over me as if towards a respite I couldn't see, or some source of alarm.

"Forgive!" Memnoch whispered.

He snatched up the monk covered with blood, his brown robes shredded, his feet blistered and burnt from deliberate fire. "In your heart, the power!" said Memnoch, "Be better than Him, better than Him, set Him an example."

"I love . . . even Him. . . ." came the whisper from the soul's lips as it suddenly dissolved. "Yes, He couldn't have meant for us to suffer so . . . He couldn't."

"Did he pass the test!" I demanded. "Did that soul pass muster in this hellish place, what he just said? Was that enough! Ignorance of God, was that enough! Or is he here scrambling somewhere else in all this filth, or did the Tunnel take him up! Memnoch! Help me."

Everywhere, I looked for the monk with the burnt feet. I looked and looked.

An explosion ripped the towers of the city and they tumbled. Was that the tolling of a bell! The huge mosque had collapsed. A man with a gun fired on those who fled. Veiled women cried out as they fell to the ground.

Louder and louder pealed the bell.

"Good God, Memnoch, a bell tolling, listen, more than one bell."

"The bells of Hell, Lestat, and they are not tolling for anyone! They are ringing for us, Lestat!"

He clutched my collar as if he'd lift me off my feet.

"Remember, your own words, Lestat, Hell's Bells, you hear the call of Hell's Bells!"

"No, let me go. I didn't know what I was saying. It was poetry. It was stupidity. Let me go. I can't stand it!"

Around the table under the lamp a dozen people argued over the map, some embracing each other as they pointed to various areas marked in dull colors. A head was turned. A man? A face. "You!"

"Let me go." I turned and was thrown against a wall of bookshelves, spines gleaming in the light, books tumbling, striking me on the shoulders, dear God, my limbs couldn't take any more. My fist went through the glittering globe of the world, mounted on its fancy arc of wood. A child with bent knees sat staring up at me with empty eye sockets.

I saw the doorway and ran.

"No, let me go. I cannot. I will not. I will not."

"Will not?" Memnoch caught me by my right arm, dark scowl looming over me, the wings flexing and rising, blotting out the light again as they closed to enfold me as though I were his own. "Will you not help me to empty this place, to send these souls to Heaven?"

"I can't do it!" I cried. "I won't do it!" Suddenly my fury rose. I felt it obliterate all fear and trembling and doubt; I felt it rush through my veins like molten metal. The old anger, the resolve of Lestat. "*I will not be part of this, not for you, not for Him, not for them, not for anyone!*"

I staggered backwards, glaring at him. "No, not this. Not for a God as blind as He, and not for one who demands what you demand of me. You're mad, the two of you! I won't help you. I won't. I refuse."

"You would do this to me, you would abandon me?" he cried, stricken, dark face convulsed with pain, tears shimmering on his shining black cheeks. "You would leave me with this, and not lift your hands to help me after all that you have done, Cain, slayer of Brothers, slayer of the Innocents, you cannot help me—?"

"Stop it, stop it. I won't. I can't support this. I can't help this to happen! I cannot create this! I cannot endure it! *I cannot teach in this school!*"

My throat was hoarse and burning, and the din seemed to swallow my words but he heard them.

"No, no, I will not, not this fabric, not these rules, not this design, never, never, never!"

"Coward," he roared, the almond-shaped eyes immense, the fire flickering on the hard black forehead and cheeks. "I have your soul in my hands, I hand you your salvation at a price that those who have suffered here for millennia would beg for!"

"Not me. I won't be part of this pain, no, not now, not ever . . . Go to Him, change the rules, make it make sense, make it better, but not this, this is beyond human endurance, this is unfair, unfair, unfair, this is unconscionable."

"This is Hell, you fool! What did you expect? That you'd serve the Lord of Hell while suffering nothing?"

"I won't do it to them!" I screamed. "To hell with you and with me." My teeth were clenched. I seethed and stormed with my own conviction. "I will not participate in this with them! Don't you see? I cannot accept this! I cannot commit to it. I cannot abide it. I'm leaving you now, you gave me the choice, I'm going home! Release me!"

I turned.

He grabbed my arm again and this time the fury in me knew no bounds. I hurled him backwards over the dissolving and tumbling souls. The Helpful Dead turned here and there to witness and cry out, their pale oval faces full of alarm and distress.

"You go now," Memnoch swore, even as he lay still on the ground where I had thrown him. "And as God is my witness you come back my pupil and my student on your knees at death, and never again this offer to make you my prince, my helper!"

I froze, staring over my shoulder at him, at his fallen figure, his elbow digging into the soft black underdown of his wing as he rose to his cloven feet and came at me again, in that hobbled monstrous walk.

"Do you hear me!"

"I cannot serve you!" I roared at the top of my lungs. "I cannot do it."

Then I turned for the last time, knowing I would not look back, with only one thought in my mind, Escape! I ran and ran, sliding down the loose marl and the slippery bank, and stomping through the shallow streams and through the clumps of astonished Helpful Dead, and over wailing souls.

"Where is the stairs? Where are the gates? You can't deny it to me. You have no right. Death has not taken me!" I shouted but I never looked back and I never stopped running.

"Dora! David, help me!" I called.

And there came Memnoch's voice almost at my ear. "Lestat, don't do this thing, don't go. Don't return. Lestat, don't do it, it's folly, don't you see, please, for the love of God, if you can love Him at all and love them, help me!"

"NO!" I turned and gave him a great shove, seeing him stumble backwards down the steep stairs, the dazed figure amid the huge fluttering wings awkward and grotesque. I pivoted, turning my back on him. Ahead, I could see the light at the very top, the open door.

I ran for it.

"Stop him!" Memnoch cried. "Don't let him out. Don't let him take the veil with him."

"He has Veronica's veil!" cried one of the Helpful Dead lunging at me through the gloom.

My foot nearly slipped, yet on I ran, step after step, bounding, legs aching. I could feel them closing in, the Helpful Dead.

"Stop him."

"Don't let him go!"

"Stop him!"

"Get the veil from him," Memnoch cried, "inside his shirt, the veil, the veil must not go with him!"

I waved my left hand, driving the Helpful Dead in a soft shapeless clatter against the cliff. High above loomed the door. I could see the light. I could see the light and I knew it was the light of Earth, brilliant and natural.

Memnoch's hands clamped on my shoulders and he spun me around.

"No, you don't!" I snarled. "God forgive me. You forgive me, but you're not taking me or the veil!" I roared.

I raised my left arm to stave off his reaching, clawing hands, and shoved him again, but against me he flew as if his wings now came to his aid, and he almost pressed me back against the steps. I felt his fingers plunge into my left eye! I felt them drive open the lids, smashing my eye back into my head in an explosion of pain, and then the gelatinous mass slipped down my cheek, through my trembling fingers.

I heard Memnoch gasp.

"Oh no. . . ." he wailed, his fingers to his lips, staring in horror at the same object at which I stared.

My eye, my round blue eye, shivering and gleaming on the stair. All the Helpful Dead stared at the eye.

"Step on it, crush it," cried one of the Helpful Dead and rushed forward. "Yes, crush it, step on it, smear it!" cried another, swooping down upon the sight.

"No, don't do that, don't! Stop, all of you!" Memnoch wailed. "Not in my kingdom, you will not!"

"Step on the eye!"

That was my moment, that was my chance.

I flew upwards, feet scarcely touching the steps, I felt my head and shoulders plunge through the light and the silence and into the snow.

And I was free.

I WAS on earth. My feet struck the frozen ground, the slippery sludge of snow.

I was running, one-eyed and bleeding, with the veil in my shirt, running through the driving storm, through the drifts of snow, my cries echoing up the buildings I knew, the dark, obdurate skyscrapers of the city I knew. Home, Earth.

The sun had only just set behind the dark gray veil of the descending storm, the winter twilight eaten up in darkness by the whiteness of the snow.

"Dora, Dora, Dora!"

On and on I ran.

Shadowy mortals slouched through the storm; shadowy humans hurried through small slippery paths, automobiles crawled through the blizzard, beams searching the rising, collecting whiteness. The snow was in such thick drifts that I fell and then scrambled to my knees; yet on I went.

The arches and the spires of St. Patrick's rose before me. St. Patrick's.

And beyond, the wall of the Olympic Tower driving upwards, its glass like polished stone, seemingly invincible, its height monstrous as if like the Tower of Babel it was trying to reach directly to Heaven.

I stopped, my heart about to burst.

"Dora! Dora!"

I reached the doors of the lobby, the dizzying lights, the slick floors, the press of mortals, solid mortals everywhere, turning to see what moved too swiftly to be seen. Woozy music and lulling lights, the gush of artificial warmth!

I found the stairwell and rose like a cinder going up a chimney in my flight, and crashed through the wooden door of the apartment, staggering into the room.

Dora.

I saw her, smelled her, smelled the blood from between her legs again, saw her tender little face, white and stricken, and on either side of her like goblins out of nursery rhymes and tales of hell, Armand and David, vampires, monsters, both staring at me in the same stark wonder.

I struggled to open the left eye that was no longer there, then turned my head this way and that to see the three of them distinctly with the one eye, the right eye, that I still had. I could feel a sharp tiny pain like so many needles in the empty tissues where my left eye had been.

Oh, the horror on Armand's face. In his old finery, he stood, heavy shopwindow velvet coat, modern lace, boots spiffed like glass. His face, the Botticelli angel still, torn with pain as he looked at me.

And David, the pity, the sympathy. Both figures transfixed in one, the elder Englishman and the young fine body into which he'd been locked, smothered in the tweed and cashmere garments of winter.

Monsters clothed as men but earthbound, real!

And the shining gamine figure of my Dora, my slender, yearning Dora with her huge black eyes.

"Darling, darling," Dora cried, "I am here!" Her small warm arms went round my aching shoulders, oblivious to the snow falling from my hair, from my clothes. I went down on my knees, my face buried in her skirts, near to the blood between her legs, the blood of the living womb, the blood of Earth, the blood of Dora that the body could give, and then I fell backwards onto the floor.

I could neither speak nor move. I felt her lips touch mine.

"You're safe now, Lestat," she said.

Or was it David's voice?

"You're with us," she said.

Or was it Armand?

"We're here."

"Look, look at his feet. He's got only one shoe left."

". . . at his coat, torn . . . the buttons are gone."

"Darling, darling." She kissed me.

I rolled her over gently, careful not to press her with my weight, and I pulled up her skirt, and I lay my face against her hot naked thighs. The smell of the blood flooded my brain.

"Forgive me, forgive me," I whispered, and my tongue broke through the thin cotton of her panties, tearing the cloth back from the soft down of pubic hair, pushing aside the bloodstained pad she wore, and I lapped at the blood just inside her young pink vaginal lips, just coming from the mouth of her womb, not pure blood, but blood from her, blood from her strong, young body, blood all over the tight hot cells of her vaginal flesh, blood that brought no pain, no sacrifice, only her gentle forbearance with me, with my unspeakable act, my tongue going deep into her, drawing out the blood that was yet to come, gently, gently, lapping the blood from the soft hair on her pubic lips, sucking each tiny droplet of it.

Unclean, unclean. They cried on the road to Golgotha, when Veronica had said: "Lord, I touched the hem of your garment and my hemorrhage was healed." *Unclean, unclean.*

"Unclean, thank God, unclean," I whispered, my tongue licking at the secret bloodstained place, taste and smell of blood, her sweet blood, a place where blood flows free and no wound is made or ever needs to be made, the entrance to her blood open to me in her forgiveness.

Snow beat against the glass. I could hear it, smell it, the blinding white snow of a terrible blizzard for New York, a deep white winter, freezing all beneath its mantle.

"My darling, my angel," she whispered.

I lay panting against her. The blood was all gone inside me now. I had drawn all of it from her womb that was meant to come. I had licked away even what had collected on the pad that had lain against her skin.

She sat up, modestly covering me with her crossed arms, bending forward as if to shield me from their eyes—David's, Armand's—never once having pushed at me, or cried out, or recoiled, and she held my head now as I cried.

"You're safe," she said again. They said we were safe. They all said Safe, as if it had a magic charm. Safe, safe, safe.

"Oh, no," I cried. I wept. "No, none of us are safe. And we will never be, never, ever again, ever. . . ."

22

I WOULDN'T let them touch me. I mean, I wouldn't give up anything just yet, not my torn shoe, nothing. Keep away your combs, your towels, your comfort. I clung to the secret inside my coat.

A shroud, that's what I asked for, some heavy thing to wrap about myself. They found it, a blanket, soft, woolen, didn't matter.

The place was almost empty.

They had been steadily moving Roger's treasures south. They told me. Mortal agents had been entrusted with this task, and most of the statues and the icons were gone down to the orphanage in New Orleans, and housed there in the empty chapel I had seen, where only the Crucified Christ had been. Some omen!

They had not quite finished these tasks. A few precious things remained, a trunk or two, boxes of papers. Files.

I'd been gone the space of three days. The news was filled with tales of Roger's death. Though they would not tell me how it had been discovered. The scramble for power in the world of the dark, criminal drug cartels was well under way. The reporters had stopped calling the TV station about Dora. No one knew about this place. No one knew she was here.

Few knew about the big orphanage to which she planned to return, when all Roger's relics had been moved.

The cable network had canceled her show. The gangster's daughter preached no more. She had not seen or spoken to her followers.

In newspaper columns and in bites on television, she learnt that the scandal had made her vaguely mysterious. But in the main, she was considered a dead end, a small-time television evangelist with no knowledge of her father's doings.

But in the company of David and Armand, she had lost all contact with her former world, living here in New York, as the worst winter in fifty years came down, a snow from Heaven—living here among the relics and listening to them, their soft comfort, their wondrous tales, uncertain of what she meant to do, believing still in God. . . .

All that was the latest news.

I took the blanket from them and walked, one shoe gone, through the flat.

I went into the small room. I wrapped the blanket around me. The window here was covered. No sun would come.

"Don't come near me," I said. "I need to sleep a mortal's sleep. I need to sleep the night through and the day and then I'll tell you everything. Don't touch me, don't come near me."

"May I sleep in your arms?" Dora asked, a white and vibrant blood-filled thing standing in the doorway, her vampiric angels behind her.

The room was dark. Only a chest was left with some relics in it. But there were statues still in the hall.

"No. Once the sun rises, my body will do whatever it will to protect itself from any mortal intrusion. You can't come with me into that sleep. It's not possible."

"Then let me lie with you now."

The other two stared over her shoulders at my empty left eyelids fluttering painfully against each other. There must have been blood. But our blood is staunched fast. The eye had been torn out by the root. What was its root? I could still smell the soft delicious blood I had from her. It laid on my lips, her blood.

"Let me sleep," I said.

I locked the door and lay on the floor, knees drawn up, warm and safe in the thick folds of the blanket, smelling the pine needles and the soil that clung to my clothes, and the smoke, and the bits and pieces of dried excrement, and the blood, of course, the human blood, blood from battlefields, and blood from Hagia Sophia when the dead infant had fallen on me, and the smell of the horse manure, and the smell of the marl of Hell.

All of it was wrapped up with me in this blanket, my hand on the bulk of the unfolded veil against my bare chest.

"Don't come near me!" I whispered one more time for the ears of the immortals outside, who were so confounded and confused.

Then I slept.

Sweet rest. Sweet darkness.

Would that death were like this. Would that one would sleep and sleep and sleep forever.

23

I REMAINED unconscious the full twenty-four hours, waking only as the sun died behind the winter sky the next evening. There was a fine outlay of my own good clothes for me displayed on the wooden chest, and a pair of my own shoes.

I tried to imagine who had made this selection from amongst all that David had earlier sent here for me from the nearby hotel. Surely he was the logical choice. And I smiled, thinking of how often in our lives David and I had been utterly entangled in the adventure of clothes.

But you see, if a vampire leaves out details like clothes, the story doesn't make sense. Even the most grandiose mythic characters— if they are flesh and blood—do have to worry about the latchets on sandals.

It struck me with full force that I was back from the realm where clothes changed shape through the will of the clothed. That I was covered in dirt and did have only one shoe.

I stood up, fully alert, removed the veil carefully without unfolding it or chancing to look at it, though I thought I could see the dark image through the cloth. I removed all my garments with care, and then stacked them together on the blanket, so that not one pine needle would be lost that didn't have to be lost. And then I went into the nearby bathroom—the customary chamber of tile and ferocious steam—and bathed like a man being baptized in the Jordan. David had laid out for me all the requisite toys—combs, brushes, scissors. Vampires need almost nothing else, really.

All the while I had the door of the bathroom open. Had anyone dared to step into the bedroom I would have leapt from the steamy downpour and ordered that person out.

At last I myself emerged, wet and clean, combed my hair, dried carefully, and put on all of my own fresh garments from the inside out, that is from silk shorts and undershirt and black socks, to the clean wool pants, shirt, vest, and double-breasted blazer of a blue suit.

Then I bent down and picked up the folded veil. I held it, not daring to open it.

But I could see the darkness on the other side of the fabric. This time I was sure. I put the veil inside my vest, buttoning the vest tight.

I looked in the mirror. It was a madman in a Brooks Brothers suit, a demon with wild, frenzied blond locks, his collar open, staring with one horrible eye at himself in the mirror.

The eye, good God, the eye!

My fingers moved up to examine the empty socket, the slightly wrinkled lids that tried to close it off. What to do, what to do. If only I had a black patch, a gentleman's patch. But I didn't.

My face was desecrated by the missing eye. I realized I was shaking violently. David had left for me one of my broad, scarflike ties, of violet silk, and this I wrapped around my collar, making it stand up like a collar of old, very stiff, the scarf surrounding it with layer after layer as one might see in some portrait of Beethoven.

I tucked the tails of the scarf down into the vest. In the mirror, my eye burnt violet with the violet of the scarf. I saw the blackness on the left side, made myself look at it, rather than simply compensate for it.

I slipped on my shoes, stared back at the ruined clothes, picked up a few bits of dust and dried leaf, and laid all that carefully on the blanket, so that as little as possible would be lost, and then I went outside into the hallway.

The flat was sweetly warm, and full of a popular but not overpowering incense—something that made me think of Catholic churches of old, when the altar boy swung the silver censer at the end of his chain.

As I came into the living room, I saw the three of them very distinctly, ranged about the cheerfully lighted space, the even illumination making a mirror of the nightwalls beyond which the snow continued to descend upon New York. I wanted to see the snow. I walked past them and put my cye up against the glass. The whole roof of St. Patrick's was white with fresh snow, the steep spires shaking off as much as they could, though every speck of ornament was decorated in white. The street was an impassable valley of white. Had they ceased to plow it?

People of New York moved below. Were these only the living? I stared with my right eye. I could see only what seemed to be the living. I scanned the roof of the church in a near panic, suddenly, expecting to see a gargoyle wound into the artwork and discover that the gargoyle was alive and watching me.

But I had no feeling of anyone except those in the room, whom I loved, who were patiently waiting upon me and my melodramatic and self-indulgent silence.

I turned around. Armand had once again decked himself out in high-fashion velvet and embroidered lace, the kind of "romantic new look" one could find at any of the shops in the deep crevasse below us. His auburn hair was free and uncut and hung down in the way it used to do in ages long past, when as Satan's saint of the vampires of Paris, he would not have allowed himself the vanity to cut one lock of it. Only it was clean, shining clean, auburn in the light, and against the dark blood-red of his coat. And there were his sad and always youthful eyes looking at me, the smooth boyish cheeks, the angel's mouth. He sat at the table, reserved, filled with love and curiosity, and even a vague kind of humility which seemed to say:

Put aside all our disputes. I am here for you.

"Yes," I said aloud. "Thank you."

David sat there, the robust brown-haired young Anglo-Indian, juicy and succulent to behold as he had been since the night I made him one of us. He wore his English tweed, with leather-patched elbows, and a vest as tightly buttoned as my own, and a cashmere scarf protecting his neck from the cold to which perhaps, for all his strength, he wasn't yet really accustomed.

It's strange how we feel cold. You can ignore it. And then very suddenly, you can take it personally.

My radiant Dora sat next, opposite Armand, and David sat facing me between them. This left me the chair with its back to the glass and the sky if I wanted it. I stared at it. Such a simple object, a black lacquered chair, Oriental design, vaguely Chinese, mostly functional, obviously expensive.

Dora rose, her legs seeming to unfold beneath her. She wore a thin, long gown of burgundy silk, just a simple dress, the artificial warmth surrounding her obviously and keeping her safe. Her arms were bare and white. Her face was filled with worry, her cap of shiny black hair making two points on either side of her face, mid-cheek, the fashionable bob of eighty years ago and of today. Her eyes were the owl eyes, and full of love.

"What happened, Lestat?" she said. "Oh, please, please tell us."

"Where is the other eye?" asked Armand. It was just the sort of question he would ask. He had not risen to his feet. David, the Englishman, had risen, simply because Dora had risen, but Armand sat there looking up at me, asking the direct question. "What happened to it? Do you still have it?"

I looked at Dora. "They could have saved that eye," I said, quoting her story of Uncle Mickey and the gangsters and the eye, "if only those gangsters hadn't stepped on it!"

"What are you saying?" she said.

"I don't know if they stepped on my eye," I said, irritated by the tremour in my voice. The drama of my voice. "They weren't gangsters, they were ghosts, and I fled, and I left my eye. It was my only chance. I left it on the step. Maybe they smashed it flat, or smeared it like a blob of grease, I don't know. Was Uncle Mickey buried with his glass eye?"

"Yes, I think so," Dora said in a daze. "No one ever told me."

I could sense the other two scanning her, Armand scanning me, their picking up the images of Uncle Mickey, kicked half to death in Corona's Bar on Magazine Street, and the gangster with the pointed shoe squashing Uncle Mickey's eye.

Dora gasped.

"What happened to you?"

"You've moved Roger's things?" I asked. "Almost all of them?"

"Yes, they're in the chapel at St. Elizabeth's, safe," Dora said. "St. Elizabeth's." That was the name of the orphanage in its lifetime. I had never heard her say it before. "No one will even think to look for them there. The press doesn't care about me anymore. His enemies circle his corporate connections like vultures; they zero in on his bank accounts and floating bank drafts, and safe-deposit boxes, murdering for this or that key. Among his intimates, his daughter has been declared incidental, unimportant, ruined. No matter."

"Thank God for that," I said. "Did you tell them he was dead? Will it all end soon, his story, and what part you have to play in it?"

"They found his head," said Armand quietly.

In a muted voice he explained. Dogs had dragged the head from a heap of garbage, and were fighting over it beneath a bridge. For an hour, an old man watched, warming himself by a fire, and then gradually he realized it was a human head that the dogs were fighting over and gnawing at, and they brought the head to the proper authorities, and through the genetic testing of his hair and skin discovered that it was Roger. Dental plates didn't help. Roger's teeth had been perfect. All that remained was for Dora to identify it.

"He must have wanted it found," I said.

"What makes you say that?" asked David. "Where have you been?"

"I saw your mother," I said to Dora. "I saw her bottle-blond hair and her blue eyes. It won't be long before they're in Heaven."

"What on earth are you saying, my darling?" she asked. "My angel? What are you telling me?"

"Sit down, all of you. I'll tell you the whole tale. Listen to everything I say without interrupting. No, I don't want to sit, not with my back to the sky and the whirlwind and the snow and the church. No, I'll walk back and forth, listen to what I have to tell you.

"Remember this. Every word of this happened to me! I could have been tricked. I could have been deceived. But this is what I saw with my eyes, and heard with my ears!"

I told them everything, from the very, very beginning, some things each of them had already heard, but which all of them together had never heard—from my first fatal glimpse of Roger and my love for his brazen white-toothed smile and guilty, gleaming black eyes— all the way to the moment I had pitched myself through the door of the flat last night.

I told them everything. Every word spoken by Memnoch and God Incarnate. Everything I had seen in Heaven and in Hell and on Earth. I told them about the smell and the colors of Jerusalem. I told them and told them and told them. . . .

The story devoured the night. It ate the hours, as I paced, raving, repeating those parts I wanted to get exactly right, the stages of Evolution which had shocked the angels, and the vast libraries of Heaven, and the peach tree with both bloom and fruit, and God, and the soldier lying on his back in Hell, refusing to give in. I described to them the details of the interior of Hagia Sophia. I talked about the naked men on the battlefield. Over and over I described Hell. I described Heaven. I repeated my final speech, that I couldn't help Memnoch, I couldn't teach in this school!

They stared at me in utter silence.

"Do you have the veil?" Dora asked, her lip quivering. "Do you still have it?"

So tender was the tilt of her head, as if she'd forgive me in an instant if I said, No, I lost it in the street, I gave it to a beggar!

"The veil proves nothing," I said. "Whatever is on the veil means nothing! Anyone who can make illusions like that can make a veil! It proves neither truth nor lies, neither trickery nor witchery nor theophany."

"When you were in Hell," she asked, so kindly, so gently, her white face shining in the warmth of the lamp, "did you tell Roger you had the veil?"

"No, Memnoch wouldn't let me. And I only saw him for a minute, you see, one second it was one way, and then it was another. But he's going up, I know he is, he's going because he's clever and he's figured it out, and Terry will go with him! They will be in the arms of God unless God is a cheap magician and all of this was a lie, but a lie for what? For what purpose?"

"You don't believe what Memnoch asked of you?" asked Armand.

Only at this moment did I realize how shaken he was, how like the boy he must have been when made a vampire, how young and full of earthly grace. He wanted it to be true!

"Oh, yes, I do!" I said. "I believed him, but it *could all be a lie*, don't you see?"

"Didn't you feel it was true," asked Armand, "that he needed you?"

"What?" I demanded. "Are we back to that, arguing whether or not when we serve Satan we serve God? You and Louis arguing about that in the Theater of the Vampires, if we are children of Satan, are we children of God?"

"Yes!" said Armand. "Did you believe him?"

"Yes. No. I don't know," I said. "I don't know!" I shouted it. "I hate God as much as I ever did. I resent them both, damn them!"

"And Christ?" Dora asked, her eyes filled with tears. "Was He sorry for us?"

"Yes, in His own way. Yes. Perhaps. Maybe. Who knows! But He didn't go through the Passion as a man alone, as Memnoch had begged Him to do, He carried His cross as God Incarnate. I tell you their rules are not our rules! We have conceived of better rules! We are in the hands of mad things!"

She broke into soft, sorrowful cries.

"Why are we never, never to know?" she cried.

"I don't know!" I declared. "I know they were there, that they appeared to me, that they let me see them. And still I don't know!"

David was scowling, scowling rather like Memnoch could scowl, deep in thought. Then he asked:

"And if it was all a series of images and tricks, things drawn from your heart and your mind, what was the purpose? If it was not a straight proposition that you become his lieutenant or prince, then what could have been the motive?"

"What do you think?" I asked. "They have my eye! I tell you not a word of it is a lie from me. They've got my bloody eye, damn it. I don't know what it was all about, unless it was true, absolutely true to the last syllable."

"We know you believe it's true," said Armand. "Yes, you believe it completely. You bore witness. I believe it's true. All of my long wandering through the valley of death, I've believed it was true!"

"Don't be a common fool," I said bitterly.

But I could see the flame in Armand's face; I could see the ecstasy and the sorrow in his eyes. I could see the entire galvanization of his form with belief, with conversion.

"The clothes," said David thoughtfully, calmly, "in the other room. You've gathered them all up, and the evidence will tell some scientific tale."

"Stop thinking like a scholar. These are Beings who play at a game only they can understand. What is it to them to make pine needles and dirt cling to my clothes, but yes, I saved those relics, yes, I've saved everything but my goddamned eye, which I left on the steps of Hell so I could get out. I, too, want to analyze the evidence on those clothes. I, too, want to know what forest it was where I walked and listened to him!"

"They let you get out," said David.

"If you could have seen his face when he saw that eye on the step," I said.

"What was it in his face?" Dora asked.

"Horror, horror that such a thing had happened. You see, when he reached for me, I think that his two fingers, like this, went into the eye socket, overshooting the mark. He had merely meant to grab me by the hair. But when his fingers plunged into the socket, he tried in horror to draw them out, and out came the eye, spilling down my face, and he was horror-stricken!"

"You love him," said Armand in a hushed voice.

"I love him. Yes, I think he's right about everything. But I don't believe in anything!"

"Why didn't you accept?" asked Armand. "Why didn't you give him your soul?"

Oh, how innocent he sounded, how it came from his heart, ancient and childlike, a heart so preternaturally strong that it had taken hundreds of years to render it safe to beat in the company of mortal hearts.

Little Devil, Armand!

"Why didn't you accept!" he implored.

"They let you escape, and they had a purpose," said David. "It was like the vision I saw in the café."

"Yes, and they had a purpose," I said. "But did I defeat their purpose?" I looked to him for the answer, he the wise one, the old one in human years. "David, did I defeat them when I took you out of life? Did I defeat them somehow some other way? Oh, if only I could remember, their voices in the beginning. Vengeance. Someone said that it wasn't simple vengeance. But it was those fragments. I can't remember now. What's happened! Will they come back for me?"

I fell to crying again. Stupid. I fell to describing Memnoch again, in all his forms, even the Ordinary Man, who had been so extraordinary in his proportions, the haunting footsteps, the wings, the smoke, the glory of Heaven, the singing of angels . . . "Sapphiric . . ." I whispered. "Those surfaces, all the things the prophets saw and sprinkled throughout their books with words like topaz and beryl and fire and gold and ice and snow, and it was all there . . . and He said, 'Drink my Blood!' I did it!"

They drew close to me. I'd scared them. I'd been too loud, too crazed, too possessed. They stood around me, their arms against me, her fiery white human arms, the warmest, the sweetest of all, and David's dark brow pushed against my face.

"If you let me," said Armand, his fingers slipping up to my collar, "if you let me drink, then I'll know. . . ."

"No, all you'll know is that I believe what I saw, that's all!" I said.

"No," he said, shaking his head. "I'll know the blood of Christ if I taste it."

I shook my head. "Back away from me. I don't even know what the veil will look like. Will it look like something with which I wiped my blood sweat in my sleep as I dreamt? Back away."

They obeyed. They were a loose triangle. I had my back to the inner wall so that I could see the snow on my left side, though I had to turn my head to the left now to do it. I looked at them. My right hand fumbled inside my vest, it drew out the thick wad, and I felt something, something tiny and strange which I could not explain to them, or put into words even for myself, I felt the weave, that weave of cloth, that ancient weave!

I drew out the veil, not looking myself, and held it up as if I were Veronica showing it to the crowd.

A silence gripped the room. A motionlessness.

Then I saw Armand go down on his knees. And Dora let out her long, keening cry.

"Dear God," said David.

Shivering, I lowered the veil, still held wide open with both hands, and turned it so I could see the reflection of the veil in the dark glass against the snow, as if it was the Gorgon and was going to kill me.

His Face! His Face blasted into the veil. I looked down. God Incarnate staring at me from the most minute detail, burnt into the cloth, not painted or stained, or sewn or drawn, but blasted into the very fibers, His Face, the Face of God in that instant, dripping with blood from His Crown of Thorns.

"Yes," I whispered. "Yes, yes." I fell on my knees. "Oh, yes, so very complete, down to the last detail."

I felt her take the veil. I would have snatched it back if either of them had tried. But into her small hand, I entrusted it, and she held it up now turning round and round, so that all of us could see His dark eyes shining from the cloth!

"It's God!" she screamed. "It's Veronica's Veil!" Her cry grew triumphant and then filled with joy. "Father, you've done it! You have given me the Veil!"

And she began to laugh, as one who had seen all the visions one can endure to see, dancing round and round, with the veil held high, singing one syllable over and over again.

Armand was shattered, broken, on his knees, the blood tears running straight down his cheeks, horrid streaks on the white flesh.

Humbled and confounded, David merely watched. Keenly, he studied the veil as it moved through the air, her hands still stretching it wide. Keenly, he studied my face. He studied the slumped, broken, sobbing figure of Armand, the lost child in his exquisite velvet and lace now stained with his tears.

"Lestat," Dora cried, tears gushing, "you have brought me the Face of my God! You have brought it to all of us. Don't you see? Memnoch lost! Memnoch was defeated. God won! God used Memnoch for his own ends, he led Memnoch into the labyrinth of Memnoch's own design. God has triumphed!"

"No, Dora, no! You can't believe that," I shouted. "What if it isn't the truth? What if it was all a pack of tricks. Dora!"

She shot past me down the corridor and out the door. We three stood stunned. We could hear the elevator descending. She had the veil!

"David, what is she going to do? David, help me."

"Who can help us now?" asked David, but it was without conviction or bitterness, only that pondering, that endless pondering. "Armand, take hold of yourself. You cannot surrender to this," he said. His voice was sad.

But Armand was lost.

"Why?" Armand asked. He was just a child now on his knees. "Why?"

This is how he must have looked centuries ago when Marius had come to free him from his Venetian captors, a boy kept for lust, a boy brought into the palace of the Undead.

"Why can't I believe it? Oh, my God, I *do* believe it. It is the face of Christ!"

He climbed to his feet, drunkenly, and then he moved slowly, doggedly, step by step, after her.

By the time we reached the street, she stood screaming before the doors of the cathedral.

"Open the doors! Open the church. I have the veil." She kicked the bronze doors with her right foot. All around her gathered mortals, murmuring.

"The Veil, the Veil!" They stared at it, as she stopped to turn and show it once more. Then all pounded on the doors.

The sky above grew light with the coming sun, far, far off in the maw of the winter, but nevertheless rising in its inevitable path, to bring its fatal white light down on us if we didn't seek shelter.

"Open the doors!" she screamed.

From all directions, humans came, gasping, falling on their knees when they saw the Veil.

"Go," said Armand, "seek shelter now, before it's too late. David, take him, go."

"And you, what will you do?" I demanded.

"I will bear witness. I will stand here with my arms outstretched," he cried, "and when the sun rises, my death shall confirm the miracle."

The mighty doors were being opened at last. The dark-clad figures drew back in astonishment. The first gleam of silver light illuminated the Veil, and then came the warmer, yellow electric lights from within, the lights of candles, the rush of the heated air.

"The Face of Christ!" she screamed.

The priest fell down on his knees. The older man in black, brother, priest, whatever he was, stood openmouthed looking up at it.

"Dear God, dear God," he said, making the Sign of the Cross, "That in my lifetime, God . . . it's the Veronica!"

Humans rushed past us, stumbling and jostling to follow her into the church. I heard their steps echoing up the giant nave.

"We have no time," David said in my ear. He had lifted me off my feet, strong as Memnoch, only there was no whirlwind, only the risen winter dawn, and the falling snow, and more and more shouts and howls and cries as men and women flooded towards the church, and the bells above in the steeples began to ring.

"Hurry, Lestat, with me!"

We ran together, already blinded by the light, and behind me I heard Armand's voice ring out over the crowd.

"Bear witness, this sinner dies for Him!" The scent of fire came in a fierce explosion! I saw it blaze against the glass walls of the towers as we fled. I heard the screams.

"Armand!" I cried out. David pulled me along, down metal steps, echoing and chiming like the bells pealing from the cathedral above.

I went dizzy; I surrendered to him. I gave up my will to him. In my grief, crying, "Armand, Armand."

Slowly I made out David's figure in the dark. We were in a damp icy place, a cellar beneath a cellar, beneath the high shrieking hollow of an empty wind-torn building. He was digging through the broken earth.

"Help me," he cried, "I'm losing all feeling, the light's coming, the sun is risen, they'll find us."

"No, they won't."

I kicked and dug out the grave, carrying him with me deeper and deeper, and closing the soft clods of earth behind us. Not even the sounds of the city above could penetrate this darkness. Not even the bells of the church.

Had the Tunnel opened for Armand? Had his soul gone up? Or was he wandering through the Gates of Hell?

"Armand," I whispered. And as I closed my eyes, I saw Memnoch's stricken face: *Lestat, help me!*

With my last bit of feeling, I reached to make sure the Veil was there. But no, the Veil was gone. I'd given Dora the Veil. Dora had the Veil and Dora had taken it into the church.

You would never be my adversary!

24

WE SAT together on the low wall, Fifth Avenue, edge of Central Park. Three nights had passed like this. We had watched.

For as far as we could see uptown the line formed, five and six deep, men and women and children, singing, stamping their feet to keep warm, nuns and priests hurrying back and forth offering hot chocolate and tea to those who were freezing. Fires burned in large drums at intervals of so many feet. As far as the eye could see.

And downtown, on and on it went, past the glittering displays of Bergdorf Goodman and Henri Bendel, the furriers, the jewelers, the bookstores of midtown, until it wound its way into the cathedral.

David stood with folded arms, barely leaning on the wall, his ankles crossed. I was the one who sat like a kid, with my knee up, my ravaged one-eyed face upturned, my chin on my knuckled fist, resting my elbow on my knee, just listening to them.

Far ahead one could hear screams and shouts. Someone else had no doubt touched a clean napkin to the Veil, and once again the image had been transferred! And so it would be again sometime tomorrow night, and maybe once the night after and how many times nobody knew, except that the icon made the vera-icon out of the cloth touched to it, and the face blazed from cloth to cloth, like flame touched from wick to wick.

"Come on," David said. "We're getting cold here. Come, let's walk."

We walked.

"Why?" I asked. "Up there, to see the same thing we saw last night, and the night before? So that I can struggle to get to her again, knowing that any show of force, any preternatural gift only confirms the entire miracle! She won't listen to me ever again. You know she won't. And who is gathered on the steps now, who will immolate himself at dawn to confirm the miracle?"

"Mael is there."

"Ah, yes, the Druid priest, once a priest, always a priest. And so this will be his morning to fall like Lucifer in a blaze."

Last night it had been some ragged vagabond blood drinker, come from God knows where, unknown to us, but becoming a preternatural torch at dawn for the banks of video cameras and newspaper photographers. The papers were filled with the pictures of the blaze. Filled with the pictures of the Veil itself.

"Here, wait," I said. We had come to Central Park South. The crowd here was all singing in concert that old solemn, militant hymn:

Holy God, we praise thy Name
Lord of All, we bow before thee!

I stood staring at them, dazed. The pain in my left eye socket seemed worse but what could be changing there, except that with each passing hour I felt the depth.

"You're fools, all of you!" I shouted. "Christianity is the bloodiest religion that ever existed in the world. I can bear witness!"

"Hush now, and do as I tell you," David said, pulling me along, so that we vanished amongst the ever-shifting people on the icy sidewalks before anyone could have turned to look. Over and over he had restrained me this way. He was weary of it. I didn't blame him.

Once, policemen had laid hands on me.

They had caught me and tried to pull me out of the cathedral as I was trying to talk to her, and then when they had me outside, slowly they had all backed away. They had sensed I wasn't alive, the way mortals do. They had sensed, and they had muttered about the Veil and the miraculous, and there it had been, my impotence.

Policemen were all over. Policemen everywhere stood on guard to help, to give out the warm tea, to put their pale shivering hands out over the flames in the drums.

Nobody noticed us. Why should they? We were just two men, drab, part of the crowd, our gleaming skin was nothing much in this blinding whiteness of snow amid these ecstatic pilgrims, wandering from valley to valley of song.

The bookstore windows were piled with Bibles, books on Christology. There was a huge pyramid of a lavender-covered book called *Veronica and Her Cloth* by Ewa Kuryluk, and another stack of *Holy Faces, Secret Places* by Ian Wilson.

People sold pamphlets on the street, or even gave them away. I could hear accents from all parts of the country—from Texas, and Florida and Georgia and California.

Bibles, Bibles, Bibles, being sold and given away.

A group of nuns gave out holy pictures of St. Veronica. But the hottest items were the color photographs of the Veil itself, snapped in the church by photographers and then reprinted by the thousands.

"Amazing grace, amazing grace. . . ." sang one group in unison, rocking back and forth as they held their places in line.

"Gloria, in excelsus deum!" burst from a long-bearded man with his arms outstretched.

As we drew nearer the church, we could see little clusters and crowds engaged in seminars everywhere. In the midst of one, a young man spoke, rapid, sincere:

"In the fourteenth century, she was officially recognized as a saint, Veronica, and it was believed that the Veil was lost during the Fourth Crusade when the Venetians stormed Hagia Sophia." He stopped to push his glasses back on his nose. "Of course the Vatican will take its time to rule on this, as it always does, but seventy-three icons have already been derived from the original icon, and this before the eyes of countless witnesses who are prepared to testify before the Holy See."

In another place, there were several dark-clad men, priests perhaps, I couldn't tell, and around them rings of those listening, eyes squinting against the snow.

"I'm not saying the Jesuits cannot come," said one of the men. "I just said that they aren't coming in here and taking over. Dora has asked that the Franciscans be the custodians of the Veil, if and when it leaves the cathedral."

And behind us, two women rapidly concurred that tests had already been done, the age of the cloth was beyond dispute.

"They don't even grow that kind of flax anymore in the world; you couldn't find a new piece of such fabric, the fabric itself in its newness and cleanness is a miracle."

". . . all bodily fluids, every part of the image, derived from fluids of a human body. They have not had to hurt the Veil to discover this! This is . . . this. . . ."

". . . enzyme action. But you know how these things get distorted."

"No, not *The New York Times*. *The New York Times* isn't going to say that three archaeologists have ruled it authentic."

"Not authentic, my friend, just beyond present scientific explanation."

"God and the Devil are idiots!" I said.

A group of women turned to stare at me. "Accept Jesus as your Savior, son," said one of the women. "Go look for yourself at the Veil. He died for our sins."

David pulled me away. No one paid us any mind. The little schools continued far and wide, the clumps of philosophers and witnesses, and those waiting for the spellbound to stumble down the steps from the church, with tears running down their faces.

"I saw it, I saw it, it was the Face of Christ."

And back against the arch, cleaved to it, like a tall spidery shadow, the figure of the vampire Mael, almost invisible to them perhaps, waiting to step into the light of dawn with his arms outstretched in the form of a cross.

Once again, he looked at us with sly eyes.

"You too!" he said, under his breath to us, sending his preternatural voice secretly to our ears. "Come, face the sun, with your arms outstretched! Lestat, God chose you as his Messenger."

"Come," David said. "We've seen enough for this night and many nights hereafter."

"And where do we go?" I asked. "Stop, stop pulling my arm. David? Did you hear me?"

"I've stopped," he said politely, lowering his voice as if to instruct me to lower mine. The snow fell so softly now. Fire crackled in the nearby black iron drum.

"The books, what happened to them?" How in God's name could I have forgotten.

"What books?" he asked. And he pulled me out of the way of the passersby, against a shopwindow, behind which a little crowd stood, enjoying the private warmth inside, looking towards the church.

"The books of Wynken de Wilde. Roger's twelve books! What happened to them?"

"They're there," he said. "Up there in the tower. She left them for you. Lestat, I've explained this to you. Last night, she spoke to you."

"In the presence of all those others, it was impossible to speak the truth."

"She told you the relics were yours now."

"We have to get the books!" I said. Oh, what a fool I was to forget those beautiful books.

"Be calm, Lestat, be quiet. Stop making them stare at you. The flat is the same, I told you. She hasn't told anyone about it. She has surrendered it to us. She will not tell them that we were ever there. She has promised me. She has given the deed to the Orphanage to you, Lestat, don't you see? She has cut all ties with her former life. Her old religion is dead, abolished. She is reborn, the custodian of the Veil."

"But we don't know!" I roared. "We'll never know. How can she accept it when we don't know and we can't know!" (He pushed me against the wall.) "I want to go back and get the books," I said.

"Of course, we will do this if you wish." How tired I was.

On the pavements the people sang: " 'And He walks with me, and He talks with me, and lets me call Him by name.' "

The apartment was undisturbed.

As far as I could tell, she had never returned. None of us had.

David had come to check, and David had been telling the truth. All was as it had been.

Except, in the tiny room where I had slept there stood only the chest. My clothes and the blanket on which they'd lain, covered with the same dirt and pine needles from an ancient forest floor, were all gone.

"Did you take them?"

"No," he said. "I believe she did. They are the tattered relics of the angelic messenger. The Vatican officials have them, as far as I know."

I laughed. "And they'll analyze all that material, the bits of organic matter from the forest floor."

"The clothes of the Messenger of God, it was already in the papers," he said. "Lestat, you must come to your senses. You cannot blunder through the mortal world like this. You are a risk to yourself, to others. You are a risk to everything out there. You must contain your power."

"Risk? After this, what I've done, creating a miracle, like this, a new infusion of blood into the very religion that Memnoch loathed. Oh God!"

"Sssshhhh. Quiet," he said. "The chest, there. The books are in the chest."

Ah, so the books had been in this little room, where I had slept. I was consoled, so consoled. I sat there, my legs crossed, rocking back and forth, crying. Oh, this is so weird to cry with one eye! God, are tears coming out of the left eye? I don't think so. I think he ripped away the ducts, what do you think?

David stood in the hallway. The light from the distant glass wall made his profile icy and calm.

I reached over and opened the lid of the chest. It was made of wood, a Chinese chest, carved deep with many figures. And there were the twelve books, each wrapped as we had wrapped them so carefully, and all padded and safe and dry. I didn't have to open them to know.

"I want us to leave now," David said. "If you begin crying out again, if you begin trying to tell people again. . . ."

"Oh, I know how tired you are, my friend," I said. "I'm sorry. I'm so sorry." From riot after riot, he'd torn me and dragged me out of the sight of mortal eyes.

I thought about those policemen again. I hadn't even been resisting them. I thought about the way they backed off one by one, as if from something so inherently unwholesome that their molecules told them to do it. Back off.

And she spoke of a Messenger from God. She was so certain.

"We have to leave it now," he said. "It's done. Others are coming. I don't want to see the others. Do you? Do you want to answer the questions of Santino or Pandora or Jesse or whoever might come! What more can we do? I want to leave now."

"You believe I was his fool, don't you?" I asked, looking up at him.

"Whose fool? God's or the Devil's?"

"That's just it," I said. "I don't know. You tell me what you believe."

"I want to go," he said, "because if I do not go now, I will join them this morning on the church steps—Mael and whoever else is there. And there are others coming. I know them. I see them."

"No, you can't do that! What if every particle of it was a lie! What if Memnoch wasn't the Devil, and God wasn't God, and the whole thing was some hideous hoax worked on us by monsters who are no better than we are! You can't ever think of joining them on the church steps! The earth is what we have! Cling to it! You don't know. You don't know about the whirlwind and Hell. You don't know. Only He knows the rules. Only He is supposed to speak the truth! And Memnoch over and over described Him as if He were Mad, a Moral Idiot."

He turned slowly, the light playing with the shadows of his face. Softly he asked, "His blood, Lestat, could it truly be inside you?"

"Don't start believing it!" I said. "Not you! No. Don't believe. I refuse to play. I refuse to take either side! I brought the Veil back so you and she would believe what I said, that's all I did, and this, this madness has happened!"

I swooned.

I saw the Light of Heaven for an instant, or it seemed I did. I saw Him standing at the balustrade. I smelled that fierce horrid smell that had arisen so often from the earth, from battlefields, from the floors of Hell.

David knelt beside me, holding me by my arms.

"Look at me, don't fade out on me now!" he said. "I want us to leave here, we're to go away. You understand? We'll go back home. And then I want you to tell me the whole story again, dictate it to me, word for word."

"For what?"

"In the words we'll find the truth, in the details and in the plot we'll discover who did what for whom. Whether God used you, or Memnoch did! Whether Memnoch was lying the whole time! Whether God. . . ."

"Ah, it makes your head ache, doesn't it? I don't want you to write it down. There will only be a version if you write it down, a version, and there are already so many versions, what has she told them of her night visitors who brought her the Veil, her benign demons who brought her the Veil? And they took my clothes! What if there is tissue from my skin on those clothes?"

"Come now, take the books, here, I'll help you, here, there are three sacks here but we need only two, you put this bundle in yours, and I'll take the other."

I obeyed his orders. We had the books in the two sacks. We could go now.

"Why did you leave them here when you sent all the other things back?"

"She wanted you to have them," he said. "I told you. She wanted me to see that they were put in your hands. And she's given you all the rest. All ties are cut for her. This is a movement drawing fundamentalist and fanatic, cosmic Christians and Christians from East and West."

"I have to try to get near her again."

"No. Impossible. Come. Here. I have a heavy coat. You must put this on."

"Are you going to care for me forever?" I asked.

"Perhaps."

"Why don't I go to her now in the church and burn up the Veil! I could do it. I could do it with the power of my mind, make the Veil explode."

"Then why don't you?"

I shuddered. "I . . . I. . . ."

"Go ahead. You don't even have to go in the church. Your powers go before you. You could burn it up, maybe. It would be interesting if it didn't burn, wouldn't it? But suppose it did, suppose it just went black and burnt up like the wood in a grate when you light it with the telekinetic power of your mind. What then?"

I broke into weeping. I couldn't do such a thing. I couldn't do it. I didn't know for sure! I just didn't. And if I had been the dupe of God, was that God's will for all of us?

"Lestat!" He glared at me, or rather I should say, he fixed me with his authoritative gaze. "I'm telling you now, listen to what I say. Don't get that close to them again! Don't make any more miracles for them. There is nothing more that you can do. Let her tell the tale her way with her angel messenger. It's passed into history already."

"I want to talk one more time to the reporters!"

"No!"

"This time I'll be soft-voiced, I promise, I won't frighten anyone, I swear I won't, David. . . ."

"In time, Lestat, if you still want . . . in time. . . ." He bent down and smoothed my hair. "Now come with me. We're going."

25

THE ORPHANAGE was cold. Its thick brick walls, bare of all insulation, held the cold, and made it colder within than the winter outside. Seems I remembered that from before. Why had she given it to me? Why? She had given over the deed to me, and all his relics. What did it mean? Only that she was gone like a comet across the sky.

Was there a country on earth where the news networks had not carried her face, her voice, her Veil, her story?

But we were home, this was our city, New Orleans, our little land, and there was no snow falling here, only the soft scent of the sweet olive trees, and the tulip magnolias in the old neglected convent garden throwing off their pink petals. Look at that, pink petals on the ground.

So quiet here. No one knew of this place. So now the Beast could have his palace and remember Beauty and ponder forever whether Memnoch was weeping in Hell, or whether both of them—the Sons of God—were laughing in Heaven!

I walked into the chapel.

I had thought to find drapery and heaps and cartons and crates.

Rather, it was a completed sanctuary. Everything was placed properly as it should be, unwrapped, and dusted, and standing there in the gloom. Statues of St. Anthony, St. Lucy with her eyes on a plate, the Infant Jesus of Prague in his Spanish finery, and the icons hanging on the walls, between the windows, look, all neatly hung.

"But who has done this?"

David was gone. Where? He'd be back. It didn't matter. I had the twelve books. I needed a warm place to sit, perhaps on the altar steps, and I needed light. With this one eye, I needed just a little more than the night's light leaking in through the tall stained-glass windows.

A figure stood in the vestibule. Scentless. Vampire. My fledgling. Has to be. Young. Louis. Inevitable.

"Did you do all of this?" I asked. "Arrange things here in the church so beautifully?"

"It seemed the right thing to do," he said. He walked towards me. I saw him clearly, though I had to turn my head to focus the one eye on him, and stop trying to open a left eye which wasn't there.

Tall, pale, starved a bit. Black hair short. Green eyes very soft. Graceful walk of one who does not like to make noise, or make a fuss, or be seen. Plain black clothes, clothes like the Jews in New York who had gathered outside the cathedral, watching the whole spectacle, and like the Amish who had come by train, plain and simple, like the expression on his face.

"Come home with me," he said. Such a human voice. So kind. "There's time to come here and reflect. Wouldn't you rather be home, in the Quarter, amongst our things?"

If anything in the world could have truly comforted me, he would have been the thing—with just the beguiling tilt of his narrow head or the way that he kept looking at me, protecting me obviously with a confidential calm from what he must have feared for me, and for him, and perhaps for all of us.

My old familiar gentleman friend, my tender enduring pupil, educated as truly by Victorian ways of courtesy as ever by me in the ways of being a monster. What if Memnoch had called upon him? Why didn't Memnoch do that!

"What have I done?" I asked. "Was it the will of God?"

"I don't know," he said. He laid his soft hand on mine. His slow voice *was* a balm to my nerves. "Come home. I've listened for hours, to the radio, to the television, to the story of the angel of the night who brought the Veil. The Angel's tattered clothes have been given over to the hands of priests and scientists. Dora is laying on hands. The Veil has made cures. People are pouring into New York from all over the world. I'm glad you're back. I want you here."

"Did I serve God? Is that possible? A God I still hate?"

"I haven't heard your tale," he said. "Will you tell me?" Just that direct, without emotion. "Or is it too much of an agony to say it all again?"

"Let David write it down," I said. "From memory." I tapped my temple. "We have such good memories. I think some of the others can remember things that never actually happened."

I looked around. "Where are we? Oh, my God, I forgot. We're in the chapel. There's the angel with the basin in its hands, and that Crucifix, that was there already."

How stiff and lifeless it looked, how unlike the shining Veil.

"Do they show the Veil on the evening news?"

"Over and over." He smiled. No mockery. Only love.

"What did you think, Louis, when you saw the Veil?"

"That it was the Christ I once believed in. That it was the Son of God I knew when I was a boy and this was swampland." His voice was patient. "Come home. Let's go. There are . . . things in this place."

"Are there?"

"Spirits? Ghosts?" He didn't seem afraid. "They're small, but I feel them, and you know, Lestat, I don't have your powers." Again came his smile. "So you must know. Don't you feel them?"

I shut my eyes. Or, rather, my eye. I heard a strange sound like many, many children walking in ranks. "I think they're singing the times tables."

"And what are those?" Louis asked. He squeezed my arm, bending close. "Lestat, what are the times tables?"

"Oh, you know, the way they used to teach them multiplication in those days, they must have sung it in the classrooms, two times two makes four, two times three makes six, two times four makes eight . . . isn't that how it goes . . . They're singing it."

I stopped. Someone was there, in the vestibule, right outside the chapel, between the doors to the hall and the doors to the chapel, in the very shadows where I had hidden from Dora.

It was one of our kind. It had to be. And it was old, very old. I could feel the power. Someone was there who was so ancient that only Memnoch and God Incarnate would have understood, or. . . . Louis, maybe, Louis, if he believed his memories, his brief glimpses, his brief shattering experiences with the very ancient, perhaps. . . .

Still, he wasn't afraid. He was watching me, on guard, but basically fearless.

"Come on, I'm not standing in dread of it!" I said. And I walked towards it. I had the two sacks of books slung over my right shoulder, the fabric tight in my left hand. That allowed my right hand to be free. And my right eye. I still had that. Who was this visitor?

"That's David there," said Louis in a simple placating voice, as if to say, See? You have nothing to worry about.

"No, next to him. Look, look more deeply into the blackness. See, the figure of a woman, so white, so hard, she might as well be a statue in this place?

"Maharet!" I said.

"I am here, Lestat," she said.

I laughed.

"And wasn't that the answer of Isaiah when the Lord called? 'I am here, Lord'?"

"Yes," she said. Her voice was barely audible, but clear and cleaned by time, all the thickness of the flesh long gone from it.

I drew closer, moving out of the chapel proper and into the little vestibule. David stood beside her, like her anointed Second in Command, as if he would have done her will in an instant, and she the eldest, well, almost the eldest, the Eve of Us, the Mother of Us All, or the only Mother who remained, and now as I looked at her, I remembered the awful truth again, about her eyes, that when she was human, they had blinded her, and the eyes through which she looked now were always borrowed, human.

Bleeding in her head, human eyes, lifted from someone dead or alive, I couldn't know, and put into her sockets to thrive on her vampiric blood as long as they could. But how weary they seemed in her beautiful face. What had Jesse said? She is made of alabaster. And alabaster is a stone through which light can pass.

"I won't take a human eye," I said under my breath.

She said nothing. She had not come to judge, to recommend. Why had she come? What did she want?

"You want to hear the tale too?"

"Your gentle English friend says that it happened as you described it. He says the songs they sing on the televisions are true; that you are the Angel of the Night, and you brought her the Veil, and that he was there, and he heard you tell."

"I am no angel! I never meant to give her the Veil! I took the Veil as proof. I took the Veil because. . . ."

My voice had broken.

"Because why?" she asked.

"Because Christ gave it to me!" I whispered. "He said, 'Take it,' and I did."

I wept. And she waited. Patient, solemn. Louis waited. David waited.

Finally I stopped.

"Write down every word, David, if you write it, every ambiguous word, you hear me? I won't write it myself. I won't. Well, maybe . . . if I don't think you're getting it exactly right, I'll write it, I'll write it one time through. What do you want? Why have you come? No, I won't write it. Why are you here, Maharet, why have you shown yourself to me? Why have you come to the Beast's new castle, for what? Answer me."

She said nothing. Her long, pale-red hair went down to her waist. She wore some simple fashion that could pass unnoticed in many lands, a long, loose coat, belted around her tiny waist, a skirt that covered the tops of her small boots. The blood scent of the human eyes in her head was strong. And blazing in her head, these dead eyes looked ghastly to me, unsupportable.

"I won't take a human eye!" I said. But I had said that before. Was I being arrogant or insolent? She was so powerful. "I won't take a human *life*," I said. That had been what I meant. "I will never, never, never as long as I live and endure and starve and suffer, take a human life, nor raise my hand against a fellow creature, be he human or one of us, I do not care, I won't . . . I am . . . I will . . . with my last strength, I won't. . . ."

"I'm going to keep you here," she said. "As a prisoner. For a while. Until you're quieter."

"You're mad. You're not keeping me anywhere."

"I have chains waiting for you. David, Louis—you will help me."

"What is this? You two, you dare? Chains, we are talking about chains? What am I, Azazel cast into the pit? Memnoch would get a good laugh at this, if he hadn't turned his back on me forever!"

But none of them had moved. They stood motionless, her immense reservoir of power totally disguised by her slender white form. And they were suffering. Oh, I could smell the suffering.

"I have this for you," she said. She extended her hand. "And when you read it you will scream and you will weep, and we'll keep you here, safe and quiet, until such time as you stop. That's all. Under my protection. In this place. You will be my prisoner."

"What! What is it?" I demanded.

It was a crumpled piece of parchment.

"What the hell is this!" I said. "Who gave you this?" I didn't want to touch it.

She took my left hand with her absolutely irresistible strength, forcing me to drop the books in their sacks, and she placed the little crumpled bundle of parchment in my palm.

"It was given to me for you," she said.

"By whom?" I demanded.

"The person whose writing you will find inside. Read it."

"What the hell!" I swore. With my right fingers I tore open the crumpled vellum.

My eye. My eye shone there against the writing. This little package contained my eye, my eye wrapped in a letter. My blue eye, whole and alive.

Gasping, I picked it up and pushed it into my face, into the sore aching socket, feeling its tendrils reach back into the brain, tangling with the brain. The world flared into full vision.

She stood staring at me.

"Scream, will I?" I cried. "Scream, why? What do you think I see? I see only what I saw before!" I cried. I looked from right to left, the appalling patch of darkness gone, the world complete, the stained glass, the still trio watching me. "Oh, thank you, God!" I whispered. But what did this mean? Was it a prayer of thanks, or merely an exclamation!

"Read," she said, "what is written on the vellum."

An archaic hand, what was this? An illusion! Words in a language that was no language at all, yet clearly articulated so that I could pick them out of the swarming design, written in blood and ink and soot:

To My Prince,

*My Thanks to you for a job
perfectly done.*

with Love,

*Memnoch
the Devil*

I started to roar. "Lies, lies, lies!" I heard the chains. "What metal is it you think can bind me, cast me down! Damn you. Lies! You didn't see him. He didn't give you this!"

David, Louis, her strength, her inconceivable strength, strength, since the time immemorial, before the first tablets had been engraved at Jericho—it surrounded me, enclosed me. It was she more than they; I was her child, thrashing and cursing at her.

They dragged me through the darkness, my howls echoing off the walls, into the room they had chosen for me with its bricked-up windows, lightless, a dungeon, the chains going round and round as I thrashed.

"It's lies, it's lies, it's lies! I don't believe it! If I was tricked it was by God!" I roared and roared. "He did it to me. It's not real unless He did it, God Incarnate. Not Memnoch. No, never, never. Lies!"

Finally I lay there, helpless. I didn't care. There was a comfort in being chained, in being unable to batter the walls with my fists till they were pulp, or smash my head against the bricks, or worse. . . .

"Lies, lies, it's all a great big panorama of lies! That's all I saw! One more circus maximus of lies!"

"It's not all lies," she said. "Not all of it. That's the age-old dilemma."

I fell silent. I could feel my left eye growing deeper and stronger into my brain. I had that. I had my eye. And to think of his face, his horror-stricken face when he looked at my eye, and the story of Uncle Mickey's eye. I couldn't grasp it. I'd start howling again.

Dimly I thought I heard Louis's gentle voice, protesting, pleading, arguing. I heard locks thrown, I heard nails going through wood. I heard Louis begging.

"For a while, just a little while. . . ." she said. "He is too powerful for us to do anything else. It is either that, or we do away with him."

"No," Louis cried.

I heard David protest, no, that she couldn't.

"I will not," she said calmly. "But he will stay here until I say that he can leave."

And they were gone.

"Sing," I whispered. I was talking to the ghosts of the children. "Sing. . . ."

But the convent was empty. All the little ghosts had fled. The convent was mine. Memnoch's servant; Memnoch's prince. I was alone in my prison.

26

TWO NIGHTS, three nights. Outside in the city of the modern world the traffic ran along the broad avenue. Couples passed, whispering in the evening shadows. A dog howled.

Four nights, five nights?

David sat by me reading me the manuscript of my story word for word, all I had said, as he remembered this, stopping over and over again, to ask if this was correct, if these were the very words I'd used, if this was the image. And she would answer.

From her place in the corner, she would say, "Yes, that is what he saw, that is what he told you. That is what I see in his mind. Those are his words. That is what he felt."

Finally, it must have been after a week, she stood over me and asked if I thirsted for blood. I said, "I will never drink it again. I will dry up like something hard made of limestone. They will throw me into a kiln."

One night Louis came, with the quiet ease of a chaplain into a jail, immune to the rules yet presenting no threat to them.

Slowly, he sat down beside me and folded his legs, and looked off as though it was not polite to stare at me, the prisoner, wrapped in chains and rage.

He laid his fingers on my shoulder. His hair had a reasonable and fashionable look to it—that is, it was clipped and combed and not full of dust. His clothes were clean and new, too, as if he had perhaps dressed for me.

I smiled to myself at that, his dressing for me. But from time to time he did, and when I saw that the shirt had antique buttons of gold and pearl, I knew that he had, and I accepted that the way a sick man accepts a cool cloth on his forehead.

His fingers pressed me just a little harder, and I liked this too. But I didn't have the slightest interest in saying so.

"I've been reading Wynken's books," he said. "You know, I picked them up. I went back for them. We'd left them in the chapel." And now, he did glance at me very respectfully and simply.

"Oh, thank you for that," I said. "I dropped the books in the dark. I dropped them when I reached for the eye, or did she take my hand? Whatever, I let the sacks fall with the books. I can't budge these chains. I can't move."

"I've taken the books home to our place in the Rue Royale. They're there, like so many jewels strewn out for us to gaze at."

"Yes. Have you looked at the tiny pictures, I mean, really looked?" I asked. "I've never really looked. I just . . . it was all happening so quickly, and I didn't really open the books. But if you could have seen his ghost in the bar and heard the way he described them."

"They are glorious. They are magnificent. You will love them. You have years of pleasure ahead with them and the light at your side. I've only begun to look at them and to read. With a magnifying glass. But you won't need the glass. Your eyes are stronger than mine."

"We can read them perhaps . . . you and I . . . together."

"Yes . . . all his twelve books," he said. He talked softly of many miraculous little images, of tiny humans, and beasts and flowers, and the lion lying down with the lamb.

I closed my eyes. I was grateful. I was content. He knew I didn't want to talk anymore.

"I'll be down there, in our rooms," he said, "waiting for you. They can't keep you here much longer."

What is longer?

It seemed the weather grew warm.

David might have come.

Sometimes I shut my eyes and my ears and I refused to listen to any sound that was deliberately directed to me. I heard the cicadas singing when the sky was red still from the sun, and other vampires were asleep. I heard the birds swooping down on the limbs of the oaks on Napoleon Avenue. I heard the children!

The children did come. Singing. And sometimes some one or two speaking in a rapid whisper, as if exchanging confidences beneath a tent made from a sheet. And feet on the stairs.

And then from beyond the walls, the blaring, amplified noise of the electric night.

One evening I opened my eyes and the chains were gone.

I was alone and the door was open.

My clothes were in tatters, but I didn't care. I stood up, creakily, achingly, and for the first time in a fortnight, perhaps, I put my hand to my eye and felt it secure there, though of course I'd always seen through it. And I'd stopped thinking about it long ago.

I walked out of the orphanage, through the old courtyard. For one moment I thought I saw a set of iron swings, the kind they made for children on old playgrounds. I saw the A-frames at each end, the crossbar, and the swings themselves, and the children swinging, little girls with blowing hair, and I could hear them laughing. I looked up, dazed, at the stained-glass windows of the chapel.

The children were gone. The courtyard was empty. My palace now. She'd cut all ties. She was long gone to her great, great victory.

I walked a long time down St. Charles Avenue.

I walked under oaks I knew, on old pavements and stretches of brick, past houses new and old, and on across Jackson Avenue into the curious mix of taverns and neon signs, of boarded-up buildings and ruined houses and fancy shops, the garish waste that stretches to downtown.

I came to an empty store that had once sold expensive automobiles. For fifty years, they'd sold those fancy cars in this place, and now it was a big, hollow room with glass walls. I could see my reflection perfectly in the glass. My preternatural vision was mine again, flawless, with both blue eyes.

And I saw myself.

I want you to see me now. I want you to look at me, as I present myself, and as I swear to this tale, as I swear on every word of it, from my heart.

I am the Vampire Lestat. This is what I saw. This is what I heard. This is what I know! This is *all* I know.

Believe in me, in my words, in what I have said and what has been written down.

I am here, still, the hero of my own dreams, and let me please keep my place in yours.

I am the Vampire Lestat.

Let me pass now from fiction into legend.

THE END

9:43 February 28, 1994

Adieu, mon amour